I Dreamt of You

I Dreamt of You

Bekki Vowles

I Dreamt of You

Copyright © 2023 Bekki Vowles

All rights reserved. No portion of this book may be reproduced, copied, distributed or adapted in any way, with the exception of certain activities permitted by applicable copyright laws, such as brief quotations in the context of a review or academic work. For permission to publish, distribute or otherwise reproduce this work, please contact the author at bekkivowles@gmail.com

The story, all names, characters, and incidents portrayed in this production are fictitious. No identification with actual persons (living or deceased), places, buildings, and products is intended or should be inferred.

First Edition 2023

Website: https://author.bekkivowles.co.uk/

To Aaron who believed in me before I did xxx

Acknowledgements

When I look back when I first started thinking about writing this book I was so worried that my awful spellings, punctuation and grammar would be enough to put anyone off. But then you get that friend who loves that stuff and offers to read the entire book, keep it secret and help with it all. Holly, thank you, from the bottom of my heart, even if your handwriting is like trying to decipher code that has been written by a four year old, I'm eternally grateful for everything you have done. I hope you're ready for more.

A little note from me...

Two things light up my soul: the first is writing the stories that just pop into my head; the second is being a life coach. The journeys we go on to discover who we are is fascinating.

I'm a firm believer that we create our destiny. When we put our minds and souls to something we really want and love then our dreams do come true, no matter how scary it is, how vulnerable we feel, we can do it. And the results are always better than we expect.

This is my first book, something I had put aside for a long time because I was too scared of what others thought of me. But then moments pass and you realise you need what you do to make you happy, this was a huge part of that for me.

So here it is, the first of what I hope will be many romance novels to come.

– Bekki Vowles x

Contents

Chapter 1: Escape   1
Chapter 2: Meeting You   5
Chapter 3: Thank You   11
Chapter 4: The Final Move   20
Chapter 5: A Rude Awakening   29
Chapter 6: A Ghost From The Past   37
Chapter 7: Shock   47
Chapter 8: The Fight   57
Chapter 9: My Mistake   64
Chapter 10: Electricity   74
Chapter 11: The Plan   87
Chapter 12: Control   101
Chapter 13: High & Low   112

Chapter 14: Panic	125
Chapter 15: I Have To Tell Her	135
Chapter 16: She's Gone	145
Chapter 17: I Trust You	156
Chapter 18: A New Beginning	165
Chapter 19: Party Time	174
Chapter 20: I Fucked Up	183
Chapter 21: Fire	202
Chapter 22: No Going Back	213
Chapter 23: Fantasy	224
Chapter 24: Big News & Fights	243
Chapter 25: So Much Worse	256
Chapter 26: Full of Surprises	270
Chapter 27: Uneasy	290
Chapter 28: It's Over	304
Chapter 29: A Split Second	321
Chapter 30: Sickness	333
Chapter 31: Shit Hits The Fan	343
Chapter 32: Fears & Nightmares	348
Chapter 33: Waiting	357
Chapter 34: Awake	363
Epilogue	374

Life isn't a fairy tale. It's a journey and you have to make it.

Chapter One

Escape

Holy shit, I'm doing this. Am I doing this? Yes, I am doing this! Looking at myself in the mirror, I can feel my heart pounding. My breathing's unsteady; it's like I'm going to have another panic attack. Placing my hands on either side of the sink to steady myself, I take a few deep breaths to calm my nerves. *Get a grip! Anything is better than this. No matter where you end up, it will be better than this!* My whole body shakes with fear and excitement about what my future may hold from the moment I step out of this door, about finding out who I am without a man in my life. No man will ever hurt me like this again. It's time to be me, I just need to figure out who that is.

It's been eight months since I realised who I had become at the hands of a man, who I wholeheartedly thought loved me, seven months, three weeks and six days since I made my list. The list that will change my life, and that has already changed it for the better.

Okay, it's time. Carefully standing up straight, I take one last look in the mirror. The marks on my face are still visible, even though I've tried to cover them with makeup.

Collecting my last few things from the bathroom, I add them to the single small suitcase on the bed. I'm not taking much, it all holds bad memories for me now. Some of the worst moments of my life were in this house, my family home. Most of my stuff was bought by him to apologise for the many ways in which he has been a dick over the last few years, and that's putting it nicely, he was always making me feel like I wasn't good enough but at the same time making me feel loved and that he could not live without me. My head is a mess, but I know what I need to do. Closing my suitcase, I sit on the bed and put my pumps on, brushing my fingers across the bruising showing on my legs. My hands are still shaking and in all honesty, I'm a little sweaty. Being nervous always makes me sweaty, and this is one of the most nerve-racking moments of my life so far. I'm sure there will be many more, but today is day one.

The taxi's on its way. They said it would be fifteen minutes. Everything has been planned down to the last detail, so I can leave without him being around. He has no idea what I am up to, or at least I hope he doesn't.

Making my way downstairs, suitcase in one hand, phone in the other. My mind slips back to thinking over the last eight months and how I have had to keep so much to myself. It's been so hard, no one knows. I have friends at work, but even they have been won over by him, and I know that if I told them, or even hinted about leaving him, then it would get back to him, or they would try to make me stay. So I kept quiet, made my plans and kept them secret, hid everything at work to start with but a few months into my plan I found Andrea going through my desk to find something, she was the biggest gossip going, and had a real crush on him, would tell him everything I did. She asked me what the file was for, and all I could say was that one of the new recruits was looking for a place to go on holiday. I said it looked like a great mini-break and asked for details. When in fact, it was a property listed for rent in North Wales, with details of the area and any jobs I thought might be worth looking into. It was so off the cuff that she believed it. I didn't know I could lie so easily. So from that moment on, I had to think outside of the box, and that box ended up being a locker in the gym. Not very exciting, I know but I'd only just joined, and he was happy I was looking after myself for him... I never took anything back home. I knew what it would mean for me.

This morning had gone to plan so far, Glen (that's his name by the way) had left for work at seven am as usual with no clue that when he arrived home later, there would be a letter waiting for him, and me well away from here.

This was the debate I had had many times in my head. Do I tell him face to face on the day I leave and brave what I knew would come, and risk him persuading me to stay, or worse? Or do I do it the weak way and just go? Well, I opted for the weak way. I'm too much of a wimp to tell him to his face, and I know for sure that if I told him to his face that I would never leave, he would find some way to make me stay. So I wrote him a letter, very British of me I know, but what else could I do? I couldn't just leave without saying anything, he would think I had gone missing and contact the police, send out a search party, put it all over Social Media that I was missing and that would just make me feel guilty, wasting police time and all that. So this was the one way I could have my say, tell him what a dick he really is and I hope he rots in hell.

As soon as he had gone, I checked the train times, booked my taxi, and told them there would be three stops; where I work, I needed to hand in my resignation, then off to the gym to collect all my things, some new clothes, my list and some money. It was like moving in slow motion, it's only been an hour since he left, but it feels like it's been three. I'm so scared he will come back. But I know he is working in Manchester today, so that gives me plenty of time, all day in fact, but I want to be gone well before he gets back. He is a creature of habit you see; he will finish work at five, then go to the pub for a few before he comes home, where he will be expecting me to be cooking dinner. Well, that's not going to happen; *takeaway for one tonight,* I chuckle to myself.

Packing my things was easy, and getting ready was easy; it's just the thought of leaving that makes me want to panic, but I know I need to do this for my own safety and to try and live a normal life.

I hear the familiar "beep, beep" of the taxi, which pulls me from my thoughts. I watch it as it pulls up outside the house. Walking to the kitchen, I place the letter on the side by the kettle, propping it up, knowing he will see it there first. I grab my suitcase and take one last look at what I have called home for the last four years with that man, and a lifetime of memories from my family home. *This is it, time to put things into action.* Taking a deep breath, I close the door behind me.

Chapter Two

Meeting You

All this started with a dream I had about eight months ago. I woke in the middle of the night, all hot with heavy breathing, like it was the real thing happening all over again. It was bliss, pure heaven, just thinking about it now – the way his hands felt on my skin, the way they made me tremble with the slightest touch, to relive what we did was turning me on. It was just one afternoon, but it was the best single afternoon I have ever had. It had been six years since that afternoon of pure indulgence but the dreams kept coming. I could feel every touch, making me want him all over again.

    I had been on holiday with friends in Ibiza, living my best life, dancing, drinking, laughing and having the best time. Charlie was my best friend at the time and we were there for her hen night. It was actually her third bachelorette party or rather just an excuse to go away for a week before the wedding to top up our tans, and look magnificent for the wedding day, a week after we got back.

I was so wrapped up in being the Maid of Honour, loving organising and planning everything with her, and making sure all of the plans were kept, and that Charlie was having a great time.

It was the last night and we decided to go all out and do a theme night. The two other girls were Charlie's friends from work, Anne and Clara. We hit it off immediately and decided to dress up in superhero costumes for the night. To my surprise, Anne was Thor. I had never laughed so much when she walked out of the room with that costume on. I actually laughed so much that I almost wet myself. She was a tall, beautiful, blond solicitor and the costume just hung off her, fake muscles and everything, it was so funny. We, on the other hand, went with the slightly more sexy versions of the characters. Clara was Superwoman, and the costume clung to her fabulous curves; Charlie went with Batwoman making those long legs look even longer, and I decided that Wonder Woman was probably the best fit for me. I was the shortest of them all, with a few more curves than the others, but in the right places. I loved my figure. We took so many photos before we went out, having a few pre-drink drinks to get in the mood for the amazing night ahead. One of the best parts was that people wanted photos with us, and we were happy to oblige. We created scenes and posed – it was hilarious. We hit the bars and then headed to the clubs.

"Charlie! I'll get some drinks," I said, pointing to the bar since I knew she couldn't hear me over the DJ. I weaved my way through the crowd and decided to head to the loo first, as the queue for the bar was massive.

Leaning against the wall, I unlocked my phone and started looking at a few of the images we had taken before we left, feeling a little more than tipsy and really needing a wee now. I continued to scroll, giggling at our faces and some of the positions we had posed in, trying to be superheroes, when this hand landed on my waist, and a man stood in front of me.

"Now that's what I'm talking about," I heard.

I looked up from my phone to see a pair of dark eyes looking over me, like he wanted to fuck me there and then. I could smell the booze on him.

"Erm, excuse me?" I said, trying to move away from his hand on my waist. But instead, he put both his hands on me, almost pinning me to the wall. I tried to move but the force of his hand on me kept me stuck.

"You know you want it, and I'm going to give it to you," I froze for a split second as his face came towards mine, trying to figure out how to handle him…and what I thought was about to happen. "I don't think so, get off me!" I screamed, ducking my head and shoving my hands against his chest, in some sort of attempt to move him so I could get away.

"Don't be like that sweetheart, I just want to give you what you want," his face was so close to mine, I could smell the whisky on his breath, his skin sweaty. I moved my head to the side, but I couldn't move. Pushing him again, I managed to knock him off balance. I made a break for it, ducking under his arm, but he grabbed me just as I broke away from him. "Let go of me!" I said, trying to pull my arm free, "I don't think so love, you're all mine," he sneered at me with a god-awful smile on his face as he pulled me back. "Oww, let go of me!" I shouted. As I was struggling to escape, I lost my balance while pulling away from him and fell back against the wall, hitting my head on it with a thud. That's the last thing I remember before I collapsed and it all went dark.

Shit that hurt, I thought, opening my eyes and putting my hand on the back of my head where it was sore. It was all too fuzzy but I could feel his hands on me again, trying to pull me up.

"Fuck off, let go of me…" I shouted, attempting to get away from him.

"It's okay," I heard another man's voice instead, "he's been dealt with, and won't be bothering you again."

Looking up, I saw the softest, brightest blue eyes I had ever seen. It was like looking into crystal clear waters, they took my breath away. For the first time in my life, I was speechless.

"Are you okay? I saw it happen from across the room, and came over to help." His hands were gentle on my arm, lifting me slowly. "Did he hurt you in any way?" his eyes were full of concern, taking a look at me to see if I was okay.

"No," I said, " I just hurt my head when I lost my balance, I'm okay." Looking around me, I saw the other guy on the floor. "Shit… What happened? Did you knock him out?" I must have looked really confused as he gave me the sexiest half-smile I had ever seen, and lifted me from the floor.

"Let's get you checked out, I think you may have blacked out for a few moments. Come with me." I swayed a little as I tried to walk and he pulled me to his side to steady me. *Wow he feels good, solid, umm…smells good too, he's so much taller than me, easily over six foot.*

"What? Really? What about him?" I asked as we stepped over him, "Don't worry about him, my guys will escort him out when he wakes up. We need to make sure you are okay," he said, looking down at me.

"You did knock him out!" I said, looking at him with shock

"Hi, could you tell me if... Jack is about please?" I hesitate before saying his name, hoping I heard it correctly last night. "He was working last night," I add, just in case they don't know who I mean. The guy behind the bar smiles at me.

"He's not working today, but he lives in the villa just next door," he says, pointing to the left. "Thanks," I say with a smile and head in its direction. As I turn the corner, I see that it's not just any villa, it's massive, and looks more like a whole complex. It's beautiful, with big white walls, and large glass windows, and there are at least three balconies that I can see from here. Looking up at the building in front of me again, I feel small standing here in my little white sundress as I smooth it down before reaching for the doorbell. I have no idea what I'm going to say, that's if he will even talk to me. I bet he sees this sort of thing way more than he should. I'm not sure any of those girls would be ringing on his doorbell the day after to say *thanks for helping me last night, I'm not really sure why I'm here, but as I am, could you tell me what happened, fill in the little blank bit for me, where when I opened my eyes after losing my balance I saw you, and those breathtaking blue eyes, and the guy who was trying it on with me, was lying on the floor, knocked out.* Ha, I suppose I do know what I'm going to say, although I don't think I'll mention the bit about his eyes.

The sound of the door opening pulls me from my morning reverie, and I'm looking into those breathtaking blue eyes again. It takes me a second to snap out of them, "Hi, um...." *I can't think, what was I going to say? Get your words out!* But before I can, he says, "Hi, you're the girl from last night, Millie right?" His hand goes up and rubs the stubble on his perfectly tanned face as he leans against the door frame. I drink him in, only this time it's better; his hair is dirty blonde and tied up at the back

Chapter Three

Thank You

I woke up the following morning with a massive headache, Charlie sleeping next to me. It always made me chuckle when she acted all motherly. I reached up and found an egg-shaped lump on the back of my head. It was still sore, but in the grand scheme of things, it could have been so much worse if it had not been for him. Jack, he never did tell me what actually happened after I lost my balance. He obviously worked at the club, but we didn't get much of a chance to talk before Charlie burst into the room and whisked me away. Making a split-second decision, I got up, leaving Charlie to sleep in, and got ready to go find and thank him.

As I walked into town, I decided to head over to the club and see if I could find him there. The club is still a club, day or night, so it's busy, but with a more chilled feel to it. There are people lounging outside when I walk up to the front and head to the bar.

"It's okay," he said, standing up quickly, "I helped her out of a situation. She hit her head pretty hard, I brought her back here to make sure she was okay." He was holding his hand up in defence as Charlie continued towards me, he backed away. I didn't want him to move. It felt so good having him next to me, I felt safe.

"Well…whoever you are, thank you but I can take it from here," and with that, Charlie helped me stand. I was still a little dizzy, and leant on her for support as we walked from the room.

"It's Jack by the way…" I heard him say as we left him standing in the office. In the taxi on the way back to the apartment, Charlie called Anne and Clara to tell them what had happened and said she was taking me back to make sure I was okay.

"I'll be fine if you want to go back out, I won't mind, it is your last night, we fly back tomorrow evening, I don't want you to miss out!" I said, still clutching the ice-pack to my head.

"There is no way I am leaving. You could have a concussion, I'm staying with you, and checking on you while you sleep," she said, smiling at me. "Weirdo," I said, glad I have someone like Charlie to watch out for me.

"Just a little, it didn't take much really, he was out of it," There *is that half-smile thing again, oh shit, that's cute,* mixed with a small amount of stubble covering his chin. I felt dizzy – not sure if it was the alcohol, banging my head or how amazing this man smelt (like warm spices and fresh air rolled into one, it was intoxicating.)

He led me to his office, where he sat me down on a large soft leather sofa. I sat back and rested my head, closing my eyes for a few seconds to take in what had just happened. He was sitting across from me, on the edge of a desk, just looking at me, all manly and…

"Here put this on your head, it will help with the swelling. You hit your head pretty hard, how do you feel?"

"Um.. a bit dizzy, but that might be the alcohol, and the heat, what happened? I didn't see you come over, and ….I'm sorry…who are you?" I lifted my head to look at him, *WOW!* This man was all man, he was slim but muscular, wearing a fitted white shirt that showed off his physique, with his tie loosened and top button undone, dark blue suit trousers hugging everything. I could feel myself going dizzy again, so I laid my head back on the sofa to try and compose myself. When I felt him sit next to me, I could smell him, making me want to lean closer, breathe him in.

He moved closer, his hand brushing my face as he put the ice-pack on my head. "How does that feel?"

"Cold," I replied, taking in a deep breath, and there it was again, that small smile that made my insides tingle.

"Millie? Are you okay? I saw you being taken in here by that man. What's happened? Get your hands off her!" Charlie shouted as she burst into the room.

(not in a weird way, in an action movie, superhero way like Thor, it's hot). He tucks a stray hair behind his ear and I can feel myself blushing. I feel like I have stopped breathing. *Stop staring Millie, I look down quickly to try and gather my thoughts, fuck me he is stunning, a perfectly sculpted man...I can feel my heart pounding, breathe... just breathe.*

"Um... yes, um...that's me, Millie, um....you're J-Jack?" *What is wrong with me? I feel all weird, like I'm star stuck, but I have no idea who he is. Why won't my words come out like a normal person?*

Oh god, he's just looking at me, and there it is, that small smile, like something amuses him, and it reaches his eyes, they go a deeper blue and my insides tingle at the response. I'm just standing there looking at him, well, staring actually...

"Are you okay?" he asks. I feel sparks of heat from his hands through my dress and the feeling runs over my body like a delicious shiver and all at the lightest touch he places on my side.

"Yes, thanks um..." *Get a grip of yourself!* "I just wanted to ask you about last night, and say thank you".

"There is no need to thank me," he says, "but I'll tell you what I saw, it's not much though, come in and have a drink?" he gestures for me to go inside, and his hand touches my arm, I feel the same sparks again, as I walk past him. I can feel his gaze, I turn and catch his eyes on me, checking me out as if I am something brand new but off limits. He snaps out of it as soon as he realises I'm looking back at him. He walks past me, his arm brushing up against me. God he smells good, a mix of aftershave and manliness, if that is even a thing – it's intoxicating.

"What would you like to drink? I have a huge...selection, name it and it's yours," he says with that small smile again, I swallow slightly, not sure what he was insinuating, or even if he was insinuating something.

"Um, I'll have a gin and tonic please, large." *I need a drink, what is with me? I'm never like this, maybe it's my head, maybe I hit it harder than I thought.* I reach for my head instinctively, and I see him watching me.

"Does it still hurt?" Jack says, reaching for the glasses from the bar, his voice is full of concern.

"Not really, it's just a little sore," I say. He hesitates for a moment before handing me my drink. Maybe he is thinking it's not a good idea for me to be drinking. I grab it before he thinks twice, and drink it in one go. He chuckles to himself, while watching me place the glass back on the bar – it's a deep rumble, a sound I want to hear over and over again.

"Can I have another?" I say, needing something to calm my nerves

"Sure, same again?"

"Please. So what happened? Um…all I remember was the guy being a bit too keen, then I lost my balance and hit my head, and when I opened my eyes, I saw you." My cheeks flush slightly with embarrassment when I remember what I was thinking about him.

"Well from what I saw, he knocked you over, you never lost your balance," he says as he takes a seat at the bar, gesturing for me to sit next to him. I try to sit gracefully on the bar stool and fail miserably. Being a shorter person, it's not easy when you have to hop up onto something. I almost slide off the other side, my dress riding up my legs as I try to steady myself, when I feel strong hands on me, one coming to my waist and the other landing on the top of my thigh, holding me, and bringing me back up. But his hands don't move; the instant I look at him, I know what that deep blue in his eyes means, and I feel it right back – I want him.

His eyes are asking for permission, and I nod and in an instant, he is kissing me, his lips on mine as if he had been waiting to do that for a while. He pulls me off the stool and onto his lap, in one smooth motion, my legs on either side of him. I can feel him beneath me, how hard he is, and wow!

Lifting his lips from mine, he says, "I've been thinking about this since last night." His lips inching closer to mine, "I couldn't get you out of my head." His lips brush mine and I feel a spark of pure energy run from my lips to my core. I take a quick sharp breath, while craving the feeling of his lips on mine again.

"When that guy attacked you last night, I saw red, I moved as quickly as I could but you were already on the floor, so I knocked him out. I've seen it happen a hundred times with other people, but I've never done that. My security team has always dealt with it….but there is something different about you…" With some confusion on his face, as if he can't make sense of what was happening to him, he places a tender kiss on my lips. "You taste so good!" His voice sounds drunk on his own need as his hand moves further up my thigh. He starts moving his fingers in small circular motions and I feel pure pleasure shooting through me. A small moan escapes my lips and he kisses me harder, pulling me closer to him. His fingers move under my dress touching me, there, where the heat pools, and another moan leaves my lips just as he presses harder and finds my sweet spot through my panties. He circles it, rubbing it and sending wave after delectable waves of pleasure through me. He kisses me harder, with a hunger that I've never felt before – he wants this just as much as I do. He stands, wrapping my legs around his waist and starts moving across the room, holding me in place. We move to another room, his fingers still on me, as he lays me down me on a large sofa, stepping back to look at me like he can't get enough, devouring me with his eyes like no man has ever before.

"Do you want this to happen? I mean, we can stop." The look in his eyes tells me he would, if I asked him to. There was no way I was going to pass up this once-in-a-lifetime opportunity. Who would when you have a man like this between your legs?

"I want this, I want you, I don't know why I..." That's all it takes, and he is with me, on me, kissing me deeply, like there is nothing else he needs at that moment but to be with me. Moving his hands over my body and sending chills of pleasure through every cell, he slowly unbuttons the front of my dress, revealing the white lace bra and panties. A deep groan comes from his throat as he traces the edge of my bra with his fingers, lowering his head and licking and teasing my already hard nipples through my bra. I squirm under him, feeling his hot breath on me, wanting him more. When he grazes my nipple with his teeth, I can feel my juices pooling where I want him the most. I have never felt so desired or wanted in my entire life. I close my eyes the pleasure taking over me, as he continues to graze, lick, and suck on my pink cherry-like nipples with his warm mouth. His hand slowly moves down to my stomach, moving along the line of my panties. I quiver in anticipation as his fingers move over them to my sweet spot once again, and move my hips, wanting more. He lowers his head to kiss me, and this time, he nips my lips, making me want him even more. I can feel his hardness on me, so I move my hips to meet his, and he pushes it further into me. "Oh god!" I hear myself crying out, but it doesn't sound like my voice; I can feel myself building already.

"Open your eyes," he commands and when I do, I see the raging flame of desire in his ocean-like eyes. I run my hands over his broad, smooth muscular shoulders; not having the words, I nod as his eyes meet mine and he slowly moves panties down my legs and rubs his finger down my wetness. I hear a hiss come from his lips when he slides his finger inside me. "Wow," I cry out as he moves them in and out of me. I can't think as the intensity builds with every thrust of fingers. Just then, I feel him add another finger, and I almost lose it. He kisses his way down my body, sucking my nipples and making me scream with pleasure. His tongue leaves a hot trail down my stomach until it finds my spot, licking me up and down, while his fingers work their magic. I explode with the most intense pleasure, my whole body soaking up the release. I feel the pleasure I have never felt before, as wave after wave hits me, as I ride the high of my orgasm. All I hear is, "I'm not finished yet, this time you're having me." *There is no way it can get better than what I have just felt,* I think.

I watch him as he takes off his clothes, his ripped body, tanned in the most god-like way. I can see how hard he is as he rubs his hand up and down his length. He reaches for a condom and, in one smooth motion, puts it on. He is on top of me, kissing me harder, and it's divine. I can taste myself on him, "Are you sure?" he says, looking at me for reassurance with those deep blue ocean-like eyes of his. "Yes," is all I can manage to say, and his kiss deepens as he positions himself over me, teasing my entrance. I move my hips wanting him; he feels so good already, hot and so big. He enters me slowly, and I can already feel myself building again with how good he feels. He fills me completely, and it's amazing.

He kisses me deeply, my body reacting to his, my hips move in rhythm with his when he starts thrusting into me. "You feel amazing," he says, breaking the kiss, "I'm not going to last long," as he thrusts harder into me. It's like nothing I have experienced before. I come closer to falling apart again with every thrust, and when he can't hold it any longer, he thrusts one last time and I'm gone. We come together, and my mind and body want to cry with the pure ecstasy that I feel.

Well, what can I tell you next? We did a few intense, incredible and mind-blowing repeats of that over the next few hours. We talked and did it again and finally drifted off to sleep in his bed after having the best shower of my life. When I woke, I realised I needed to leave; my plane was leaving in a few hours, so I left him there, asleep, looking like the god he was, my hero. I sneaked out the door and took the wildest memories home with me.

That's when I realised I had changed; I was so different then, twenty-two years old, carefree, living life to the fullest. I loved myself, I loved who I was and who I was going to become.

I had plans...to be honest, it was like having someone smack you in the face. I had let a man change me from who I was, and I loved who I was.

This man who lies next to me, the one I have been in a relationship with for the past five years, has changed me, and not for the better, but for a weaker, more fragile shadow of who I used to be. This was when I knew things had to change; I had to change; I sat there for hours just looking at him, crying silently and thinking about how it had all happened and that I hadn't noticed the changes in myself, everything he had ever said to me, to make me this pathetic person I had become. There had been no big changes, they all came little by little, the odd comment that would make me think for days on end. I never knew if he was joking or not, and slowly I started to believe everything he said about me. I would never amount to anything; who would want to have someone like me? I was stupid, incapable of doing a simple task properly. He made me step away from my friends because he didn't like them; they were all immature and needed to grow up if they wanted to have a real relationship like we had. Ha, can you believe I fell for it? Well I did.

Then things changed for the worst, I had nowhere to go, no one to turn to.

I didn't sleep that night after the dream; how could I have? I knew I had to do something about it, the person I had become, but what? I couldn't just go, I had nothing.

That's when I made my list, a list of all the things I wanted, things he told me I could never do, stuff I would never be able to achieve without him.

The trouble was I gained confidence the moment I made that list. It was the best and the worst thing that had ever happened to me. The more I stood up for myself, the angrier he got.

Chapter Four

The Final Move

"All done," I sigh with relief. "Main street gym please." It's all falling into place; I didn't stay long at work, I just dropped my letter off and walked back out again. Everyone looked at me like I was mad, probably wondering why I was walking out when I had only just walked in. I know I didn't need to print off my resignation letter. I have also emailed a copy to them, just in case they think it's a joke. I've worked there a long time, my second job after I finished uni. I liked it, so I stayed. It was never really the plan, the plan was to move onwards and upwards, but then I met Glen…. and over time, he convinced me that I was just not quite good enough to move up in the world, and it would be best if I stayed where I was. I mean, who would want me… the truth was he never liked it when I made more money than him, and I did, a lot more.

After I left work, we (me and my taxi driver) drove to the gym, where I hid everything from him. I headed in and collected my things from the locker, making sure everything was there. Moving over to the front desk, I asked if I could cancel my membership. I could feel my emotions rising as I told them was moving away, and won't be able to use it anymore. This place had been sort of my safe haven, a place I was able to come and be myself. I never worked out, just did a few classes, mainly yoga or pilates, or sat in the sauna. A place I could hide for an hour before heading home, to him questioning where I was and who I was with. I would always get changed there even if I was just going to sit in the locker room, but it's just something else I won't need now, something else I am removing from my life. But now... now I'm off to start the life I should have had. Or to try and be the person I once was, or maybe the person I should have been, if I had taken a different path, *Uhh*, I have no idea really, I'm just going to have to take each day as it comes, see where I end up, and hope it works out.

I never planned where I was going to live, or stay for that matter. I have a small amount of money saved, which will get me by for a while, but after that...oh man, I hope things work out. Letting out a breath, I think I have been holding for a while, the last stop now as I get back into the taxi.

"To the train station please."

As I enter the train station, I realise what I am doing all over again. It has taken me almost eight months to get to this point, it's been hard being excited about what I was doing and not being able to show it. When I did start to stick up for myself, things just got so much worse for me, so much so that my heart would always have a barrier around it. I'm not sure I would ever be able to let anyone in again, not after what he has done.

Get yourself together, I say, shaking off the feelings that keep trying to rise within me as I walk over to the coffee shop; I need to decide on where I want to go.

I take out my list when I sit at the table and ponder over the first two…

1. Get away from him
2. Go somewhere he nor you has never been before

I have absolutely no idea, I look up at the boards in front of me, telling me what trains there are, but even then it confuses me. So I start looking at the map on my phone. Where would I like to go? A new city? No, I need something different. A country village? Nope, I'm not sure I want to do that alone, then I need something that fits in the middle. I have always liked the seaside, there is something calming about it… and we never went together. I know he doesn't like the sea.

"Decision made!" I say out loud with a small smile, I just need to figure out where, so I spend the next thirty minutes looking at seaside towns, and I come across one on the south coast. It looks beautiful, just the right amount of everything, so I book my ticket, and head to the platform. It's over three hours away, but that works well for me.

Three hours and forty minutes later, I arrive at the most beautiful seaside town I think I have ever seen. I step out of the train station and I am immediately hit by the smell of clean air, and I let it fill my lungs. I stand soaking it up for a few seconds. I can see shops, restaurants and offices as I start walking toward the letting agents I googled on the train. It's really beautiful, even on a day like today when the weather matches my mood – overcast and threatening to rain, not a bad day for mid-April.

You can see the sea from almost everywhere you turn. It helps that the town is on the top of a hill, with one main street down the centre lined with boutique shops, florists, cafes, restaurants and loads more I can't wait to discover.

Looking at the map on my phone, I can see that I'm almost there. It's not on the main high street, it's a few roads back, but I don't mind the walk after being sat on the train for the last few hours. I'm not holding my breath about what I will be able to get; I don't have much money, only what I have managed to save. I also don't have a job, which is not ideal, but I will take what I can get. When I open the door to the letting agents, a bell dings and two faces look up at me – one guy goes to get up, when a stunning tall, blonde girl tells him to sit down and she comes over to me.

"Hi, I'm Emma, how can I help you?" She has the brightest smile.

"Hi," I say, "I'm looking to rent a place immediately. Do you have anything?"

"Come and sit down and I'll take a look at what we have," she points to her desk and I wheel my case over and sit down on the plush seat she has in front of her desk.

"Comfy," I sat with a smile.

"Good, can I get you a drink?" she offers.

"Yes please, I've not had one since I left. It's been a while. Coffee please"

"Sure, Andy? Will you make our customer a coffee please? Where have you come from?" Emma asks while she does something on her laptop.

I look over at Andy when he sighs and stands up. He looks at me like he can't be bothered and heads out the back.

"Sorry, you will have to excuse him, he has no manners, and doesn't want to be here, he retires in a few months," she chuckles.

I like her, she seems nice and puts me at ease. Luckily she forgets that she asked a question. I don't want anyone to know where I've come from.

"Okay, I have a few, but I need to know a few more things before we can go ahead," she says, looking at me.

We spend the next few minutes going over the details, and she comes up with a few places that she says we can view today, but as I don't have a job, they will have to take a bigger deposit, which is fine, and what I expected.

"Most of them are one-bedroom apartments, but when I say apartment, they are tiny… and not in a great part of the town," she says with a sad sort of smile, giving me the bad news.

"I don't care, as long as it's available and I can afford it, it will be good for me," I say and she looks at me, wanting to ask more questions, but she stops herself.

"How far away are they? I don't have a car, but I can walk and meet you there?"

"Don't be silly, we can go together, the first viewing is in about twenty minutes."

Andy walks in and hands me my coffee, I won't have time to drink it now but I say, "thank you" anyway. Emma rolls her eyes and I giggle, shocking myself. I don't remember the last time I giggled, and then it hits me all over again why I'm here, what he did. And I have to force back the fear, and the tears that threaten to come.

"Are you okay?" Emma asks, and I see the confusion on her face. I realise she is looking at me properly for the first time, and I hope she can't see what I'm trying my hardest to hide.

"Yes, Sorry, I'm fine," I say, not so convincingly. She looks at me like she knows otherwise but doesn't press me, which I'm grateful for, as I think I would fall apart if I had to recount everything.

"Right, we had best be going, don't worry about the coffee, Andy makes a shit cuppa anyway."

And I giggle again, this time enjoying the feeling, and her bluntness.

Viewing the apartments didn't take long; there wasn't much to see really. All three apartments were basically just two rooms, bedroom/lounge/kitchen with a small shower room to the side. I went for the cheapest one, it was basically an attic room of a three-storey apartment block. There was an apartment below me, and another on the ground floor, the only downside (well it wasn't the only one) was that it was in a bit of a rough area and I couldn't move in until Friday afternoon, almost five days, something about paperwork, etc. I don't mind that it's the smallest, I don't have much, only what's in my case, and the apartment comes furnished, which means I will be able to save even more in the long run. But as I can't move in till Friday, I'll have to stay in a hotel or B&B, which will cost me a small fortune. I never even considered having to buy the basics like bed and cooking stuff.

As we get back into the car, I ask Emma if there are any cheap hotels or B&Bs she could recommend, as I need somewhere to stay until I get the keys.

"There are a couple of B&Bs just down the hill, but they won't be cheap. There are more hotels at the top, depending on what you are after; some are great, some are not great though. There is one I wouldn't recommend, called the King's. It's the kind of place you would stay if you are not going to be there much, there is a reason why it's so cheap." She chuckles, and I know where I will be staying. I don't tell her that though, I already feel embarrassed about it all.

After talking through the details back in the office, and paying a month's deposit, on top of three months up front, I am basically left with nothing in the bank. Well, that's not true, but it's a lot less than what I did have, and with the bill for the hotel for the next four nights I'll have to pay, I'm going to need to get a job ASAP, doing anything I can.

I have no idea why, but when I left the letting agent's office, I acted like I was going to stay in one of the B&Bs at the bottom of the hill. I even went down the hill to check them out, and I could tell they were out of my price range, so I headed back up the hill, wheeling my case with me, to find the hotel Emma doesn't recommend I stay in. I know it's silly and she was looking out for me, but I can't risk spending more money than I need to because what if I can't get a job? What happens then? It's not even worth thinking about.

When I got to the top of the hill, I could see it. It was run down, and from what I could see, it was mostly used by students and stag-do goers. The place smelled like stale alcohol and didn't look much better. At the reception desk, I booked my room for four nights and paid in advance so I wouldn't have to talk to the man on the desk again, he gave me the creeps. He kept checking me out, looking me up and down, so much so that I almost ran to my room, and locked the door behind me.

When I turn around after switching the lights on, I feel a sense of relief wash over me. It's not a great room, or a great hotel, but here I am, safe. Looking around the room, it's clean-ish, and very basic, but for fifty pounds a night, I'm not going to argue. I should really eat. I'm not sure when I last ate, maybe yesterday? I don't remember, my stomach has been in knots knowing what I was about to do, but I feel too tired to even go out to look for food. It's only five pm but all I want to do is shower and go to bed. I know Glen will be getting back soon, *I hope he just lets me go.* Although deep down, I know for sure he will be pissed at me, I don't know what he will do, and that scares me the most.

I grab my case and lift it onto the bed; I take out what I need for my shower and place them on the bed. Walking into the bathroom, I realise there is no shower, just a bath. I loved having showers, the feel of the hot water running down my body, cutting off any noise around me, washing away the mess, the stress and generally cutting out life for a short while.

It's all too much, I feel the stress and emotions of the day catch up with me like I had been holding them back just trying to get where I needed to be without thinking. I sink to the floor as the tears start to flow down my face.

'*I have nothing,*' I say to myself as I sob, questioning if I have made the right choice to leave him, to leave my home, my lovely home, for this. I can't stop the tears and I don't want to, so I crawl back to the bed, take off my clothes and climb in, sobbing uncontrollably and trying not to think about how I will do this on my own. When tiredness overtakes me, I feel myself drift into a restless sleep.

The Letter

"What the fuck is this!" Grabbing the note by the kettle, my knuckles turned white with force. Unfolding the paper, I see her handwriting and read it.

I hate you. You're not worth the effort anymore, I don't need someone like you in my life. I wouldn't even call you a man. No man would ever lay a finger on someone they loved. I've taken your abuse for too long, you thought you broke me, but I'm so much stronger than you will ever know!

Don't look for me, you'll never find me.
Fuck you!
Millie

"HOW FUCKING DARE SHE LEAVE ME?!" I shout, screwing the note up in my hand. "I'll find you Millie, and when I do, you'll pay for what you've done!"

Chapter Five

A Rude Awakening

The next morning I'm rudely awoken by someone banging at the door. It takes me a few minutes to realise where I am, the thudding gets louder, panic sets in when I realise…what if he's found me? Don't be stupid, I have to tell myself. Whoever that is at my door will go away in a minute.

"Thomas, where the fuck are you?" he shouts through the door, and I relax a little, knowing no one knows me, or knows I'm here. I don't want to get out of bed, but whoever that is at my door doesn't sound like they are going to give in until I answer.

"Let me in, Tom!" I hear a man beg from the other side. He doesn't sound angry, just annoyed. "I'm not in the best of moods, given what you did to me last night, I need my keys back, so I can get to work," he says, still banging on the door.

Swinging my legs out of bed, I grab an old t-shirt from my suitcase and put it on as I walk over to the door, I step back before I place my hand on the doorknob and take a few deep breaths, I know it's stupid to be scared but I am, I don't know anyone here. Just as I unlock the door, he must have been leaning on it because he stumbles in, hands stretched out in front of him. I'm not quick enough to move out of his way. And before he or I can do anything about it he knocks me over.

"Oh shit," I hear him say as I land on my ass with a thud. He looks at me with an odd expression, then looks around the room.

"I'm so sorry," he says, reaching for me but I flinch out of his way, covering myself. I stand up as quickly as I can. I know my face has gone red with embarrassment. I realise he's looking at what I have been trying to cover up for a long time, so people don't give me that look. The look he is giving me now, I can't cover them not with this t-shirt...

"Get out, please," I beg him. He turns and heads for the door, but he stops by the door frame, turns around and looks back at me...he looks concerned. I don't want his pity.

"Are you okay?" he says as his eyes go to my face, where there is a fading bruise. I watch as his eyes drift over my body, looking at all the cuts and bruises I have. I feel so ashamed of myself right now, and try to cover myself up again with no luck.

"I'm fine, could you please just leave?" I say when my courage finally comes to me. I place my hands on his chest and shove him away, not that it does much good but he moves anyway. I grab the door, almost slamming his fingers in it, trying to get rid of him. All I hear him say is "sorry" as I close the door behind him.

Locking the door behind me, I hear him mutter under his breath, something about what an idiot he was. I don't agree. *How did he know what was behind the door?* I lean myself against it, letting out a huge breath I didn't realise I was holding. No one has ever seen them before. I stopped looking at them a long time ago; each faded bruise was soon replaced by another one, a day, week or a month later. But the look of confusion, and then pity on his face, as he looked at me and realised what he was seeing, was just awful, and I never want to see that look again. I grab a glass of water, then decide to climb back into bed and sleep for a few more hours, to try and forget what just happened... that look, my ex, this mess, this place.

Walking out of the room a few hours later, I decided today needed to be better. Start as you mean to go on, they say... So, okay, it didn't start great, but when I woke up and felt free, I had no one to tell me what to do, how to behave, what to wear, and it felt amazing. I can feel the smile on my face.

I head down the hall to the stairs and make my way out of the building, the reception now smells like smoke, not the legal kind. A few more days and I'll have my own place. But I need to look for work and quickly, I will take anything.

Just as I'm about to pass the reception desk, I hear a male voice call out. I ignore it, it can't be for me, who would want to talk to me? So I keep walking and head outside; I wrap my coat around me, it's colder than it was yesterday, even though the sun is shining, and there is barely a cloud in the sky.

"Excuse me, hello... Miss, hello," I hear the voice again; it seems to have followed me outside, so I turn around and watch as a guy jogs up to me. As he comes closer, I realise it's the guy from this morning, the one who knocked me on my already sore ass. I start walking a little faster, I don't want to talk to anyone, not in the least him.

"Hi," he says, catching up to me. I don't want to speak to him, but I'm also not rude....

"Hi," I say back to him, trying not to look at him.

"I'm sorry, I just wanted to say I'm sorry." He shakes his head, realising how that sounds. "I feel bad about what happened this morning. My mate nicked my keys so I couldn't drive back last night, when I knocked on your door, well I thought it was his, the stupid staff there, I swear they do it for fun." I can feel his eyes on me, so I stop walking and he almost walks into me again.

Holding his hands up, he says, "Wow, again? Almost," and he chuckles. It's a sweet sound, and I find myself smiling at him. He's a lot taller than I am, with dark hair and has a great tan for this time of the year.

"Made you smile," he says, grinning at me, and I can't help but smile again.

"Yeah, you did, look if you don't mind I have to go, I need to find a job today, so I need to get going." I'm not sure why I told him that.

"Sure, I just wanted to ask if you were okay." I can see the concern coming back on his face, so I blurt out the first thing that comes to mind.

"Yes, I'm fine, I was in an accident a few weeks back, but I'm on the mend now, look I really have to go." By the look on his face I can see that he doesn't believe me; the look he gives me says it all and that makes me want to run and hide with shame. As I start to walk away, he goes to grab my arm and I flinch away from him. Shaking my head, he gives me an apologetic smile.

"Look if it's a job you're after, there are a few going at the Manor House Hotel if you're interested, I could…"

"No thank you, I don't need any help," I say, turning around and walking away, leaving him standing there.

I can do this on my own.

I have spent the last three days painstakingly looking for work; I've asked everywhere, shops, hotels (not the one that guy mentioned) and I've managed to pick up a part-time job in a local pub, not far from my new apartment. It's nothing fancy, just collecting glasses, and helping out where I can, the hours are awful, but for the time being, I can't complain. It will give me the days to myself as my shifts don't start until five on Thursday, Friday and Saturday nights. The Manager, Mike said I won't finish until at least twelve or one in the morning. My first shift starts tonight, I'm a little nervous, I don't want to mingle too much; I'm going to try and keep myself to myself until I heal and feel a bit stronger. The last few nights have been awful, I've not slept much. I keep dreaming he is coming after me, and I can't escape, and it happens all over again, as soon as I close my eyes. Then I wake up panicking, barely able to breathe. So I just sit there and listen to what's going on outside, and wait. I'm so tired, my body aches all over. Getting my own place is going to be a dream! My own space, somewhere I can be me, or at least find out who me is, even if it's not the best, it will be mine.

I don't have long to wait, I move in tomorrow, but I also have to work tonight, which is not ideal, as I'll have to set up with no or little sleep, not that I have much. I've packed everything up ready so I can move first thing in the morning. I can't wait to go shopping to pick out some new stuff; I've been eyeing the shops up and down the hill for some of the basics I'll need and making lists of everything I will need to get. I literally have to start from scratch again – pots, pans, bedding, you name it, I need it; I've not bought anything yet. I have no way to move it all and doing some shopping will be nice. Oh that reminds me, I need to see what's next on my list; pulling my pad out from the suitcase, I open it...

1. ~~Get away from him~~
2. ~~Go somewhere he or you have never been~~
3. ~~Find a place to stay~~
4. ~~Get a job~~
5. Learn what I love
6. Do things outside of my comfort zone
7. Try new things
8. Build my own business
9. Learn who I am
10. Be myself (whoever that is)
11. Learn anything I want
12. Sell my house

Learn what I love, ha, where do you even start with that? I don't remember the last time I did something for myself, something I enjoyed doing. It was always something he wanted; even if I suggested something, he would say, "Why would I want to do that?" and I would be made to feel stupid, and inadequate all over again. So I stopped making suggestions. It's going to be a learning curve for sure. I guess I will just have to wait and see, try new things, learning what I love and doing things outside of my comfort zone, I guess all rolled into one. I'll keep my eyes open and see what is there to do around here, see what takes my fancy, so to speak.

There is one thing that scares the shit out of me, and I'm not sure I'm ready to do it yet. I know it will tip him over the edge, but it's mine, not his like he told everyone; I need to sell my house. I can't go back there; I have nothing to go back for, I have no friends there, or family. It's just me, I just need to figure out how I can do it without being there. Maybe Emma will know, but that means telling some of what I don't want anyone to know. So I add it to my list to deal with later.

Two hours later, I'm at the pub; Mike has spent the last hour showing me the ropes. It's not rocket science, but it's what I need, I can blend in without being noticed. It's Thursday night, and even though it's only eight o'clock, it's busy. Mike introduced me to Dale and Sammy, who work on the bar and has left me to it. They seem really nice. It's obvious they already have a thing for each other. It's cute to watch.

I have not stopped, it's already eleven, and it took me a while to get into a bit of a routine. I also started helping the guys in the kitchen when it started to get really busy earlier, just so I'm not around people so much. I know it sounds stupid, the likelihood of him finding me here is like…one in a million, but what if someone knows him? He travels the country for his work, and I'm sure he never told me everywhere he went. What if he finds me? My heart starts racing, starting to panic, so I quickly excuse myself from the kitchen and make my way outside to get some air, when I collide with someone. He grips my arms to stop me from falling back, and I flinch from the pain, "Ow!" I look up to see who it is and… Oh my God, how… I can't think, my mind goes blank, what do I say…

"Fuck… I'm so sorry," is all I manage to say. I can't believe it, it has been six years but I would know him anywhere. I can't look at him, how can I still feel like this? Oh man, the feel of his hard chest beneath my hands, it's so warm even through his shirt, the way he is holding me. I can't do this, not now, I look away. I don't want him to see me like this; I step back and walk away as quickly as I can and sneak back into the pub. Once I'm back inside, I lean my back against the door, and let out a shaky breath. "What the fuck!" One thing is for sure, he has no idea who I am. Why would he even remember me? I'm nobody. I was a one-night stand, technically a one-day stand, an amazing one-day, one that rocked my world. How can he even be here? He of all the people I could literally run into, the man I have sex dreams about, the best sex I have ever had, the man who started this whole thing, my reason for being here. I spend the rest of my shift hidden from customers, and only show up in the bar once it's closed.

Chapter Six

A Ghost From The Past

Jack

"Wait…Mi…." is all I can manage to say…ha…it can't be her, no way, not my home town. "Wait," I say again as I spin round to take another look, but she's gone. I try looking for her as I walk back into the pub, but there's no sign of her. Maybe I imagined it. I run my fingers through my hair in frustration. I can still feel where her hands were, the sensation, that feeling of her hands on me, just like that day back in Ibiza. If it was her, she looked… scared, and so fragile, that's not the Millie I knew. Well, yeah I only knew her for one day, a fucking great day, but even so, something's not right, I can just feel it.

"What's up bro? You look like you've seen a ghost." Em says when she brings a drink back from the bar.

"Have you just bought those?" I say, taking the focus off me. If it was her, Millie, I need to see her again. Where would I even start to look? Although everyone knows everyone around here. I'm sure I can find out where she's staying, or maybe I will wait and see if I see her again. The first option may be a little stalkerish, but I need to know if she's okay. I know it's an odd way to react…but…that woman has invaded my dreams before; if I can get the real thing again, then I'm going to try. Something just feels off though, she looked panicked, like she was in trouble. I need to find out, even if it's just to settle my own conscience.

"Yep, why?" Em looks at me in confusion when she realizes, "Oh man, I keep forgetting you just bought this place, oh well I'll add to your profits." She laughs and hands me my drink.

"Where's Dan? Is he not joining us?" Dan is my sister's soon-to-be husband; that's one of the reasons I'm back – the wedding and buying this place. It holds a lot of memories. I've known Dan for a long time, ever since I can remember. He has been my right-hand man since I made the move to buy my first pub, club and hotels in the UK and abroad. He doesn't travel as much with me anymore since hooking up with Em, but he's happy, and most of all, he makes her happy. I've met some of the blokes she dated and girls he so-called dated. I'm happy for them, couldn't get a better match if you ask me. As for me, I've been single for a long time, that's not to say I've not had my fun, but it's never been serious. There was a moment a few years back when I met her, Millie; she just felt different, everything about her was so breathtaking. She was all I could think of, the moment I saw her in that outfit. What was it again? Oh yeah, one of my favourite superheroes, Wonder Woman. Man she looked hot… I need to stop thinking about her, I can feel myself getting turned on already, and this is not the ideal place, sitting next to my sister.

"He's on his way, don't worry, you won't be stuck with just me for much longer, so how long are you in the country for this time?" she says, taking a sip of her wine.

"A few months I think. I've got the apartment set up at the hotel. I need to see things through here, then there's your wedding, but after that it's back to sunshine and....sand," I say, grinning.

"You recovered from that well. We all know what you get up to out there. There may be sunshine and sand but there will be sex, lots of it, if I know my brother well enough," she grimaces a little.

"Please, let's not talk sex, you're my sister and it's weird no matter how old we are." We raise our glasses and clink them just as Dan walks in. He waves and heads over.

"I'll grab you a drink," I say, and head to the bar.

"Another round please Mike."

"Sure, boss," he chuckles. "Sounds weird calling you boss, I remember you and your mates coming in here years ago, and even then, you said one day you would own this place."

"For starters, please don't call me boss. Only Dan does that; I've even told him not to. Are we still on for our meeting tomorrow morning? Say about 11.30?"

"Yep, I'll be here, ready with the paperwork. Oh we have just taken on a new gal, only part-time, glass collecting, general help where it's needed, do you want to meet her?" he said, handing me our drinks.

"No, it's a social visit tonight, I'll meet them all in a few days when we do the introductions."

"Right-o, I'll carry on, see you in the morning." And he walks away to serve another customer. I like Mike, I'm glad he will be staying on; the punters love him. Easy going, hard-working and a good listener. Everything you could want in a pub manager.

As I head back over, I see Dan and Em are deep in conversation.

"Everything alright? You guys look serious."

"We're fine, we were just talking about the girl Dan literally bumped into the other day, when he went to get the keys from Tom at that horrid hotel at the top of the hill."

"Why, what happened?"

"I think it might be the same girl that rented that dive of an apartment I was telling you about, she sounds similar," Em says, almost hugging her wine to her.

"Are you going to tell me, or do I have to guess?" I say.

They spent the next fifteen minutes or so telling how Tom had taken Dan's car keys as a joke. Dan went to the hotel, well if you can call it a hotel, it's awful. They gave him the wrong room number... and Dan had managed to barge in on this poor girl in her hotel room, managing to knock her over on her ass in the process.

"It was awful man, she was covered in cuts and bruises, some were massive, on her legs, arms and face, and when she realised I was looking at them, she tried to cover herself up and shoved me out the door. I caught up to her later when she came out. I was still there waiting for Tom to come back to life, she said she had been in an accident... but I don't know, something about her was off, made me think otherwise," Dan finished and hung his head like he couldn't wrap his head around it, or figure out what was wrong.

"That is shit, the poor girl, what was her name? Did you manage to get it?"

"No," she never said, said she had to look for a job, and walked off. Got the impression she didn't want anyone to know anything about her," he said, shrugging his shoulders.

"Emilie! That's the girl that rented the apartment. She moves in tomorrow; we're meeting at ten, to hand over the keys," my sister says matter-of-factly. "It was hard getting any info from her. She has no job, and little savings from what I could tell. Only had a small suitcase with her too. Maybe her stuff will be delivered later... who knows," she finishes.

I'm frozen on the spot, I'm not sure I can breathe, what if it's her... Emilie, Millie, it's possible. *Oh shit, what if she is hurt badly. She flinched when I bumped into her, was that from the bruises? Did I hurt her even more? Oh god!* I stand up abruptly, and they both look at me.

"Just remembered, I need to check a few things out before tomorrow's meeting. Meet you back here at eleven?" I nod to Dan, he nods back, looking a little confused. "See you later Em," and I head out the door.

Why do I feel like this, this... almost primal instinct to find her and make sure she is okay? I walk for ages to try and settle this feeling I have, and find myself back at my hotel. I'll wait till tomorrow and head over to her hotel, and see if she comes out. I've not seen this woman since before she left my apartment six years ago, what would I even say to her?

I can't even voice it, this situation. Not even to Dan or Em, because I know how crazy it all sounds. How crazy I sound right now!

I've barely slept, and in what sleep I did have, I dreamt about her. When we were last together, the taste of her lips, her body, her sweet, sweet juices, the way she came in my mouth, it was the sexiest thing I have ever done and seen in my life. The first time we had sex, it was quick, but fuck me, it was… I take in a deep breath remembering the feeling, something I have never felt again since. Then she goes and blows me, sucks me, and I watch her do it. She was naked. I was naked, I felt like I had died and gone to heaven. Every time, every position was better and better. I watched her every time she came; it was beautiful, she was beautiful; and the hours we spent together, enjoying each other in any and every way possible – her silky smooth skin, the way it felt under my touch, her hard nipples in my mouth, and with each tug she would moan, and arch wanting more. Just that sound alone would almost send me over the edge. When she climbed on top, and I slipped inside her tight walls, she rode me. I had the best view watching her move up and down on me. I held her breast in one hand and her ass in the other, filling her deeper and deeper with each movement. Hours passed in bliss, and we both eventually fell asleep, wrapped up in each other, but when I woke up, she was gone.

And the rest is history. I tried looking for her, but it was like she had disappeared. She must have flown home that day. The island isn't that big, and when you know everyone like I do, it's not hard to find someone. So I carried on, oh man, listen to me, I'm acting like I actually had a fucking relationship with her; this is ridiculous. What am I doing?

Stomping out of bed, after tossing and turning, and not getting the release I need, I'm already in a bad mood, so I head over to the bathroom to take a very, very long cold shower.

An hour later, after having to sort myself out in the shower, I'm walking up the hill towards the worst hotel in town, when I decide on a better plan than stalking and hanging out outside of the hotel, waiting to see if it's the same girl. It has to be, I want it to be.

The main street hill is steep, with shops lined on both sides; it's a great little town, seaside resort and country living all rolled into one. Even though I travel around the world a lot, and I'm not in the UK much anymore, I've always called this place home.

I head to Bruno's coffee shop to grab a cup of coffee before I stalk a girl I once slept with, mentally shaking my head at myself. This place is a little odd, and Bruno is certainly a man of character. He's in his 60s and has the most unique style you could ever see. He has always dressed like he is still in the '60s – smart, bold colours, tweed, everything tailor-made, brown leather jacket; he even rides a vintage Vespa in orange, it's got all the mirrors, and it's in pristine condition. I'm a little jealous, in all honesty, although with my six-foot-four frame, I think I would look a little out of place on a tiny Vespa. Anyway, the cafe is as vintage and '60s as its owner.

"I can't stop this morning, I'll have my usual and a latte for Em please, Bruno," I say as I walk through the door.

"Black coffee and latte coming up, where are you off to in a rush, it's only nine thirty?" he asks jokingly, smiling at me.

"I've been up for hours, just meeting a friend, or an old friend." I'm not sure what I should call her…

"Well whatever you're doing, and whoever you are meeting, have a good one. I've thrown in a treat for you both. Say hi to Em for me," he says, passing me my coffees and a small bag. Straight to the point as always, he eyes me from the side while he serves the next customer, knowing I'm not telling him everything.

"Thanks, will do," I say, lifting my cup and nodding to him as I turn and leave. Like I said, the whole town knows everyone, and everyone's business, personal or not, and when you work in a cafe and have been here as long as Bruno has, well, he knows when something is up, or in my case when someone is not telling him everything. He is one of the biggest gossips in town.

I walk into Emma's office a few minutes later and place our coffees on her desk. When she walks out from the back room, she rolls her eyes at me. "And what do I owe the pleasure of your company this morning?" she says while sitting down.

"I bailed last night, so I thought I would bring you coffee, and Bruno sent you a little something else, it's in the bag," I say, handing it to her. I know it's a massive use of my sister, but I remembered what she said last night about meeting Millie, or Emilie, here today, so I thought what the hell, this way I don't look like a creepy stalker and I get to spend some time with my sister too. I need to know if it's her or not.

"Ahh, he knows me so well, pain au chocolat," she pulls out two and hands one to me. I shake my head, this woman would eat chocolate all day if she could.

"Nothing worse than chocolate in the morning," I say, frowning at her

"All the more for me, brilliant". She smiles, popping the other one on her desk for later, and biting into the other.

There is one thing I know for sure that I can keep her talking about, and I won't even have to speak after I ask her.

"How's the wedding planning going?" I ask with a smirk on my face.

"You really want to know?" She frowns at me, like I'm joking with her.

"I'm here aren't I?" I say. Although I have already heard everything I need to know from Dan, just the main details: time, date, dress code, I know she will tell me all the bits in between… and she does. Twenty minutes later, we are still on the invites and who has and hasn't RSVP'd, when I hear the door ding open. It has to be her!

"You have a customer, I'll grab another coffee for when you're done," I don't even look behind me. I just walk out the back to the small kitchen, and flick the kettle on and just listen.

"Hi, it's Emilie, I'm here to collect the keys to 29 Bench View?"

Bench fucking View? That's not a great place to live, the landlord is a right dick. What is Em thinking, letting her that place?

"I remember who you are Emilie, come and sit and I'll fetch the keys. We need to sign a few things, then you can be on your way."

"Thanks," Emilie says. She sounds tired so I sneak a look round the corner and my heart almost stops at the sight of her. She has changed so much, still just as beautiful, but so fragile. She's lost so much weight, her clothes almost hang off her. The jumper she has on looks huge but the jeans, they fit well, hugging her legs, and her hair is still fiery red and curly. I remember running my fingers through it a few times when we were... um stopping that train of thought. I just watch her for a little while longer as they talk about the details of the apartment, she seems on edge, like she can't settle. Looking up, I eye the clock.

"Shit," I say out loud, I'm going to be late. I go to grab my keys and realise they're still on Em's desk, sitting right in front of Emilie. I contemplate for a moment on different ways to get them, but end up with nothing serious, so I opt for just walking out...

"I'm late Em, I'll see you later. We can talk more about the wedding then," I say smoothly, giving her a quick kiss on the head, and placing her coffee on the desk. I walk around the desk and pick up my keys.

It all happens in slow motion then, as I move away from Em's side, Emilie looks up, her face freezes, and I can see her cheeks turn pink as I look back at her. She knows who I am! What a relief! She takes a deep breath, her eyes staring right into mine.

"Millie," I nod to her, my eyes raking over like I need to absorb everything about her... that's all I say as I walk out the door and head to the pub.

Chapter Seven

Shock

Millie

Emma looks at me like something's funny, her eyes gleaming at me. I can feel my face getting hotter the more she looks at me, how is this happening?!

He remembers me, remembers my name. I can't speak. All I want to do is leave. I almost stand up, then I remember why I'm here and stay seated, trying not to show the shock and the embarrassment on my face from not only seeing him, but remembering him, for so long it-he-felt like an illusion, maybe even a figment of my imagination. Even bumping into him last night, I didn't think it was real, but shit me… he remembers my name.

He looked even better than in my dreams. That smile makes my insides tingle. The last time I saw that smile was, well, before it went somewhere very private and I enjoyed every last second of it … oh my god, he said something about a wedding, they must be getting married. Why did he do that? Get engaged, I mean look at her, she is literally stunning, tall, blond and successful, shit I would if I swung that way. Why would he even acknowledge me? Say my name, like nothing happened between us. But the way he said my name… Millie, no-one has called me Millie in such a long time…it feels so nice. Oh crap I can feel myself getting redder by the second, from just thinking about it all. I lower my head even further, I can't look at her now.

"You okay?" Emma says, clearing her throat and smirking at me.

"Um, yes, I'm sorry," I say, trying to regain some sort of composure if I'm talking to his fiancée.

"No need to apologise, how do you know Jack?" she says with a raised eyebrow, her eyes almost bulging out of her head.

"Well…" What do I tell his fiancée of all people? Oh you know, we had amazing sex over and over again about six years ago. Now I have wild dreams about him, about what he did to me, so much so that I left my shitty life and even shittier boyfriend behind to start afresh, only to bump into Mr Sex God himself here of all places. No I can't say that, so I say, "We met when I was on holiday once in Ibiza with a bunch of friends. He helped me out of a…situation," which was the truth, just twisted a little bit with a few omissions.

"Oh wow really? That's odd, he has never mentioned you, how long ago was it?" She really looks interested and not pissed off, which I expected, and that confuses me a little bit.

"About six years ago maybe? I'm surprised he remembers me really, we only met a couple of times." Still the truth.

"I definitely want to know more about this," she says, pointing at me. "And you, but I have another meeting and you need to move into your new place," she points at me again. I realize I have loads to do tonight before I start work later, plus I need to get some much-needed sleep.

"Oh sorry, yes, sorry I didn't mean to take up so much of your time, sorry."

"There is no need to apologise. Here are your keys, this one is the main door, this one is for the apartment, you're all set. Fancy meeting for a drink tonight?" Wow, I was definitely not expecting that, is this some sort of trick? Maybe… maybe not… she's been so nice, I don't want to say no.

"Thank you, you have been wonderful. I'm actually working tonight, but another time? You have my number." Nodding at the computer, she smiles back at me.

"Brilliant, I'll call you tomorrow, we can catch up," she said, looking excited.

"I need to ask actually," I hesitate for a moment, but I know I need to get this sorted. "Can I book another appointment with you? I would like your advice on another property?"

"Now I'm intrigued, let's do it over a drink, say…" she glances at her screen "Sunday afternoon?"

"Sounds good to me, where?"

"Do you know a place called the Brasserie?"

"Funnily enough I do, five okay for you?" It's where I work, I don't tell her that though.

"Perfect, see you then, Millie," she says with a chuckle, like she knows something I don't.

After leaving Emma's office I head back to the hotel. Packing my things up in my room, I head over to the apartment. I can't wait to get in, but before I do, I need to grab a few things first. I head to the department store just down the road and pick up some basics, a new duvet, pillows, and a cover set with some sheets. All I want to do is make sure that when I finish my shift tonight, I can go to bed. I desperately need sleep, I can start getting some other stuff tomorrow, but for now, that will be enough.

When I reach the main entrance of the apartment block, I can see that the main door is broken, the lock hanging off, like someone has broken in. So no need to use my key. I walk up the three flights of stairs with my case and my shopping bags, only to find that my door is open too, I look inside and see a man there, he looks at me.

"You must be... Emilie?" he says after looking at the sheet in his hand.

"Yes, that's me, who are you? And what are you doing?" Stepping inside and looking around the small space.

"I'm Phil, your Landlord. We're just taking the furniture out of your way, we won't be long, just getting the last few pieces out for you." *What the hell...*

"What do you mean? I thought it came furnished?" I look around and there is nothing left. The sofa has gone, no table, and they are just dismantling what looked to be the bed, *fuck*. I want to cry. Why is this happening to me?! I can feel my composure sliding, but the look on his face says he doesn't care. They push past me to get the bed out of the room, and they start heading down the stairs.

"No, only part furnished, which means you get the kitchen stuff and washing machine, come on lads, let's leave her to it," he says, laughing to himself.

"But…what am I supposed to do..?" It falls on deaf ears and they leave, carrying away the last bit of hope I had of getting a good night's sleep. I walk in and close the door behind me. It's empty, I have nothing. I sit on the floor, I put my head in my hands and just cry. I can't hold it back anymore, it's all too much.

An hour later, I pick myself up off the floor and take a look around. It takes me all of two minutes. It's a studio apartment, so the kitchen, living room and bedroom are all in the same room, with a small shower-room to the side. It's more like a bedsit really. And it needs a really good clean. I have three hours left until my shift starts, so I'll clean. At least it will be better when I come back later. I'll have to see if I can buy something to sleep on tomorrow.

Two hours later, after a trip to the shop to get some cleaning things, it's all done. I'm exhausted – the feeling runs deep into my bones, like an ache I just can't get rid of. There's no time to sleep now though, not that I have anywhere to sleep, but on the positive side I have a roof over my head, and a place I can call home for a while. Just the smell of the place makes me feel better.

I head to the shower to wash the cleaning smell off me and fully enjoy the feeling of the water running over me, losing myself for just a few minutes. How I have missed this! It's only been five days, but this is heaven. I wash my hair, pull on some jeans and a shirt and flick the kettle on to make coffee before I go to work.

The walk to Brasserie only takes me fifteen minutes, which means no having to spend money on taxis. The coffee didn't help much, I'm still struggling to keep my eyes open. I carry on anyway, knowing that when I get home, I can fall into a blissful sleep on the mock bed I have made out of a duvet and my pillow. I have a feeling that as soon as my head hits them, I'll be out cold. The temperature has dropped this evening, I can barely feel my fingers as I walk into the pub to start my shift. Mike greets me with a big smile, "You okay love? You look tired!" Great, that's all I need, someone telling me I look as bad as I feel.

"Thanks Mike," I say, shaking my head at him. "I'm okay. It was a moving day today, so just a little tired from it, that's all."

"Okay sweet, if that's all it is, then okay. Make sure you grab a coffee before you start, that will warm and wake you up a bit. You all get to meet the new boss tonight, he'll be here about 8ish."

"Oh, I thought you owned it?" I ask him

"Used to, finalised the sale a few days ago. I'm staying on as manager though, just a little less responsibility for me." he looks really pleased. That settled the uneasy feeling I had a little. Who knows what a new boss would do, last in, first out and all that? Maybe I should keep my eyes open for a new job anyway, just in case this new boss doesn't like me.

"He's a good guy you know, hard when it comes to business, but a good guy." He must have read my mind. "Well known around here too," he added for good measure.

I nod at him and start cleaning the tables and tidying up for the busy Friday night ahead. The next few hours pass quickly. I'm just in the kitchen helping prep when I hear Mike call us all out to the bar to meet the new boss.

I can hear him start introducing people just as I'm washing my hands. There are a lot of happy voices, they must all know him well.

"Where is she?" I hear Mike say just outside the door. I'm the last one to come out and be introduced.

"Just coming, sorry, I needed to wash my hands," I say as I walk out the door, head down, drying my hands on my jeans.

"Jack, this is Emilie," I freeze instantly, not really wanting to look up but I have to; I know it's him. When I do, I can feel my face going red already, heating at the sight of him. God damn it, he is everywhere!

"We have actually already met Mike, nice to see you again Millie." There's that smile as he reaches out, taking my hand into his. I instantly regret letting him, as he closes his fingers around my small hand, engulfing them with his warm touch. The spark of his hands on mine runs up my arm and I pull away, shaking my hand and moving it behind me, like it's burned me. I can see him staring at me, I move to the back of the room, behind the other staff so I'm not as close to him. I can't do this. The way my body reacts to him, it's embarrassing… He's engaged to one of the only people I kind of know here, well I don't know her yet, but I'd like to.

Keeping his eyes on me, he addresses the rest of the staff as I try to hide. Pressing down the feelings as best I can, but not having much luck.

"I know many of you already know who I am, but some of you don't. I'm Jack. Mike and I have come to an agreement about what's going to happen here. Mike will be staying on as manager, with me in the background, taking some of the responsibility off of Mike. You will see me around from time to time but Mike is still your go to person. Do you have any questions?"

Most people shake their heads, some ask if anything will change, and he answers them all while I sneak away back to the kitchen, pressing myself against the wall, and covering my face with my hands. All I want to do is leave, but I know I can't run from everything. I also can't afford to now that I need to buy furniture. So I busy myself with work, and try to carry on like nothing has happened. I can't face questions right now, not about me, or what I've been up to. I have nothing against him, I just need… who knows, I just want to hide and let this night pass like it never happened. I know it sounds stupid, but I've not processed what happened to me yet. I've been in autopilot for so long that I need to catch my breath, and heal.

"Millie?" I hear him say beside me, startling me. I must've been so deep in thought I didn't hear him come into the kitchen.

"Jack," I flinch when he gets closer to me and touches my arm. It still hurts from what that bastard Glen did to me, and I just don't like being touched anymore.

He moves his hand away, looking and frowning at me.

"Are you okay, Millie?" I can see him eyeing me, checking me out, looking to figure out what's wrong with me. He won't guess, no one ever does, I've kept it well enough hidden for the last three years. Nothing will change now, only that there will never be anything else to cover up again.

"Um…Yes, I'm fine, how are you?" I say, taking a step away from him. He looks confused, "I'm sorry boss, I need to get back to work, I can't have you thinking I'm a slacker."

"I'd never think that, and don't call me boss, I don't like it," he says, shaking his head at me.

"I'm sorry, I didn't mean to upset you," I can feel the panic rising. I know it's not him, but I can't shake the same feeling of panic, knowing what used to happen when I said the wrong thing.

My head instantly drops and my eyes close as I try to calm myself down and slow my breathing.

"Why would you upset me?" he asks, looking even more confused, tilting his head to the side slightly. "I just wanted to say we are having a drink to celebrate me being the new owner, if you want to join us, the drinks are on me. Well one drink as you're all at work," he says with a smile.

"Oh, that would be nice, thanks!" I say, looking at him and heading for the door, I can feel him close behind me as we walk out together.

Mike hands me a drink of champagne when I walk out of the door. It tastes wonderful. Standing with Mike and a couple of the girls from the bar while we have a drink and chat about general stuff. It's nice, I feel sort of... normal again.

Before we know it, we have to put the champagne glasses down as it starts to get busy and we are rushed off our feet. I keep feeling a little light-headed as I make the rounds, but carry on. I think the drink may have gone to my head. Being tired probably doesn't help; I'll rest up tomorrow.

The whole night seems to be going in slow motion, every time I look around the pub, there he is, always watching me, like he's trying to figure something out, watching me work and chat with the people that come in. Maybe I'm talking too much, maybe that's his problem, so I stop chatting to the customers and just nod at people when they try to talk to me.

When I hear shouting and a few screams, I look over my shoulder to see a fight that's broken out between two guys. The guy by the bar has been punched in the face; both of them are drunk, you can just tell by the way they stumble around each other when more fists start flying. One guy hits the other and stumbles over towards me. Before I can move out of the way, I'm knocked over. As I try to get up, I see a fist flying towards me, as the other guy moves out the way. I know it's not aimed at me, but it sure does hurt when it hits me square in the chest and I fall into the table beside me. Sharp pain spreads across my ribs as I land on the floor. I can't breathe, I keep trying to stand to get out of the way as the fight continues around me, but it hurts too much. I can't get up. I can't suck enough air in… my head spins, I can't focus… I know I'm starting to panic. I need to get out, bad memories flood in, I can't deal with this. Everyone's looking at me, I hear my name being shouted, but I can't focus on where it's coming from. Before I know it, one of the guys has fallen on me, he's so heavy, like a dead weight… it feels like he's crushing me, I can't catch my breath, it hurts too much, the pain…

Chapter Eight

The Fight

Jack

Walking back into the bar, I hear shouting, "I step out for two minutes to take a piss and look what happens," I mutter under my breath. My first official night as owner, now look what I've got to deal with. I was kind of hoping it would be a slow night so I'd get a chance to talk to Millie again. She seemed almost scared when I touched her arm earlier out the back, the way she flinched again, and almost withdrew herself… there's something wrong, I just need to find out what it is.

I look around while I walk over to the fight to help try and break it up, I can see some locals trying to help but the fight is bad; these two really have it out for each other. I look to see if all the staff are okay, but I can't see Milllie, maybe she's out the back, I wouldn't blame her.

As I get closer to the guys fighting, I see her, she tries to move but she's not fast enough and the guy punches her in the chest full force, fuck… I start running, almost shoving people out of the way as they watch what's happening. I watch as she smacks into the table beside her. She clutches her chest and lets out a cry of pain. I start running faster towards her, "Millie," I shout, but she can't see me. She tries to focus, but the guy lands on her, shoving her back down onto the floor. She can't move, she can't breathe. I move in and grab the guy by his shirt and haul him off her, letting everyone else deal with him. Kneeling down on the floor, I go to pick her up but she flinches away from me.

"Millie, it's Jack, let me help you?" I ask. I can see the fear in her eyes as she tries to get up but can't, struggling to get a full breath in. When I move closer, I can see she's panicking, still unable to catch her breath. I need to get her away from all this and see how badly she's hurt. When I pick her up, she cries out in pain but then curls up in my arms as I carry her through the crowd and into the office. I'll call an ambulance when we're inside. She feels so small in my arms, so fragile. All I want to do is protect her. Glancing at her every few seconds, I notice the bruising on her arms showing just underneath her shirt. They're a lighter shade of purple, but some are yellowy. All across her wrist like a band. I can see them on her neck too. *What hell has she been through to get these? She's tried to cover them up but they still show. Are they from the accident Dan told me she'd been in?*

When I place her on the small sofa in the office, she winces. She's in so much pain, her breathing is staggered, like she can't get enough in.

"Millie, try not to move, I'm calling you an ambulance, we need to get you seen too."

"No..." her eyes dart to me, "Don't call..."

"But you're hurt real bad Mil, you may have broken something, you can hardly breathe." I pull out my phone and dial 999, I go through the motions and one is on the way, or should be soon.

"Why... did you do that?" You can tell each word she says hurts, but she carries on, "It's only a fractured or bruised rib..." wincing in pain.

"I don't understand, how do you even know it's a fracture? They'll be here soon anyway, so you have no choice but to see them".

"It's nothing... I've not dealt with ... a few times before." She lets out a steady breath

"What the fuck does that mean?" I can feel myself getting angry, but my words come out calm. *What does that mean? She has dealt with broken ribs before, a few broken ribs? Was it the accident?*

"Nothing... I mean... um... I was in an accident a few weeks back... I broke a few ribs, that's all."

Bullshit, I know what Dan meant now when he said he could tell she was lying. I get this feeling in the pit of my stomach like dread. I want to help her, but I'm not sure she is going to let me.

"Was it bad, this accident?" I walk over and sit next to her, her breathing a little more even now.

"Yep, it was bad." She starts to cry, tears streaming down her face. Reaching out, I put my arm around her, she tries to move away and screams in pain again, so I move away. "Sorry, I just... don't want to talk about it," she says, looking at me with such sad eyes.

Mike knocks on the door and walks in.

"Ambulance has just pulled up, how are you Emilie?'" Unfortunately it's not the first time someone has been hurt in the pub when a fight starts, not usually staff though. Mike looks as concerned as I do, when she doesn't speak, we both glance at each other, not knowing what to do. I watch as her head falls to the side and suddenly, she slumps over, passing out. I grab her before she falls off the sofa and lay her down just as the paramedics walk in.

"She's just passed out, she was fine, well not fine, but talking, she was struggling to catch her breath, but then she slumped over," I tell them, moving back so they can do what they need to do. Mike does the same, we both just stare at her.

"What happened to her?" One the paramedics asks, I tell them everything I saw, then they ask us to give them a few minutes with her, so we both leave the office and wait outside, letting them do their thing.

"Mike, how much do you know about Millie?" I ask him. She may have told him something that could help me understand what's happened to her in those six years.

"Not a lot really, I know she has just moved here, moved into her new place today. She looked exhausted when she came in today, but she said it was just from the move. I think it's more than that though, I have a feeling she is running from something or someone, why do you ask anyway? How do you two know each other?"

"In all honesty, I don't know that much about her, we met in one of my clubs a few years back, and we… hit it off, so to speak, but I look at her now and she has changed so much. She was confident, bold, full of energy, this Millie is not the same Millie I knew then, and I don't know what to do. She is so fragile, almost broken."

"I think you hit the nail on the head there my friend, she is broken, you can see something in her eyes, and it worries me what she has been through. You can see she is hiding cuts and bruises too."

I leaned my head back on the window and let out a long breath, "She told me she was in an accident. But why would you hide them if it was an accident?"

"I have no idea…" At that moment, the paramedics open the door; one steps close to us, and asks if he can have a chat.

"Emilie has regained consciousness, but is now refusing to go to hospital. Her rib is more than likely fractured, if not badly bruised. There's not much we can do about it, we have strapped it up, and she will need to get some medication to ease the pain… is there anything else we should know? She has bruises and marks on her arms and chest, a few weeks old and some older ones…?" He stops talking while waiting for us to say something.

"We know just as much as you. She only moved down here this week, I knew her a long time ago, but other than that I've not seen her for years. She did say she was in an accident a few weeks back when we noticed the bruising on her arms and the ones she has tried covering up on her face, but she won't talk about it."

"Okay, that's… hmm, right she will need help over the next few weeks. I take it she has no family close by?" We both look at him blankly. "Thought so, can one of you help? She needs to rest for a few weeks until the fracture or bruising starts to heal. She needs to take it easy, no heavy lifting, that sort of thing." He opens the door and gestures for us to go in.

"Okay, I'll help her, it's the least I can do really."

"Good, we have given her something for the pain, but she is refusing to go to hospital, we will take her home."

"I'll take her, my car's out the back."

Millie looks at me and rolls her eyes, I don't give a shit what she thinks, "I'm taking you home."

"You don't need to, I'll walk it, it's not far." She pushes herself up like nothing has happened, but I can see the pain in her eyes,

"Millie, let me help you, you can hardly stand up, it hurts so much." *Why is she acting like this?* I turn to the paramedics and thank them before they leave, reassuring them she will be taken care of.

"Mike, I'll pull my car round the front, can you stay here and make sure she stays put?" Another eye roll from her and I chuckle, knowing it's slightly annoying her how much I want to help her. Mike nods and sits at the desk, watching over her.

"I'll be back in a few." Walking out to the car park around the back, I see the paramedics still parked up and head over. Knocking on the window, I wait till they roll it down.

"Can I have a word?" The guy nods at me, indicating for me to carry on. "The bruises she has, what do you think they are from? I'm worried about her." I say simply, and they give each other a look.

"Look, I've been doing this job for a long time, and I've seen those sorts of injuries more than I would like to admit. They are not from an accident, and I'd say she has been getting those sorts of injuries for quite some time." I fully understand what he's trying to say. I know he can't say much, but I appreciate what he's telling me. No matter how brutal it is to hear, she's been on the receiving end of someone's fist… *what sick bastard would do that to her?* My face falls into a grim line; I don't know how to deal with this.

"I had my suspicions, but I never imagined this…" I rub my hands over my face. *How can anyone do this to her? She's perfect, the fucking bastard.* It makes me feel sick to think what she could have been through at the hands of another person.

"If you really care about her, and I think you do, she's lucky she has someone like you to take care of her." And with that, another call comes through and they leave.

Chapter Nine

My Mistake

Millie

I must have passed out, as when I wake up, Jack and Mike are not in the office, and the paramedics have me on the floor. It startles me when I look down and I realise they have checked me fully over, my shirt is undone, and they are examining all the cuts and bruises I have.

"Hello, Emilie, I'm Jane and this is Dave, we are the paramedics looking after you."

"I don't need any help, I know I have a fracture, maybe bruised rib…did I pass out?"

"Yep, that's what we were told by the owner, Jack?" I nod, signalling she has it right.

"When was the last time you ate Emilie?" Jane asks me,

"Um, maybe yesterday? Things have been a bit unsettled and it just slips my mind." It may have been longer, but I'm not going to admit that, am I? "Is that why I passed out, do you think?"

"I would say it's in the mix of a few things," Dave says, looking at me sympathetically.

"Have you been getting much sleep?" I think he can tell from the bags under my eyes that I've not been sleeping.

"No, keep getting these dreams. They wake me up, I can't settle after that." I didn't say they were bad dreams, they are the best kind of dreams to have, or they were until I found out he was engaged. Now I just feel guilty for having them.

"Well, we will need to take you to the hospital to get your ribs x-rayed and get you some painkillers. Does it hurt when you take a deep breath in?"

I try to take a deep breath and I feel a sharp pain that radiates over my chest and ribs. They can tell from the look on my face that it hurts like hell. *Why does this happen to me?* I let out a sigh feeling sorry for myself, then wince when even that hurts.

"We will give you something now for the pain."

"Thank you, I'm not going to the hospital with you though, I know how it goes and I will be fine." They share a look, but don't argue with me.

"You'll need to sign a few forms, but okay." Dave's not pleased about it, I can tell.

"Let's get you up and back on the sofa and dressed again." I know they know what the bruises and cuts are, but I don't care anymore. They can't say anything to anyone, so it's still my secret to keep.

Dave steps outside and I can hear them talking in low voices. After a few minutes, they all come back in.

"Okay, I'll help her, it's the least I can do really," I hear Jack say to Dave.

"Good, we've given her something for the pain, she is refusing to go to hospital, but we will take her home." I shake my head, I don't want to waste any more of their time; I'm about to say something when Jack beats me to it.

"I'll take her, my car's out the back," Jack says, looking directly at me, so I roll my eyes at him. It would be better if the paramedics drove me back. I don't want him to take me back and see where I live and that I have nothing there when I get back.

"I'm taking you home," he says again, with raised eyebrows, wanting me to challenge him, so I do.

"You don't need to, I'll walk it, it's not far." I try to push myself up from the sofa but the pain is intense and I sit back down again, clutching my side.

"Millie, let me help you, you can hardly stand up, it hurts so much."

Why is he being so nice to me? I don't understand. I've not seen him in six years, now he is everywhere I look, wanting to look after me. I can't deal with having a man in my life right now, not after Glen. I can't trust them.

Jack turns around and thanks Jane and Dave for helping me.

"Mike, I'll pull my car round the front, can you stay here and make sure she stays put?" I eye roll him again, annoyed at how much he wants to help me. If he takes me home, he can't come in, there is no way I'm letting him in, but I know deep down there is no way I will be able to stop him. I don't want him to see where

I live, let alone that I have nothing when I get there. *How am I going to sleep now?* I have no idea.

"I'll be back in a few," he says as he walks off.

I try to stand again, and this time manage it. The pain seems to have eased a little, the painkillers must be working already. I'm sure I can walk home.

Jack has been gone for a while now. Mike keeps looking at the time.

"Mike, you don't need to babysit me, I'll wait here for him. I can barely move, even if I tried to walk out of here, I wouldn't get far." I give a smile and he seems to take it.

"I'll be back in ten minutes, I'll just check to see where he's gone."

"Okay, see you in ten." Watching him walk out the door, I notice him walk to the front of the pub, then head outside. I take that as my cue and slowly and very painfully move to the back door, unlock it and move outside. I start walking in the opposite direction to the carpark. I know it loops back around; I have to steady myself every few steps and catch my breath, the tablets have taken the edge off the pain, but it's still bad. This is going to take a while. *Not such a great idea Millie, you could've had a lift home, or insisted Mike give you lift, but no, you and your stubbornness got in your own way once again.*

After about half an hour of walking and stopping, I realise how this was a massive mistake. It hurts so much, I lean against the wall for support but that hurts even more, so I slide to the floor. I'm just about to stand up when my phone starts ringing. It can only be one of three people, Jack, Emma or Mike. I take my phone from my pocket and see it's a number I don't know, so it must be Jack. I send it to voicemail, then send Mike a message.

> *Me: Hi Mike, sorry, I'll be in tomorrow at my normal time, I'm home already. Thanks for everything this evening. Emilie.*

> *Mike: Don't be so F***ing stupid, you are taking a few weeks off, you need to rest.*

> *Mike: also... Jack went mental, he was not impressed you left to walk home this late at night by yourself, but it's even worse in the state you're in, he is currently out looking for you.*

Oh shit!

> *Me: Thanks Mike, I'm not sure why he went mental, I'm not his responsibility, and I can look after myself.*

> *Mike: Jack's number, call him, tell him you're home. 079812349760*

> *Me: Okay.*

Fuck, I'm so stupid, it's going to take me so long to get home. I cry to myself, I'll call him now, well, maybe in a few minutes, at least he can think I'm safe, instead of looking for me. I sit for a few more minutes, but it's eating me up, knowing he's out looking for me... I feel guilty... I don't feel panicked at all, knowing he's looking for me. That's new. Before now, if I went out, or was out longer than intended, Glen would come looking for me... even if he knew where I was, he would drag me back home and well... it never ended great for me – memories I would rather forget then keep reliving. But this feeling I have...

No, I can't... he's engaged to what seems like an amazing woman! Move on...

Okay, I can't put it off any longer. I copy the number over and call it, holding my breath.

"Thank fuck, where are you? I'll come and get you!" You can hear the relief in his voice; it's actually nice to hear. I can feel myself relax a little and smile... maybe he actually cares about me...is that so far-fetched?

"I'm home," I say with confidence, "just getting into bed."

"Really? Is that so..? You managed to walk home faster than I could drive to your apartment, sneak past me, waiting outside the main door, which is broken, by the way... then climb into bed." I think I've been rumbled...

"Oh, shit, um, yes? I can be very sneaky." I almost laugh, but remember just in time, it would hurt like hell if I did.

"Sneaky you may be, but home you are not! Where are you? It's been well over half an hour since you left, you should be back by now."

He sounds so grumpy.

"I sat on the floor to rest, and I can't get back up... yet... I've tried. I'll manage it, though, at some point... oh brilliant it's raining, that's the perfect way to end this shitty day, what else can happen now, oh yeah I forgot I don't even have a…" I stop suddenly when I realise what I was going to say.

"If you have finished ranting, I'd like to know where you are so I can come and get you. And put you to bed myself".

I freeze, what the fuck, did he just say that?

"Shit, ha, that came out wrong, sorry, just tell me where you are please?" He doesn't sound sorry though, he sounds husky… and sexy and all things… nope.

I try to stand up again but it hurts too much and I cry out. I can hear him on the other end of the phone getting agitated when I don't answer.

"Mil, please, just tell me, I want to help you."

"Okay okay…" I say in defeat. I know I won't make it home on my own. "I don't know the name of the road, but it's about four streets down from the pub, I didn't get far." I tell him, sighing down the phone to him.

"I'll find you, I won't be long, stay on the phone with me, so I know you're okay." I almost break down on the phone. I've not had this feeling for a while, it feels nice. He actually wants to help me, like he cares for me.

"I'm not sure how much more I can take of this," I say, sinking back into the wall. Closing my eyes, I let the rain fall on my face, it feels nice.

"What do you mean Millie?" He says softly

"It's just been a rough few months, that's all."

He doesn't say a word, but I know he is there.

A few minutes later, I hear him say, "I can see you" over the phone. I hear a car pull up and a door open; I open my eyes to see Jack almost running to me, I summon everything I have to stand up before he gets to me, but I can't do it. I've got nothing left, I just want to sleep. I feel his arms move around me. It feels warm and safe as he lifts me to my feet as gently as he can, scooping me up into his arms.

"I've got you Millie," I hear him say into my hair as he places me in the car. We start to drive to my new shitty home in silence. I don't know what to say to him. Our paths have crossed for the first time in six years, and he takes care of me, like we're old friends or lovers. It all feels too much, but right at the same time and it scares me so badly I can feel myself shaking.

When we arrive, I go to get my keys out but he takes my bag from me. I try to protest, but the look he gives me says, 'don't even try'.

"Can you help me out?" I ask as he opens my door, I swing my legs around and he pulls me up out of the car and tucks me into his side so he can help me walk, which I'm grateful for. When we reach the main door he stops looking for the key.

"It's broken, remember, you don't need the key," he looks annoyed and opens it, as we walk up the stairs. I can feel his hands on me, helping me up the three flights. Every step and every breath hurts, but it doesn't take my mind away from his hands on me, with every touch, I can feel sparks; it's like a painkiller, it's what I need, but I know I can't have.

When we get to my door, I stop and turn around to face him. He fills the small staircase with his huge god-like statue body of all men. All I want to do is touch him, but each time I think of him, I think of Emma. I back into my door, trying to take a step away from him.

"Thank you, you have done more than enough for me tonight, I can see myself to bed." I chuckle and wince, even laughing hurts. This sucks.

"Ummm, I wouldn't mind tucking you in Millie." Lifting his hand, he brushes my cheek. I close my eyes and enjoy it for just a split second, the way he says my name, it sends a wonderful zing through me. I want this so bad, but he's engaged. I can't. I'm not that girl.

"Um, no, plus that was a really cheap line." I smile at him, putting a stop to whatever he was about to do. But when I turn around to open my door, I drop the keys. I instantly reach to catch them then cry out as pain spreads across my chest. I almost double over as he grabs me, pushing me back up as carefully as he can, then leans down to pick them up.

"Let me," he says as he picks up the keys and opens the door before I have a chance to say anything. He walks in and switches the light on, he turns around and looks at me, he walks over to the only door in the apartment, opens it, breaths out a massive sigh, he walks back over to me, eyebrows raised. I shrug slightly, I have nothing to say, it is what is, I will make do.

"No way," he says, shaking his head at me, "you don't even have anything to sleep on, where is all your stuff? I thought you moved in today? You couldn't even get up off the floor a few minutes ago, what are you going to do, sleep on the floor?" He says it sarcastically, but my eyes move to the makeshift bed on the floor and he looks to where I'm looking.

"Fuck no, no way." I laugh at him, he looks so serious.

"I have no choice," I say to him, annoyed. "When I arrived, my brilliant new landlord was taking all the furniture away. I thought it came furnished, but apparently I was wrong about that too. Look, can you just leave now? I've had a really shitty day. I've not eaten, I feel dizzy, I'm so tired, I just want to be left alone to sleep. It's taking everything I have right now to stay standing. I can't take much more."

"I can't do that, I can't leave you alone like this." He's standing there looking at me like I've lost my mind, towering over me, his eyes a deep blue and unwavering in watching me.

"Yes, you can, just walk out the door, that's all you have to do. I've had so much worse than a broken rib before now, I'll be okay." *Not making the situation any better, are you?* I scold myself. It's like I've got verbal diarrhoea around him, it just comes out. I lean against the wall, and wince, not helping myself prove my point. He takes my hand, and brushes his thumb over my knuckles, he looks at me. I melt… those eyes.

"You have just stood there and told me, you don't have anything to sleep on, you feel dizzy, you haven't eaten, and you have had much worse than a broken rib before, then you expect me to just walk out the door? I don't know what type of man you think I am, but no, you are coming home with me until you get better, I'm not taking no for an answer." I think I melt some more… so commanding, but this time it's sexy as fuck.

Wow, shit, what can I say to that? So that's what it feels like when someone wants to care for you. It's been so long, I'd forgotten. Glen never cared for me. I don't know why he was with me if he hated me so much and did what he did. It makes no sense to me… but this… Him… Jack… I don't know what to say, so I just nod.

Chapter Ten

Electricity

Jack

She fell asleep in the car on the way back last night. She didn't say much after our little chat in her apartment. I can't believe she was going to sleep there and not say a word about any of it, having no bed… I mean what the fuck! *Does she really have nothing?* I know she doesn't know me, or any of us. We don't know anything about her situation, we've guessed at what has happened and the most likely horrific option, I just don't want it to be true. I can't and don't want to imagine what she has been through to get to this point in her life, but god damn it, I want to make things better for her.

After carrying her up to my suite in the hotel, I put her in my bed, only taking off her shoes. She looks exhausted and so restless.

I wake up this morning still in the chair I fell asleep in last night. Millie was still sleeping. Running my fingers through my hair, I head to the shower. I've got a full day today and I'm still in yesterday's clothes. Dan will be here at nine and we need to sort some stuff out for the hotel, pub and restaurant. I need to get clean and have a coffee before I deal with Dan. I know how he'll react when he finds out Millie stayed the night.

No matter how much I try, I can't help but think about some of the things she said to me last night, it really scared me. I'm not sure I could handle the truth about what she's been through. I think it would kill me to think of all the things that could have happened to her. That's if I'm right about it all, I hope to god I'm wrong about it. I just hope she never has to go through it again, any of it. It could have all been so different if I had found her back in Ibiza six years ago.

Even in the shower, she's invading my thoughts. I can't stop thinking about her. I'm not sure what's happening to me. I've never acted like this over any woman before, not even the ones I've slept with a few times. But there's something about her. I just want to wrap my arms around her and tell her everything will be okay. I get this sick feeling when I think about what she may have been through. I keep replaying last night in my head. I couldn't understand why she wouldn't accept a lift home. I assumed it was her being stubborn. When I walked back into the pub and she was gone, I freaked out. I went ape-shit at Mike for leaving her alone. I suppose I had been gone a while but I needed a few moments to process what the paramedics had said to me about what they thought her injuries were. I knew she would never be able to make it home on her own. And just like that, I'm pissed off again.

I flew to my car, my heart racing, thinking the worst. I drove straight to her apartment, looking for her on the way, sitting outside the main door. I've never been so worried, I felt helpless. Had she disappeared on me again? I want to see her every day. It made my day yesterday when she walked out of the back of the pub when I introduced myself to the staff. I couldn't help but smile at the shock on her face, that pink blush that crept up her cheeks, it made me laugh. All night I'd been thinking of ways I could be at the pub more, just to see her, get to know her a little better. I had a similar feeling back in Ibiza with her, I just wanted to keep her next to me, have her with me, it felt… good. I'm not sure I want to lose that feeling. Being close to her last night before I opened the door to her apartment, it felt like electricity between us. Her skin was like silk beneath my fingers. I meant what I said to her about putting her to bed. I could feel myself getting hard just being close to her. I wanted to touch her, feel her, and do so many things, but she shut me down. I don't blame her, given the night she had.

Walking into her apartment, I could see why she did what she did. She knew I would never let her stay there. She has nothing, even though she doesn't know me well enough, she knew I would want to help her.

Bringing her back here last night was the best decision I could have made. Placing her in my bed felt right. Fucking hell… I was planning on sleeping in the spare room, but I watched her sleep for a while, sitting in the chair by the window. You could see her dreams were tormenting her. She was restless, every time she turned, she was in pain. She also said my name, which I enjoyed, it made me watch more but she seemed to fall into a deep sleep after that. I may ask her about it later. I must have dozed off sometime after that, only waking up when my internal body clock chimed.

Wrapping the towel around my waist, I head back over to grab some clothes when she stirs and tries to sit up, clutching her side in the process.

"Shit, I forgot for a second," she says, lying back down on the bed.

"I'll grab you some painkillers, try and get some rest. Go back to sleep," I say, sitting on the edge of the bed.

"Thank you," she says simply, staying where she is. Her red hair fanned out on the pillow behind her.

When I walk back up she's trying to get up again, I give her a look; she doesn't need to move today.

"Don't look at me like that, I need to pee really bad, do you mind if I also take a shower?" she says shyly.

"Be my guest, this place is yours for as long as you need it Millie, let me help you up," I move closer to her, and holding her gently, I lift her up so she's sitting, but leaning against the back of the bed.

"Take these before you get in the shower, it will help," I say, handing her the painkillers and water.

Walking over to the wardrobe, I grab a few things and lay them on the end of the bed. She struggles to get off the bed but doesn't ask me for help. I watch her walk to the bathroom, clutching her chest and side.

"Towels are in the cupboard, next to the sink," I say as she closes the door. What I wouldn't give to be in there with her. That makes me hard all over again… there is something seriously wrong with me, she's in pain and all I can think of is my dick.

"Shit," I mutter to myself. I need to try and keep that under control as I look down at the reaction I get just thinking about her, imagine... No, don't imagine. Forcing myself to get dressed, I head to the kitchen and make a coffee. When she opens the bedroom door ten minutes later, I'm surprised to see she's still dressed.

"Umm... could I ask you something? You can say no." She looks embarrassed and really uncomfortable. "Forget it, don't worry, it's too much...I'll just..."

"Ask me, what do you need?" I cut her off as she tries to back out of saying it to me.

"I need some help..." Her cheeks flush that wonderful shade of pink again. "I can't... I can't get... I can't get undressed. It hurts when I bend, or move..." She drops her head and holds her side.

"Sure, tell me what you need me to do." Walking over to her, she turns and heads back into the room. Following her, I close the door behind me, just standing there waiting for her to say something. When she doesn't, I move a little closer and hold her hand.

"Don't be embarrassed Millie, I'll help you."

"Okay... but..." She's shaking a little. "Could you not look, or look away please?"

"That might be difficult, I'll need to see what I'm doing, but I promise I won't look at the best bits." She laughs, then winces.

"Aww... Don't make me laugh, it hurts," She mutters, standing awkwardly "This is so embarrassing!"

"Sorry, promise I'll be good."

The next few minutes are the most tense of my life. Dropping my hand, she turns around and unbuttons her shirt standing in front of me, hiding herself. *Where has the Millie I knew gone?* She never hid her body from me six years ago. *What has this guy done to her?* My hand moves up to her shoulders and I slide the shirt down her arms. The bruising she has is clear, all over her arms and back. Most of it faded, there are cuts and scars old and new. I don't make a sound, but my mind only goes to one place. I want to hurt the bastard that did this to her. I unclip her blue lace bra and she holds it in place with one arm while she undoes her jeans. I'm still standing behind her, my hands on her shoulders. I lightly touch one of the bruises.

"Please don't..." she whispers to me, her voice so small and so sad. "I'm not the person I used to be Jack." I'm glad she can't see my face right now, it's torn in two completely different directions, lust and hate. She's still so beautiful, yet she can't see it. It's hard to look away when I pull down her jeans, my fingers lightly brush the backs of her thighs, and it's taking all the power of the gods to hold me back from touching her more. I don't know what to say, so I don't say anything.

I hook my fingers in the side of her knickers but she steps away before I can help her.

"I'll do that, thank you. It's more than you should be doing, given the circumstances."

I leave her to it after that; I don't want to upset her or overstep where I'm not wanted but so desperately need to be.

In the kitchen, I make some more coffee. Dan walks in right on time, ready for the day, when he hears the shower running. His eyes light up like a puppy, knowing he is going to get a treat.

"And how was your evening?" he says, nodding towards the shower, a smug smile on his face.

"Mind your own business, here, have a coffee." I hand it to him, but his eyes are trained on the door to my room. I know he is waiting to see who comes out.

"Sit down, it's not what you think." Sitting at the table, I start to run through my day.

"No, of course not, the man who doesn't do relationships has someone in his shower, and you expect me to believe you didn't have a good time last night? Who is it? Anyone I know?" I ignore him. He'll see soon enough, if she's brave enough to come out of the room.

"Paperwork for today, this is yours, what else do we have on? I'd like to try and free up this afternoon if I can, and maybe the next few days?"

"You mean you want some time off? Are you okay boss?" I know he's joking. He's known me long enough to know I don't have time off.

"Yes, I want some time off. Is that so bad? I've got a few personal things I'd like to take care of."

"Personal things? Really? This just gets better. Who is she? I don't remember the last time I saw you with someone, let alone someone who stayed the night."

"Work," I scold him. He chuckles and gets on with plans for the day. Half an hour later, my bedroom door opens and Millie steps out wrapped in just a towel. I stand up, almost knocking my chair over, when I see her. Dan's mouth is wide open when he realises who she is.

"Ha, that's twice I've seen you almost naked!" he says. She stops in her tracks, turns around and walks back into the bedroom.

He just looks at me with a massive smile on his face, nodding his head.

"You're an idiot! Like I said, it's not what that stupid sappy brain of yours is thinking... I'll tell you more about it later. I'll just check on her," I said, almost stomping away from him. I can hear him laughing at me.

When I open the bedroom door, she is pacing the room. "Sorry about Dan, he's a little bit special, but a good bloke. He's marrying my sister actually," trying to keep my voice casual.

"I need my case, did we pick it up last night? I can't find it?"

"No, it didn't even cross my mind, sorry, you can borrow something of mine, and I'll grab your stuff on my way back later," I say, gesturing towards the wardrobe.

When I walk back out the door, Dan chomps at the bit for more information. I ignore him and carry on working.

"I've already texted Em to tell her, she is going to love this. You know they're having a drink together tomorrow at the pub right?"

"Do you two tell each other everything?"

"Yeah man, it's great, although it's normally Em with the juicy stuff. Not this time though!"

Millie walks back out a few minutes later wearing one of my t-shirts, and I think it's the hottest thing I have ever seen. I'm not even sure she is wearing underwear, which only makes me want her more.

"Sorry, I didn't mean to interrupt." She looks down at herself when she sees me looking at her, my eyes following every move of hers. "I had a little trouble getting dressed, do you have any coffee?"

"I don't think Jack minds, and yes the machine is over there," Dan points and smirks at me.

I kick him under the table and he laughs at me. I feel like a school kid looking at his crush.

"I'm Dan by the way, Emilie, Jack's right-hand man, best friend, business partner and soon to be brother-in-law."

"Nice to put a name to the face," she says and almost sighs when she sees how far away the coffee machine is.

"Take a seat, I'll get you a coffee."

"I'll stay standing, thanks. It may take me a while to stand back up again after last night."

Dan almost sprays his coffee everywhere at her words, I chuckle and Millie just looks so confused.

"Did I say something funny?" she asks, frowning at Dan.

"Dan has the wrong end of the stick," how can I put this…"He thinks we spent last night doing… each other" Millie's face somehow pales then goes red almost at the same time.

"Do I? Really? She comes out of your room half naked, then tells me that! NO way, you two didn't do the nasty last night!" I'm not sure Dan will let this go; the smile on his face is huge.

"You put me in your room?" she says, looking directly at me and avoiding any eye contact with Dan.

"Why do you ask?" Now I'm confused. *Why would that matter?*

"You're engaged, that's why I'm asking. What will she think? Oh god!" she turns away, too embarrassed to look at me.

Now I'm really confused. *Where would she get the idea that I'm engaged from?* I've definitely not given the impression I'm with someone else. The way I've been with her, definitely says I'm single.

"Emilie, you keep making this day get better and better," Dan says, laughing still. "Why would you think Mr No Relationships would be engaged?" A little harsh, but also true.

"Who do you think I'm engaged to?" I can't help but laugh, and I see her face get redder when she turns around to face me, the colour almost matching her long curly red hair. She looks down, embarrassed, like she is questioning herself.

"The other day…? In the estate agents?"

But before she can finish, Dan interrupts, leaping up at the same time, coming to stand next to me. Putting his arm over my shoulder. He is having so much fun right now, he will be talking about this for weeks.

"You think he is engaged to Emma?" He's trying his damnedest to not laugh.

"She is pretty hot if you ask me," he says, eyeing me from the side.

"Get off," I say to Dan, shoving him off me, "and no, I'm not engaged to anyone and especially not Emma. That's my sister!" I pull a face letting her know just the thought of what she has said makes me want to vomit.

Millie lets out a little giggle, and it sounds amazing and I just watch her for a second.

"I'm so sorry, it's just the way you said you would talk about the wedding later, then gave her a kiss on the head, I just assumed she was your fiancée. Sorry."

"Sit down Mil, I think we need to clarify a few things, here I'll help you." Setting her coffee on the table, I move towards her and take her arm, helping her sit down at the table.

"Would you like to tell him what happened last night? Or should I?" She looks withdrawn like she doesn't want anyone to know what's happened. None of it's her fault; she has nothing to be ashamed of. Taking a deep breath, she lets it out.

"Um, I got punched in the chest last night, then fell into a table and possibly bruised or fractured my rib, an ambulance got called, I passed out then…"

"I brought her here, as she could barely walk or breathe, the paramedics said she should not be left alone, so here she is."

Dan is stunned into silence, his eyes going between us, trying to see if we are telling the truth.

"Well that killed my fun, Em's going to be disappointed when I tell her what actually happened."

"Oh, so you're marrying Emma?" You can see it all clicking into place the way she is looking at him.

"I'm so stupid, I'm so sorry, look at all the shit I've caused you already, I'm sorry."

"No need to apologise, it's not your fault."

The moment I say it, she looks at me like what I have said is the most ridiculous thing she has heard and shakes her head, pushes herself up, well tries to, so I give her a hand.

"I've got some calls to make and I need to get some stuff sorted out, but I'll be out of your hair soon."

"You can stay as long as you need to, there's no rush. I've got work this morning but I'll be back at some point this afternoon, I'll help you get things sorted."

"Thank you, but you don't need to, I'll manage, nice to see you again Dan." I let go of her and she walks off slowly, my eyes following her as she walks away closing the bedroom door behind her. I let out a sigh and when I turn back to the table, Dan's eyes are on me, like he can't believe what he has just seen.

"I never thought I would see the day that Jack Lucas actually has feelings for a woman!" He whisper-shouts at me.

"What? Don't be ridiculous, how can you have feelings for someone who you only slept with once six years ago?" Oh shit, I've said it, I can't take it back now, and from the look on his face, his eyes are about to pop out of his head. I know I'm in for it today, I will be hounded with questions from him and Em.

God damn my big mouth!

Gone

I trailed her as far as I could, but she's disappeared. She won't get away with this. After everything she's put me through, the humiliation, the betrayal, how could she? She doesn't get to be happy.

Chapter Eleven

The Plan

Millie

Walking into the bedroom, I close the door behind me, I'd sit on the bed, but I struggle to get back up. So I just stand there, like the stupid dick I am. I've made such an idiot of myself, and caused Jack and the pub so much trouble, I'm not sure I can face them. I'm still pacing the room when I hear Jack and Dan leave. I can feel myself relax a little but not enough, my mind is all over the place. I can't think straight, I just want… "Ahhh," I don't even know what I want. Well let's be honest, I do, but I'm so not ready to even have that thought yet. But he is single, I feel like he really cares about me, and he is so goddamn sexy I could just… No, that can stay in my dreams for a while longer.

Putting those thoughts to one side for the time being. Maybe I just need to get practical about this. Where's my notebook? Of course, it's in my case, back at that shithole of a place I'm meant to call my home, where I don't have anything. I'm losing the plot, I need to get out of here.

I grab my jeans from last night and slowly pull them on. It takes a while, every time I bend over, it hurts like hell. I take one of his jumpers from the wardrobe and gradually pull it over my head. It smells like him, warm spices and fresh air, I like it. It takes me a good twenty minutes but I manage to get dressed. I know I can't walk far, so I'll get a taxi back to my place and grab a few things. I'm still not sure about staying here at Jack's but at least I have a bed to sleep in. I'll move out when my new bed arrives, when I order one, that is. I may be staying here, but I don't want him doing anything for me. I need to do this my way. By myself.

Walking out the front door, I suddenly realise I don't have a way to get back in, but before I can hold the door it clicks closed. "Shit," now I'm locked out. It just gets better, and I feel myself start to crumble a little more… this was not how it was all meant to go. I'm not sure how it was actually meant to go, but this was not it! I suppose it's a nice day, cold but still nice. Walking out of the lift on the ground floor, I spot Jack, but thankfully he doesn't see me. I have a feeling he would make me go back upstairs to his suite.

"Hi, would you be able to call me a taxi please?" I ask the receptionist

"Sure madam, where shall I tell them you are going?"

"Bench View."

"Okay, you can wait over there, what name shall I book it under?

"Millie please, oh also, I'm staying with Jack," I say, eyeing him. "Is there any way I can get a key to the suite? He forgot to leave me one when he left."

"I will have to speak with Mr Lucas first, but I don't think it will be a problem."

"He looks busy, don't worry, I'll call him myself when I get back, I'll wait outside for the taxi."

Back in the apartment, I grab my case and head back out. I don't feel comfortable here. Maybe it will be better once I have a few things of my own. Who knows, this is better than where I was. I have to keep telling myself that.

I asked the taxi man to wait while I grabbed my things. When I got back, he asked me, "Where to?" and I had no idea where I wanted to go. I had not been anywhere yet to find a nice spot to sit in.

"Can you recommend somewhere I can sit and stay for a while, somewhere with a view maybe?"

"The Manor Hotel, where I picked you from, has comfy garden seating with heaters, and the grounds are beautiful. How does that sound?"

"Sounds great, means I don't have to walk far with a broken rib," I say smiling.

"If you had told me that love, I would have carried your case down the stairs for you!" Shaking his head in the mirror, he pulls away.

"There is also Bruno's. Next time you're out and about, it's a great coffee shop."

"Thanks, I'll check it out." He talks about all the places I should visit and I write them down in my notebook, deciding to see a few of them over the next few days.

"If I want to find things to do, like creative things, where would I go?"

"You're best off going to the small biz hub, it's like a centre where they have stalls, and all that stuff, it's down by the sea front."

"Who needs the internet when we have you!" I can feel myself feeling better as the morning goes on. I feel a plan starting to click into place, I'm excited, and I don't remember the last time I felt excited to be on my own, to be free.

Walking back into the hotel, I head to the cafe and order a really big coffee and a piece of chocolate cake. Once I have them, I walk out to the garden and find the comfy sofas the driver talked about. Clicking on the heater, I settle in. *Fuck me, these are comfy.* I sink into the seat as it wraps around me, this is amazing. Taking my notebook out of my bag, I place it on the table. I need to clear my head and get a plan in place. Decide on my next step, what I want to do and have and how I will get it. I take a look at my list and decide to write a fresh one. It's a new start, so a new list would be appropriate.

I scratch off the old list and start again, but this time I start thinking about how I want my life to be, who I am, what I love, and also the many things I would have loved to do/get done when I was with Glen, but he would never allow me to, so the first thing I write is:

1. *Create my own design company*

I trained as a fashion designer. I loved creating funky images and applying them to all manner of clothing and bags. I was so close to starting my business when I met Glen, but he instantly took a dislike to it, and said I would never be able to do it, that I lacked everything you needed to run a business appropriately. Well I'll show him, I just need to figure where to start with it, and how I will finance it. I know I can support myself with the job I'm doing. It's not much but I can make it work, if I get another job. I remember Dan saying they had jobs going here, I'll ask at reception on my way back.

2. *Do some yoga*

I may not be able to do some right now, or join a class. I know that will work out to more money, but I'm sure there will be an app I can use to get me started. It's the one positive thing I can take from my relationship with Glen. He liked that I was willing to work on myself. I was bigger than the other girls he knew. And he always reminded me of how much slimmer they were compared to me, so I took a few exercise classes but I enjoyed the yoga the most and stuck with it.

3. *Get my dream tattoo*

I remember designing one once, it was a beautiful simple floral design. I wanted it to run over my shoulder, down my back and arm, tiny flowers, hundreds of them clustered together like a vine. I have a picture of it on my phone, I'll see how much it would be to get done.

4. *Sell my house*

This one still scares the shit out of me, I have no idea how I'm going to do it, but I need to do it. It's the only thing that ties me to that place, and him now, and I want rid of it.

5. *Buy my own place*

I can't do this until I sell that... I sigh a little, this is not a short term plan.

6. *Always stand up for myself, be independent*

The rest speak for themselves, I'm excited, but so nervous at the same time, also a little angry at myself for not doing these things before and letting him control me and treat me the way he did for such a long time. But now I have a plan, something to focus on, which I have been missing this last week, it feels good.

Sitting back, I take a good look at the view, the gardens look down onto a huge lawned area filled with trees, beautiful flowers, and shrubs, it all looks out on the seafront. The place has such a relaxing feel to it, it's stunning. I might stay out here all day, but I need more coffee first. Eventually I manage to stand up and head back inside. Fifteen minutes later, I have my second delicious coffee in hand and I slowly walk back outside. The sun is still shining when I sit back down in my cosy spot and pull one of the blankets over my lap. The sun may be shining but it's still cold. Leaning back in the oversized chair, I close my eyes and start to relax, feeling the warm sun on my face, and it feels wonderful.

When I open my eyes again, the warm sun is fading and I realise I must have dozed off. Oh well, it can't have been that long, I reach for my phone to check the time.

"Oh crap!" It's been hours, literally hours, since I sat down. I never even drank my coffee, it's stone cold. I have three missed calls and one text message all from Jack from two hours ago. I click on the message.

> *Jack: Mil, let me know you're safe x*

My heart melts and my stomach does a funny, twisty, fuzzy thing, it makes me feel... NO, I'm not going there. I squish the feeling back down, and put it to the back of my mind. Taking a deep breath, I reply to him.

> *Me: I've not gone far, still in the hotel actually.*

> *Me: Well, I did go back to my apartment to get my case...but I've been back for ages, and don't worry, I took a taxi, I didn't walk this time.*

> *Jack: Where are you?*

Straight to the point... well if he is not up for a chat, he can wait. I've had such a nice afternoon. I have enthusiasm about what I want to do, no one will stop me this time, and I certainly won't let a man get in my way.

> *Me: Not telling you, you will spoil my vibe!*

> *Jack: I'll find you.*

Now that statement has me a little excited. It's strange, I can feel myself becoming me again already. As bad as things are here, with the very little money I have, a shit apartment, no furniture, and a broken rib, which also means I can't work for a while, *damn it, how has that only just occurred to me, I won't even get sick pay, shit...* but it's so much better than how it was! I'm free, I've made these decisions, me on my own. Just that thought gives me a sense of almost peace.

I sit back and close my eyes again. I'll figure the money stuff out, I always do. My thoughts drift to Jack and how different he is from Glen. I have a feeling he would do anything for me, protect me, nothing like what Glen did, he nearly killed me. I can't let myself go there with Jack. I want to, I want to see if my memories and dreams are right, I want to feel him, touch him and get lost in him again. But I'm not sure I can let anyone in. It hurts too much to even think about what Glen did to me. I loved him, and he... I shake my head at the thought, what if Jack... tears spring to my eyes, and spill over and I let them fall. That pain will never go away.

"Millie, what's wrong?" I know it's him. It sounds so good, a deep rumble that melts my insides. I feel that pull, deep in my heart, pulling me from my thoughts. I wipe my tears away with the back of my hand and open my eyes. I don't want him to know how weak I was, that I couldn't fight back. I just look at him, I don't know what to say.

When he sits down beside me I want to curl up next to him, pretend what Glen did never happened.

"Tell me Mil, I want to help you," he says, wrapping my hand in his. I still don't speak; *how do you tell someone your ex-boyfriend did horrible things to you... so much so it almost killed you?* I wouldn't know where to start, so I don't, I change the subject.

"How did you find me? This place is huge!" I can tell he is annoyed that I have changed the subject, but it's my story, and if I do decide to tell it, it will be when I'm ready.

"I thought I would try my favourite spot first, turns out you like it too!" His eyes are searching mine for answers; I can't look away, his eyes have me locked in place.

"I've got the rest of the day off, would you like to do something?" His smile makes me want him even more. It's like I'm constantly contradicting myself; my mind says no, while my body says yes please, take me now! I don't know what to do. It terrifies me to think that someone could do *that* to me again, I can't handle that though, not a relationship.

"Okay, I have a great idea, fancy watching a movie? I've not seen one in ages."

"Sure, I'll book us some tick..." I cut him off.

"I don't mean go out, I mean from the sofa, with popcorn, chocolate, and wine."

As much as I want to go to the cinema, the thought of being in a dark room with this man beside me has me wanting to do more than just watch a film. I mean just look at him… those deep blue eyes, looking at me like he wants it just as much as I do. The first few buttons of his shirt are undone, showing just the smallest hint of toned, tanned chest. If I could just slide my fingers in and open up his shirt and feel his skin on mine… he is even wearing a tailored suit, showing off his broad shoulders and chest, his muscular arms and rock-hard thighs. His hair is tied back in that man-bun, wow, letting out a sigh, I hope I will have some good dreams tonight. There are not many men that get away with it, but he just looks godlike. Strong, masculine, and fucking sexy as hell.

I may have been staring for a while because he clears his throat, looking at me. He gets that small smile on his face that I remember so well, and it does crazy things to my insides. I take a deep breath in, trying to rid the thoughts of jumping on him, kissing those lips and...

I immediately turn a deep shade of red when he laughs and moves his hand to my thigh, making small circles with his fingers, edging further up my thigh just a little, sending waves of electricity through me. Oh my god, I almost explode with pleasure. My eyes flutter closed for a millisecond, that feeling runs up my leg right to my core. He lets out a deep sigh and moves his hand away. I can't help but feel a loss, I can still feel where his hand was on me, all I want him to do is touch me again.

"Movies on the sofa sound good to me," he says, *maybe it was not such a good idea, I'm not sure I can control myself.*

"What are we watching?" he says and I have no idea,

"I don't know, you can choose," leaving the decision to him.

"Really... you want to watch this, I thought you would have been an action guy?" I can't help but laugh at his movie choice. It's definitely not what I would have picked, a cheesy romcom with Sandra Bullock in it. But it was his choice.

"Hey, you said it was up to me, and this is what I want to watch. Next time you can choose."

When we got back, he took my things to his room and insisted I stay there, saying it was the better bed, and I'd be more comfortable, but surely the beds are the same? It's a hotel, and it means he will have to stay in the spare room when all his stuff is in here. I'll move my things to the spare room tomorrow when he goes to work.

"I'll call down to reception and ask them to bring a few things up for us, and to get you a key to the room, what do you want?"

"Don't get it from the hotel, it will be expensive, I'll pop to the shop down the road and get a few things," I say standing up, grabbing my purse.

"It's on me, the hotel has loads of this stuff. Now what would you like?" Picking up the phone, he dials reception.

"Just some chocolate please." When reception answers, he asks for two bottles of white wine, some beers, chocolates, popcorn, crisps, and a pizza to be delivered later on. I shake my head at him, but he just smiles at me.

I'll leave him some cash tomorrow; being here for the next few days may work out expensive if he carries on like this.

"Oh damn it, I forgot to ask about a job at reception on my way up, I'll be back in a few minutes." Making my way to the door, he looked at me, confused for a moment.

"You have a job, why do you need another? He is leaning against the island in the kitchen with his arms folded, like he can't understand why.

"As much as I like working at the pub, that only covers my flat rent, bills and not much else. I really need to earn some more money if I want a fresh start, so I need another job."

"What were you doing outside anyway?" he says, changing the subject.

"I was making plans, I'll tell you all about them one day, but first I need to see if I can get another job." Grabbing the door handle, I pull and walk out the door.

When I get downstairs, the receptionist is on the phone, she mouths she won't be a moment. I hope they have something, something where I can sit down, meaning I can start as soon as possible, even with my rib the way it is.

When she comes off the phone, she hands me a key card. She looks at me with a smile, she is a slightly older lady, with greying hair, "Mr Lucas has asked me to give you this, so you can get back into the suite."

"Oh, thank you." A little taken aback, I look at her name badge, it reads, 'Mary, Manager'.

"Mary, Could I ask if there are any admin positions going at the hotel please?"

"Let me take your name and number down honey, I know we have a few vacancies. I'll call you tomorrow with some details if that's okay? We are a little short-staffed today, otherwise I'd go through them with you now."

"Mary, that's wonderful, thank you, do you need some help with anything, I can always help out now?" I say as I hand her my name and number on the paper she gave to me.

"No dear don't be silly, you get back to Mr Lucas and we will talk tomorrow, I'll call you in the morning."

Thanking her, I make my way to the lift. I would have skipped back to the suite if I could have. If I can get one of the jobs they have, I can start to save and put my plans into action. Eeeek I'm so excited.

When I walk back into the suite, Jack is pouring out two glasses of wine in the kitchen. When he glances over, he has that sexy smile on his face. It makes me feel all those things I don't want to feel, but also really want to feel at the same time. *Damn it, why!* Trying to be normal, I walk over to him; he turns slowly towards me, his eyes travel the full length of me. I can feel my cheeks flushing, knowing pretty much what he is thinking. He chuckles to himself, then turns to me, handing me my glass of wine. He places his hands on either side of my waist, facing me, my back softly pressing against the counter. When he leans in, I feel his warm breath on my neck, my eyes close and my breath hitches, his lips skim my neck and he says, "I like seeing you in my clothes, there is something really sexy about it."

He glides a hand to the small of my back and presses me closer to him. My body reacts before I do, arching to him, wanting to feel more. Relishing in the feeling, I can't stop my free hand from roaming his back, feeling the strength it holds beneath his shirt. I can feel how turned on he is, I can feel his length pressing into me. He bends his head so his cheek touches mine and places a small kiss right below my ear on my neck. I can't think straight, his body pressed to mine, brings back all those feelings, all those dreams, images run though my head of our time together, but he stops and steps back. *What the fuck!* I let out a breath of frustration and squeeze my legs together to try and find some release to the feelings he has so easily stirred up. I watch him close his eyes and take a deep breath. Stepping further back he says, "Let's watch this film… they sent everything up while you were out." I look round and see that he has set all the snacks out on the coffee table with another bottle of wine on ice.

"Let me get changed." Pushing myself away from the counter, I head towards the bedroom, I need a few moments to myself after that. And now I have to sit and watch a stupid movie with him, I feel like crying. My body so badly wants to be with him, but my mind and heart are telling me otherwise. *Would it be so bad to just maybe sleep with him, no strings attached? Can I be that person?* I've only ever been that person once, and that was with Jack. It was hard to leave him the last time, even though I knew I was nothing more than a one day stand to him. What we did felt right, but can I do it again? I'm not ready for a relationship, I don't want a relationship, not again, I know what can happen when you trust someone, they break it, and you get hurt.

Lifting my glass to my lips I take a massive gulp of wine… *maybe that is the best way?* Grabbing my case, I open it and find my PJs. I look at them and they feel so soft and cosy, but I put them back, deciding to wear one of his t-shirts and a pair of sexy lace french knickers. I'll see how far he is willing to go, no-strings, no pain, no hurt. Eyeing myself in the mirror I let my hair down, curly red locks fall over my shoulders, the t-shirt comes down to the top of my thighs, leaving my legs bare, you can still see the bruising, but that's okay. I take a deep breath, grab my wine and walk back out the door.

Chapter Twelve

Control

Jack

It was fun to watch her reaction to me. I know she's as turned on as I am right now, but I will not go any further. Man I want to, I really want to, I want to do it all, but she needs time to recover from whatever has happened to her and start again with her life here. I don't want her to run, not again, plus with her rib the way it is, it would be not fun to see her in even more pain while we… *all thoughts stop, I can't… fuck.* My eyes dart to the bedroom door, "Millie. My, what?" She is wearing my tee and what looks like nothing else, fuck, I can't look away, so I stand up.

"I need some more wine," she says as she walks over to the coffee table and bends down reaching for the wine bottle. My jaw just hangs open, as I catch a glimpse of her tiny black lace panties hugged to her fantastically rounded bum, when the tee rides up while she bends over. I've stood to attention in more ways than one, *what is she doing? What happened in that room?* I can't move my eyes away, I can see where the top of her legs meet the sweetness of those panties and her silky skin, that place where I long to be, long to run my fingers, and make her scream my name. I'm hard. So hard I can't move. Putting into practice what I have just been telling myself, is going to be even harder than I thought. I was going to keep teasing her, I mean, I'm only human, but if she carries on like this, with those sexy legs, her hair down and loose, making me want to run my fingers through them, I won't be able to help myself. Taking a deep breath, I sit back down and automatically reach out to touch her legs. When she glances at me, a smile creeps up her face, and her eyes dance with amusement.

Oh she knows what she is doing. Moving my hand back to my lap, I adjust myself. *Why is she doing this?*

"What are you trying to do?" I say, my voice coming out all harsh and husky.

"Just getting some more wine, why?" she says as she sits next to me crossing her legs so I can still see those delicious panties, and traces of what's under them.

"No," I manage to say, shaking my head.

"No, what?" she said, looking a little confused

"Just no. I know what you are trying to do, just what I did to you when you walked through the door, and it's not going to happen."

"I have no idea what you are on about, press play so we can watch the movie." This is going to be tough. I know what she is trying to do, I won't give in to her. I want more than just sex, and

I know she is not ready for that, not by how her reactions have been before now. I can't, I won't take advantage of her like that, she's vulnerable.

"I won't sleep with you, not like this" not even I sound convinced.

She sits up and flinches at the same time, holding her side, "What do you mean *like this*? You started it, I'm just egging you on, do you not want to play with me?" she says as she slides her legs over mine, making it impossible to think of anything else but playing with her, but there is a look in her eyes that I can't figure out.

"Oh I want to play, but not like this, not until you are healed, I can't, I won't."

"Sounds to me like you're trying to convince yourself, I'm ready when you are." She leans back and the tee lifts up past her legs showing more than I have seen before, tiny black lace just about covering the area I want to be in most, and when she stretches up it rises past the top of her panties over her stomach revealing a small tattoo of a lizard, I don't remember seeing before. I want to trace it with my finger and feel how soft she is.

"Fuck…this is…no. Not going to happen, tell me about the tattoo. Why a lizard?"

"That's a secret for another day, it's a bit personal…"

"Tell me, I'm intrigued." I need something to distract me.

"Umm… okay, but don't laugh. It represents one of the most amazing times of my life. Before it went to shit." she sighs. "It's kind of a symbol of a country I fell for and someone who changed me for the better."

"Why would I laugh at that? Sounds like a great place. Tell me where?"

"Oh hell no," she laughs. I love the sound of it.

"Okay, but I'll find out one day." I need to make a mental note to look up what countries have lizards as a symbol.

"I won't tell you," she chuckles. I press the button for the movie to start but all I can think of is how much I want to touch her. Feel her skin on mine, taste her sweet spot and drive her crazy. I think watching movies with her has just become my new favourite thing to do, especially when she is dressed like that.

I place my hand on her legs and automatically move it up, caressing her skin, this simple little touch is driving me insane. Pleasure runs from my fingers all over my body, the feeling of warmth spreads across my chest, relaxing me, all the while Millie sits and watches the movie like nothing is happening. *How can this affect me so much, and not her?* It's insane what she's doing to me.

The entire evening is like torture; every time she moves or picks something up, I see more of what I so badly want. Suddenly there's a knock at the door, a welcome distraction I need.

"I'll get it," she says, getting to her feet and adjusting the tee to cover her ass.

"Not dressed like that you're not!" Walking past her, I open the door, where our pizza is waiting for us. I tip the guy and close the door before he can get an eyeful.

"Great, I'm starving, I feel like I haven't eaten in days." She props herself up against the bar stool, and perches on the edge, legs and panties in full view.

"Are you trying to kill me? Look at you..." Flinging the pizza on the side next her she opens the box and grabs a piece.

"No idea what you're talking about." The smirk on her face says differently, and when she takes a bite of pizza, licking her fingers and lips, I can't take it anymore.

"That's it..." I pick her up with my hand wrapped around her waist, she squeals with excitement as I sit her down on the sofa, careful not to hurt her.

"I'm not going to sleep with you, but I will make you scream my name." I kiss her, giving her everything I have. Her soft lips part and our tongues meet in a fever of passion and need. Leaning into her, feeling her body against mine, drives me further. The need for her, to taste her, it's like nothing I have felt with anyone but her. I can't stop. Sliding my hand to her back and lifting the tee over her head, revealing her to me, I move back an inch and take her in – all of her, her body, the bruises, scars, all of it. *How could someone have done this to her beautiful body?* She's perfect, lying against the cushions, her deep red hair tumbling down her shoulders, her hand resting on my shoulders, the warmth spreading through me. Our eyes meet and all I see is beauty, deep within those hazel eyes, and for a quick second, I see an odd emotion in her eyes, before she closes them.

I bend down, taking a sweet plump nipple into my mouth, still looking at her, even though her eyes are closed. Flicking it with my tongue then sucking the bud. She moans, so I do it again, and she arches to me, pressing my length against her, so she knows how I feel. Millie grabs my shirt, and I pull it off, gliding my hands back to her. I slide my fingers under her panties and find her wet. My hard cock twitches, aching to get out and be buried deep within her. She moans again, when my thumb finds her clit, I glide my finger over her and she curses. That's what I want to hear. It turns me on more than I have ever been in my life, circling her most sensitive spot, bringing her higher. Her breathing becomes heavy as I apply a little more pressure, teasing her, making her moan and curse. Sliding her panties down her legs I see her in her full glory. I want to taste her, have her in my mouth, while she screams my name. I place her legs over my shoulders and press tender kisses down her abdomen, squeezing her nipples with one hand while I hold her with the other. Trailing the kisses lower, I nip at her skin, she arches, needing more from me. I kiss down to the parts I've dreamt about and kiss her, right there, inhaling deeply as she puts her hands in my hair and work her, bringing her closer to the edge, when she says my name I insert my finger deep into her. She's so wet, her walls clamp down on my fingers. She screams my name again and again; looking up I see the most beautiful sight I have ever seen as she comes apart, my fingers and tongue still caressing her, bringing her over the edge. She convulses around my fingers and I watch as wave after wave washes over her, leaving her breathless, while she lays back on the sofa, arms covering her face.

"Don't hide yourself from me!" I trail more kisses up her stomach, and take a nipple in my mouth sucking it until she moans again. My fingers are still inside her, moving them slowly, in and out, pressing my thumb to her clit, she arches craving more.

"I could do this all night, watching you come. You're the hottest, sexiest thing I have ever seen. I hope you're ready for more."

"Jack," she says in a faint whisper. I can feel her building again, I tug her nipple with my teeth and she lets out the most amazing sound I have ever heard. My fingers move a little faster now, in and out making her insane with need. She starts moving her hips to get more friction, riding my hand making me watch every move. I kiss her as she climbs higher, thrusting harder giving her what she needs. Her hands grip my hair as she comes apart again in my arms, saying my name while I kiss her hard. Resting my head on her chest I can hear her heart beating fast, she feels and smells intoxicating. It's taking everything I have not to go further, bury myself in her, and feel her come around me, while finding my own release in the process, I know it would be bliss. She wraps her arms around me, flinches slightly when she moves under me.

"I'm so sorry, are you okay?" *What have I done? How could I have been so stupid? I've hurt her even more.* Guilt washes over as we lie down together. I watch while she recovers. I can't help but touch her, she feels amazing. Opening her eyes, she lifts her head to mine, kisses me softly and cuddles into me. We stay like this for a while. Not saying anything.

"This may sound stupid, but thank you."

"Have you just thanked me for making you come, twice?" There's a massive smile on my face, that I can't hide.

"Yes and no, I mean, that was earth shattering, and we didn't even have sex, but the way you made me feel…even if this never happens again, you have made me feel wanted, and sexy. Something I've not felt in a very long time, so yes, thank you, even if I am unable to move tomorrow through the pain in my rib, it has been worth it."

What do you say to that? I'm stunned into silence. *How could she not feel wanted, and sexy? Look at her..* I can see all the marks that cover her body, the scars, the bruises, and cuts. I kissed them, caressed them, wished they were not there. She's beautiful. I help her to her feet, and she walks over to the kitchen to grab her things from the floor where they landed when I threw them. When she bends down, she whimpers and doesn't move, you can see the pain all over her face. I shoot up and grab my tee, helping to pull it over her head. I can see the tears in her eyes. She turns her head, grabs the pizza box, and walks back to the sofa. I help her sit and get comfy. *Shit, I've done this to her! I've made it worse just to inflate my own ego.*

How can she not be sexy? How could someone not want her?

"What happened to you Millie? How did you end up here?" I say, turning to her, placing my hand on her bare leg. She looks down like she is considering something, there is a flash of pain in her eyes, then it disappears as quick as it arrived, and she takes a deep breath in..

"Like I said, I was in an accident about five weeks ago." She shuts down, as soon as the words come out.

"Bullshit, but if you're not ready to talk about it, that's okay, I'm here when you are."

Leaning back on the cushions, I close my eyes, drawing small circles with my fingers along the inside of her thigh. Leaning into me, she lays her head on my shoulder, her fingers playing with the hem of the tee. I can smell her sweet scent like oranges and mangos, when she places a hand on my chest, and lets out a breath.

"You're right," she whispers, "it is bullshit, but I'm not ready to go there, not yet, it's too painful."

"Okay." It's all I manage to say. I can feel the anger swelling up inside me, I have a really good idea what happened to her, and it infuriates me. *How anyone can do that to a woman?* I have no idea, I want to find and catch the bastard that did it, but for now I wrap my arm around her shoulders, and hope she feels safe.

The next few days Millie spends in bed, our little sofa catch up has made her ribs worse, so I've ordered her to stay in bed. I've not taken any time off work but I have been working from my dining room in the suite so I can keep a close eye on her. She keeps trying to do things by herself, and I have to keep reminding her I can help, and that she is not alone anymore.

The hotel arranged for her to have a phone interview rather than going out. I explained about her ribs and they were happy to accommodate. It helps that I'm the boss, but I'm not sure she realises I own the place. I can't wait for her to find out, I think it will piss her off. Anyway, she got the job and starts on Wednesday. She will be purchasing manager, all from the office downstairs. I also have a little surprise in store for her. I know how much she needs her space. She keeps telling me. So I have decided to sort something out for her with the hotel. But she will be staying with me for next week until she can do a few more things by herself, like sit up without swearing.

"Sweet motherfucking...a-hole!" I hear her from the bedroom.

"Everything okay there?" I say walking over and opening the door. "What are you trying to do?" I see Millie sitting naked, on the floor, legs crossed and looking pissed off. She tries to cover herself when I walk in.

"Don't cover yourself just for me, you know I like what I see." She rolls her eyes at me, and I laugh, "I've helped you in and out of the shower for the past few days, helped you get dressed and seen more of you than this from our little bit of foreplay on the sofa. You have nothing to hide, I like it." She rolls her eyes again, but holds out her hand.

"Help me up, I was trying to get myself dressed, and fell on the floor. I have a few things I want to organise for my apartment today." Oh shit… I need to stall her.

"Now, about that. Don't rush into buying anything. I asked Em to take a look at the contract for you, try and get him to put the furniture back, but you are staying with me for at least a week."

"You did that for me? Why?" I ignore her, rolling my eyes at her this time. I'm not willing to let the reason why even enter my thoughts. She has been back in my life for less than a week, and I'm acting like a possessive boyfriend. I want her to stay with me for as long as she likes, but I know how much it means to her to have her own place. "Leave it a few days before you start doing anything, see what Em comes up with," I say as she sits on the bed. "Do you want me to help you get dressed?"

"No, but I think, you think, you need to." She looks sad, all I want to do is make her happy.

"Okay, nice knickers. Are you sure you want to get dressed? I can help you back to bed?" Kneeling in front of her, I glide my hand over her thigh, but she slaps it away. I look up and give her my best puppy dog eyes.

"No," she laughs, it's a sound I love to hear. Her smile reaches her eyes, a little playful, and it's wonderful. I just stare at her.

"Are you going to help me? Or do I have to try and do it myself and keep swearing profanities at you?" She laughs again, so I start to help. We work together to get her dressed. I help when she can't bend down or reach where she needs to; it has to be the best morning I've had in a long time.

Chapter Thirteen

High & Low

Millie

It's been over a week and it's been challenging, to say the least. After Jack devoured me on the sofa, I have been in more pain than I have been letting on. But it was worth it. Oh my god was it worth it! I haven't felt so good about myself in years, he really made me feel wanted. Desired. Even sexy. Oh god it sounds so stupid. But it's boosted my confidence so much, I feel I could take on the world. Jack, on the other hand, has had other ideas. He hasn't let me leave the bedroom for three days. It's not what you think either... he's not touched me, other than to help me. He's only just agreed to let me leave the room. He's based himself in the dining room to work, and has been waiting on me, hand and foot ever since, which has been wonderful but also slightly annoying. I'm not one for sitting around, I like to be doing things, and he has not let me do anything… nothing, zip, zero, zilch. It's frustrating, but also really sweet at the same time. I keep having to tell him that I need my space. I'm not sure he completely understands though. How could he?

When I went to take a shower the following morning, I couldn't do it by myself; he found me sobbing in the bathroom, just stood there like an idiot, and I had to admit to him how much pain I was in. But instead of looking at me in disgust and leaving me alone like Glen had done many times before, he helped me get undressed, helped shower and wash my hair, he even helped me dry my hair and put my (his) tee on.

He's been so kind to me, I don't know what to think, maybe he's feeling bad about what we did and the consequences of that, even though I enjoyed every tantalising second. I'm not teasing him again though, I made that decision the moment I woke up the following morning alone. I can't be that girl, I have never been able to be that girl. I have to do this on my own, I have to find myself again without a man. I just hope Jack understands.

I feel a little bad for him, I didn't even get to repay the favour he so wonderfully, and expertly bestowed upon me. If it hadn't been for my ribs that night, who knows where the night would have led to. But then again, if it wasn't for my ribs, I wouldn't be in Jack's hotel suite, would I? But I can't and won't be that girl who sleeps with someone for fun. My feelings for him are already growing, and it scares the shit out of me, I can't trust another man. My heart is so fragile that if anything happens, I'm not sure I would ever recover. So I'm taking a step or two back. I can't do it; deep down I know he won't hurt me like Glen did, but I still can't shake that feeling of my heart being broken. Trusting anyone again will not be easy.

Yesterday he told me not to order anything for the apartment, as Em was working on getting some furniture back for me, which is great. Fingers crossed, I'll be back there soon, in my own space, to find out who I am and start my life the way I intended, man free. Every time I say this to myself, I feel a little pinch in my chest, but I ignore it and try focusing on something else.

The thought of leaving also makes me feel so... sad. I want to have my own space, I need to feel free, and staying in a hotel suite being waited on hand and foot by this godlike, adonis of a man is not gaining me that feeling. So why do I feel like this? So sad? No... I'm not ready to answer that question. Pushing that feeling down again, I grab my notebook and start working on my new idea. I signed up to some free design software, and have bought myself a second-hand laptop. It does what I need for now, my first pay cheque should cover what I have spent, after leaving some money for Jack to pay him back for everything he has done.

So with not being able to move from the suite for the last week, today I decided I needed to get out. I have dressed myself, with no help needed from Jack, much to his disappointment, and I have settled on the sofa.

Jack's not touched me since that night. He teases and talks about it but never sees it through. It's nice, I think.

Anyway, I've focused my energy on building my business, I've been working on a few fabric designs, and it feels amazing. I have even thought up a name for my business, 'Milliecan.' Because I can, I've been told I couldn't do anything for so long. It's nice to know I can and I will. I have not told Jack yet about my business; he keeps asking what I'm up to. All I'm telling him is it's a new project I'm working on. He keeps trying to sneak looks while I'm working, but I just shut it down. I will tell him when I'm ready, I just want it to be mine for a little while, enjoy the feeling of being creative again.

I had to cancel my meeting with Emma last Sunday, but I have arranged to meet her tomorrow after work. I can't believe I got the purchasing job. It's great, well paid, Monday to Friday, so I can still work at the pub, Thursday, Friday and Saturday nights. Things are looking up.

My first day at work today came around like a flash. Mary, the manager, has been amazing, she has shown me everything, and I've taken to it easily. Doing everything that needs to be done and a little more. In true Jack form, he sent me lunch, followed by a bunch of flowers wishing me good luck, which was really sweet. I messaged him saying:

> *Me: Thank you, but I can get my own lunch.*

To which he replied:

> *Jack: "You're welcome, I know you can, I want to make sure you're eating."*

Ha, well, if it hadn't been for him sending me lunch, I would not have eaten. I would have just worked through like I normally would have. It's like he knows me already, which scares me even more.

A few minutes later, there is another delivery of a massive piece of chocolate cake, accompanied by a very large coffee. I eat the cake and drink the coffee, take a picture of the empty plate and send it to him, turning my phone off so I carry on working. By the time I look back up from the computer, it's already 5.15 pm and it's time for me to clock off, but before I go, I make a list of everything I need to get done tomorrow, say a quick goodbye to Mary and head to the suite to get ready to meet Em at the pub.

It's been so nice to get back to some normality today. It really feels like some of the weight has been lifted off my shoulders. There is still so much I need to sort out with the house, my business and my apartment that my head still feels a little overwhelmed. But knowing I now have two jobs is putting my money worries at ease a little. Hopefully, Em will be able to help me take a step forward with the house. I don't want Jack to know yet, I want this to go as smoothly as possible, and I know as soon as he finds out, he will want to help. But this is definitely something I need to do on my own. Once the house is sold, I can buy a new place, set up my biz from there and look to the future properly. I'm so excited about it all.

When I walk into the suite, Jack's not there, which is great; I can get changed and go out without having him worry. I'll send him a message that I've gone to meet Em.

"Oh shit," I say out loud to an empty bedroom. I totally forgot to turn my phone back on. A swell of panic and fear rises in me, my thoughts instantly go to Glen, and what he would do when he found out I switched it off. I hurry to turn it on, almost crying, and then it hits me all over again. I chuckle to myself, realising I don't have to worry anymore. My panic calms slightly, I sit on the edge of the bed with my head in my hands and take a few deep breaths, tears still streaming down my face, but tears of relief this time; he won't hurt me ever again. It's hard to get my head around that, my head knows I've left him, but my body is reacting like I'm still there. I suppose it will take time for these things to stop happening.

After a few minutes, I head into the bathroom to take a long shower. Once I'm dried off, I step into the bedroom and dress in a long green flowing skirt and black cami. I unpin my hair from its high bun and tame the waves as best I can, plaiting one side to keep it out of my face. Heading out to the kitchen, I grab a bottle of wine and a glass and take it to the living room. I have half an hour or so before I need to meet Em, so I decide to sit and relax with a glass of wine. It's so nice I have two glasses before I leave and plan on drinking the rest when I get back. It's now almost 6.30 pm and the evening air is crisp and fresh. Hugging my leather jacket closer to me, I walk the short distance to the pub, still a little early.

"Emilie, you look good, how are you feeling? Jack said it will still be a week or so before you can come back to work?" Mike says when he spots me walking in.

"Thanks Mike," I say with a smile, shaking my head at the thought of Jack talking to Mike for me. I know he means well, but this is my life, not his.

"Forget what Jack says I'll be back tomorrow for my shift, I'm feeling much better thank you." I walk up to the bar and lean against it.

"Only if you're sure, we will keep you out the back this week, then next week back to normal?" He doesn't sound sure at all, I'm betting Jack will have something to say about it. But he is not the boss of me, well technically, he is here… damn it. Oh well he'll just have to live with it.

"Sounds perfect, no need to run it by Jack, I'll let him know, could I get two glasses of wine, one for me, one for Em please?"

"Sure can," he says as he pins me with a worried stare. "Should you be drinking on those painkillers?" Honestly, it is like having my dad back; it feels nice to have people worry over me. I have only known them for a few weeks and they are already feeling like close friends.

"Yes, Dad," I tease, rolling my eyes at him. He smirks at me and pours the drinks.

"On the house," he says as he sets the drinks down in front of me. Taking a sip, I thank him, then move over to a table a little out of the way, where I know we will be able to chat away from the busy bar.

"I'm so sorry I'm late, my stupid boss made me catch up on all my emails before I left!" Em says as she sits down opposite me, reaching for the glass.

"I thought you were the boss?" I think she's messing with me, but I'm not sure.

"Ha, I am yes, I can be mean as hell to my staff sometimes," she says with a wink, then laughs at me, taking a sip of her wine. "I'll get us another, keep us going for a while." When she stands to leave, I let out a breath... I'm nervous.

I feel so uncomfortable. I've not been out with a friend for such a long time; it feels almost alien to me, what will we even talk about? I can feel my anxiety levels going up slightly.

The last time I went out with one of my friends was almost three years ago, just after... well it all started to go south. I met Charlie, my best friend at the time for a few drinks and we never saw each other again after that night. I'm not even sure what happened, we had a great night together just like we always did, then she never responded to any of my messages or calls, and after a few weeks, I gave up. Glen said I was better off without her, but clearly, he didn't want anyone on my side and Charlie always looked out for me.

"You look deep in thought, penny for them?" she says, placing another glass of wine down in front of me.

"I was just thinking of an old friend, we lost touch a few years ago, we were great friends once upon a time, I'm not sure what happened."

"Then reach out again, no time like the present. If you were good friends once, it would be like nothing had happened," she says softly.

"That's a good idea, a toast to new beginnings, and old friends." I hold up my glass.

"And new friends," she says with an eager smile.

We toast and sip our wine and talk like we have been friends for years, I had no reason to worry. Before you know it, we are a few more glasses of wine in. I know all about Emma, how she and Dan got together behind Jack's back in secret for a whole year before they told him. They had been friends before that, a true love story, sneaking around, fun and sexy, and how he made her feel so loved. She knew for years, even before they got together, that one day she would end up with him. What did I do so wrong for Glen to treat me like he did?

"Tell me about your wedding, I want to know all the details, it's soon isn't it?" I ask to stop my trail of thoughts.

"Oh yes, my favourite subject," she says with a laugh. "It's eight weeks and two days away, most of it is all planned, it's going to be at the Manor Hotel actually, under the huge rose arch in the garden. We have gone simple and elegant, with white, hints of green, black and gold. As much as I want the big wedding, all I really want is to marry Dan, soppy or what?"

"It's not soppy, it's beautiful you have found your one!" I almost yelled at her, "I thought I had mine a few years ago, but things changed, or rather he changed." I sigh, I'm trying not to think about him at all but it's so hard. He's affected so much of my life and none of it in a good way.

You can see the concern on her face almost instantly. I shouldn't have said anything.

"Is that why you are here? Because of a man?" Curiosity lacing her voice, she reaches over and squeezes my hand. It's a small gesture but it means a lot.

"Yes and no, I needed a fresh start, and this is it! Oh that reminds me, I need your advice, but I was hoping you wouldn't tell Jack?" A quick change of subject. I hope it's not too obvious.

"Sure, I love knowing more than he does, it will wind him up something rotten! What do you need?" Em laughs.

This is it, a massive step for me; as soon as the words come out of my mouth, I can't take them back; I have to do this.

"I have a house in London, and I need to sell it, but there is still someone living in it. Do you know how I can do it without…um, being there?" leaning forward a little towards me, she asks.

"Oh my god, is this the man you need a fresh start from? Is he still living there?"

"Um…yeah," my palms are sweating so much. I feel like I want to back out already, but I know I can't. He is going to be so pissed when he finds out, I'm not sure what he will do. That chills me to the bone. He was unpredictable at best of times, short-tempered; you never knew what would set him off. But I'm sure this will send him to boiling point. Not that I'll tell Em any of this.

"Tricky, is the house in both names?" You can literally see her switch to business mode, even the way she sits is different, almost straighter.

"No, my parents left it to me after they passed away a few years ago, so it's mine."

"Okay, the best way would be to get him out, change the locks so he can't get back in and sell from there. You would need to get a solicitor, and speak to a local estate agent to get images and sort the evaluation out. I know a good estate agent. I'll get in touch and ask him to contact you. Would that be okay? I'm sure we can get this done between us." She reaches out for my hand and gives it a squeeze. "But why don't you want to tell Jack? He would be more than happy to help you."

"It's just he's done so much for me already, and I'm not even sure why. We only met once six years ago and… well, he has more than enough on his plate, with taking over this place. I don't want to trouble him anymore than I have to." My hands are fumbling with my glass, as soon as I said about meeting him six years ago, I could feel the heat rising in my cheeks, and now I'm having trouble looking her in the eyes.

"You really have no idea why he is helping you? I can tell you now, I have never seen him like this with anyone… tell me how you met?" Her eyes go wide with mischief, like she knows but wants to hear it from me, so I tell her about the man that tried to attack me, and how Jack came to my rescue.

"He stepped in and knocked him out cold? Really?" Her expression is a little shocked, but also proud of what her brother did for me.

"Yes, really, he took me to the office but before I could even say thank you, my friend Charlie stormed in and shouted at him and took me back to the hotel," laughing at the memory, and remembering the look on his face as she pulled me away.

"That's awesome, she sounds like a good friend, is that the one you lost touch with?"

"Yeah, she is, she was pretty awesome. Always looked out for me, anyway I went back to the club the next day, to say thank you and..." I can feel my cheeks getting hotter by the second, at the thought of what we did together, the memory, the dreams, "Well, one thing led to another, we spent the afternoon together, I knew I was only a one-day stand for him, so I left when he fell asleep, flew home that day."

"Wow, I'm a little grossed out as it's my brother, but WOW!" she says, sitting back in her chair.

"What do you mean.. wow? There is nothing unusual about it, just a standard one-day stand" I'm a little confused by the comment.

"Well, let me explain something to you. Dan has told me a few stories about Jack over the years, but there was one that always sticks in my mind. And it's how he tried to find a girl he slept with and looked for an entire day around the Island. He knew everyone so it was easy to ask questions and find someone if you needed to, that was about six years ago…he told Dan that she had been different to all the others."

"All the others?"

"That's what you take from what I have just said?" she said with a chuckle, "Not that he tried to find you, said you were different to all the other girls he has slept with."

"How do you even know it was me? It could have been anyone, no, no, no..."

It all feels too much, I can feel myself wanting it to be me he looked for, I want that connection, I want to feel wanted, but at the same time, an overwhelming fear sweeps over me, almost crushing me, clutching my chest in a vice grip, I can't. *What if... what if it all happens again, what if he hurts me... what if he tears me apart just like Glen did? What if... no...* my head's spinning. I can't focus...

"Are you okay? You've gone pale?" I can't see her, my vision's clouded, I can't get enough breath in.

"No, not really, I'm not feeling great, I think I'm going to head home," my words come out in a rush.

"If you can wait fifteen mins, Dan will give you a lift back..."

"Thank you, but I think the walk will do me good. I'm so sorry... I'm not used to drinking, this is the most I have had in a long time, plus I've not eaten since lunch." My hands are starting to shake, I need to go, I know what's going to happen and I need to get out here, now.

"Okay, it's not far, text me when you're back at the hotel."

As I stand up to leave, my anxiety hits me on a level I've not felt in a long time. I almost died at the hands of a man who I thought loved me. I can't even entertain the thought of another man in my life, one who wants... more. I'm on the edge, about to fall over, and I can't stop it..

I lift my hand to wave and head for the front door, holding it together as best I can. I don't want anyone to see me like this, weak and pathetic. The moment I step outside, the cold air hits me and I realise just how much I've had to drink. My head spins and my legs feel weak, I need to go.

I make it a few streets down just before I'm in someone's garden, stumbling all the way back, supporting myself on the wall as my panic attack gets worse.

It feels like it's taken me forever to get back to the hotel, no matter how much I try, I can't calm myself down. I think Mary waves at me from the front desk and I force a smile on my face, heading to the lift hoping for my own sake I don't see anyone else.

I step out onto the suite floor, my hands are shaking so bad that it's hard to grab the key card from my purse. The pressure in my chest as my panic rises is so intense, it's almost crippling. When I walk or rather stumble through the door, it is agonising. All I want to do is hide, go to bed and try to ride it out.

When I look up, I see him standing there in the kitchen, looking at me.

When he steps towards me, I drop to the floor and pray he won't hurt me, my hands come up to protect me, and I cry.

"I'm sorry, I'm sorry, please don't hurt me…"

Chapter Fourteen

Panic

Jack

"Your stag do is planned and no, I'm not telling you what we're doing or where we are going."

"Oh come on, Em will kill me if I don't tell her where I'm going, or what you have planned for me, is it bad?"

I love tormenting him, he deserves it for marrying my sister. Just the look of slight worry on his face at what I could have planned for him, is worth it. Em knows everything I have planned, but I want him to suffer a little, and she finds it hilarious.

"Really bad, stuff you should only really do when you are single, if Em finds out…well, I'm sure she would be fine with it eventually."

"Oh fuck, you do realise I'm marrying your sister, you best be fucking with me…" He has been pacing the living room of his house for the last fifteen minutes, trying to think of what I could have planned for him. He has guessed it right a few times, but I'm not letting on; where would be the fun in that?

"Do you honestly think I would put your relationship with my sister on the line, for a stag do?" I'm sitting on their sofa, coffee in hand, watching him pace and enjoying every second of it.

"Right now, this second, I'm not sure, you have the best poker face I have ever seen, you could have booked us all to go to Vegas, with strip clubs, biker bars and god only knows what else, I would never be able to tell"

"Now that's an idea, biker bars, imagine how much trouble we could get into there!"

"I can't stand not knowing what is going on, you know I like to be the one who knows everything!"

"Yeah, I know, that's why we are not telling you." Laughing now, he settles back down when my phone rings.

"Em, we were just talking about the stag do, he hates not knowing, it's hilarious to watch, would you be okay, with Vegas, strip clubs and biker bars?" Em chuckles down the phone, and says, only if she can go, and that it sounds like a great stag do, then asks to put her on speaker.

"Dan, if you even step into a biker bar they will eat you for breakfast. But on a more serious note, um can someone pick me up please?"

"Yeah sure, I'll pick you both up." Dan says.

"Um.. Just me, Millie left a few minutes ago, I think I may have said something, something that may have had her running? She looked pale, when I spoke about some things, namely your feelings Jack, and she could not get out of here fast enough. Oh, she is also drunk; we shared at least two bottles of wine but she said she would text me when she got back to the suite."

"Fucking hell Em, why? What could you have said to her that made her run? Dan's on his way, I'll head back now and see how she is."

When I get back, she is not there; I'm not worried, she has almost fully healed now. Even if she is a little drunk the way Em said, she would not appreciate me turning up and trying to haul her into the car. She has been a little off over the last few days, like she regrets what we did. Maybe it was too much too soon, but the way she kept teasing me, I couldn't control myself. One look at her and I'm hard, thinking of all the ways I can be with her, make her mine. Shit, that sounds very caveman, but who cares I want her, any way I can have her. Walking to the kitchen I grab a cold glass of water, when I hear the door handle go, it takes her a minute to open it, but when she does she almost falls in. Chuckling to myself I move forward, but she moves back, drops to the floor, her hands moving up to cover her face.

"I'm sorry, I'm sorry, please don't hurt me again... I won't survive this time, not after what you did, it almost killed me." she cries out, shit she must think I'm him. My brain goes into overdrive, she said killed me; he almost killed her? I take a step back; my brain can't handle the information. She has pressed herself up against the door, trying to protect herself, from him, from me?

"Millie, it's Jack. I won't hurt you. It's me Jack," I blurt out. I stay away holding my hands up, trying my best to remain calm, when I can feel the anger build in my chest as her words sink in. I want to find that bastard and hurt him like he hurt her.

"It's Jack, Mil, I've never hurt you, never will, I want to help you." She looks at me with wide eyes through her hands. Who could do this to her? Reduce her to this – panicked and submissive—it's so wrong. The woman I once knew is in there somewhere, with bright eyes and full of confidence.

Keeping my voice soft, I look her directly in the eye, "I will never hurt you Millie, why would I? I…" Shit I was about to say the L word, do I? No, too soon. Stupid thought, but my heart is pounding like it knows better.

"It's Jack." I move towards her and she flinches away, the panic in her eyes, she looks almost wild. My heart is thumping so loud; I crouch down on the floor and just sit there for a moment.

"I'm sorry, I'm sorry, it won't happen again."

"Millie, you have nothing to be sorry for, I would never hurt you, let me help you up, I think we need to talk."

She backs away. "Jack?" she cries, and I'm there next to her in a flash. I move her hands away from her face; her breathing is ragged, like she can't get enough air in. Her hands are shaking, tears keep sliding down her cheeks, she can't stop them.

"I think you are having a panic attack, let's get you off the floor." In one swoop she is in my arms; I can feel her relax against me, her head landing on my chest as she takes in a deep breath to try and settle herself. Sitting on the sofa I place her on my lap, she curls up even more, a sob leaving her lips as I stroke her cheek with the back of my hand.

Millie

I could barely breathe, I thought it was him, but all my senses tell me it's Jack. When he picks me up into his arms, I can feel the panic sliding away, but the tears still come. It's like I can't turn them off; the smell of his aftershave calms me, his arms wrapped around me, and I snuggle in closer, welcoming the warmth and the feeling of safety he brings to me.

"Millie?" he whispers into my hair and I can feel his heart pounding; it's like a sleeping pill, lulling me under, my eyes feel heavy.

"I think we need to talk."

"Not now," I say and I feel myself get pulled under into a restful sleep, still wrapped in his arms.

My head feels like it's going to split, I can't and don't want to open my eyes. The memory of last night returns, what I did, how I reacted to Jack, how I thought I had seen Glen standing there in the kitchen, and how I freaked out when he stepped towards me.

I feel so ashamed of my reaction to him; embarrassment washes over me as I try to block out the memory, groaning and pulling the covers over my head. When I do, I feel an arm wrap around my waist, and I feel those delicious tingles run through my body; Jack pulls me to him, still asleep. My back pressed to his front, I can feel his erection pressing into my back; the warmth of his skin feels wonderful on mine. His hand trails up my hip, my eyes shoot open and I freeze on the spot. I realise I'm naked, taking a peek under the covers, well almost naked, I still have my pants on. He must have got me undressed; this just got worse, I don't remember him doing it. Maybe I did? I need to get out, I can't handle this, as much as I love the feeling of him next to me, I just can't do this. it's too much for me to handle, let alone anyone else.

As I slide his hand off my hip, he groans but stays asleep. I slip out and head to the bathroom, quickly shower and gather my things. When I walk out the bathroom ten minutes later, he's not there, but I can hear him taking a shower in the other room. As quickly and quietly as I can, I grab my case, shove my stuff inside and wheel it to the door. I manage to get the case outside before he opens the bedroom door.

"Millie? Where are you off to this early?" he says with a questioning look in his eye..

"I've got some stuff to do before work..um…thanks for last night Jack, and I'm sorry," I say, hanging my head in shame. *How can I even be around him when I react like that?* I feel ashamed, he doesn't deserve that from me, not after everything he has done. I know he is not Glen, but I can't let myself be in another relationship. I need time to …. I don't know the answer to that, I just need to get away, clear my head, be me.

"What are you sorry for exactly?" He goes to move towards me but I move myself out the door.

"All the trouble I have caused you," I say in a faint whisper and close the door behind me.

I almost run to the lift so he doesn't see me leave, I know he will try and stop me.

When I get down stairs, I ask Mary to call me a taxi.

"Where are you off so early?" She asks, glancing at my bag and back at me. *What is with the questions?* She has been on the night shift. It's only 7 am, and not many people are around.

"Going back to my apartment today, I thought I would go and set it up for when I finish work later."

She looks at me puzzled, "I thought you gave up your apartment?"

"No, what makes you say that?" I frown at her.

"Maybe I have my wires crossed, it was just something Jack said last week, that's all." Her brows draw together in a frown, just like mine.

"Well, I still have my apartment, and I'm moving back in today." I can't help but feel a little worried at her expression. She looks almost anxious, I shake off the feeling, must be work stuff.

"I'll be back in an hour for my shift, see you in a bit." Walking away, I take a quick glance back I see her reach for the phone. "Oh and please don't tell Jack!" I shout, she looks at me and places the phone back down, staring at me, with a confused and worried expression on her face.

As I pull up out the front of my apartment block, I see five police cars parked outside. When I walk up to the door, an officer walks up to me, and stops me in my tracks..

"Do you live here?" he says

"Um yes, moving back in today, why?"

"What apartment number are you?" he asks, flipping through a pile of paperwork in his hand.

"Number 3A, my name is Millie. Sorry, Emilie."

"I don't have you on the residents list, sorry, you can't go in," he says, shaking his head at me.

"What do you mean? I don't understand? I paid for a six month lease? How can I not be on the list?" I say, trying to look at his paperwork, as he moves it away.

"Sorry I don't have you on my list, maybe you should call the landlord, see if he can help."

"Okay, what's happened? Why can't I go in?"

"Unfortunately Miss, someone was found dead here this morning, no-one is allowed in unless they live here," he says walking away.

"Oh my god, I'll ring the landlord!" Grabbing the phone from my bag, I dial his number, I have to call him twice for him to answer.

"What?" *Rude.*

"It's Millie, from apartment 3A on Bench View. The police won't let me in the building saying I'm not on the residents list. Can you just confirm with them that I am, so I can get back in please?"

He huffs down the phone. "Why would I do that? You gave notice, and moved out last week, you don't live there anymore," he yells at me and he hangs up.

"What the fuck?" I say out loud, and the officer looks at me.

"Everything alright?" he asks

"No, not really, but in the grand scheme of things, it will be. I just have to find somewhere else to live, cuz apparently I don't live here anymore, fucking rat of a landlord."

I don't want to call another taxi. So I decide to walk to calm the anger that seems to be taking over me.

I head back into town, how could this happen? I never gave my notice. Now I have nowhere to go, well I do but my humiliation from last night is still so raw, I can't face being there. It will be bad enough when I see him around work, knowing what happened. He will try and help me, giving me those pitying looks that I can't stand.

As I walk into town I decide to pop in and see Em; she will know what to do, but when I reach her office, she's not there.

Shit what am I meant to do now? Homeless is the word that pops into my head. I have nowhere to go, other than back to that hotel. It won't be for long, but I'm now down five months' rent/deposit. I'll have to put a few things on hold with the business for a month or two, that should sort me out. I need coffee and cake, maybe that will cheer me up. As I walk down the road, I see Em coming out of Bruno's cafe, I wave and head over.

"I just want to say sorry for last night, I ran out on you."

"What happened? One minute we were talking and having a great time, the next you looked like you were going to explode and ran. Talk to me!" Her hands come up to my shoulders as she hugs me tight.

"I will tell you, later maybe, but first I need your help, a massive favour, if I could? I need you to help me look for another apartment. For some reason my landlord just told me I don't live there anymore. I only found out because the police found a dead body there this morning, and they have restricted access to residents only!" I say moving away from her hug.

"Wow, that was a lot of information to take in! Why aren't you staying with Jack? I thought he said you were going to be with him for a while?"

I sigh and dip my head; I need to tell her, if I don't, she won't understand and think I'm being stupid and stubborn for no reason.

"Oh shit, okay. Let me grab a coffee and get us a cake. Is there somewhere we can talk privately?"

Chapter Fifteen

I Have To Tell Her

Emma

We walk back into Bruno's and Millie orders two coffees and two pieces of chocolate cake to go.

It's been bugging me since last night why she left so suddenly. I kept asking myself if I had said something out of turn, but I was only telling her how much my brother really wants to be with her. He has been bugging me for weeks, talking about her non-stop, going out of his way to help her, and even taking time off work for her. I think that's the biggest surprise, he has never taken time off, and always worked so hard.

First, when our mum passed away suddenly from a heart attack, he helped support Dad when he had his breakdown. He worked any job he could, and then two years later, Dad was diagnosed with bowel cancer. Unfortunately, it was way too far gone to help him much. Just under two years later, Dad passed away in hospital.

It was such a hard time; Jack was only nineteen but he kept working, sorted it all out. He said I never had to worry about him. But I did, all the time. When our inheritance came through, Jack made sure everything was taken care of. We sold their house, and bought two smaller houses, one for each of us. When I went off to college, Jack had his master plan, and nothing would stop him from achieving it. When I went away to University, he left with Dan and built his empire, using some of the inheritance money. He never let himself relax, always moving onto the next property, the next business adventure, never a personal one. I think he saw too much pain, when it came to relationships. I think seeing our dad the way he was after Mum died, he never wanted to go through that, even though our parents' marriage was a happy one.

There was a glimpse of hope when he first met Millie for that brief moment. I remember Dan telling of how he looked all over the island. It's like his guard just went down and he let her in. That was a few weeks after Dan and I started seeing each other. God I loved that, sneaking around! Every time he flew back from Ibiza, he would stay with me; we would call and talk every day he was away. I would fly out every chance I got. After a year of doing this, we decided to tell Jack. Dan was so scared, I found it hilarious; his hands were shaking, and he kept trying to back out, saying we could wait, and that Jack didn't need to know. Apparently, there is some bro code saying you don't date your best friend's sister; she's off limits, beatings were implied, and friendships were put in jeopardy. When we told him, he laughed and said that he had known about it for about six months, and it was fun watching us try to hide it. He hugged us both and said that we made a great couple, but if Dan ever hurt me, he would kill him.

"Hello? Em, you in there?" Millie says, pulling me from my thoughts.

"Sorry, I was just thinking about when Dan and I told Jack we were dating, it was so funny."

"What was his reaction? Was he pissed at Dan?"

"Quite the opposite," I chuckle. "He said he had known for six months, found it funny watching us try and hide it, but did say he would kill Dan if he ever hurt me." I laugh some more.

"Sounds like you have a great big brother."

"I do, I really do. Anyway, enough about me, let's go for a walk. So you can tell me all about it."

"Can we go somewhere a little more private? It's not something I have talked about before, so I may get a little, um...." She takes a big breath and sips her coffee, "Emotional, let's say." Watching her, I can see her hands shaking a little, every time she brings the cup to her lips.

In all honesty, I'm a little on edge, almost feeling scared about what she could be about to tell me.

"Okay, I have a great place, just down by the seafront, it's quiet and secluded, we should be okay there," I reassure her.

She nods and I lead the way. It takes us about ten minutes to get there, and when we do, Millie looks so nervous that she's picked her empty cup to shreds.

She also rang work and told them she would be late, saying there was a problem with her apartment, so she didn't lie, although it wouldn't matter anyway.

I nod towards the seating area at the edge of the walkway. We walk over and sit on the bench; it looks over the sea in one direction and has wonderful evergreen trees surrounding it, making you feel safe. I used to use this place when my parents passed away, needing time to be by myself. This place would calm me down when the reality hit that I didn't have my mum or dad anymore. Only Dan knows about it, he would always be the one to find me here and bring me home.

Millie takes in a few deep breaths to try and calm herself. I can see she's still shaking, so I reach out and hold her hand. When she looks up at me there are tears in her eyes but she's trying to blink them back. When a single tear falls onto her cheek, sliding down her face, I have an idea of what she is going to tell me, but I don't know the extent of it.

She tells me everything, from the day she met him to the day she left him. I cried with her and for her as she let it all out, told me and trusted me with what that evil prick had done.

I don't know how she is even standing or how she survived and managed to leave him. It feels like it's been hours, hours of horrific stories, stuff you would never even imagine. No wonder she freaked out at me and Jack last night; if I had known, I would never have said anything.

"I'm so sorry Millie, if I had known I would not have said anything to you about Jack," I said to her, crying and Millie hugs me for comfort. I don't want her to let me go. She looks worn out, tired of it all, and how it keeps affecting her. I don't want to let her go.

"It's okay, well it's not okay, but you know what I mean." Sighing, she stands and pulls me up with her, looking me straight in the eye.

"Now you know why I freaked out so badly, but please don't tell anyone else. I can't stand the pity looks, they make me want to hide away, it's humiliating. And if I do that, he's won."

I grab her for another hug, *how can she be so strong?* I need to pull myself together, it's not my story and yet I feel like I've been through it with her; my emotions are all over the place.

"Can I ask you one thing?" I say in her ear, "Please tell Jack, even if things don't happen between the two of you, he needs to know, so he can understand."

"But it's so humiliating. He would never look at me the same way. I'm weak, broken and damaged, not the girl he first met. She was… a dream that… got squished."

"How can you even think that way? You're right in a way though." She looks at me like I've offended her, but I'm not finished yet. "You're not that girl anymore, you're better, stronger and so much more, you just need to realise it yourself. You had the courage to stand up for yourself and leave that absolute arsewipe of a man! That's the bravest thing you could have ever done." Standing back a little I look her in the eyes, so she knows I'm serious.

"Thank you, and thank you for listening, it's not a nice part of my life, and I'm trying so desperately to forget about it." She drops her head when she talks about it. It breaks me even more.

"Are you going to take the rest of the day off?" I ask, hoping she will.

"No, I'm going to dump my bag at the hotel, then head to work, I need all the money I can get right now, until the house is sold."

"Well, okay I need to head back anyway. I've got a few clients I need to see, as well as look into your house sale." I smile and hug her again.

As we walk back up the hill, we go our separate ways after hugging each other one more time. I watch as she heads further up as I walk into the office.

I can't get it out of my head, it's like a nightmare I keep replaying. *How has she coped with this?* It's not happened to me, yet the thought of what she has had to deal with day in and day out is unthinkable.

Sitting back at my desk, I try but I just can't concentrate. So I make a few calls and leave and head home, where I can try and deal with what she told me for the rest of the day.

The door opens for me when I get home; I am a little surprised to see Dan working from home today.

We both look at each other in surprise.

"What are you doing home so early?" We say at the same time, then laugh, but my laughter suddenly turns to tears. Dan scoops me up in a great big hug and leads me to the living room. He places me on the sofa and sits beside me, looking at me like I've lost my mind.

"Em, what's up?" He trails his hand over my cheek, concern etched on his face. I'm not a crier, never really have been; I'm good at compartmentalising and dealing with stuff, but this… It's a whole new level of… I don't know.

"I've been with Millie this morning," I say through sobs, "she told me… everything," sinking back into the sofa a little more.

Dan moves closer, taking my hand in his. His other hand rested on my thigh, caressing it with his thumb.

"What do you mean? Why does it make you so upset?" His head is resting next to mine now.

"He hurt her so badly Dan, I mean most people would go to prison for a very long time after what he did to her, and not just once either, multiple times, over and over and over again. Then the last time he almost killed her," I tell him, losing whatever composure I had left again. Sobs come easily every time I think of it all.

Leaning forward, he puts his head in his hands, like he can't process just how bad it was for her. So I tell him everything while I cry. He gets angry, then cries himself for how she was treated and it just makes me love him so much more, how he wears his heart on his sleeve.

"I knew it wasn't a car accident! Just the way she behaves, that bastard! How could he do it? How could anyone do that to someone? It's sick!" he shouts.

"I know, she asked me not to tell anyone, so you can't let on that you know. I know it's going to be hard for you, but please, she needs to trust us. And I don't want to let her down, not after what she has been through."

Dan looks at me and laughs, "You know that's going to be impossible, right? I have never been able to hide how I feel. How do you think Jack found out about us? My heart is forever on my sleeve," he sighs. He was right, it's one of the reasons I love him so much, that and his big kid side, it's refreshing.

"Alright, I'll let her know you know. It makes you think though doesn't it, just how easy it could have been for me, or one of my friends to end up in a situation like that."

"I would never hurt you, you know that right…"

"I know you would never hurt me, Jack would kill you if you did, and you love him and me too much for that to happen." I chuckle, reaching for his hand.

"I'll show you just how much I love you, and how I can't wait for you to be my wife," he says, tackling me to the floor and pinning me underneath him, claiming my mouth with his.

He moves his hand eagerly up my leg, lifting my skirt and gliding his fingers over the apex of my thighs. He moves his fingers under my panties, slowly and agonisingly taunting me. I let out an eager moan while his mouth moves down my neck. He kisses me tenderly as his finger finds my clit, circling it, making me moan louder. He spreads my legs, giving him more room to play, while I tug off his shirt. *I should come home early more often if this happens,* I think to myself.

"Oh my god babe, you're so wet, can I… you know?"

"Do whatever you want to me. The way I'm feeling right now, I want you however I can have you," I tell him and with that he rips my panties off, slides two fingers inside me and sucks my nipples through my blouse. *God I love him so much.* I can feel myself climbing, my muscles clamping down on his fingers as they move in and out of me, curling up inside of me to get to my sweet spot. His fingers are coated in my juices, when I feel him rub my back passage with a finger, and he slides it in, the sensation makes me climb higher, I grab his hair pulling his lips to mine and kiss him hard. I scream his name as he makes me come, wave after wave sweet high washing over me. Before I can come down, or even catch me breath, he slides his finger out and I feel the tip of his cock at my entrance. He slams into me, letting out a groan and stills himself.

"Fuck," he says kissing me, before he thrusts into me again, building me up higher again.

My back arches to him, and he takes a nipple in his mouth, nipping at it and sending a shock of ecstasy through me. He thrusts into me harder and faster, meeting his own needs as well as mine. I can't hear anything; my mind is full of pleasure, I feel light. As he fills me up, I hear myself moan in a way that doesn't sound like me. I can feel myself climaxing when he thrusts one last time, and I fall apart around him. He stills and we reach our high together like always. I explode and slump to a frazzled, happy mess on the floor with Dan lying on top, kissing every part of me he can. I cup his face and kiss him back.

"I love doing that with you," Dan says into my ear as he rolls off, and we lie on the floor together, me on his chest.

"I *love* doing that with you too!"

"Good, you have me forever, so get used to it." I laugh and sit up, realising the time.

"We need to go, we have our sample menu to eat, Marco has made it specially for us."

"Nice, no need to cook then, even better. Oh just going back to our conversation, does Jack know about what happened to Millie? Has she told him?"

"No, she's only told me, I did ask her to tell him, but she feels humiliated and she's ashamed of herself for letting it happen I think."

"Oh man, that's awful, I know you would have told her not to be so silly." I love how he knows me; I nod in agreement, and try to stand up, but my legs feel like jelly still. I laugh and look at him, lay there, his tanned toned body, naked beside me.

"Need a moment, even after all this time, you still make my legs turn to jelly."

Chapter Sixteen

She's Gone

Jack

I woke up this morning and she was gone. I can't get what happened last night out of my head. She asked me to lay with her so I wrapped my arms around her and held her. That's all I could do. I wanted to comfort her better, but I didn't know how. *How can I?*

I can't get over what she said. What did he do that almost killed her? Did he almost kill her? I mean fuck, I'm not questioning what she said, it's just so hard to take in. Who could do that?

I need to talk to her but she has been avoiding my calls and messages all day. I haven't seen her in the office at all this morning. Mary keeps saying she has popped out, which annoys me more. I know something is up but I have no idea what.

Just before lunch, I head out to the gym, to try and work out some of this pent-upness I feel. Whatever that is. Frustration maybe, because I am definitely sexually frustrated. Having her so close to me over the past few weeks and seeing her naked while helping her recover has been so hard, in more ways than one. That body is just to die for. Last night as she moved against me and snuggled in, all I could do was wrap my arms around her. There was nothing I could do about my erection. It was instant, pressing into her back most of the night, throbbing and painful; it was heaven and hell at the same time. I'm a sick bastard for even thinking about it. I know she needs time to recover, but my body wants her close and my mind dreams up all the wonderful things it wants to do to her…and my mind likes to play games.

I work hard at the gym, doing extra rounds on the weights and running machine. I even stay longer than usual, but nothing works. I can't get rid of this feeling that something's not right.

She should be getting lunch now; I've had it sent to her every day from Marco, the chef. I know for a fact that if the food was not placed in front of her, she would only eat cake and drink coffee all day. The woman lives on sugar and caffeine. I'll head over and check the office again when I'm done.

Heading off to the shower, I strip off and run the shower cold for a few moments to see if that helps get rid of the frustration. It takes the edge off but I have to take matters into my own hands, literally. Again, I hate and love that she makes this happen, I just wish she could be here to help me. Having these thoughts about her doesn't help my current situation.

Feeling a little more refreshed after my shower, I dress and head to her office to see if she is enjoying her lunch, except when I walk in, she is still not there.

"Mary, where is she?" I yell as she walks past. She stops dead and looks down, a little nervous.

"She is around somewhere, why? Can I help you with something Mr Lucas?" She's turned very professional this morning, she's hiding something.

"No, has she been in this morning? I've not seen her and she is avoiding all my calls and messages." When she looks away again, I know she's definitely hiding something from me.

"Spill, now," I tell her, moving in front of her so she can't get away.

"She left this morning, then rang in saying there was a problem she had to deal with and she would be there for a few hours. That was just before she was meant to start at eight, I've not seen or heard from her since, sorry," she says, a little defeated. I know there's more to the story, but I don't dig any deeper.

"But it's almost one pm, what was the problem? Did she tell you?" *What could she need to deal with that would take over five hours?*

"No, just said she would make up her hours and work late tonight instead."

"Hmm, alright, sorry I barked at you Mary. It's been a stressful few days." I wasn't lying, they have been, just not work-related this time.

"That's okay, we have all been there," she says as she walks off.

What does that mean?

I don't see Millie at all for the rest of the day. She is definitely avoiding me. My mood has been shitty, even Dan couldn't stand to be around me this morning. He left early and went home. Too bad for him because we are all having dinner together later.

I don't even want to be around me today. I have to force myself to stop working; if I let myself, I would work sixteen-hour-plus days. There is always a lot to do, but tonight, there is nothing that can't wait until tomorrow, closing my laptop. I grab my phone and walk out.

It's six o'clock when I head back to the suite and get changed, looking forward to taking my mind off Millie for a while and getting a few beers down my neck while we talk wedding plans, or while Em talks wedding plans and we listen. I had planned on asking Millie to come to dinner tonight but I figured that's not going to happen now. It would have been good to spend some time with her tonight, without the pressure.

I go downstairs, and just as I'm about to call a taxi to take me to Em and Dan's house, I spot her. She sees me and almost runs for the office. Her red hair trailing behind her. *Why would she do that?* Walking over, or rather stomping, I open the door. I was a little pissed off she was MIA all day. But that soon disappears when I see her.

"Hi." That's all she has to say, hiding behind her desk.

"You have been avoiding me all day, I've tried to call and I've messaged you, are you okay? After last night…" She cuts me off.

"I don't want to talk about it, I can't, it's humiliating." The sadness in her eyes says it all. I move and sit on the edge of her desk. *How can she think like that?*

"There is nothing humiliating about last night, I want to help you, why won't you let me?" It's getting frustrating that she won't let me help.

"Because I don't want your help, it's too much. I barely even know you. Yet you want to do all these things for me, and I don't understand why, I'm not worth the effort Jack." Her voice breaks when she speaks those last words.

"Please don't say things like that. You are worth it. I.. I just want you to feel safe and be happy Millie, I want to help you!" I'm pleading with her now, I can't help it. I'll win her around, even if it takes everything I have.

She rolls her eyes at me; it annoys me and turns me on at the same time. I do want her to feel safe and happy but I also want her to be next to me all the time. I want to see her every day, I want more, something I have not really ever wanted.

I run my hand over my face in frustration. I don't know what else to say to her. I know if I say what I actually want, it will scare her. Especially after what Em said last night, I can't and won't do that to her.

My eyes fall on her face, which she's been trying to hide behind her screen. Her eyes are red and puffy like she has been crying. Shit, she's been crying! *Where has she been? Why is she so upset?* Moving around the desk, I pull her chair toward me and cup her face in my hands. "You've been crying. What's wrong, what happened?"

She closes her eyes briefly, but then moves back away from me, shaking her head and closing herself off. She won't even look at me.

"Fine, don't tell me, but I will find out one way or another." Standing up, I pace the room; she is so frustrating.

"Jack…There's nothing wrong, it's just been an emotional day, it seems like last night has had a lasting effect that I can't shift." She leans her head back on the chair and closes her eyes. My eyes fall on her face once again; she looks so sad, almost like she has given up on something. When I reach to touch her, she pulls away again, tears brimming in her eyes.

"I need to get some work done before my shift at the pub, could you leave please?" A single tear glides down her cheek.

"What have I done Millie?" I ask, moving away to the door; I don't expect an answer, it was more of a question to myself.

"It's not you Jack, you're perfect, I'm just…not." She says, then carries on busying herself with work. I'm not sure I was meant to hear it, but I leave, making the promise to do everything within my power to make her happy, and bring out the woman I know is in there.

When I walk into Em and Dan's half an hour later, I'm in an even worse mood than I was before. I feel deflated, confused, frustrated but eager to prove I can make her happy. It's confusing. She is the one I want. I know that for sure. I'm not letting her go again. I'll wait as long as it takes. But it's like talking to a wall! If she doesn't talk to me, I don't know what I'm supposed to do. My face must look like thunder when I walk into the house.

"Not you as well, we all seem to be in a shit mood this evening," Dan says and hands me a beer when we walk into the kitchen.

"Why are you both in a shit mood? Did it not go well with Marco? He's been working on those sample menus for months!"

"Oh nothing to do with Marco, he is pure magic, if that man can cook like that, I wonder what he's like in the…" Em says.

"Um, no, you have a soon-to-be husband right here. Stop talking like you're single, get your mind out of the gutter!" She winks at Dan, he is so jealous of any other man that looks at her, that it's funny to wind him up. I like that he will always look out for her.

"So why are you two in a bad mood? You should be all happy I'm getting married in… however many weeks kind of thing!" Bringing my bottle to my lips, I welcome the cool beer. I may need a few more of these tonight.

They share a look between them, that tells me it has something to do with me and it's not great news. Placing my bottle on the counter top I ask, "What is it?" a little too impatiently. "I've had it with people keeping stuff from me today. Millie won't talk to me and has been avoiding me all day. She even told me to leave earlier. So what is it?" Having already drained my beer, I grab another and sit on the bar stool. They just look at each other, then Em finally moves and perches on the stool next to me.

"I spoke to Millie today, I saw her this morning, after she found out someone had handed in notice on her apartment; now she thinks she has nowhere to go. She has asked me to look for another place for her."

"What do you mean, why was she at Bench View?" It's like I'm in a different world. "I don't understand why she would be there when she is staying with me."

"Now don't lose your shit, but I didn't understand why she was asking either." She squeezes my arm.

"I'm glad we're on the same page. She has me, and somewhere safe to stay. That place is bad news!" I almost yelled.

"Yep, even more so now, when they discovered a body there this morning. Hence why she had to ring the landlord, to try and clear up with the police why they would not let her in as she was not a resident on the list they had." Oh shit. "So, long story short, she was angry that someone is trying to control her life, without her knowing!" Double shit. "Also I know it was you who paid off the landlord to get her out of the lease." Fuck… I cringe a little, maybe that was a bit forward, but she was never going to stay there again, so I dealt with it. There was no point in her paying rent when she was staying with me. "You should look uncomfortable right now, but I know why you did it. Anyway, I also wanted to know why she ran out on me last night, why me talking about you, and how funny it was to see you really interested in someone, really freaked her out. Well…" She lets out a sigh and tears start to pool in her eyes, and I bring her in for a hug.

"What's the matter, why are you about to cry? You never cry." Looking over at Dan for answers. Em sniffs and a small sob escapes her lips, so Dan takes over.

"Millie told her everything…we have all had an idea of what we thought she had been through but…" Even Dan looks like he could cry. *What is going on? How can it be worse than beating her up?*

"When you say everything…?" I say, worry seeping through me like a bad tequila.

"I mean everything," Em says, "everything from start to finish, what he did to her, everything."

"Tell me Em. I need to know, last night when I got home, she freaked out, had a panic attack. I think she thought I was him. She kept saying sorry over and over again, saying don't hurt me. She literally fell to the floor in fear, she also said," I say, taking a deep breath in, "that it almost killed her… is that true? Did he?" My voice breaks when Em nods at me. I can't breathe, how could he… I knew it was bad but hearing what Emma had been told was gut-wrenching, even without the details. How could he hurt her like that? The fear, the anger, the sick feeling I have, I can't just sit down.

"I can't tell you anymore, it's not my story to tell, but she needs you, more than she realises, you need to get her to talk to you," Em says softly.

"I will, I promise, I'll do anything I can help her."

"I know you will, you love her."

"Oo, woo, hold your horses. I never said I loved her, I just really, really, really like her a lot." *Who am I trying to kid?*

"Yeah, yeah, we know. Anyway, how are you going to get her to talk to you?"

"I have a plan, I think."

"Don't go all caveman on her, that's not what she needs. She needs you to be honest with her, and sneaking around behind her back doing what you think is best is not the right thing to do."

I have to admit she's right, my plan was to just turn up and drag her back, and 'caveman style' as my sister put it. But I know that won't work, not now. *Be open with her? Can I do that?*

We spent the rest of the evening talking about the wedding. I just sit there nodding when I think I need to; my mind is elsewhere. I've never wanted a relationship, not after what happened with Mum and Dad. I never want to feel what they went through. I don't want to lose her though. *Maybe what I'm feeling is love? Maybe it's worth it?*

We all have a slight gloom hanging over us, I get back to the suite just after midnight. Millie should be back by now. Her shift finished at eleven and she normally heads straight back home. When I knock on her room door, there's no reply. Opening the door, I take a peek inside and find it empty. Taking a closer look, I notice all her stuff is gone.

I'm on the phone within seconds, calling Mike, Dan and anyone else I know to see if they know where she is, and bingo, she is staying at that shit hole again. It's good to be me sometimes, especially when you know everyone.

Unfortunately, it didn't take much to get the room number off the reception desk, which is a little alarming and I will be reporting it tomorrow. With the lift out of order, I climb the stairs and reach her room; I hadn't really thought about what to do after this point. It's almost one in the morning. I'm standing outside about to knock on the door, when it flies open and out comes Millie in my t-shirt and nothing else. The look of shock on her face when she sees me is priceless. She almost walks into my chest.

"What are you doing here?" She looks angry and relieved at the same time. Her red hair is tied up in a bun on top of her head, and she is looking up at me, wanting an answer.

"What are you doing out of the room looking like that?" I say, glancing down at what little she is wearing. I know she has no underwear under that top, I can see everything.

She laughs but doesn't move; she just places her hands on her hips, looking at me.

"What are you doing here Jack?"

"I am trying to look out for you, but you are making it very difficult. You can't stay here Millie. It's not safe, I only had to ask what room you were in and they gave me the number," I say gesturing to the stairs where I came from.

"You don't need to worry about me Jack. I'm okay," she replies, taking a step back from me.

"You see, you're wrong, I do. I can't help it." I sigh, stepping towards her and putting my arm around her waist. I pull her in as close as I can.

"Jack…I…" Her breath hitches as she places her small hand on my chest.

"Look, can we talk? I want to be honest with you."

Chapter Seventeen

I Trust You

Millie

I suppose it's now or never; if I tell him everything, he will see me for the weak-ass person I have become. I need to tell him why I am the way I am, why I freaked out. I think he already knows, but I doubt he knows the extent of the abuse. At least he will know how fucked up I am; I suppose I can't feel any more ashamed about it than I already do.

Stepping back, I walk back into the room, knowing he will follow me. I gesture towards the chair and he takes a seat, leaning his elbows on his knees. As humiliated as I am, I can't help but drink him in, he looks amazing even at this time in the morning. His blond hair is tied up in a man-bun, showing the shaved sides hidden underneath. There is a hint of stubble on his jaw that makes him look even more rugged. His sculpted arms and chest are covered in a well-fitted blue hoodie, and his jeans, my god those jeans hug him in all the right places. I sit across from him on the bed but before I can say anything, he looks me in the eye.

"I'm sorry," he says, shaking his head, "it's all my fault, it was me who handed in the notice on your apartment. I got your money back, it should be in your account. I just wanted you to be safe, and that place isn't. Fuck…I have also found another place for you to live, although I would like you to stay with me if you want to." that's a lot to process, but weirdly, it all makes sense, and surprisingly, I'm okay with it. Frowning at myself, I take a minute to answer.

"That's okay, I understand. I just wish you would have told me, but I can't stay with you. There are reasons why…I…" I stop myself mid-sentence; I just need to find the right words. *Just start at the beginning,* I think to myself, let him know everything and he can decide from there. *He won't want me after I tell him.*

"Just listen, don't say anything. I'll tell you everything. It's not a happy story, but it's mine." Taking a big breath, I start talking and it all comes out. "A year or so after I met you in Ibiza, I met him – Glen. He was wonderful, handsome, fun, caring, he really wanted to be with me… and I, with him. A few months later, both my parents died in a car crash, and I went to him as I didn't have anyone else. I was devastated. He helped me and we were good together. Not long after the will was read, he started to change. I was the sole beneficiary of the estate. I was their only child."

"I'm so sorry Mil." He reaches out and touches my hand.

"Anyway, it all happened so slowly. I didn't see it coming, didn't know what was happening until it was too late. He would make snide comments about my weight, how I looked, how he wanted me to look, what I ate, my work, my life, my friends, my job, how I was just not enough, and how I would never make anything of myself. As you can tell, my confidence disappeared, I became nothing. He would get angry if I went out, and turn up to get me just after I had gone out. He would be angry if I wasn't back at the time I told him. Then all my friends stopped talking to me, one by one they disappeared, and I was alone. But he was my whole world, I just couldn't see what he was doing. He would act like the anger he had towards me was him worrying for my safety. Charlie tried to warn me a few times saying I had changed but I said she was being silly; I thought she was jealous I had found someone, which was ridiculous because she was married." A little laugh escapes my lips, and I hear Jack sigh.

"Then about two years later, one evening we were out with work friends, all his friends. I had quit my dream job, and started working for the same company as him. I think it was so he could keep an eye on me. I was office-based and he was on the road. But he would check in, call me, call others in the office and see if I was there. Anyway…when we were out, I made a stupid joke about how I was the man of the house, as it belonged to me. We all laughed it off but that night, he followed me to the bathroom in the restaurant and hit me, punched me in the stomach. I couldn't believe it had happened, the pain, not only from the punch but my heart almost broke me."

"Mil…I…" I can see the pain in his eyes as he hangs his head.

"Just let me get it out…I want you to know everything. That night I cried myself to sleep, and the following morning he brought me breakfast in bed. At this point, he would apologise, say it would never happen again. That's how abuse lasts so long, you believe what they say. It was like nothing had happened. But he must have liked what he did because he kept on doing it, beating me, abusing me mentally and physically. Every chance he got, he would punch, slap, kick and throw me around, apologise, 'make it up to me'. It became our normal. One night after work he came back drunk, he got in my face the moment he walked in, telling me I was worthless." The memory of this is so painful, I have to take in a deep, steadying breath before I can get the next bit out. "He... grabbed me by the throat, with his one hand and threw me against the wall. He then made me stand back up, pinning me against the wall again, I could hardly breathe. He started to punch me, over and over again, in my stomach and ribs. He walked away into the kitchen, and I thought it was over. But instead, he grabbed a glass off the side in the kitchen, smashed it and...and used it to cut me. He pinned me down while I was on the floor and cut along my stomach. I couldn't fight back...He hurt me so badly that night I wasn't able to go to work for over a week, it hurt too much to do anything. I had no one to run to nowhere to go. I was a regular in hospital, he would always come with me, saying I fell, or some other lame excuse." Lying back on the bed, I close my eyes, remembering everything he did. Tears well up and spill down my cheeks, I can't stop them. When I feel the bed dip, I look to see Jack climbing on the bed, lying next to me, still holding my hand in his. I need to carry on otherwise I'll let it all out.

"I was broken, unable to do anything, go anywhere without him. He had broken my ribs nine times, my arm twice, my cheekbone three times and countless cuts, bruises and split lips." Jack squeezes my hand, but I don't move.

"Then just over twelve months ago I...I found out he had been sleeping with someone else, and still sleeping with me, well

I let him, but I didn't want him to. It felt wrong, but I knew what would happen if I didn't."

"Fuck…are you saying…he would rape you?" I nod and I can see the tears in his eyes. His whole body goes tense, but he holds my hand gently but firmly.

"Well after that I had the most wonderful dream. A dream about what my life was like before I met him, how I was, who I was.. and this dream, well it kept coming back. I dreamt it every night, and eventually one night, I woke up and looked at the man beside me, saw him for who he truly was. He wanted my money, the lifestyle and nothing else. He was so jealous that I made more money than him. This was what got him the most I think. So that very night, I made a list of what I wanted, how I was going to get away. I was excited for the first time in years. But it was also the worst. He could sense something was up, I got more confident the more plans I made, and unfortunately, the more confident I got, the worse the beatings got."

"I'm so sorry, Millie if only I had…" I hold my hand up. I need to get this last bit out, then he will know everything.

"Unfortunately I'm not done. About two months ago, we were out for the evening with his friends, having a meal and drinks. When I say to one of his friends that I made more money than him, I could see the anger in his eyes, we were sat next to each other with six other people around us at the table. His hand went to my thigh, and grabbed me so hard I knew it would bruise, but I kept still. He then dropped one of the steak knives on the floor and asked me to get it, I knew what was coming, he kicked me under the table, getting me right in the stomach, when he pulled me up he made sure I hit my head hard on the table making me cry. His friends were all like him, too self-obsessed to take any notice. I passed him the knife, he kept it in his hand while I struggled to get up and sit back at the table.

That's when I felt my skirt lift and he pressed the knife into my leg, while he was talking happily with his friends. I stood up abruptly and felt the knife cut me deeper down my leg." My hand goes to the scar without me thinking and Jack traces the scar with me, his touch sending warming and comforting sparks through me.

"When I stood up I made my excuses and left. He stayed, and I could hear him laughing with his friends. I ran. I didn't know where to go. I wanted to leave but I had nothing on me, so I went back to the house, not really believing what he had done. My heart was already broken. I could feel the blood dripping down my leg, the pain starting to seep in. I needed to leave.

"When I got back to the house, I grabbed my case and packed everything I could, but when I got downstairs, he was walking through the door. He grabbed me around the throat and threw me across the room. I landed on the glass coffee table, glass piercing my back and hands, but he didn't stop. He kicked, punched and shouted in my face how worthless I am, how weak and pathetic I am, how he wished I would just die. I was a rag doll in his hands. At some point, I stopped feeling the pain. Every kick and punch just stopped hurting. I must have passed out at some point because when I regained consciousness…Shit…I was being put in the boot of his car. My hands and feet bound together…I knew I was going to die, and the man I thought loved me was going to be my killer, I even hoped it would be over soon." I let out a sob and Jack's arms wrapped around me, tugging me closer.

"But do you know the worst thing? He dumped me on the road outside of the hospital. I was barely able to see, my face was smashed up, someone apparently found me a while later, and I ended up in hospital having lost so much blood, I almost lost my life." I let out another sob. "But he came in when he was called, looking shocked, crying and angry, saying he would kill the person who had done it to me. They all believed him. I said I couldn't remember what had happened. And after over a week in hospital, I was sent home, back to him. He didn't touch me again, I think he thought I had finally learnt my lesson. That was six weeks ago." My hands are shaking, it's like I am reliving it again. Jack pulls me closer to him and we lay there on the bed in silence, while he lets it all sink in.

"So now you know...I'm weak and pathetic, I couldn't and didn't defend myself. I'm not worth the hassle, but I want to thank you for everything you've done, looking after me when I had no one, and I'm sorry for freaking out on you like I did, it was humiliating." I want to curl up in a ball and just hide away.

Jack sits up and looks at me with a look I've not seen before. He pulls me up so I'm sitting in front of him, still holding my hands.

"What happened to you is unforgivable. That rat deserves to die a long and painful death, at my hands. But what you did is nothing less than magnificent. Even after he did all those... things to you, you still stood up and walked away Millie. You are the strongest woman I know, let alone intelligent, funny, beautiful and sexy as hell." He lets out a shaky breath, "I was stupid to try and do those things without asking, but please believe me, I will do everything in my power to make you happy. I... I love you, I have been in love with you since we first met I think, it's always been you." He dips his head and kisses my hand. I'm speechless, he just told me he loves me...I mean, what?

"What? After everything I just told you...you..."

"Yep, I told you I love you," he says again. Holding his hands up, he moves off the bed. "I'll wait for you Millie, I'll help you and I'm going to make you happy." He says with that small, sexy smile.

"But I'm..."

"You're perfect, then and now, you will always be perfect to me." *How can he say that, the man is delusional...*

"I've not gone mental." It must have been the look on my face, or *can he read my mind? How could he want me...no...love me?*

"I'll spend my life showing you just how much you mean to me. First of all, let's start with getting you out of here, if you would like to." I'm in shock, not sure how we went from my past to my future so quickly.

"I don't understand...how can you love me after what I just told you?"

"Easy, I loved you before you told me, and after you told me it made me love you more, and want to protect you more, if you will let me." His face is all cute and serious at the same time.

"Huh, that's definitely not how I thought this conversation would go." Moving to sit cross-legged on the bed, I just look at him.

"You don't need fixing, you're not broken. I'm going to find out more about that bastard, I'll get him, and he will never hurt you again. I promise that." He's looking me dead in the eye and I believe every word he says.

Just hearing those words makes me soften a little. He actually still wants me, loves me, in fact.

He pulls me up off the bed, so I'm standing in front of him, his hands resting on my waist. Lowering his head, he presses his nose to mine, his intoxicating scent filling my nostrils. I inhale deeply, letting it wash over me; just his smell alone is doing wondrous things to my body.

"May I kiss you Millie?" He whispers against me, his soft lips gently touching mine.

I nod, feeling breathless. "I need your words Millie, I will never do anything to you without your permission." His hand slowly moves up my back toward my neck; his fingers tangle in my hair.

"Yes..." my voice comes out in a soft whisper.

His lips caress mine the second he hears me say it. He kisses me softly, with so much feeling behind each touch and caress it melts my insides. Gently sucking on my lower lip, I let out a whimper when he pulls away, resting his forehead against mine.

"Will you come with me? Just come back to the suite tonight, then tomorrow I will show you your new place, and if you don't want it, I will understand." He looks almost remorseful for the actions he's taken; it's nice, although there is no need for it.

"I'll come back, just for tonight, I need time to process what's happened to me Jack, and be just me for a while." I sink my head down but he lifts it back up with a finger.

"That's okay, I said I would wait for you and I mean it, I will."

Chapter Eighteen

A New Beginning

Millie

"It's a cottage!" I'm stating the obvious right now, I know that, but when he said he found me a place to live, I thought it was, or would be, another apartment, somewhere safer perhaps, but this is…

"Way too much, I can't afford this. It's beautiful. I can't take it, how much is it? I bet you it's more than what I was paying a month for the apartment." I know I'm rambling. But my mind can't process what I'm seeing right now.

Jack laughs at me; we've not even made it to the cottage yet, he has only pointed it out from across the field. From here, all you can see is the front and a walled area to the left-hand side of the property. But it's so beautiful. A stone cottage with a red tile roof, with what looks like an annex on the side and a sloping red roof to match. All the windows and doors are a pale sage green; picture-perfect comes to mind.

"Everything is more expensive than what you were paying for that apartment, but this is free." *Oh my god this man, he is going to kill me with kindness, but this I can't accept, it's way too much.*

"No…just no, I can't live in this stunning cottage for free! Are you crazy? Have you lost your mind?" Spinning around to look at him, I almost trip over but he catches me before I fall; he shakes his head.

"Be careful. And wait until you see the inside before you turn it down, it needs some work."

I stayed the night as his last night, we stayed in separate rooms, but during that night, I had some crazy, scary dream that left me screaming, and he came running. He burst into the room looking like…wow, he only had boxers on! His tattoo was showing, and he looked like the magnificent man he is. He calmed me down and took care of me, but when he went to leave, I could feel the panic rising, so I asked him to stay. Nothing happened, other than my own vivid imagination taking over. I just feel safer with him around. And after his confession last night about how he loves me, I am seeing things a little differently today. I know he is not Glen, I know Jack will never hurt me, but those feelings of hurt and betrayal are still there. I'm not sure they will ever truly leave me. Even so, we seem to have a better connection today, like we are both on the same page.

It's amazing what a bit of communication can do. Smiling to myself, I walk a little faster to see the cottage he wants me to have. He keeps pace with me and when we get to the front door, we step inside, and my eyes well up at just how perfect this is. There has been some work done but I think it's just decorating, from what

I can see that needs to be finished. It's stunning! I can feel Jack close behind me. Walking in through the door, you enter the living room; there is a huge fireplace that covers the longer wall on the right-hand side, with a log burner bang in the centre, and huge wooden mantel over the top. It is perfect, all the walls are plastered and ready to be decorated. Moving through to what I think should be the kitchen, I see that it's empty except for the walls and doors. That then leads out to the walled garden, which is currently so overgrown it's taller than me. I open what I think is a cupboard and find it's a set of stairs leading up to two rooms and a small bathroom that needs work, but the other rooms are good to go. Heading back downstairs, I open another door in the kitchen to find a small toilet/utility room. This place is unbelievable.

"Why did you have to show me this?" I laugh, knowing it is well out of my price range. "I want it, and now nothing else will compare, I love the location, I love the space, I love the feel, why would you do this to me?" I would sit down but the place has no furniture, so I lean against the wall, running my hands down my face.

Jack just laughs at me, which I don't really find funny, but I'll humour him for now.

"So tell me what the rent is on this place?" I say, giving him the evil eye.

"Like I said, it's free."

"I'm not having you pay for my living accommodation Jack, that's ridiculous."

"I'm not paying for it, I promise. It came with The Manor; there are a few of these dotted about the estate, all being renovated."

"So how much is it? I am not staying here for free, no way. I will pay what it costs because I'm going to live here, I love it!" Jack gives me a stern look and moves a little closer. I can also see the relief in his eyes.

"I'm not going to win this one, am I?" I ask him, and he shakes his head, the corner of his mouth twitching like he's trying to hide a smile.

"Ok, what if I continue renovating it? I pay for the stuff that's needed?"

"No," he says flat out, "everything has been ordered, it just needs to be fitted, plus it's owned by The Manor, it's… their responsibility, so it's free." He is just as stubborn as me.

It's been three weeks since the first day at the cottage and so much has happened. I'm all moved in; the bathroom and kitchen were installed a few days before I moved. Jack and I agreed to disagree about paying for the renovations. I've been ordering the things I want for the cottage, but he keeps leaving cheques in the kitchen to pay me back for them. When he realised I was not banking them, he set up payment directly into my account. I think it's a losing battle, which he will win no doubt.

I love being in the cottage. It feels like home, something I've not felt in a long time. I'm exhausted though, working two jobs, doing the renovations and working towards the next step in my business. I'm working all the hours I can. I want to make this place look amazing, I want it to be mine. We spent last weekend cutting down the overgrown forest in the little walled garden; it's so beautiful. I can't wait for summer to come around so I can plant a few flowers and create a little sanctuary all of my own.

Oh and my ribs have healed; I can move, bend and do everything again! With that in mind, I've started yoga at the local studio. It's wonderful! I do it most mornings before I start work. It sets me up for the day. I love it.

Today I've skipped my yoga class, and I'm so excited! I'm getting my tattoo. I've not told anyone about it yet, I want it to be a surprise. I found the images I designed before I met Glen. And that's the exact design I'm having today. I still loved it even though it's been years since I originally designed it.

Jack and I are getting closer; we see each other almost every day. However, he and I have been busy over the last few days, so we've not spent as much time together. I like where we are though; he's giving me the space I need, although he's still there. If we don't see each other, we speak on the phone or text every day. It's given me a little hope that I can have a relationship again.

Today is not only a good day for me, but Dan, Jack and a few of the other guys fly to Ibiza for the stag do. Em, a few of her other friends, and I are heading up to London for a few days for her hen do tomorrow.

We've also put a plan into place for selling the house. Well it's just the start of a plan; I've not figured the rest out yet. Jack is none the wiser, I feel a little guilty about keeping him in the dark, but I know how he would react. He works so hard and I don't want to spoil the weekend he has planned with the boys. And I have to do this, for myself

There's more... I'm meeting with Charlie first thing in the morning; we've been talking on the phone, and I'm nervous and excited. It's been years since I saw her last, so much has happened. Most of which she knows now, not all the details but a summary of sorts. She has also agreed to help me with the sale of the house.

I'm not going near it; Charlie and Em will be doing the lock changes and estate agents stuff, only after it has been staked out to make sure he is definitely not there. I don't want to be seen, or be around if he comes back. I don't like putting them through this, I'm worried he will come back and catch them. I know how he would react to me, but I'm not sure what he would do to them, and that scares me. They have insisted it's the best way to get it done, which I'm not happy about.

Not telling Jack was also at the insistence of Em, as we know he would want to be part of it, but that would only make things worse if he was there and he would hate the idea even more than me. Anyway, afterwards, we'll join the girls at the Sky Lounge in the Shard for drinks, followed by more drinks, cocktails, food, clubs and dancing. I can't wait to be out with the girls; it's been so long. It's all been organised and booked by Em's friend, Jane. We met briefly at Em's last weekend. I have a feeling she doesn't like me much, but I'm at this hen party for Em, not her.

But first, my tattoo, the design I have chosen is an old one I designed myself; it will be big, down my arm and across the top of my back. Flowers of all sizes joined with stems. It's really delicate. It's going to take a good few hours but it's only a line drawing with no filling. Hopefully it will be finished today so I can travel up to London tomorrow.

"Where are you going?" Em catches me when I walk past her office on the way to see Matt, the tattoo guy.

"To get a tattoo," I say simply and her eyes almost pop out of her head before she laughs and says, "No really, where are you off to? Fancy some coffee?"

"If you want to join me you can, but I'm getting my tattoo today," pointing to my arm and the tattoo place just past her office.

"Oh my god, you're serious!" she squeals.

"Yep, I've wanted one for so long, it's on my list of stuff to get me back to me." I told Em about the list last week, didn't say what was on it, but she loved the idea and has helped me find some classes I want to take. She helped me find the yoga class, it's more spiritual than other ones, which I absolutely needed.

"I'm so coming with you, I'll grab us some coffee and meet you there!" She almost squeals at me, wandering off to get our drinks. We have become quite close in the short time I have been here. It's nice I can talk to someone who knows everything, even if she is Jack's little sister.

I'm four hours in, and we are almost done. Matt has been amazing; Emma stayed for about an hour then had to get back to work. We ate cake while Matt worked on my arm; I'm feeling really tired; sitting in the same position for four hours is not good for anyone. But from what I can see so far it looks amazing! I can't wait to show Em tomorrow.

"All done," Matt says, pushing back his chair and giving me a hand to get up. "Go and take a look in the mirror, it looks great, your artwork is beautiful." He says, taking his gloves off. Matt is a great-looking guy, slightly too skinny for me, but has that boho, rocker man vibe going on, long hair, tattoos. It's a good look on him.

"Thank you!" I laugh a little shyly.

"You're welcome, go on, take a look."

I'm almost lost for words! "Matt, it's amazing! Thank you!" I reach out and hug him.

My tattoo is beautiful; Matt has made it come to life, the detail he has added in is amazing. I wonder what Jack will make of it, and then the same feeling washes over me and makes me feel sick. *What if… what if he…*

"Everything alright over there?" Matt says from behind the counter, breaking my train of thought.

"Yes, yes it's stunning, you've added some magic to it Matt. Thank you," I say, squashing down my rising panic.

"The pleasure has been all mine." I pay Matt and start heading back to the cottage after he wraps it for me.

It's much further to walk than before, but I don't mind. I'm starting to get a handle on my negative thoughts. The yoga teacher I have been going to has taught me a few things about meditation, and how just noticing your thoughts, accepting them and moving on can really help you. It's not easy but I feel a small shift in the way I think about it all now.

My phone rings in my pocket and I take it out. It's Jack.

"Where are you? I wanted to see you before I go."

"Where is the "Hi Millie, what have you been up to today, I've not seen you in two days," I say sarcastically and he sighs.

"Hello beautiful." He laughs down the phone, and I instantly smile. My stomach is doing little flips, even though we've seen each other almost every day. He has been a true gentleman, which is getting a little annoying, if I'm totally honest. I think it really freaked him out how badly Glen hurt me. I can't blame him really, but he seems to have taken it that if he touches me, I may break. I mean we sit on the sofa watching movies and he moves away from me when I have wandering hands. I need to sort this out, I'm so horny, it's ridiculous, and now he is away for three days, maybe I should give him a little treat before he goes…

"I'm on my way back now, I've got a surprise to show you, I should be there in half an hour," I say but can hear his sigh on the other end. "What time are you going?" I ask.

"The limo has just pulled up, we are off in about five minutes." I can hear how sad he is.

"I'm sorry, my surprise took a little longer than I thought. I won't get to see you for three more days!" I hate the thought. It'll be five days since we've not been able to see each other! It sucks.

"Five days… I'm not sure I'll survive not seeing you for that long." This makes me smile.

"Nor me…"

Chapter Nineteen

Party Time

Jack

"I'm not fucking wearing that!" Dan shouts and laughs at the same time. We flew out to Ibiza yesterday afternoon. When we landed, I had him blindfolded and handcuffed to an inflatable blow-up man. I've rented an exclusive villa just outside of the main strip, perched on the seafront with an infinity pool looking out to the sea. We could have stayed at my place but there are twelve of us, it's going to get messy and I like my villa the way it is.

Yesterday, we took Dan to a few bars and clubs; some of the locals and other bar owners gave us VIP treatment because we know them so well after almost ten years of being on the island. He was so drunk we had to carry him back!

I actually think he is still half-cut today! The main event has not even started yet; god forbid I ever get married because payback will be a bitch after what I have planned for him! I know he is marrying my sister and all, but I have to get revenge somehow. Plus Em knows all about it, she even helped me plan it. Chuckling to myself, I look over to see Dan's face, a picture of shock, excitement and maybe a little fear.

"No way, is it just me dressing up? You can't do this to me? Please?" Everyone was looking at the outfit; they had no idea what I have planned because none of them can keep a secret.

"We all have something to wear, it's not just you, but yours is by far the worst." I laugh as they all turn and look at me at the same time.

"But it's a rainbow tutu, fairy wings, fake boobs in a bikini top and a tiara." I'm not sure he believes what he is seeing.

"Oh, don't forget these..." I hand him a bag he has to carry for the night; it's a furry kitten bum bag, and inside are the tasks he has to complete over the weekend, nothing too offensive, and a few extras "take a look, see what's in it".

"You have got to be kidding me, face glitter, hair clips, and...oh my god! I can't do these things, Em will have my balls on a plate if she ever finds out! You do remember who I'm getting married to don't you?"

Taking a swig of my beer I tell him, "All Emma approved." We clink bottles, this is the best reaction I could have hoped for.

A few hours later, we are all dressed in rainbow-coloured t-shirts, each with a different picture of Dan on it, ranging from drunk photos, naked baby pics, and life events over the last few years, all slightly humiliating to him. We ordered pizza at the villa along with waitresses, a fully stocked bar, and a little light entertainment before we head out for the night. Dan is so embarrassed by all the attention, it's great. Just watching him get pulled up to dance, and be made a part of the firebreather entertainment while dressed as a fairy is one of the best moments ever. All throughout, I am taking plenty of photos and sending them to Em.

There is a nice surprise for him later though, one I had not planned but will work well for us both. I can't help but smile to myself.

Millie

To my utter surprise, everything went really well; meeting Charlie was almost like old times. We talked and have promised to keep in touch; she even said she would come down to see me when it's all settled to celebrate with me. I can feel my old self coming back, just having her around for a few hours today has brought back so many good memories of who I was and who I want to be again.

She checked out the house while I stayed back but there was no sign of him. The locks were changed by the locksmith, and a new security system was put in place, all of which Charlie and I have control over.

Em arranged for the estate agent to meet us there and it's all sorted. They know the details and the house will be on the market as of Monday morning. I know it will make him angry when he gets back and finds he is locked out, but it's my house and was my parents' before that. It was a happy home, before him.

As we are heading back in the cab, Em's phone starts ringing. It's her best friend Jane on the other end and from the look on her face, something has gone wrong.

"What? You have to be kidding me, how can they do that? It's my hen do." Tears stream down her face as she talks.

"What's wrong?" I ask, trying to guess what has happened.

"It's all been cancelled!" she says between sobs, "how…how could they? Why?" Her hand coming up to her face, and slumping back in the seat.

"What? Why?" *How could they ruin her day like this? What are we going to do?*

"What did Jane say? Give me your phone, I'll talk to Jane to see if we can sort something out."

Five hours later, we are stepping off a private jet! Yes, a freaking private jet, where we were all served champagne and snacks, fancy snacks at that. We sat on beautiful cream leather seats and listened to music, starting the hen do in style.

I'm still not sure it's real, maybe this is a dream and I'm still in bed in the cottage, so I pinch myself. *Ouch, nope not a dream.* And guess what, Jack organised everything, the jet, the limo, the villa, everything. When I called him and told him what had happened, he just said, "Leave it with me." He took care of it, all of it, or at least someone did. Now we are here in Ibiza, being escorted to the villa in a limo where there is supposedly a surprise waiting for us.

"It's stunning, how on earth did Jack manage to get this sorted in such a short space of time?" The villa is breathtaking; there are six of us in total, but this place must have at least ten bedrooms, two bars, a pool, you name it, it has it. It's all white set against the breathtaking blue sky, sun and crystal clear sea background.

Em laughs like there is an inside joke and says, "I'll let Jack explain it to you."

"What does that mean?" I ask, looking confused.

"Ask him and he can tell you. Now let's get this party started. I need more drinks & cocktails."

Just at that moment, three men wearing just tiny aprons walk from the outhouse towards us, where we are all sat by the outside bar. Em screams with excitement, clapping her hands as the other girls join in.

"Hello ladies, we," he says, gesturing towards the other two men, "are your naked butlers for the next few hours. Who would like a drink?" Oh my god, when they turn around to head for the bar, we see almost everything, tight bums, all toned and smooth-skinned. I have to say I really want to pinch one, I won't but I want to. I wonder if Jack would ever be a naked butler…just for me? That image almost sets me on fire, so I push it back for later, when I'm all alone.

For the next few hours, we were all served cocktails and canapes. It's one of the best afternoons I have ever had and it's only just started.

Em comes out of the villa dressed like the sexiest fairy you have ever seen, in a short tutu, bikini, wings, waving her wand like she is a true fairy. I snap a photo to send to her later; Dan is one lucky man, she looks amazing, and ready to move on to our next surprise.

"Me and Charlie came here a long time ago, it was great then we had the best time, but it's even better now, VIP treatment is the only way to go," I chuckle, talking to Sam, sitting at Cafe Mambo enjoying more cocktails while the DJ plays some awesome music. I'm not sure how much more I can drink, I'm already drunker than I've been in a long time.

"Is your brother around Em?" Jane says with her back to me slyly.

"Somewhere," she says, "he said he would stay away from us. Dan's on his Stag Do this weekend too, and Jack wants to keep it separate," Em replies, eyeing me with a slight eye roll.

"That's such a shame, I remember that last time we met up here, Jack was so..how should I put it..." she places a finger to her lips, "*attentive.*" She giggles and the other girls laugh. There is a weird sensation in my chest that I don't like; I don't like what Jane is implying, maybe it's the alcohol making me feel weird.

"That was a long time ago Jane, plus please don't talk about my brother like that in front of me. It's gross." She moves to talk to another friend on the couch opposite me, and mouths an apology. There's that feeling again, but there is nothing to apologise for; I know he has a past, it's not like I am the only one he has slept with. Shrugging off the feeling in my chest, I lean my head back and enjoy the music, then decide to get another drink as Jane's still talking to whoever will listen about how good Jack was, what he did to her – in great detail, and how she can't wait for it to happen again, as they have been texting one another since a few months ago.

This time, the feeling comes back, but it's mixed with a heavy feeling in the pit of my stomach. I feel like I can't breathe; we've not slept together, Jack has been keeping his distance like that. We see each other, but it's during work, or sitting on the sofa watching a movie. *Maybe he thinks we've moved into the friend zone? Oh God…since he told me he loved me, has he been texting someone else?* Nothing has happened between me and Jack since the night on the sofa. I thought he was giving me space. Maybe I misread it, maybe he thought telling me he loved me was a sure thing. And when it didn't happen…shit, I'm so confused, my chest hurts, and it gets worse the more I think about them together, I can't stand it.

"I'm off to the bar, I'll send a round of drinks over," I say to Em. She looks at me, a little confused, "Millie, we have table service, you don't need to go to the bar!" she says, but I'm already standing up and on my way. The only way I am going to survive this evening and make sure Em has a hen do to remember is to try and ignore Jane, and enjoy myself, while getting as drunk as possible. It's the only solution. When I reach the bar, I ask for a round to be sent to our table and ask for a few shots for myself, drinking them one after the other while the barman watches me frowning. I order two more and do the same thing. I love the warm feeling of them sliding down my throat, and the fuzzy feeling spreading throughout my body, numbing the feelings that were slowly creeping in.

I make my way outside to the beach, where people are dancing and sitting on the sand. I watch for a while and decide if I want to be a bit more me, and forget about how she was describing what positions they had done it in. I'm not sure I can remove that image from my mind. I need to do a few things on my own. So I step down, kick off my sandals and feel the sand on my feet, feeling the beat of the music on my chest. I close my eyes, enjoying the freedom, the warm setting sun on my skin and falling back in love with myself just a little as the music washes over me. I dance for what seems like forever; I'm in just a bikini and a short green skirt, my new tattoo in full view for everyone to see. My hair is down and wavy, tickling my back as I move. We all have rainbow colours on, as part of the hen do theme.

I feel someone come up behind me, their hands on my hips, pulling me closer to them, but when I turn around, it's not who I want it to be, and my heart sinks, that feeling in my chest coming back again. I shake my head and move away, walking over to the edge of the water, where I sit and feel the cool water tease my feet and legs. I put all this other stuff to one side; this is bliss, this place. I could become addicted to this, the sun, the sea, the air. Lying back on the sand, I close my eyes, basking in feelings I had forgotten. Freedom, just to be me for a little while, soaking it all in.

Peeling open my eyes, I check the time. I've been MIA for almost two hours. I should head back inside and join the rest of them, but I plan to disappear again later just to get this feeling back, which I have missed so much.

It's so much busier now; when I try to get back in the bar, it's rammed and I have to push past people to get to where everyone is still sitting. Our group seems to have gotten bigger, it looks like the boys joined us anyway. I spot Em and Dan, and burst out laughing. They are wearing identical outfits, even down to the matching tutu and fairy wings; only Dan looks as ridiculous as Em looks stunning, with her long, lean legs and tanned skin; she looks so happy.

I scan around to see if Jack is here; when I spot him, I stop laughing, the smile wiped from my face when I see that Jane was right, it might happen tonight for her. She's sitting with her legs draped over Jack's, his hand resting on her ankle, her arm around his neck, playing with his hair while she says something into his ear. He turns towards her and they laugh, his hand still on her ankle. They're even wearing matching colours. My chest has that feeling again, my hand comes up to my chest to try and protect it from whatever is happening right now. A noise escapes my mouth and I realise it's a sob; I can't breathe, my eyes close for a second and when I open them, Em is looking at me, with apprehension written all over her face. She looks from me to where my eyes are trained on Jack, but before she looks back, I'm gone.

Chapter Twenty

I Fucked Up

Jack

"What the fuck?" Em shouts in my face. "Have you lost your mind? Jane, I love you but get off my brother. It's not happening; he wants someone else, or I thought he did until I saw this," she says, stabbing me in the chest with her finger, rage all over her face, directed at me, and I have no idea why.

"What the hell are you talking about, what's not going to happen with Jane?" Jane has scurried off to the other couch, and is now talking to one of the other guys.

"You told me, you were giving her space to heal, you told me that you loved her! Yet you go and do this." She gestures between me and Jane, I'm even more confused. "That, right in front of her. The most delicate and vulnerable person we know, and you go and break her further after everything that has happened to her, you do this!" She is red in the face, getting louder the angrier she gets. Dan is behind her, holding her steady, and I still have no idea what's going on. I peer around at Dan, looking for answers; he shrugs, he knows when to stay out of it, some best friend he is.

"Em, what the fuck I have I done?" I ask, shifting a little in my seat, I'm still clueless. I've not seen her this mad since, well I can't remember. She leans forward, getting in my space and I lean back slightly, not knowing what to do. She lowers her voice so only I can hear her.

"What do you think Millie saw when she came back to the bar a few minutes ago, huh? After she disappeared about two hours ago because she couldn't stand to hear Jane talk about how she was going to, and has already, had her way with you, highlighting the details of your past encounter together. Then she walks back in to find Jane wrapped around you like the limpet she can be, laughing, with you touching her up! Are you fucking stupid?"

"I…" I have no words; that was not what was happening. *For fuck sake, I've worked so hard to gain her trust, have I just ruined it?* I've stayed away from anything romantic; it's been so fucking hard. Every time we sit on the sofa to watch a movie, I'm hard just with the slightest touch. I watch her at work, and get jealous of everyone she speaks to. I've been rude to the guys on staff when I catch the way they look at her and make comments about her. It's nothing I've not thought about myself, but she's mine, only I'm allowed to think of her in that way.

I've just been there for her. I wanted her to heal like Em said, to trust me after the stupid things I did, and the stuff that has happened to her, and now…now I may have lost it all, by not seeing what was happening right in front of me.

"Fuck!" I'm so stupid. "You know how I feel, I need to find her!" I say, moving Em to the side so I can stand up.

"She has already left, she went out by the beach, you are such a dickhead!" she says, and gets her phone out of her bag.

"She says she is okay, that she has gone out to another bar, and will keep me updated on where she is." I relax a little, knowing she's messaged Em, but I need to find her.

It's been an hour, I've called her eight times, sent her messages asking where she is, saying that I need to talk to her. I know she has read them, but she's not messaging me back. I feel like I'm going out of my mind. I'm worried for her safety; we are in another country for fuck sake. *What is she doing? What might someone else do to her...fuck, I can't even let my mind go there.*

"Fuck!" I run my fingers through my hair and head to the club where we first met. I can't lose her again. Maybe I'll have some luck there.

I greet the guys when I walk through the door and take a seat at the bar. Issac hands me my usual drink, whisky on the rocks. The club is rammed, which is great. I don't know what to do, I feel useless, I feel awful for leaving my sister and Dan's celebrations. They were having a great time. I made sure of that, it is my best friend and my sister, after all. I reassured Em I would find her and explain everything to her.

I can't think and I need to think. Grabbing my drink, I push past everyone having a good time, dancing and drinking. Making my way up the stairs towards the office, that's when I see her in the middle of my club. I lean over the rail a little, my hand clutching onto it, and I watch her. Her hair is falling down her back as she dances, guys trying and failing to touch her. She is the sexiest thing I have ever seen, I watch as she moves to the music, her hips swaying from side to side to the beat, her sweet little ass in that tiny skirt, I can't take my eyes off her, she turns around and my eyes almost pop out of my head, that…bikini, the small triangles just about covering her perfect boobs.

Then I watch as a pair of hands curve around her stomach; I feel sick, that bastard is trying it on, I can't blame him, but that's my girl. What I see next amazes me, she turns around and looks him in the eye and within seconds, he is gone, I was ready to kick the shit out of him, but she is handling it.

Moving back down the stairs, I walk towards her, watching her dance with her eyes closed, beautiful, that's all I can think. Of course I have a massive hard-on; I'm starting to get used to having a bad case of blue balls. It's getting embarrassing how quickly it can happen from a single thought of her.

I must look like a right dick but I just stand and watch her some more from a few feet away; she looks like the girl I first met six years ago, she looks happy, carefree and loving life. This is how I remember her, the first time I saw her, with her friends dressed up like superheroes, enjoying the night, laughing and being free. It's why I watched her then, and why I can't take my eyes off her now. Some lad tries to grab her ass but I step forward, grabbing his shirt just before he touches her, "She is mine, hands off!" I tell him and he backs away as quickly as he came over, hands up in defeat.

Standing behind her, having those hips sway right where I want them to be, I'm mesmerised. Reaching out, I move some of her long, red, wavy hair back from her shoulder, sliding it through my fingers, exposing her neck. I feel her as she freezes. I lean down, inhaling her scent; it drives me crazy, my nose tracing her neck and ear. I hear her take a sharp inhale. It takes me a few moments to realise something is different, I've been too focused on the way she moves and the pricks trying it on with her to notice a beautiful new intricate design that runs over her shoulder and arm.

"You have a new tattoo," I smile, lightly tracing the small flowers with my fingers down her other arm, as she turns to face me.

"I'm not talking to you," and she moves away towards the stairs. Leaving me standing there alone on the dance floor. Catching up with her as quickly as I can, I grab her hand.

"Come to the office with me, so we can talk please?" I beg.

"Let go of me, and no, I saw what I saw." I let go and she goes up the stairs to the bar and orders three shots. I ask Andy for some water and my usual and tell him it's on me; she shoots me daggers, drinks her shots and walks away again, flaunting her ass and driving me crazy. *Ahh...* I scream in my head.

"Please just hear me out, Millie please."

"No. Why should I? It's not like we are in a relationship, you can do whatever you want with whoever you want." Her tone is calm, annoyed but calm.

"I don't want anyone else, I want you!" I say but she is walking away again. I need to get her alone, she will hate me for this, but what else can I do? I stride past her, stop in front and she almost walks into me. Placing my hands on her hips, I lift her over my shoulder in a fireman's lift. With her sweet ass in the air, she screams but also laughs at the same time as I move us towards my office.

"People can see everything," she shouts at me, trying to hold herself up, her hands on my lower back, but she falls back over my shoulder. I move my hand up to cover where her short skirt has come up over her delicious ass. I can feel the heat between her legs; she gasps and stops wriggling.

When we reach my office, I put her down and she stumbles back onto the sofa.

"Well, that was rude, there was no need to do that." She stands up but sways a little.

"There was every reason to do that, you wouldn't listen. How much have you had to drink?"

"None of your goddamn business," she says, steadying herself on the arm of the chair. "Whatever you have to say....I don't want to hear it," she says with her hands on her hips. *Fuck, she's sexy when she's angry.*

"Look..." I step forward and stand in front of her. She looks up at me with defiant eyes and moves away from me. "What you saw was Jane trying it on as normal; what you missed was me telling her to back off as I'm into someone else. She laughed it off, and I, the stupid dick I am, carried on, not noticing what she was doing, because I'm not interested in her! I'm sorry!" *Fuck, I hope she listens.*

"Oh, really? That's your normal is it? Girls falling over themselves for you, and you pretending not to see what's going on! You were touching her, your hand was on her leg, for fuck's sake!" She was shouting at me, her anger rising, her hands in the air, looking me in the eye. "I thought you were different," she says, fighting the tears back. "I will not be treated like this. I need someone better, I can't go through... all that again." A tear slips and glides down her cheek as she holds in a sob. I reach out for her but she moves back, "Don't...I..."

"Millie, please, I'm not like that, like him, please listen to me, I love you! I was trying to move her off me." I really want to touch her, hold her close and make it all better.

"I know you're not him," she says in a whisper, softening a little, she closes her eyes. "You're like my own personal brand of sunshine," she says, draping herself on the sofa, putting her legs up over the arm, like she can't take it anymore. I smile, I know I shouldn't but I can't help it. I'm not sure she realised what she said. *So I'm her personal brand of sunshine? Well fuck me!* I can't hide the smile spreading across my face right now or the swell in my chest.

"Do you know how sexy you are when you're jealous?" I say, kneeling down next to her on the sofa. She looks like a goddess, the way she is laid out in front of me, long shapely legs, almost ivory with a hint of blush from the sun, freckles everywhere; I want to count them, kiss them. The natural curves on her body, the way her breasts swell when she breathes, I can see the outline of her nipples through the thin fabric of the bikini. It's been so hard to stay away from her.

"I'm not...really? Huh," she puts her hands over her face, "maybe I am a little jealous...the way you were touching her, laughing with her, I want it Jack. I'm not ashamed to say it, although it may be the drink talking, making me brave...I want you Jack, I want you to touch me. I want..."

I don't let her finish, I move her hands and cup her face in mine, tracing my thumb across her bottom lip. I'm so close I can feel her warm breath against my face. We haven't touched since the night she told me about him. I promised I would give her time, but now, maybe I should have done things differently.

"I'm going to kiss you Millie, if you will let me?" Moving my hand, I tip her head up towards mine so I can see her eyes and those tempting pink lips.

"Yes." It's the faintest whisper.

Lightly brushing my lips with hers, I tease her lips apart with my tongue. As I lean over her, her arms wrap around my neck, pulling me closer, wanting more. Her scent fills me, and I crush my lips on hers, unable to contain myself. Tasting her, my hands drift down her body, exploring her breasts, stomach and hips like it's the first time all over again. She moans, arching up to meet me, wrapping her legs around me and pushing me back so I lay on the floor. Millie is straddling me, while we are still kissing each other with a feverish need to get more.

"Door..." she says, coming up for air.

"Locked." It's all I can manage to say. I can feel her heat through my shorts, there is no hiding how much she wants this. She presses herself down on my length, feeling how hard I am. *Fuck, I'm not sure how much longer I can last if she keeps that up.*

"Good," she says, her hands moving down my stomach, unbuttoning my shorts. I help her take them off, she pulls my boxers down, freeing me and my erection springs up. Her eyes are full of lust, and she slides down my body and to my utter surprise, she takes me in her mouth. *Fucking hell.*

"Fuck...Millie...You...don't have...to...Ahhh!" She kisses the top of my erection and then sucks it, taking me deep into her wet mouth. I grab hold of her hair, careful not to hurt her, or force her to do anything, but I need to hold on to something.

"Hmmm," is all she says, the sensation that sends through me is something I have never felt before, this is …fuck, the best goddamn blowjob I have ever had. When I look down, she is looking up at me, and it almost sends me over the edge. I reach down and pull the triangles of her bikini down and find her nipples hard with desire. I pinch the first one, then move to the next and she moans while sucking my dick harder. Lifting her face, she stops and I grab her legs and pull them towards me, spinning her around. She gasps when I make her straddle my face; she laughs but carries on where she left off, sucking me in the most exquisite way. This time she adds her hand to stroke my full length while sucking and teasing me with her tongue.

Her knees are on either side of my head, I tease her by dragging my tongue over the tops of her thighs. She smells insane, I can see she's already wet when I glance up. My fingers trace the line of her apex to where I want my tongue to be and I hear her moan again around my straining dick. I pull her bikini bottoms to the side, exposing her to me, and she wiggles, like she needs me to go quicker. I'm going to take my sweet time, I want her calling my name and begging for me to be inside her. *She's so wet and this is just for me, no one else,* I think to myself. I glide my finger over her folds and she groans and moves, wanting more. I kiss her sweet spot and thrust a finger inside her while I play with her clit. The sounds she makes have me stiffening and I almost come right there; those are the sounds I want to hear for the rest of my life, god how I have missed them.

She has me deep in her mouth and every vibration makes me harder. Adding another finger I work her up into a frenzy. I can feel she is close; her legs shake, my cock forgotten, as she bends and arches with need. I wrap my arm around her waist to keep her in place and pick up speed, moving my fingers in and out and curling them to reach her spot, licking and sucking on her clit until she explodes. I feel her walls clench around my fingers, as I move them faster with my mouth sucking her clit and my tongue lapping at her juices. She rides my face and my fingers and collapses when her orgasm finally subsides. Before she's fully recovered, I move us to the sofa, and lay on top of her, teasing and pulling at her nipples and taking her mouth with mine, so she can taste herself on me; she runs her fingers through my hair.

"Millie…" she looks at me under hooded lashes, "I want you…here." I press my cock up against her opening, she arches up in response, taking a sharp breath, but I need her words, I won't do this without them.

"Tell me…Yes…"

Rubbing her clit with my thumb and kissing her, making a trail down to her breasts and those pink buds, I take one between my teeth and gently pull, she moans again.

"Say it Millie."

"Yes…" I slowly remove her bikini bottoms with my hands while I suck on her nipple. Coming back up to face her, I place my dick at her entrance again and I hear her gasp as I slowly enter her. She is so tight, it takes my breath away, I keep going until she has all of me inside her. I bend my head down into the nape of her neck and kiss her there, she's already rocking my world, and we've hardly even started.

"Oh god!" she says panting, "I forgot how big you were…Oh fuck…Yes!" Her walls told me tight as we connect for the first time in six years, it's better than I remembered.

"Fuck, you're so tight, it's..." We just stay there for a moment, absorbing one another, while we get used to the feel of each other, then she moves, wanting more fiction, so I move out and slam back in.

"Yes, fuck...yes..." I can feel her walls tighten around me, I'm on the edge, so I do it again and she screams with pleasure, kissing me, while I pump into her again and again, as we hold on to each other like our lives depend on it. Millie wraps her legs around my back, while I cradle her in my arms and kiss her wherever I can reach. I won't last long, but I don't think she will either. I can feel her climbing, our bodies slick with sweat; the intense need we have for each other is out of this world.

"Come for me Millie," I say through gritted teeth. It only takes one more stroke of my length against her, and she falls apart around me. I can't hold back my dick swelling deep inside her and filling her to the hilt as I flow into her. She milks me of everything I have and we just lay there, tangled up in each other for what seems like hours.

"I don't want to move, but we should get back to the others," she says, trying to untangle herself from me. But I just hold on tighter.

"Jack..."

"I know, but I have waited for this for so long, I'm not ready to give it up just yet." The smile on my face says it all.

"Who said anything about giving it up, I want to do that again very very soon, just not in your office."

"Well, in that case..." I prop myself up on my elbows and soak her in, half dressed, her breasts still out, which I can't help but play with, her messy hair. *God I love this woman.*

"Whatever is running through your mind right now, hold that thought until we are alone later." I look down and I'm hard pressed against her leg.

"It's all you Millie, you make this happen," I say, eyeing myself. She giggles, sliding out from under me and turning as I continue to lie on the sofa. She plants a kiss and a playful lick on my cock before she stands up, adjusting her clothes back to their normal position and sliding her bikini bottoms back on.

"Can't I just keep you to myself?" I ask, pulling her towards me.

"No, I already feel guilty about this whole situation." She looks like she has just been fucked and I make a mental note to keep her looking like that as often as she will let me.

What I wouldn't give to just stay here, I know it's my office but no one will bother us if the door is locked.

"But…I have so many ideas on how we can make up for lost time. So many ways we can…" I don't tell her; I just trail my fingers down her body, my hands stopping at her perfect behind.

But she pushes back and stands up, pulling me up with her.

"Well, okay…" I say, planting another kiss on her lips. She watches me get dressed. *Man, I can't wait to get her alone again later; the things I'm going to do to that perfect body of hers, I'm going to make her scream with pleasure over and over again.*

Half an hour later, we walk back into the bar hand in hand, but before we head over, I want to sort out a little situation just to make sure Millie knows I'm dead serious about her.

"I'll get us a round of drinks in, I'll be over in a minute."

Millie

I can't believe what has just happened, we had sex in his office, not just sex, mind-blowing, life-altering sex. And it was so much better than I remember, better than my dreams, that brought me back to him.

Even after what I thought he had done, my mind went into shock, fight or flight, as they call it. I walked away to protect myself and he found me. He wouldn't let me leave until I had heard him out. I softened a little when he threw me over his shoulder; I had to stifle a laugh as well as being angry. I told him the truth and he apologised to me, over and over again. There was something different about how he said it, the feeling behind it was….worry, almost like he thought he would lose me.

I told him he was nothing like Glen, when I saw his face after what I said about not being able to go through that again. I know my heart couldn't take it. I'm still not ready to admit my feelings to myself, let alone anyone else.

I thought of him as my own personal brand of sunshine, "Oh shit!" I put my face in my hands when I walked over to where everyone was at the table, I said it out loud! I can feel my cheeks going red. *That's why you should never drink Millie*, I lecture myself. I can't seem to keep my thoughts in my head around him, and he told me I was jealous. I mean I was, still am, a little, if I'm honest, but that man is a fucking God, inside and out, and…wow, my body feels like it's alive after what he did to me. I'm on cloud nine, not only from feeling like I'm getting my old self back, but from the way he touches me, it's like he wants to memorise every part of me.

It's a new feeling for me, one I still need to process but I'll leave that for another day. I want to savour it now. I'm happy, totally happy and it's been a very long time since I could honestly say that to myself and it's all because of him.

When I reach the table, everyone is much drunker than when I left them, but they all look like they are having a great time. Em and Dan are still dancing together, arms wrapped around each other. When she spots me, she grabs Dan's hand and tugs him over towards me.

"You're back!" she shouts over the music, and wraps her arms around me.

"Yes," I chuckle, "I'm sorry I took off Em. I should never have left you. It's your hen night."

"Do I look bothered?" I laugh at that. "I have had a great night. I know why you went and it's okay. I gave him a right mouthful just after you left. I take it he found you? He had no idea what he had done. I don't even think he realised what the silly dick there was doing," she points over at Jane.

"It's okay, he found me and he explained it all. We're good, really good!" and my face heats at just how good we are.

"No…that's my brother, you can't have those thoughts about him…Eww." She shudders and my face flushes even more and we both burst out laughing at the same time. Em hugs me and turns back to Dan, who is waiting patiently behind her. He winks at me and whisks her back to the dance floor. God they make an amazing couple.

My eyes fly to Jane, who is sitting across from where I'm standing. Her eyes are trained on Jack, watching his every move as he comes back from the bar. If only she knew what we had just done. I watch as she mouths something to Helen with a sly look on her face.

She stands up, adjusting her cleavage so they are almost spilling out of her bikini top and heads over towards Jack, swaying her hips, like she means business.

I stand back and watch as she places her hand on Jack's arm, running her finger up and down, trying to stop him from walking away from her. I catch Em watching as well; Em then starts to move towards her, like she wants to put her in her place. When Jane rises to her tiptoes, she says something into his ear, Jack looks down at her and frowns, laughing at her and shaking his head at the same time, almost like he can't believe what she's just said. She reaches up to touch him again, but he moves away, leaving her standing there, walking directly to me. The smile on his face when he sees me is so spectacular it makes me weak in the knees.

When he reaches me, he grabs my hand, tugging me to him and presses me against him so tightly, I'm wrapped in his godlike form and protective embrace. I can hardly breathe when he takes my mouth with his and kisses me so passionately, I lose myself in him again. We fall back onto the sofa with Jack on top of me, pressing me backwards into the deep soft cushions and I forget the world around me for a few moments, it's just me and him. The weight of him on me does things to my body I don't want to resist. I hear whistles and whoops around us, and when we come up for air I realise all eyes are on us.

"That should do it," Jack whispers softly into my ear, laughing, holding himself up slightly to allow me some space.

"You did that on purpose?" I question, my voice has turned to a sultry whisper.

"Yes, how else am I going to prove to you how serious I am about you? I needed to show you that I don't care who is watching. I love you Millie." His face nuzzles my neck, then I see flashes. Someone has just taken photos of us but when I look up, I see someone quickly walking away, with a huge camera around their neck.

"Why are you frowning?" Jack asks, looking at me a little puzzled. "I know you're not ready to say it back, and I'm okay with that…"

"I know, but someone just took our photo and ran off." How could he not have noticed?

"Oh shit…" he says, leaning back down, giving me a quick kiss on the cheek.

"What? Why would someone do that? It's weird," I ask him, a little puzzled but chuckling at the same time.

Propping himself up on his elbows so I'm still underneath him, he eyes Dan, like he wants to get him to do something, but decides against it. "Um…I may need to explain a few things about me."

"What does that mean?" My feelings are a little all over the place. What could he mean?

"Let's go back to the villa, I'll explain everything there. It's a little more private."

A few hours later, I'm sitting in his villa, yes, his villa. And one of many by the sounds of it. I'm a little shocked; his property portfolio on its own is worth billions!

He owns clubs, pubs, hotels, villas, gyms, offices and the press are interested in everything he does. They want to see who he will be with next. Given his reputation with women, he is known as a bit of a ladies' man. He showed me some recent articles about him. I read the headline but didn't want to read any more. *How did I not know anything about this?* I don't read the papers, or magazines; I find them a bit pointless, it's never happy news.

"I can promise you, most of it isn't true, yes I was a bit of a ladies man, but every one of them only wanted one thing…my money."

"I had no idea. This is impressive, you must have worked so hard to get this." I'm in awe of him; I knew there was something about him, the way he knows everyone everywhere we go. But this was something else. Then, it finally clicks into place…

"Wait a minute…you own the Manor Hotel?" I ask, standing up, a little annoyed because it hadn't occurred to me before.

He dips his head but looks at me, and his eyes say it all.

"Yes, I'm sorry, I should have said something, but I knew you would have never taken the job or the cottage if I had told you."

It suddenly hits me as I pace up and down the room. "My job, you got me my job? You own where I live…"

I almost stutter the words out as they sink in, I can't believe it. My mind is reeling.

"Oh no.." he says waving his hand in front of me, "don't do this. I never did it with the intention of being…" I cut him off before he can say anymore.

"It's okay," I say, grasping his hands with mine, stopping them from flapping around. "I know you wouldn't do that, and you only want to help, I get it, but…" Taking a deep breath, I tell him the truth. "I don't feel comfortable with it, so as of today, I will be paying you rent, no arguments." I said, putting my hands on my hips like I mean business. When he goes to protest, I just kiss him, taking away his words and making him moan instead.

"Is that how it's going to work with us?" he says, pulling away slightly. "You just kiss me to get your way?" I kiss him again, this time with a little more passion, and I can feel the smile on his lips.

The House

I brought my workmates back to mine for a drink after work and found that she's changed the locks and put my house up for sale.

She humiliated me in the worst possible way. That's all I can see. The laughter in their eyes, that she was able to get one over on me. Me…fucking me, of all people! *Does she not know who I am?* The rage I feel keeps crawling under my skin, making my blood boil. The things I'm going to do to her when I find out where she's been hiding, she'll regret everything. I will find her, if it's the last thing I do.

There's no going back now, I don't know how she did this, but she will never humiliate me again.

Chapter Twenty-One

Fire

Jack

We had three amazing days in Ibiza. I barely let her out of the bedroom, I just can't get enough of her. Every time we have sex, it's like the first time all over again, only better. It blows my mind and so does she.

Everything she does, I can't help but watch her, the way she moves, the way she listens, the way she is, she's just beautiful inside and out, and so god damn sexy. I have a hard time concentrating whenever she's around; my mind instantly goes to my dick and how I can make her scream my name. Even when she isn't around, I think of what she's doing, what we could be doing together instead of working. It's like I'm a horny teenager again.

When the others went home after the stag and hen do, it was just the four of us, myself, Millie, Em and Dan, and that was how I liked it. I know who I can trust and count on in that group, everyone else I always had my suspicions about. Somehow, things always get leaked to the media, like the other night. When I taught Jane a little lesson, someone snapped a picture of me and Millie. And when that got released a few days later, it was Dan that found out first.

"Jack, got a minute?" Dan pops his head in the door with a worried look on his face.

"Yeah sure, what's up?"

"Shit has just hit the fan, that picture of you and Millie. It's all over the internet, they want to know who your latest conquest is, and why they seem so special to have them as part of your private party," I knew it would happen, but I hate to think of the ramifications for Millie.

"Show me." Coming round to my side of the desk, Dan types in my name and up pops the picture with the headline, 'Who is she?' It's me on top of Millie, saying something into her neck while she looks up, enjoying what we're doing. It's not the best quality but you see it's her. And it pisses me off.

"What do you wanna do?" Dan says as he sits on the other side of my desk. "Do you think she will be okay with it? I know you told her about it all, but they can be well…nasty sometimes."

My phone rings in my pocket; when I look, it's Millie. My heart sinks a little, knowing I'm going to have to break the news to her. I'm not sure how she will react, but as soon as I answer, she says, "So, I was walking down the hill towards work and guess what I saw in the paper outside the newsagents? Huh..can you guess?" she sounds miffed and I can't blame her.

"I'm so sorry Mil, I've only just found out. I'll try and get it taken out, or get them to stop any further stories. Are you okay?"

"I'm okay, but I'd rather not be in the papers."

"And on the internet," I add with regret laced in my voice

"What…Really?" you can hear the frustration in her tone.

"Yep, Sorry," I say, hanging my head. I know what this means for her, and I can't help but think that she might be a little scared right now.

"I'll be okay, I think. Not much I can do about it now." That just makes me feel worse, I can hear the concern in her voice. We hang up after I tell her I'll do everything I can to make it right.

When I told Millie a little more about me, what I owned, and why someone would take pictures of me, or us, she was pissed, to say the least, but what really shocked me was that she was not pissed about me being a billionaire but about me trying to intervene in her life. I feel like I fuck up more than I make things better. It's a shitty feeling. I think she knows I would never do what he has done. Well, she says she knows. I suppose I'll have to let her pay me rent now. I think it will make us both feel better in the long run.

Why can't I go back to two weeks ago? Be back in Ibiza, in my bed, wrapped around each other, me diving into her most sensitive parts, worshipping every inch of her, lapping up every single bit of it.

It's been so busy since we got back, one thing after the other. Millie is still working two jobs, and trying to get her own business up and running. She won't tell me much about it yet, but I know she has set up a studio in the cottage. From what I can gather, her drawings or artwork are spectacular. I had to help her lug all the furniture up there. Those stairs are not meant for big furniture; we had to dismantle it all and rebuild at the top again. It was worth the effort just to see the smile on her face when it was all set up. Plus, we got a little sweaty after the furniture building. That brings a smile to my face.

My legal team spent the next week trying to get the photo retracted, but with no luck.

I've also been called away to my club in Ibiza; we had a fire breakout during one of our busiest times of the year. It's not ideal. It's a massive issue, I've had to fly back to Ibiza to help sort it out.

With the wedding only a month away, I've left Dan back in the UK and flown out on my own to try and figure out what's happened.

When I arrived, I realised just how fucking lucky we were not to have any injuries. The fire damage covered the staff area, bar and part of the dance floor. God we were lucky. Everywhere you look, there is smoke damage and water damage from the fire crew that attended. What was bright and colourful is now dark, dirty and wet. It is soul-destroying to see your hard work look like this; charred, black, unrecognisable.

The fire crews said that it started in the hall leading to the staff area, the only place there are no cameras, but we have a few faces to check out from other cameras that might have caught something, ones that were nearby, just not where we needed them to be. *What if it was arson, and not an accident?* We should find out tomorrow what the cause was. We just have to wait.

"Most of the damage is superficial, easy to repair. We are looking at four weeks' closure while we get it all back up and running," Bobby says to me when we sit down in my office.

"Four weeks? Can we do it any faster? This is our busiest time Bobby." My heart and stomach sank a little more.

Bobby has worked for me for the past three years. He is my go-to guy for any work that needs to be done, construction, remodelling, you name it, he can get it done. He has been great; he dropped everything to fly out with me to assess the damage.

"We can try, but I don't want to rush it. I know we were planning to remodel this winter, we could bring it forward. I have everything in place ready, materials etc., all in the warehouse ready. I just need to wait for the fire officer, chief, whatever you call him over here, to sign it off to know it's safe, then we can start."

"That's a great idea, I knew there was a reason I hired you! Alright, let's remodel like we planned, no point doing it twice. However long it takes. We're only a few weeks into the season. I'll get marketing and do a massive PR launch, get them to put a spin on it. Not the best circumstances but it should work out to our advantage, alright, let's do it." That put a smile on my face. We've worked incredibly hard over the last two years on the renovation plans. Bobby has taken the lead, working with a local designer and contractor. It's going to do wonders for this place.

"Great, I'll get everything ready. I'll let you know how I get on, how long are you here for? I can stay and supervise the whole thing if you need me to?" he added, knowing I won't be staying long.

"That would be amazing, thanks Bobby. I'm here for the next few days. Let me know if you need anything. You can stay in my villa when I'm gone, save having to stay in the hotel." He nods and walks out. I know he will do a great job, but I need to know when we can start. This happening at the start of the season will massively cut into our profits; the sooner we start, the better. The next few hours are spent talking to marketing, Bobby, as well as the staff. The fire officers who attended the fire tell me they will be here tomorrow with the final sign-off and be able to tell me the cause.

I know Dan has been talking with my security teams about how and who could have done this. I know I'm jumping the gun a little bit, but I know our club was safe. We only had the safety inspection a week before we opened and it was perfect. And I don't know who would want to do this, not anyone on the island; we are all like family, looking after one another, helping each other in friendly competition.

A few hours later, Dan calls.

"Jack, how is it going? Have you had any news yet?" You can hear the concern lacing his voice

"Tomorrow, we should be able to find out, have you managed to find anything?"

"I have about 100 faces, we need to look into them all. I've got Issac helping out, he knows faces better than anyone from working the bar. We should be able to remove quite a few."

"I know we've not heard yet, but I know it's arson. The club was safe Dan, it was only inspected a few weeks before, and it's checked out every day. Who would want to do this?" There is so much frustration coming through in my voice. Dan lets out a sigh and says "I have no idea; something is niggling at me. I've got a bad feeling about this Jack." Oh shit.

"Yeah, me too." I let out a deep breath and ran my fingers through my hair, I'm exhausted.

"Right, I'm heading back to the villa. Oh has Bobby emailed you?"

"Yep, got it a few minutes ago, onward and upwards," he chuckled

"Great, look I'll give you a call once I know the outcome, thanks Dan." With that I hang up and head back to the villa.

Dan emails me the next morning with a file full of images. Going through them, I can remove a few immediately, but that still leaves us with 20 faces to ID and check out backgrounds.

Luckily, the security cameras were not badly damaged. Once the fire took hold, you couldn't see much. But it captured the faces of those who were around that spot about the right time.

Scanning through, I spot an image of a guy who is looking directly at the camera. It unnerves me, like he's telling me something. I make a note of which one, the guy looks pissed. But there are a few others I feel who are acting suspiciously and add those as well. I need a break, so I call Millie.

"Morning gorgeous, how are you this morning?" She sounds just as tired as I am. I think I'll take her away after the wedding, to get some time just for us.

"I'm okay, I have to tell you something you won't like."

"Straight to the point," I laugh, resting my head on the back of the sofa.

"Sorry, it's been playing on my mind, I've got to go back to London."

"What do you mean back to London? Is that where you ran from?"

She takes a deep breath; fear runs through me. *Is she going back to him?*

"Yes, that's where I'm from. I put my house up for sale. The weekend we came away and there has been some interest. Charlie has been doing most of the negotiations but I need to go up and sign a few things. So I'm heading up today. I know I should have told you, I'm sorry."

My blood is boiling with all the anger I feel right now. Clenching my fist, I stand up and start to pace the room.

"What house? The house you lived in with him? That asshole…"

"Yep that very house, it's mine. Well it was my parents, they left it to me when they died."

"Are you going alone? Let me send someone with you."

"Don't be silly, it won't take long, I'll be back tonight."

"Does he still live there?" I have so many questions I want to ask, but why am I so fucking far away? She must be terrified.

"No, or at least we don't think so. We had the locks changed the weekend we put it up for sale. I'm sorry I never told you." I can tell, even over the phone, that she's chewing on her lip.

"That's okay, I just wish I could be there, make sure you're safe". It's not okay, but what can I say? I'll have someone watch out for her, she won't know.

"You need to be where you are, your businesses need you. Like I said, I won't be there long. I'm meeting up with Charlie so I won't be alone." There's something in her voice that has me worried, she sounded off.

"Are you sure you're okay? You sound a little off."

"I'm fine, I promise. I'll call you when I get there, and keep you updated."

"Okay, remember I love you."

She lets out a giggle down the phone "I know you do."

She's still not ready to say it back, I can't blame her. It won't stop me telling her though. Well shit, there goes my concentration for today, just another thing to add to the ever-growing list of things I have to worry about.

"It was arson," I tell the team around me. Bobby and Issac look shocked, a few of the bar staff, dancers and managers all look like they have no idea, which is reassuring, I suppose.

"Fuck. Who would do that? It's not just the building, they put lives at risk. People's jobs." Dan shouts over the speaker. There are mumbles around the room, the feeling of shock radiates around everyone.

"The ignition point was in the hall like we already knew, but it was started by a mix of chemicals placed with a spark, almost like a detonator, I suppose." The look on their face says it all, they love this place just as much as I do.

"Dan and Issac have been looking at footage from the security system. We've got some photos of people who were in the vicinity at the time it started, I want to eliminate anyone who is good with you guys."

"You knew it was arson?" One of the bar staff asks, looking a little taken aback.

"We had an idea, the club was safe, we check it regularly, our standards are high."

She nods her head in agreement. Then I pass out the photos of the faces. One by one, we remove eight of them. Leaving us with twelve to find. The rest will be passed to the other clubs to see if they recognise anyone, or if they club-hopped, met with friends, have a history, are drug users etc. I'm not stupid I know what goes on in and around the club. We try to eliminate it all but we can only do so much.

"Thanks guys, just to reassure you all. You'll still be getting paid, it's going to be all hands on deck while we refurbish, so if you can help in any way we would appreciate it. Speak to Bobby and he can assign you jobs. But take a few days off while we arrange everything and come back on Monday." With that, they all file out of the room, chatting, whispering, concern on all their faces.

Even with everything going on, I can't stop looking at my phone. She's not messaged me or called me since this morning, I got one of my security team guys to keep an eye on her, and he says she is still travelling. At least I know he is keeping an eye on her.

"Right, I'll be back in the UK tomorrow. Bobby has it all handled here, I'll put Issac second in command to help him," I say to Dan, picking up the phone and taking it off the speaker.

"You sound bad mate, what's wrong?" I fill him in about Millie going to London on her own, the house, but what he says next makes me want to punch him in the balls.

"I thought you knew about it, Em told me about the house, said it was like going on a spy mission. But she shouldn't be there on her own, I'll go meet her if you want?"

"You knew? Wait Em was with her when they changed the locks? I'm going to fucking kill you when I'm back!" I shout at him on the phone.

"Don't shoot the messenger, I only found out when it had been done, when we got back after the stag and hen do. I was pissed off too mate, but I thought Millie would have told you, that's some pretty big shit to deal with on your own. Look, I'll book a train ticket and meet her there." All his words come out in a rush. Trying to make amends with me. But it does not stifle the fire I have in me right now.

"I'm still going to punch you! But I have Owen on it, I know she is safe."

"Try it, you know I'll beat your ass!" he says, laughing. There was no way on earth he would be able to do that, and he knows it but it made me laugh.

"In your dreams, mate," I laugh.

"Yeah, I know. But a man can dream," he sighs, which makes me laugh even more. That's the best thing about Dan, he knows when you feel like shit and knows how to make you laugh. It's why he is my right-hand man; he keeps me level-headed and calm in most situations. After hanging up, I finally got a message from Millie.

> **Mil:** Arrived and just met with Charlie. How is your day? xx

> **Me:** Glad you arrived okay, my day is shit. It was arson, I'll tell you about it later. Call me when you are back and keep me updated xx

> **Mil:** Oh god, that's awful. Yes I'll call you when I'm back. And yes I will keep you updated xx

I can almost see the eye roll as she messages me back.

Chapter Twenty-Two

No Going Back

Millie

Walking into the estate agent's with Charlie, I find it a bit surreal that I'm about to sell my home, where I grew up, where all my childhood memories are from, where I had all the love from my parents. And being here really makes it hit home, seeing it on display in the window, ever ything how I left it. But then the images of that night come back, all I can see is what happened, how he hurt me, I can't live there anymore. Not with these memories, I just can't do it. I know I have made the right decision, but it's still hard. It's all I have left of them.

Charlie sees me looking at the pictures on the wall. She spins me around and hugs me.

"I can see how hard this is for you. Are you sure it's what you want? I mean it's the last thing your parents gave you." I know she is trying to comfort me, and I know she cares but I just…I don't know. My feelings are all over the place. So much has changed in the last few months. I've gone from almost dying at the hands of someone I thought loved me in a house I thought I would have forever to someone who has disconnected herself, moved far away, and has a man who loves me and is willing to do anything to help me.

Closing my eyes, I lean into her shoulder and take a big breath in. "Yes, it's the right thing to do," I say, turning around and pointing at the picture.

"You see that room? That's where he did it. It's all I can see, everything is broken, and if I keep it, it's all I'll ever see. I'll be living under the shadow of what happened that night. The shadow of him. And I'm done being under the shadow of him." It's like something clicks in me, I can't say what it is, but I know something has changed, and changed for the better. It's almost like the final piece of getting my life back.

"Enough said," Charlie says. She turns to the man at the desk, waving her hand.

"She'll sell to the highest bidder."

The man's face lights up, and we walk over, sitting down in front of his desk. It's not as nice as Em's offices but it works.

"That's great news," he says, typing something on his laptop. "I have a couple of things for you to look over, then I'll tell you the highest bid."

After a few minutes of papers and chat, he slides a piece of paper over to me, a list of numbers. Picking it up, I look at him, confused.

"What's this?" I ask, waving the paper around in the air.

"It's the highest offer we have so far on the house. I'm not sure you realise how sought-after a house in that area of London is. We have been inundated with offers, but this one blows them all out of the water."

The numbers don't even make sense, I can't get my head around it. I knew my parents were wealthy; they have left me a fund for when I turn 28. But this is…unexpected. I'm in shock and hand it to Charlie. When she sees it, she goes to stand up but falls off the chair backwards. The look on her face is so funny I burst out laughing.

"Well shit me!" she says in a shocked whisper, grabs the chair and sits back down.

"Sorry, did you see that number on there? It's more than I've ever seen, ever." I'm still laughing, but I look at the guy behind the desk and nod for him to accept it.

An hour later, we are all done. Charlie asks if I want to head to the house to get anything before I leave.

"No, I'm never going back there, but if you could organise a charity to come in, they can have all the furniture, anything they want." I don't want anything, I have the bits I need: photos of my parents, the keepsake stuff, the important things.

"You said it boss," she says, giving me another hug. I could not have gotten through today without Charlie by my side. A little bit of me wishes it was Jack here to comfort me. But I know he has so much going on right now; he needs to be there for his employees, making sure they get it all together and back up and running.

"Drink? I need a drink. Oh and they're on me."

"Absolutely, they are on you." Linking arms, we walk down towards Leicester Square and head to a bar.

"This feels good, doesn't it? The two of us being back together, like old times," Charlie says as we set down our fourth cocktail. I should stop. I've got a long journey back, but I'm enjoying this way too much.

I've messaged Jack a few times, telling him what I'm up to; he seems okay but I think he will feel better once I'm back, even though he is in Ibiza right now.

"It does feel good; no matter what happens from now on, I hope you will always be in my life."

"I hope so too, and I'm sorry...I should have tried harder to get to you, but everything I tried, he was there with an answer, even told me you had had enough of me pestering you, and that you didn't want to see me again. I should have known then really, that something was seriously wrong, but I could have never guessed just how bad, I'm so sorry." Tears well up in her eyes as she speaks, her shoulders slumped in defeat and regret for how our friendship ended.

"You have nothing to be sorry for; it's all in the past and we have a good future ahead of us." I chuckle.

"What are you laughing at?" she says, wiping the tears from her eyes.

"Makes us sound like a couple the way we are going on." She laughs with me, and before you know it, happy and sad tears are falling down our cheeks. It feels so good to have her back in my life. This is how it should have been all along.

After a few more cocktails, lots of girl talk and a pizza, I head back to the train station. It's already 8 p.m. I've been here a lot longer than I thought, but it's okay, I've had so much fun. It's a two-and-a-half-hour train ride with one transfer at this time of night, so three-ish hours and I should be back.

"Wow, how drunk are you?" Jack says when he calls me an hour later, you can hear the stress and anxiety in his voice.

"Very, but I have had a fabulous time. Also I have some news. I sold the house! So we celebrated, maybe a little too much, but I have pizza, water and oh that's it." Jack mumbles something I don't quite hear, but I get the feeling he's worried I'm on the train alone and drunk, maybe he has a point. Oh well, too late to worry about it now.

I'm glad you have supplies." He is a man of few words, but a good man, and so fucking fantastic in bed, well not just in bed, on the floor, on the sofa, in the kitchen, he would be amazing at it anywhere.

I can't wait to have him in my kitchen, for him to bend me over the counter, rip my dress up and pull my underwater to one side and just fuck me, take me, fill me up with his massive cock, oh god, it feels good already and I'm not even doing it, the tension between my legs feels like it's going explode the more I think about him in me.

"Mil are you still there?" he asks and my cheeks flush. I know he can't see me, but my god.

"Oh, yes, sorry, got lost in my thoughts," I hold in a laugh.

"And what thoughts are they Millie?" he asks with curiosity seeping through his voice. "Anything I should know about?"

"If you're alone, I'll tell you. I'll text you what I was thinking."

"I'm alone, in the villa, all by myself," he cuts me off and I can't help but smile.

"Okay, stay on the phone, read it and tell me what you think." I've never done this before; it feels exciting, he has no idea what I'm going to tell him, so I suppose I better make it good. I love how brave I become when I've had a drink.

> **Me:** Just a little fantasy I had, and have never lived it out…you walk into the cottage and find me wearing a long green dress. It's silk, flowing over my body like water. It has a low back, a deep plunge at the front and a slit in the side rising to my hip. When you see me, you drop everything and walk over to me, taking my mouth with yours like you can't contain yourself.

Send.

I hear a beep on his end and continue typing.

> **Me:** You slide your hands over my bare shoulders and remove the straps, letting the front of the dress fall.

Send.

Another beep.

> **Me:** *You spin me around, and push me down onto the counter, lifting my dress up around my waist, seeing I have a matching green thong on.*

Send.

I can hear him, heavy breathing.

> **Me:** *You undo your trousers and push down your boxers. Moving my thong to one side, you run a finger down my slit and slide a finger inside me.*

Send.

I can hear little noises of pleasure coming from the other end of the phone. This is turning me on so badly.

> **Me:** *Are you touching yourself?*

Send.

"Fuck yes… I'm hard as fuck." His words come out all raspy over the phone; it's good I'm wearing my earphones.

> *Me: You kneel down with your fingers still inside me. I'm so wet for you. You run your tongue over my wetness and devour me, licking and sucking at my clit. And I come in your mouth with your tongue inside me.*

Send.

"Mil...you, fuck, I'm almost there Millie. I'm so fucking hard, I'm touching myself, all I can see is you and you're all over my face. Oh fuck!" His voice can be dialled down to a rumble, I can tell how turned on he is.

> *Me: You stand up and fuck me, taking me with such urgent need thrusting into me over and over again, right there in the kitchen.*

Send.

> *Me: You make me come so hard, but we come together, hard and fast, clasping on the counter, you leaning over me... Send.*

Send.

All I hear is heavy breathing and moaning. I give him a few minutes before I speak. I'm so turned on right now. I'm alone on the train now; everyone seems to have left, so I tell him.

"I'm so turned on right now, I'm so wet, I may have to play with myself when I get home."

"Fuck Millie…yes." His breathing is heavy.

"Did you like that?" I ask, teasing him.

"Are you kidding? That will be my porn for life, you just made me come over a text message."

"I can't explain how turned on I am right now, I may need to use my vibrator when I get back, I'm so horny."

"I take it you're alone on the train?" he asks.

"I am now, yes, why?"

"Touch yourself Millie, tell me how wet you are." I look around quickly, making sure I'm alone; not even the cameras are pointing my way. So I slide my fingers down under my skirt, moving my knickers to one side and feel myself.

"I'm so wet, that was one of my fantasies I want to live out. I have the dress."

"Spread your legs Millie, open yourself."

When I do, I feel my juices coat my thighs.

"Done, I'm open for you. What do you want me to do now, I feel so good, so slick."

"Fuck Millie, I'm hard again. This time I'm going to come with you."

My breath hitches just the idea of him being hard again for me.

"Touch yourself Millie, circle that juicy clit and come for me."

I rub my clit like he asked me to and my insides start to do wonderful things. I try to stifle a moan, and it comes out as a whimper.

"That's it, I can hear you Millie. Harder, fuck yourself for me...slide those fingers inside yourself and come for me! I'm almost there Millie, tell me you're doing it."

I slide my middle finger down and press on my entrance.

"Oh fuck, Jack, it feels so good."

"Fuck yourself Millie, harder..."

I slide two fingers in and feel myself climb higher, my walls tightening around my fingers as I slide them in and out of me, building the pressure.

"Two fingers Jack, sliding in and out." I'm losing control.

"I'm coming Jack..." I can't say anymore, my mind goes blank as my eyes close, topping my head back as I come hard with my own fingers and his words.

"Fuck...yes, me too." I'm gone, but I hear him moan my name when he comes with me.

"Millie? Are you still with me?" I hear him say through my earphones.

"That was the fucking hottest thing I have ever done, and it makes me love you so much more. 1,300 miles apart and we can still have the best sex."

"Umm...I know, not just the best sex, the best phone sex! And it was the hottest thing I've ever done in my life, maybe we can do them for real when you get back."

"I have so many fantasies I want to try out, they all include you baby, and yes when I walk in your door tomorrow morning, I'm doing it to you. I'm going to bend you over, make you come with my tongue inside you, then fuck you until you see stars, then we will do one of my fantasies, one I've dreamt of for years."

"Good cuz I have a few more too."

We end the phone call half an hour later; after changing trains, I spend the next journey relishing and reliving what has just happened. The buzz I feel all over my skin just turns me on more.

So I hide myself at the back, tucked away in the corner and take a few pics for Jack to wake up to. By the time I get home, it's almost midnight and dark as hell.

When I walk through the door, I turn to put my keys in the bowl but they hit the floor instead, and I trip over something on the floor. I must still be drunk or high on phone sex. I start giggling as I remember the photos I took for him, three to be precise, one sucking my fingers, one tugging my nipple, and the last one with my hand down my pants playing with myself. Walking up to my bedroom, I get the green dress ready, and hang it on the wardrobe door ready to put on tomorrow morning.

Sleep comes easy that night, my eyes close and I dream of Jack.

Fumbling around in the kitchen the next morning, I find a few things out of place, like the small table I use to put my keys on, and the umbrella stand on the floor. I can't seem to find a few things either and it's irritating me. I've lost the key to the back door, so I can't sit outside and have my coffee. That's if I ever find it! How can I lose coffee? I can't function without it, I'll be a zombie! Let alone be in a bad mood, and I definitely don't want that, not today. I've got the day off, Jack is coming back this morning and I can't wait to see him. His flight lands in about an hour and I need to get myself ready for today… I'm so excited and horny just thinking about what his fantasy is.

"Thank god!" I shout, finding the coffee in a random cupboard. I make two cups and head back upstairs to take a shower.

Looking in the mirror thirty minutes later, I take in the green dress covering my body. It hugs me in all the right places – the back dips to the bottom of my back so I'm not able to wear a bra. The front has a plunging neckline, reaching down to just below my boobs, showing the soft curves of them. Thin straps hold everything in place. While the slit in the side of my dress runs up towards the top of my hip, with a gold brooch attached at the top, when I walk, the split leaves nothing to the imagination. I've added my gold high sandals to match and left my hair loose, the soft curls hanging down my back.

I'm ready. So I wait for him in the kitchen. He just has to walk in.

Chapter Twenty-Three

Fantasy

Jack

I've never been so fucking sexually frustrated in my entire life. Last night was something I had never even imagined possible, no, scrap that, I never even thought about it! Yet we had phone sex, while she was on the train, she made me come twice, her words on those messages were insatiable.

Then, when I woke up this morning, I looked at my phone and found three images I will never be able to erase from my mind or phone. I've been walking around with a hard-on since. I keep sneaking a look at them every now and then, and it just makes me harder. I thought about another handjob from my right hand but decided against it. I want to show Millie what she does to me, then show her what I plan on doing.

I've been travelling for the last four hours, cooped up on the plane. I can't wait to see Millie. When I step through the door of the cottage, I'm floored. I can see her standing there in the fucking sexiest emerald green dress I have ever seen. Every thought leaves my mind, my heart rate accelerates and sends even more blood pumping to my cock, making it even more painful than it has been for the last four hours. I drop everything as I walk through the living room, she turns around to say something, but her words fail as she sees my intentions written all over my face. She glances down to see my cock straining to be released, a smile spreading across her face, along with the blush rising on her cheeks.

Standing in front of her, I tangle my hands in her hair at the back of her head and pull her lips to mine. Taking everything I can, Millie lets out a moan of pure frustration, gripping me harder around my waist and pulling me to her. I know she can feel how hard I am because she gasps as I press my cock into her stomach.

"Do it!" she says and I stand back and gaze at her – this woman, this beautiful, intelligent, sexy woman. She's mine. As I take all of her in, she lets out a small moan, and I can see her thighs squeezing together to try and relieve some of the tension we are causing, the pent-up sexual arousal I can't wait to see around me. The smile that spreads across my face feels like it will break me in two; I do this to her, just like she does it to me.

I trace my fingers over her jaw, trailing them down her neck to her collarbone. Millie leans her head back, a wonderful shiver spreads across her skin, and I watch as her nipples harden through her dress.

Slowly lowering the straps on either side of the dress and letting them fall, I ease her dress over her breasts, and it falls like liquid around her waist, revealing her silky white freckled skin and two perfect pink hard nipples. Her heart rate picks up as I glide my fingers down each breast, taking each nipple one at a time with my mouth. My eyes are trained on her mouth as another gasp escapes her lips. I watch as she leans back, holding onto the counter tighter. I grasp one of her nipples with my teeth, pulling, then licking it with my tongue over and over again.

"Yes…" she says. I can smell her arousal. Moving my hand further down, I move my fingers slowly under the dress, coming in from the slit of fabric at her hip. Grazing the inside of her thighs and up to where she is so wet, I almost lose it. I can't contain the noise that escapes me. It's almost feral, animalistic.

"Oh god, yes!" Grabbing her hips, I spin her around, bending her over so her ass is perfectly aligned with my cock. Placing her hands flat on the counter, I tell her, "Don't move." Then, bending down to my knees, I find the slit in her dress again and trace the line with my hand from her ankle to the hip, moving it to one side to see the matching thong and her round ass pert and waiting.

I move the dress up her legs, resting it on her back; she almost screams with excitement.

"I'm so fucking ready for you. This is your fantasy, I'm going to make it so much more."

"Oh…fuck, I…I.." she almost cries, her eyes focused on her hands.

"Look at me Millie!" I demand as she closes her eyes. She moves so she can see every move I make while she's bent over the counter, everything on display just for me.

Grabbing her hips, I spread her legs a little wider and move her green thong to one side. We both inhale sharply; she's so ready, glistening, ready to be devoured. I slip a finger in and she moves her hips back to get more.

"I said don't move," and she stills, waiting for more.

My finger glides in and out of her, I can feel her walls tightening around my fingers, so I add another and she moans with pleasure. The need to taste her is almost overwhelming, so I dive in, my tongue lapping and circling her clit, taking her arousal, moving my fingers faster inside her. I suck and lick, bringing her higher when she stills, her walls clamp around my fingers. I can't help but take it further, bringing her climax higher, as her juices spill and I lap them up, riding out her high. She's still turned to watch what I'm doing when her back arches, her head falls back and she screams.

"Jack…" I watch her ride the waves as I stand up, my fingers still caressing her. I undo my trousers with my other hand, and pull down my boxers, feeling myself with my left hand, watching her watch me.

I place myself at her entrance, placing my hand on her shoulder; she smiles out of breath but ready.

"You're so wet, you make me so hard, I'm going to fuck you." Just as I say the words I press into her, and I don't stop until I'm all in, deep and unforgiving. I fuck her, thrusting in and out with all the passion I have built up over the last twelve hours; I fill her completely, she's intoxicating.

"Harder," she whimpers and I almost lose it, slamming into her over and over again. One hand on her hip, the other on her shoulder, holding her there, just where I need her. My hand slides around her hip to find her sensitive clit; she moans louder and louder with every thrust and every touch of her.

"I'm…coming…Jack." Through breathless words, I feel her growing higher, her hands holding on for dear life on the counter as she pushes back onto me for more, wanting more. I give it to her, and she comes apart around my cock, taking me with her. I see stars, all I hear is the low moans of her coming as I thrust in one last time, all noise lost as I swim in this feeling of release, my juices mixed with hers. I slump forward, resting on her back as she, too, slumps over the counter. I'm still inside her, it's where I always want to be.

It takes a few minutes for us to regain any strength or coherence to move, but when we do, we slide down to the floor, her legs over mine as she moves beside me, nuzzling my neck.

"Well that beats the fantasy out of the water, you literally just rocked my world." She's sweaty and flushed and looks like she has just been thoroughly fucked, just the way I like it.

"I'll fucking rock your world every damn day Millie, you already rock mine," I say back meaning every word I said. She nips at my ear, and slowly kisses down my neck.

"Since you just did me twice, it's only fair we make it even." Fuck.

She trails her hands over my body, removing my shirt, while she straddles me, her breasts in full view of where I'm lying on the floor, her perfect body on mine. And I'm hard as rock in seconds. Who knew it could be like this?

She places herself over my cock and slides down me taking me all in, a moan coming from my lips. I take her hips and move her up and down when she stops, places my hand on her breasts and rocks her pelvis on me.

"Oh fuck..this... that's..." She rotates them, moving in circles while I'm deep inside her.

When she moves off me, I whimper and try to put her back, but she leans down, taking my cock in her mouth until it can't go any further, then she takes me a little more.

"Sweet...mother fucking...fuck...Millie!" words fail me, I can't take it, I will take it but this feeling is, "Millie!"

She holds the base on my cock firm and starts pumping while she sucks me and swipes her tongue over the sensitive top. My hips want to move but I hold them firmly in place, I don't want to hurt her.

"Millie," I say again, and she moves, taking me out of her mouth, curling her tongue on the top as she does.

"Is that how you like it?" she says, teasing me. I want her to put it back in. I want to fuck her, I want it all.

"Yes," and with those words, she takes me again, the tension rising in me until I'm about to come.

"Millie, I'm going to come," I say, trying to pull back, but she holds me steady, taking me further. I come in her mouth, she swallows it all, sucking me dry. I have nothing, no words, just pure happiness.

She takes my hand and leads me up to the bedroom. I have a feeling today and tonight are going to be long.

A few hours later, we both lay on her bedroom floor, completely exhausted and elated at the same time. Our bodies glisten with sweat, but neither of us wants to move. And I'm not sure I can.

I trace the line of the scar on her leg that's wrapped around my waist while she's pressed into my side, her head resting on my shoulder.

"What's wrong? You just got all tense. What were you thinking about?" she says as I trace the scar again and she sighs.

"Oh…" she says, sitting up slightly and leaning on her elbow.

"I'm sorry, I know, but it still makes me so angry. I promise I will find him and make him pay for what he did to you Millie, you just need to tell me more."

"No," she cuts me off, moving out of my grasp and standing up.

"Jack, he is a huge part of my past that I desperately want to forget. If I tell you more about him, you will just drag it all back to life. I have enough scars already, I don't need anymore."

She walks off into the bathroom, tears in her eyes. Sitting up, I immediately regret where my mind went; I forget she has to live with what he did every day. Sitting on the end of the bed, I hear Millie turn the shower water on. Putting my head in my hands, I wonder why I keep doing this, making progress, then fucking it up.

I need to show her how much I love her, not by fucking her, but loving every inch of her, removing all the bad memories around her scars.

Standing up, I walk over to the bathroom; leaning in the doorway, I watch as she stands under the water with her eyes closed, her hands hanging down by her sides.

When I open the shower door, she opens her eyes and turns her back to me. I suppose I deserve that. I come to stand behind her, sliding my hand around her waist and holding her against me. When I reach for the shower gel and sponge, she sighs and leans back into me.

"I'm sorry," I whisper into her ear.

The soap slides down her skin as I gently clean her, taking care to reach every part of her body. Taking in each and every scar she has, like I do every time I see her naked. I need her to see herself the way I see her, her beauty.

"Can I show you something?" I ask her when I'm finished. She nods and I turn the shower off, then I lead her back to the bed and lay her down. I gently climb over her naked body, fighting the urge to sink deep into her.

"What did you want to show me, or have you got a little distracted?" She laughs and fidgets underneath me when I kiss her.

"I'm always distracted by you Millie," I say, kissing her softly.

"But I do have something that I want to show you."

Millie

"Then show me, because this feels a little like you're distracted. What are you doing?"

His finger and lips trace my skin and it feels wonderful as the tingles spread over my skin.

"Look at me Millie," and when I do, there is something so different about the way he is looking at me, the way he's kissing my skin. There is no hunger in his eyes, no lust, just... love.

"Jack, I don't understand." My eyes fill with tears as I watch him move around my body, tracing each and every mark on my skin.

"When you see these, these marks on your beautiful body." His fingers and lips trace a scar on my stomach; it's about two inches long from where a piece of glass cut into me. "I want you to think of this moment, how I make you feel." There is nothing sexual about this; my tears spill over and slide down my cheeks.

"I'll do this every day until you have no memory of him on your skin."

With each trace and tender kiss, he places on a mark or scar, I can only think of Jack. The love he is pouring into me, makes me feel special, like I've never felt before.

"Every time you look in the mirror, I want you to see that each of them is beautiful, just the way I see you." I'm crying and I can't stop the tears from falling, I don't want to. He keeps kissing every mark on my skin. It's the therapy I never knew I needed; my breath hitches as more tears come.

"Jack…I…I… don't know what to say." My voice is shaky, matching my body every time he touches me.

"You don't have to say anything." The feeling I have right now bubbling away in my heart scares me to death, the way he makes me feel, what he's doing right now for me. I think I … I can't find the words. That's not true, I know the words but they won't come out; my heart and my head feel like they are at war.

I don't say another word; I just let the tears fall, letting these feelings wash over me, as I accept each and every one of them, my marks and scars, each taking on a new meaning.

I must have fallen asleep at some point because when I wake up, I'm wrapped in the soft blanket from my bed. I stretch out and my body is aching deliciously. The soft sheets feel cool on my skin as I slide over and sit on the edge of the bed.

When I stand, I catch a glimpse of myself in the mirror. My curly red hair is messy. There is a slight glow to my skin. It's like I'm seeing myself for the first time, from head to toe. My eyes wander the full length of my body while my fingers circle the long scar on my stomach, the silver scar, the softness of the skin, the uneven edges. But what I feel shocks me. All I remember is the way Jack kissed me there, the feeling of his soft lips pressing against it, the way my body felt with each touch. A massive smile spreads across my face. That man, what have I done to deserve such an amazing man? Standing up in front of the mirror, I remember last night, the way we had sex, the way he touched me and made me come. The way he has erased the past for me. And I watch as my cheeks blush in response as I remember what we did downstairs. I can hear him in the kitchen right now, making so much noise and chuckling to himself.

Then I smell pancakes and bacon. I quickly grab his shirt from last night and slide it over my arms, buttoning a few buttons as I walk out of the room downstairs. I watch him for a minute while he cooks; I've never seen him cook before. He looks funny, he's got on a pinny with just his joggers on, top half naked. I can see his full tattoo now, tribal art all down the right side of his body, twisting around his waist and abs, curving around his arm and up around his shoulder and part of his neck. It's the sexiest thing I've ever seen. Every time I see it, I want to touch it and follow the intricate line with my fingers. A bowl crashes to the floor, bringing me back to reality.

"You best be cleaning up this mess," I say, walking over to him.

"When did you wake up? I was going to bring you breakfast in bed."

"I've been awake a while, just thinking of last night." He grabs my waist and presses me to him. He lifts my legs around his waist and places me on the countertop, leaning forward and nuzzling my neck.

"You smell amazing, you're making me want you all over again, especially when you're wearing my shirt like that." He looks down and tugs at one of the buttons, undoing it in the process. He moves it to the side to reveal one of my breasts. His thumb slowly circled it, sending instant desire where I wanted him most.

"You're relentless…" but I don't care, I want him, I want him all the time.

"I want you Jack," I undo his pinny and giggle as I do, reaching down and sliding his joggers over his tight ass and down his thighs. His cock springs free, he went commando this morning.

"I want you too Millie," he kisses my neck as he reaches between my legs, finding me wet and ready. He moans and positions his cock at my entrance, before slamming into me, filling me so deeply. The feeling is so intense, my whole body shakes as my body starts to respond to him. My skin flushes with heat as he moves in and out of me, going deeper than I ever thought possible. He grabs my ass to bring me closer, and he presses a finger to my clit and I can't take it much longer. A wave of pleasure takes over, and I hear Jack mumble something, but I'm lost.

"Fuck Millie. Come for me!" That's all it takes, and I shatter around him, my walls tighten around him, and I feel his warmth spread in me as another wave of my orgasm takes me. He rides the waves with me until it's too much and I go to fall back, but he holds me to his chest and kisses me with pure love. I fold my arms around his neck and trace the lines of his tattoo.

"Good morning," I whisper into his neck.

"Good morning, beautiful," he whispers back, "I think that was the quickest sex we have ever had."

"Two minute man." I laugh and slide off him onto the floor, heading to the toilet to clean myself up.

When I come back out, he is naked with just the pinny on, the strings tied around his waist, leaving his chest in all its fine glory for me to enjoy. I smack his ass when I walk over, making him jump and little. He almost drops the plate of pancakes.

"Oops, sorry, I just can't resist you in that pinny, it's like having my own naked butler." I laugh at him as he sets it all on the table, while I take a seat.

"All for you, Millie. Oh and to make up for my two minutes, I'm taking you out today on a date."

"I enjoyed the two minutes, I think it's the quickest you have ever made me…happy." I smile. I know my cheeks are red right now.

"I love how you blush, what happens when you think of what we did in the kitchen last night? It was one of the hottest, sexiest nights of my life." He eyes me while he shoves a pancake in his mouth and almost spits it out again, trying not to laugh as my face goes bright red, and I put my head in my hands.

"Oh my life, I don't know why it happens, it was one of the best nights of my life too and I'm not just talking about the sex." I trace one of the small scars on my arm, smiling softly, remembering how he made me feel all over again.

"I don't know why you did it, but, thank you." Lifting my head up to look at him, I realise he is frowning at me.

"Why are you frowning?"

"Because, you should know why I did that last night. I. Love. You. Millie. I don't want you to think of him ever again, so I made you think of me instead." I think I knew that deep down, but admitting it was something else.

"Thank you. So where are we off to today?" Changing the subject quickly before he can give me those sad eyes when I don't say it back to him.

"It's a surprise. We need to celebrate you selling the house, and being free, while I celebrate having you back in my life, all to myself."

An hour later, after leaving the house, we are at a farm, in a field, with a basket in each hand. It's not really the date I had imagined, but fruit picking is a nice way to spend a few hours, I've not done it for years.

"Are you ready? We are heading over to the polytunnels first to pick some strawberries." As we walk over through the field side by side, he holds my hand. It feels nice, our fingers intertwined. It's a beautiful warm day, the sun is shining. Jack looks sexier than ever, in a pair of faded jeans and a black t-shirt. I, on the other hand, not knowing where we were going, put on a green mini-dress, and a pair of pumps – not really ideal for fruit picking but it will have to do.

"Just over there, can you see?" He points to where we are heading; there are five massive tunnels, all full of strawberries.

As we walk into the first tunnel, I see rows upon rows of bright red juicy strawberries, but something catches my eye just to the left. I notice a picnic blanket set up just outside, under the large tree. I watch Jack as a smile slowly creeps over his face.

"Our first official date, what do you think?"

"Jack, it's perfect! You did this?" The picnic blanket has been laid out with cushions, a basket sat in the centre, full of fresh food, and a bottle of champagne in a cooler, with two glasses to the side of it.

"I had some help," he says, taking my hand again, leading me to the blanket, and letting me sit down.

"It's beautiful, can we still pick some strawberries?" He sits next to me and stretches his legs out in front of him, leaning back on his hands.

"Yep, we have this all day. It's just us with no one to bother us."

"How? No, don't tell me, let me guess, you own it?" That stupid smile on his face says it all.

"Yes, I own it. It supplies the hotel with its produce, the restaurant and cafe are amazing. Joe and Abby do an amazing job." He smiles.

"I love that you are so passionate about all of your businesses. Oh that reminds me, I want to ask you something about the cottage."

"You're still not paying rent."

"No, well I don't want to pay rent. How much is the cottage worth?"

"Why? Do you want to buy it?" He laughs a little like I made a joke.

"Yes, I want to buy it. Like I told you, I sold my house and I want to invest in a property here, what better one than the cottage, you know how much I love it." I feel like I'm pleading my case a little, but I need to do something with the money I'll get from the sale.

"Wait, you're serious?" He sits up, moving closer to me, putting my hand in his.

"Of course I'm serious. It means I can live there, it will be mine, and we won't have to argue about rent anymore. I know you have been putting it back into my bank account."

"You do huh." That sheepish smirk spreads across his face.

"Of course I know, I'm not stupid. It's sweet of you, but I want this. No, I need this." I do, I've needed to be independent for a while, have something that was mine, just mine. I needed him to understand.

"I know you don't understand, but this is a big deal for me. I've never had something that's all mine."

He leans back and rests his arms under his head, closing his eyes. Sitting up a little more, I straddle his lap and place a soft kiss on his lips, my hair cascading down over his shoulder.

Jack places a hand on my thigh, and runs his fingers through my hair, opening his eyes. He looks at me and smiles that smile that makes me want him over and over again. The way his lips curve up at one side, it is so sexy.

"I understand, I'll have my lawyers sort it out. How much can you afford? From what I remember, it was valued at just under £350,000. I don't want you to take on too much. You are already working three jobs."

I kiss him so deeply and I can feel his desire rising under my dress. After a minute, I come back up for air, placing my hands on his chest.

"I can afford it, don't worry, and I'll hopefully be giving up one or two of my jobs soon."

"Wait." He sits up with me, still straddling his lap, "What do you mean you can afford it?"

"The sale of my house will cover it. It made a little more than I expected. Well a lot more than I expected really, I had no idea."

"How much are we talking about? You don't have to tell me, not if you don't want to."

That's the thing about Jack, he's just curious. He doesn't want any of it, he just wants to make sure I will be okay. That's it.

"I don't mind, well it was just under seven million." I laugh as I watch his eyes almost pop out of his head.

"Millie, are you joking?"

"Nope, not joking. I'm not sure I believe it yet, but Charlie fell off her chair when she saw how much the offer was for." I can't help but smile, it matches his.

"Now I know you're not with me for my money." I go to swat him but he moves and pins me to the floor beneath him.

"I'm not sure why this makes me so happy," he says while kissing me. I think I do; it's one less thing for him to worry about. Knowing I'm not going to run myself into the ground working.

"It makes me happy too, and I can feel how happy you are," I tease and look down as he presses his erection into me.

"That has nothing to do with the money, that is all you!" He smirks and lifts up my dress, revealing my red lace underwear.

"I've never been like this with anyone before Millie. You have me under a spell. Every time I see you, I…I just want you, in any way I can have you, and I don't just mean sex."

"I know, I think about you all the time, day and night, even in my dreams."

"Oh really, in your dreams. Please do tell…" he says, sliding my underwear down my legs.

"No way…oh god…Jack!" I say when he slides his finger inside me, moving it in and out slowly.

"Tell me your dream Millie, and I'll make you come," he adds another finger, making my back arch up.

"It was you, always you, every night…" He presses a finger into me, making me cry out.

"Tell me more. I want to know."

"Oh… You're the reason I'm here, the reason I…"

"Millie…?" He stops.

"Oh god, Jack….the reason I left him was you…"

"What are you talking about? What do you mean?" he says, kissing me and I feel a tear spill over my cheek. Closing my eyes, I let it all out.

"I had dreams about you, about what we did when we first met. Every night Jack, I would wake up in a hot sweat, thinking of you. The more dreams I had, the more confidence I got to leave him. Each dream showed me what I should have had, what I could have if I left him. I woke one night after a dream of you, and decided that was it. I was going. So I made my plans. I've told you what happened in between. But you're the reason Jack, the reason I left him and ran, as far away as I could. I had no idea where I was going to go, so I stood in the station and just picked this place. I had no idea, you were just a dream."

When I open my eyes, his eyes are on mine, searching for something. Like he thinks it can't be true.

"I...had dreams about you too...for weeks before I saw you. Every night, Millie," he says, a wave of emotions washing over his face and in his eyes.

"Oh my god," I place my hand over my mouth, and cover a cry, but he removes it and kisses me, softly, like I'll break. When he moves away, he looks at me deeply, like he can't believe it.

"Let me make love to you Millie?" My heart almost stops, as I nod my head. He removes his jeans and boxers and lays back over me. Intertwining his fingers with mine, he places them over my head, resting his forehead on mine. His warm breath on my face as he lowers his head to kiss me.

"Keep your eyes open, Millie, I want to see you, I want to remember this." When his lips reach mine, they are soft. His tongue teases my lips open, and I take him in while looking into his deep blue eyes. I've never noticed the gold flecks before, it's like the sun shining on the sea, my own personal brand of sunshine. His warm breath sends shivers over my skin. He's not even touching me, and I can feel my body reacting to him. He moves to kiss my neck, and I bite my lip as tantalising shivers run over my body. His lips slowly move down to my chest, he lets go of my hands, pulling my dress over my head. I'm just in my red lace bra. My hands reach for him, holding him as close as I can, feeling the strong muscles along his back. He takes my nipple in his mouth through my bra and I gasp. He takes my hands again, lacing his fingers with mine, moving them back beside my head, and pinning me there. I open my legs for him and wrap them around his waist. He enters me slowly, and it's the most sensual feeling I've ever had, every nerve ending is set alight inside and outside of me. My skin flames like it's on fire, my breath hitches when he kisses me again, taking his time. He moves in and out of me with passion and love. My emotion is right on the surface. This is what it should have been like all along, Jack and I.

"Millie, I love you," he whispers into my ear, his breath sending warm, delicious shivers throughout my body.

"Jack, I....Oh god, Jack...this is...oh god." I close my eyes as my orgasm starts to climb.

"Open your eyes, Millie, let me see you." I do as I'm asked, and come as soon as I look into his ocean-deep blue eyes. I feel the heat, the waves, the tenderness and the love roll over me, over and over again.

"Come...with me Jack." I'm pushed over the edge, and when I feel him thrust one last time, I feel him swell and spill his warmth in me. I hold him tight as we come together, his eyes never wavering from mine. He kisses me softly, and we collapse into one another. I close my eyes and drift off, falling harder than I have ever fallen before.

Chapter Twenty-Four

Big News & Fights

Emma

"Dan, I can't be late, will you hurry up? I need to meet Millie and the girls before we go to the dress shop." How he has ever managed to keep a job, I have no idea. Oh yeah, he works for his best mate, my brother.

"Dan, seriously, hurry up." I'm waiting by the door.

"What's got your knickers in a twist? Even your tappy foot is out," he says, looking at my feet while grabbing his stuff.

"Ahhh…I just don't want to be late for my dress fitting." Men, they just don't get it. He leans in and kisses me, and it takes me by surprise.

"What was that for?" I ask as he pulls away from me.

"No reason, oh look, your tappy foot has stopped," he laughs and heads out the door. He really does know how to calm me down, but he has no idea why I'm really on edge. I can't wait to speak to Millie.

"Are you coming Em?" he says, watching me stand by the door like an idiot. Closing the door behind me, I head to the car.

"You're a dick, you know that? Why am I driving you anyway? You have a perfectly good car sitting on the drive." I say, nodding to the beautiful black Lexus just sitting there.

"What is with you this morning, have you forgotten already? It's pizza and beer night at Millie's," he says, frowning at me like I've lost the plot.

"Oh yeah, my turn to drive." I'm so excited and nervous that my memory is failing me.

"No, we said we would get a taxi back, so we could both have a drink. Are you okay? You're acting really odd this morning, are you worried about the fitting?" His hand comes to rest on me while I pull off the drive.

"A little, it's the second to last one I'll have. I've got to deal with Jane today too; I've had to demote her to bridesmaid. She's not happy, but she's done nothing but cause me trouble. She's hardly helped with the wedding stuff, while Millie has been amazing. She has worked three jobs, and helped me with the wedding, all while refurbishing the cottage. So I'm promoting her to Maid of Honour. Jane is pissed about it. Millie doesn't know, I need to tell her before we meet with the others." Dan just looks at me with wide eyes; I may have just offloaded a little.

"Sorry, that was a lot for one sentence." I smile at him and continue driving.

"Yes, it was. Let me do something to help?" My smile widens at him. I know he wants to help, but with everything he has going on with the work, the refurbishment and the other businesses, it's not fair.

"You're sweet, but no, I'll handle it. You have enough on your plate. Any news on the names of faces yet?"

"We have some, but there are still three we need to find. The police say that they are handling it, but we have more info than they do, we keep passing info to them." He laughs and shakes his head.

"I guess it's better than nothing. Any idea why someone would do it?" Dan shrugs and shakes his head again.

"I think it's personal, aimed at Jack, not the club."

"Fuck! What?" I swerve the car a little at the news. Dan holds up his hands in apology.

"Sorry, not really something I should say while you are driving. There is nothing to support it yet, I just have this feeling, and it's bad, and I don't like it." You can see it on his face.

"Does Jack know? Have you voiced it to him yet?"

"Oh god no, he is on a high with Millie right now, and I don't want to kill it. You know he will go all commando on us, amp up security, close ranks, keep us locked in."

"Man, I love you," I say, smiling at him. He never takes anything too seriously, he puts fun in everything we do. Always playful and knows exactly how to handle my brother.

Jack has been looking after us both since the day our parents died. Always overreacting, and Dan was right. He would have us all locked up with 24/7 security if he could.

"I love you too, Em." When I take a quick glance over to him sitting on the passenger side, there's a look on his face and I instantly know what he's thinking.

"Why are you looking at me like that?" I ask, knowing what the answer is.

"I want to have sex with you, you're in a weird mood, and sex would be kinky, can we go back home?"

"Are you kidding me? You want me to turn around, go home and have sex with you?"

"Yes, I'm really horny for you right now." He grabs his crotch, showing me just how horny he is.

"It would be a shame to waste it, but we're not going home." I pull the car into a lane and park behind a tree at the side. I step out of the car and so does Dan. He comes round to my side of the car, and presses me against the door.

"Yes, I love kinky," he says as I lift up my skirt and start sliding my knickers down my legs. He undoes his belt, and shoves his trousers down his legs along with his boxers. I turn around and bend over for him, pushing my ass into him. I brace myself on the car door, waiting for him.

"Fuck me baby," I say and he slides into me. "Fuck. Yes, do it harder baby." He slams into me, holding my hips with his hands, and he drives into me over and over again. I like it rough, and so does he.

"Harder…more…" He moves faster and faster. I love this man.

"Yes…baby," I reach between my legs and cup his balls while he fucks me. "Fuck yes!" he shouts.

"Touch yourself, I'm going to come hard."

I move my hand between my legs and find my clit. My head flips back, his hand meets mine and he presses hard on my clit, making me scream as I start to come. He continues to slam into me, making my orgasm even more intense. I feel him come with one last push, and he drops down on me. We both lean against the car, trying to catch our breath. He pulls out and covers me, then gets himself dressed. He spins me around, I can barely stand, and my legs feel like jelly.

"Lift your leg." I look down as he glides my knickers back up my legs. When he stands up, I grab his face and kiss him hard.

"I knew it would be kinky." He smiles down at me, kissing me back.

"Get back in the car, that wasn't kinky, I'll show you kinky later." I smile at him.

"I can't wait, princess."

"Millie?" After dropping Dan off, I walk over to Millie's office and find her deep in conversation with Mary.

"Everything alright?" I ask. Mary looks like she's gone into mom mode.

"Yes, everything is fine," Millie says quickly before Mary can get a word in.

"I was just telling her, she is working too hard, she had a dizzy spell a few minutes ago." Millie rolls her eyes at her.

"I'm fine, I just had a long night, and I need to eat something. I've only had coffee today."

"Millie!" Mary and I cry out at the same time.

"I bet you did your yoga class this morning as well, didn't you?" She looks at me, grabs her bags and heads to the door.

"Let's get to your dress fitting, and I'll grab something on the way. Would that be okay with both of you?" she says, heavy on the sarcasm.

"Make sure she does Em," Mary says and sits back at the desk as we walk out the room.

"I need to tell you something, two things actually, but not here, I don't want anyone listening."

"Exciting, I love a bit of gossip," Millie says, linking her arm with mine as we walk to the car.

"I'll tell you when we get back in the car, then I know nobody will hear me."

"That serious huh?" Her eyebrows wiggle at me. When we get in the car, I couldn't wait any longer to tell her.

"I'm promoting you to Maid of Honour and I'm pregnant. I'm sorry I couldn't contain it any longer. I needed to get it out. I've bumped Jane to Bridesmaid and I've not told Dan yet that we are having a baby…I'm having a baby!" Millie just looks at me, mouth wide open, then she leans over and wraps her arms around me.

"I'm so happy for you. Why have you told me first and not Dan?"

"I want your help with a little 'after the wedding' surprise for him, and I can't keep it at mine. Oh and don't tell Jack." I grimace at her.

"I have so many questions for you right now, just give me a minute to absorb the information." She leans her head back on the seat and closes her eyes for a second.

"Oh my god, you have a baby growing in your belly! How far along are you? What is the surprise for him? Why am I Maid of

Honour and not Jane? What happened to Jane? Oh man she will be pissed, and she will hate me more. I think that's it." She laughs at herself. I spend the next few minutes answering the questions she keeps coming up with. When we walk into the shop for my fitting, Jane is nowhere to be seen. I look at my phone to call her but she doesn't answer. Oh well, I'll try and catch her later. At least I don't have to deal with that right now.

"Are you ready? Only three weeks until the wedding, you will have one more fitting the week before, then that's it," the lady from the bridal shop says, as I'm handed a glass a fizz. Tasting the delicious bubbles, I feel so excited when I see Millie glaring at me and then looking at the glass in my hand. *Oh shit, what am I doing? I don't know what to do!*

"I'll take that," Millie says, "you need to go try your dress on." She takes it out of my hand and I frown at her. She laughs and, sits down and starts drinking the fizz herself. The girls all start chatting while the lady, who I think is called Tabitha, takes me into the fitting room. I'm only a few weeks pregnant but I have to say something, I don't know how fast my tummy will grow and this dress leaves nothing to the imagination.

"Um..." I whisper, "You need to leave a little room in the tummy area." I gesture towards my stomach, and watch as she tries to catch on to what I'm saying.

"Oh...oh gosh...really? How exciting." I hold my fingers to her lips to stop her talking, and she nods at me.

"I'm not sure it will make a difference. You have three weeks until the wedding. I'm sure you will be fine."

"Thank you, I was so worried."

"I'll go and get you another glass of fizz," and she mouths 'non-alcoholic' to me. Well, that's one thing sorted, now to get through the rest of today, with no drink, and this evening. With no drinks, this is never going to work. Everyone knows I love a drink, how am I going to pull this off?

There was a reason Millie was in my life. All afternoon, she has been going to the bar for everyone, placing most of the drinks orders, and drinking all the drinks the girls have been buying for me and she is hammered. She is the best Maid of honour ever! There is still no sign of Jane. I've called her a few times with no answer.

Millie

"Oh god, I feel sick. I can't drink anymore, please don't make me drink anymore." I'm practically lying on the sofa in the bar. I know I said the words but I'm not sure how they came out, slurred, mumbles, maybe even in another language, and not anyone I know would understand or be able to translate. Em and the others are laughing at me, they think I'm a lightweight, but I've had almost double of what they have had. Em hugs me from the side

"I don't know what I would have done without you this afternoon, you have saved me. I'm also sorry," she whispers to me.

It's not good. I'm going to be sick. I sit up too quickly and my head spins, while my stomach churns. When I stand, I swear the floor moves, so I take my shoes off; it's the safest option. I start weaving in and out of the crowd towards the loo when I spot Jane halfway there. She's walking over to me, she looks pissed. Her jaw is set, and her eyes narrowed on me. It's not a great look on her, I can't be bothered with her agro, so I move faster and walk into the ladies' loo, hoping she'll leave me alone. I'm in no fit state to deal with her shit but what a surprise, she comes in behind me and locks the door after her. Just the two of us. Great.

"What do you want Jane?" I ask, my head still spinning with every move I make. She walks right up to me, and pushes me against the wall.

"What the fuck, get off me!" I try to push her away, but she slams me back and I hit my head hard on the wall. My vision blurs for a split second, the spinning in my head makes me wobble a little.

"Jane, get off! What have I done?" Shit, I can't get free, she's so much stronger than she looks. Her hands are pushing my chest, using her full weight to keep me against the wall.

"You know what you have done, you ruined everything," she shouts in my face. "Do you think that the whole hen do was actually planned for us to go to London? I had it all planned out...and it was working, up until you got your fucking nose in the way." Wow, what a bitch! "Jack is meant to be mine! And you stole him away from me!" She grabs my hair as I try to push her away again. "And now this... you're stealing my best friend too."

"I've not done anything. Ahh... you're hurting me." She pushes me to the wall again, but I manage to push her off this time. As soon as I look up, I feel the back of her hand across my face. My head snaps to the side and I fly backwards, hitting the floor.

"You deserve every shitty thing you get in life, you dirty slut!" she says and I watch her walk out, leaving me on the floor.

Well, that was a slightly different end to the afternoon than I thought. I pull myself up from the floor, feeling slightly more sober. A massive wave of dizziness washes over me, and I stumble over to the loo and throw up.

"Why...?" I cry into the loo. *What have I ever done to deserve this shit!* As soon as I start to feel happy, I get hurt. My face feels swollen already; the bitch was wearing rings when she gave me that backhander. When I eventually stand up, my head is pounding. I feel dizzy – time to go home and be by myself.

I walk over to the sink, wash my face with cold water, and wince, my cheek starts to sting. When I look up into the mirror, my cheek is bright red, with two small cuts from where her rings caught my skin; the bruising is already starting to show.

"Fuck sake," I swear into the mirror, "I can't even sneak out." I left my bag and shoes on the table. I have a spare key in the garden; I'll walk back and hide for a few days. Jack's busy anyway, it should go down by the time I get to work on Monday. *It's only Friday afternoon, plenty of time to sort it out,* I think, completely forgetting about work at the pub over the weekend. Bracing myself on the sink, I take a few deep breaths and head out the door, a little wobbly.

I'm ready to head off when I see Jane in Emma's face. Jane looks like she is going to slap her.Oh my god..

I see red, and before I can even think about it, I'm running towards them. Janes raises her hand to Emma.. but she slaps me instead as I step in between them. The same cheek as before, and I hit the ground.

"You both deserve each other!" she screams before two guys drag her, kicking and screaming outside.

"Shit, Millie are you okay? Why did you stand in front of me?" Em asks, as she bends down to me.

"I didn't want her to hit you." I looked at her tummy and she sighed. "Besides, she already backhanded me in the loo, and smashed my head against the wall."

"Are you fucking kidding me? She did that? Your face. Shit… it's cut and swollen. I'm taking you to the hospital." I roll my eyes at her and go to grab my shoes when the room spins and I stumble forward, clutching onto the seat beside me for support.

"Em? I think… I… might… I… feel…" All the weight lifts from my body; I feel like I'm falling as blackness clouds my vision.

I can hear voices, but I can't make out what they are saying. *Where am I?* Peeling my eyes open, I realise I'm in a hospital. *Shit*. Sitting up, my head feels like it actually may explode. I hold it up with my hands and scan the room. I'm in A & E; the curtain is drawn and I can hear Em talking to someone outside. I must have a concussion; I don't think it's that bad, but the alcohol and lack of food definitely didn't help the situation. I really need to learn my lesson.

Sliding off the bed, I stand up and gather my stuff slowly, the more I move my head, the more it feels like it's going to fall off. I'll discharge myself and rest at home. I don't want to waste their time any more than I already have.

"Em…?" I say and the curtain opens. Em is standing there with the doctor.

"Get back in bed, you should not be up!" they both say at the same time. Em looks at me, then says the words I don't want to hear.

"I've rang Jack, he is on his way back, but they have had to go to London for something. He'll be there for a while."

"Why did you do that? Okay, then take me home. I know I have a concussion, I know what to do. Take me home, I'm discharging myself." I hate hospitals, too many bad memories.

Em looks at the doctor; he shrugs and says I can go, but I will need to be checked over by my GP on Monday. And if my symptoms get worse, then come back asap…blah blah blah.

"Thank you, Doc… Em, please get me home." I hate hospitals, I need to leave.

"Okay but I'm staying with you. At least until Jack gets back," she demands, coming to my side.

"Fine, can we grab some food on the way? I'm starving."

"Yes, life saver, I'll buy you as many pizzas as you want after what you did for me today, twice!" She turns me around, so I'm facing her. "I'm so sorry about what Jane did. Who knew she would turn into such a bitch over my brother!" She slumps her shoulders, dipping her head slightly. "I guess you never know what someone is willing to do to get what they want." I don't say it out loud, but I think I know more than most what people are willing to do in order to get what they want, even if it means hurting someone.

An hour later, I'm sitting on my sofa, an ice pack on my cheek; my headache is slowly going after taking the tablets from the hospital. I'm eating pizza and wincing with every bite as I chew. *I thought these days were over,* I think to myself.

Em is lying on the sofa with her feet over my lap, making me laugh as she relays the events of today. I'm smiling even though it hurts to move my face.

"You are an awesome friend. How have I lived without you? Do you think your cheek will be better by the ball next weekend?"

"What ball?" I say with a mouth full of pizza.

"You are joking right?" She bolts up from the sofa. "Jack has asked you to go, hasn't he? It's the company's annual summer ball. Employees from all over the world will be here to celebrate another good year!" She looks shocked that I know nothing about it. I wonder why he hasn't asked me.

"Nope, not been invited." I lean back on the sofa and close my eyes, "Em, can I go to sleep now? I'm tired." I've been asking since we got home, but she's not letting me out of her sight.

"No, not until Jack and Dan get back." I groan at this and give her my best evil look. "… okay, fine," she says, holding her hands up in defeat. "But you stay down here, where I can keep an eye on you."

"Fine, I'll go and get changed and come back downstairs." It's funny really, I used to long for someone to take care of me when something happened and no one ever did. Now I have Em, who won't let me out of her sight. She is that worried about me. I know Jack will be the same, and Dan. Oh God, Mary is going to give me shit on Monday too. I laugh out loud as I make my way up the stairs. I don't make it back downstairs though; I fall asleep on my bed after getting changed. I only wake when Jack gets into bed next to me, wrapping himself around me like a massive protective blanket.

Chapter Twenty-Five

So Much Worse

Jack

I've been watching her for the last few hours while she slept, my arms wrapped tightly around her waist, spooning her. The fear I felt in my chest when Em called to say that she had been attacked left me scared; my thoughts instantly went to him. It doesn't help that I've been on edge lately, trying to find the guy who set fire to my club, or at least trying to figure out why someone would take a huge risk like that, they could have hurt so many people.

Maybe I need to take some time off after the ball and renovation. Get some space for us to just relax and enjoy each other without all the hassle that seems to be swirling around us at the moment.

It pisses me off that she won't tell me any more about him. I've tried looking, but there isn't much to go on. Don't get me wrong, I understand, but it still pisses me off. I'll never admit that to Millie, she would freak out if she thought I had tried to find him. I know they lived in London together, and I know where and what house, but he was not on any paperwork for the house or social media sites, so the trail went dead. If she told me about his work, or even his full name, I'd have him.

I hate to admit it, and I know how bad it sounds, but I was a little relieved when I found out her attacker had been Jane. This whole situation is fucked up. Em told me why Jane did what she did. Who the fuck does she think she is? We had a one night stand. I don't even remember when it was.

I've updated my security team on the situation and added Jane to the minor threat list. But I doubt she will be seen again. I've got eyes on Millie now, it won't happen again, not while I can protect her.

I feel Millie snuggle in next to me, her ass grinding against me. My hands slide against her stomach and hips as I pull her closer to me, burying my face in her hair at the crook of her neck. I love how she smells, I could get lost in her for days.

"I'm not letting you out of my sight today," I whisper in her ear, kissing the soft spot just below her ear.

"Yes you are, I have to..oh…" I press my lips against her neck, trailing kisses as I pull her closer to me. I slide my hand lower, loving the softness of her skin—it's like silk beneath my fingers. Sliding them into her pyjama bottoms, pressing my ever-growing erection against her ass.

"Like I said, you are not leaving my side today, if I had my way, we would not leave the bedroom" She sighs and tries to turn to face me, but I hold her in place, moving her bottoms down, slowly revealing her ass.

"Let's not leave the bedroom then." She removes her top over her head, my hand finding her nipple as she presses herself back into me. My hand traces down the inside of her leg, lifting it slightly, opening her up to me, and as I slide my fingers back up, her breath hitches a little. I know she loves it when I tease her. I slide my erection over her folds from behind and she moans with each movement. I reach for her clit with my other hand, pressing down hard, and a moan escapes my lips when I find that she is so wet, just for me.

"Jack…"

"So wet already, do you want me Millie?"

"I always want you Jack," she grinds into me, placing me right where she needs me, and as she pushes back against me harder, I slide into her just a few inches.

"Fuck…Millie!" she does it again and I go deeper, filling her a bit more. She moves her hips and does it over and over again until I fill her completely. The feelings she invokes in me are overwhelming. She's doing this to me, for me, with her hotness all around me. So I hold her to me as tight as I can, my one arm wrapped around her holding her back to me, while my other hand plays with her clit, making her moan, over and over again. Pulling out almost all the way, I tease her a little, then slam back in, going deeper, and I feel her wall tighten around me. She feels so good, I'm on the edge, this woman..

"Yes, Jack, harder…" I pull out again and slam back into her, feeling her climb higher with each thrust, wanting more, her fingers digging into me as she holds on. Our bodies combine in a frenzied need for each other.

"Come for me Millie. I want to feel you…Fuck!" she shatters around me; every wave of her pleasure sends me closer. I keep going, listening to her come and feeling her as she screams my name, and that's it, I fall over the edge, crashing and thrusting one last time, as she takes everything I have, filling her completely. I nuzzle my head in her neck, kissing her gently as my jerky movements slow down. "I love you, don't ever scare me like that again, I thought…" It all comes out a bit breathless, and she cuts me off.

"I'm okay, it's not the worst night I've had," she says, moving around to face me, "Plus I couldn't let her hurt Em, not when…" she stops mid-way, placing her hands on her chest, like she is keeping something hidden.

"I hate it when you say things like that." I kiss her hard. Thinking of her hurt worse than this, and at his hands, it makes my blood boil. I won't say it though, she doesn't need to be reminded, she needs to forget.

"I'm sorry." She looks me in the eyes, the softness she holds in them tells me she really does care for me, or is it love? She kisses me back tenderly this time.

"That's okay, you never need to apologise to me," I say in between kisses, holding her to me.

"So what's this about a Summer Ball? Is there a reason you don't want me to go?" Propping herself up on her elbow, she raises an eyebrow at me. I can see the bruise on her cheek now, purple and green covering her cheek with the small cuts from where she was hit. Raising my hand, I brush my thumb over them, she doesn't say anything. I wish it never happened, that I could have stopped it from happening.

"I just assumed you knew we would be going together."

"I didn't know about it until Em told me yesterday. I know it's been busy at the Manor, maybe I've been too wrapped up in my own stuff to realise what was going on." She flops back down on the bed and winces a little when her head hits the pillow. I chuckle and lean over her, caging her underneath me. Fuck she looks so beautiful in the morning, I love how messy her hair gets, and add in the flushed after-sex look she has; I never what to wake up without her.

"Millie, will you do me the honour of going to the Summer Ball with me?" She looks up at me with a smile that reaches to the deepest part of my soul—*that* smile; I'll do everything in my power to keep that smile on her face.

"Yes, Jack, I'd love to go with you." lowering my head slowly, I kiss her as her hands come up and pull me closer. "I know just the dress to wear." A low rumble escapes my lips.

"I'll never get through my speech if you wear that." I'm getting hard just thinking about it.

"It's a deal then, the green dress it is!" The playful look in her eyes is beautiful. There is no way I will be able to concentrate if she wears that. She looks beautiful in it, but I'll just be thinking of what we did together when she wore it last, her legs, her ass, her breasts, that matching thong…how she tastes, the look of her bent over the counter wanting me; I clear my throat, I'm a goner. I already have another hard-on.

"You're thinking about what we did while I wore what dress, aren't you?" She grabs my cock, and starts stroking her hand up and down me.

"Always Millie…that feels good."

"We never did get to fill one of your fantasies, did we? Tell me one, and I'll do it for you."

This woman is on another level. I knew what I wanted to act out, but it would have to wait for later.

"I'll tell you but right now I need to be inside you. I need you Millie." She moves her hand from me, and shimmies down the bed under me. I watch as she disappears, her hair spread out under me. She stops when her mouth is level with my cock.

I suck in a breath when she licks the top of my cock, tasting me. She takes me in her mouth and my cock hits the back of her throat, but she takes me further.

"Fuck…Millie…" She grabs my ass and guides me in and out of her mouth. Fuck…this is…she moans and the vibrations send tidal waves of pleasure through me. I try to keep my hips still, but she moves me in and out, so I move a little and she moans more, sucking me and taking me deeper. Words can't even explain the pleasure that's building inside of me with her being under me while I fuck her mouth, her hands on my ass moving me faster and faster.

"Mil, I'm going to come." I try to pull out but she holds me in place, taking me deeper down her throat until I swell and explode in her mouth. She moves me in and out as I do, sucking every last drop out of me. When I look down at her through my arms, her eyes are looking back up at me, watching me. She gives the sweetest yet sexiest smile I have ever seen, like she enjoyed that just as much as I did.

"That was hot, but I think I may need some tablets, my head hurts," Millie says as we lay on the bed together.

"Shit…you have a concussion…I'm so sorry, I should have never…" I say, sitting up and running my hands through my hair.

"Do not apologise, I enjoyed that just as much as you. Believe me, it's my own fault."

"That's it, no more today. I can't risk hurting you. Today you're coming to work with me. I need to finalise stuff for the ball, and start to get things ready."

And with that, I move off the bed, leaving her there on the bed naked, laughing at me.

"I can't look at you like that, you're too tempting. Get dressed, I'm going to have a hard enough time today concentrating after what you just did to me. I'll get you some tablets." She's still laughing as I walk away.

I'd say it was a surprise but I should have known that Millie wouldn't just sit and relax in my office at the Manor. As soon as Dan walked in, in a flap about one of the vendors having to cancel at the last minute, and others having issues with supplies for next Saturday's ball, Millie jumped up and dived in to help, sorting it out. She was now talking with vendors, stylists and decorators, coordinating everything. She had taken over, getting all the information and sorting through Dan's non-existent system.

I'm in awe of this woman. Is there anything she can't do? I'm meant to be sorting the refurb, but I can't concentrate, the way she handles it all, it's with grace but with a boot of fierce determination slapped in. Dan looks over at me, nodding his head towards Millie.

"How? It takes me weeks to get answers from anyone, and we do this every year! How has she managed to sort out all the shit in a few hours?" He looks baffled, but also kind of pleased she's helping. It's funny to watch them work together; they make a good team. Dan just keeps nodding at her, handing her anything she needs, while she talks to employees, vendors, and caterers. She even has Dan making lists and spreadsheets so he can keep up to date with progress.

"I have no idea, but she has taken over. There is nothing for us to do for the Ball," I whisper back to him, sitting back in my seat. When she looks up at us from her phone, we both stop and look at her.

"There is plenty for you to do, I have work tonight at the pub, so I can't speak to a few people. That's your list of jobs Jack and that's yours, Dan," she says, handing us both a jobs sheet.

"It'll be done." Dan nods, "Millie you know, you have a real knack for this, don't you?" Dan says, "I may make you our events manager." She laughs at him, and I shake my head.

"I used to help my parents with the events they held a few times a year for their employees, I guess you never forget." She smiles but you can see the sadness in her eyes. She must miss them; losing them both so suddenly must have been awful.

"No way, I can't have you with four jobs, plus you are meant to be taking it easy today and I've already rang the pub and spoke to Mike, you have the night off."

She lays the list on the desk in front of me, rolling her eyes at me; her smile says she is annoyed but a little pleased. God she is cute…no, sexy as hell. She glances down again at the list she has placed on my desk, ready to grab it back when she freezes, stepping back.

She looks panicked, her face pales, going ghostly white, as her hands shoot up to cover her perfect mouth. When a sob escapes her lips, Dan and I both stand up at the same time, moving towards her. She looks like she's going to freak out. Her hand drops to her side.

"What…why…you said…" she says, her hand coming up to cover another sob, before it can escape.

"Mil, what's wrong?" I don't know what just happened, what did I say? She stumbles back, her legs hitting the sofa behind her and she sits down, across from the desk. Walking over, we sit on either side of her, looking at each other for answers. Dan is watching her face as she tries not to cry, while I am watching her whole body shake as she tries to breathe evenly.

"Why…why do you have that?" Her face is so pale, it's like all the blood has been drained from her.

Wait, the photos that are laid out on my desk, does she know one of them? Dan must have the same thought, because he stands up and walks back over to the desk, picking them up.

"Millie…do you…"

"You said…no…you promised you wouldn't…" Tears stream down her face as she says it. She is looking at me like I've betrayed her trust. The fear in my chest matches the fear I can see in her eyes.

"Mil, I don't understand, do you know one of these men?" I say as Dan places the pictures on the coffee table. She's shaking.

She nods and points to the guy on the left. Fuck, it's the same one who had given the creeps from the word go, the one who looked directly into the camera in my club in Ibiza. Her gaze lands on me, confused, looking for the truth. I cup her face in my hands when she speaks.

"You don't know who that is?" She asks, looking bewildered.

"No, I promise you I don't. These are the photos of the suspects for the arson attack on the club...who is that Mil?" I think I already know the answer, deep in my gut, I don't want her to say it. If it is him, things have just got ten times worse.

"It's him, my ex, Glen," she cries. "Oh god, I have to go!" She stands up to leave, my hands fall to my lap for a split second, trying to take in what she has just said. But I grab her and make her sit back down next to me, taking her in my arms.

"I... I can't, Jack. I need to leave, I can't do this. If he knows where I am... oh god, it's all my fault. I'm so sorry, I should never have stayed...the fire...oh my god the fire, it's all my fault!" She pulls away from me, tears streaming down her face. She stands again and heads to the door. Dan blocks it, unwilling to let her leave.

"Dan...don't...I can't risk it, if he is willing to do that, then who knows what else he is capable of! I'm not risking putting you all in danger, especially now."

Dan doesn't move, just rests his back on the door and folds his arms over his chest. He doesn't say anything. He just looks at me.

"It was him!" My words come out angrier than I expected, and Millie spins around, looking at me.

"I'm so sorry Jack, I'll leave, you don't have to worry about what he will do next. If I'm not here, he won't bother you...it's me he wants to hurt." You can hear the fear in her voice.

My head is spinning; it was him, her ex did this. Why? He could have hurt so many people. Was he really that possessive of her? What would he do to get her back? There are so many questions I have flying through my head, and all of them I need answers to.

"Dan, let me go." I can hear her saying but I can't focus on what is happening. He set fire to my club, because I'm in a relationship with Millie; he risked the lives of my staff and friends because of Millie.

"Dan, I can't stay. I need to leave before he can do anything else." I watch him shake his head, still not moving from the door.

"You don't understand!" she says, and I start to take notice of what she's saying and trying to do.

She can't leave, he will just keep finding her, then what? Kill her like he almost did last time, leaving her for dead. Snapping out of it, I stand up. I walk over to the door and grab Millie's hand, leading her back to the sofa, where I engulf her in my arms.

"You aren't going anywhere, Millie. I won't let anything happen to you."

"But…Jack…I can't…" Leaning backwards I hold her as firmly as I can without hurting her, "Not an option," I say and she sighs. My head runs through all the possibilities of what could happen as fear starts to take over me. But just like always, my mind snaps into action. Looking at Dan.

"Dan, we need to inform the police, and our security team. Get Owen down here now." Dan nods and heads out of the room; I know he will tell Em as soon as leaves. I need to put a plan together, I won't tell Millie just how worried I am. I won't tell her the extremes I am willing to go through to keep her and my family safe.

"You don't have to do this Jack, if I leave you don't have to worry." She's not crying anymore, but the tears are still falling. She keeps wiping them away with the palm of her hand. I want to protect her with everything I have. Taking her face in my hands again, I brush my fingers over her tears and wipe them away. Placing a soft kiss on her lips.

"You're not leaving Millie, I'll sort it out. Besides, he hasn't actually hurt anyone, maybe he just wants to try and scare me away from you, and that's not going to happen." I kiss her again, and she kisses me back. If I play it down, maybe she will calm down too.

"I'm so sorry Jack. If I hadn't come into your life again, this would never have happened. I can't even express how sorry I am…what can I do?" Her eyes are pleading with me.

"Just do as I ask until we find him, no more secrets, don't be alone, you have me, don't ever forget that," I say, kissing a little harder this time.

"I'll never forget that Jack," she says, pulling back, her hands slipping into the back of my hair.

"I need you Jack, right now." Kissing my neck, she undoes my belt and buttons on my jeans, moving her hand inside, taking my length in her hand.

It's like she knows what I need, I need her too, so much. I moan when she straddles me, her skirt moving up over her legs as she wraps them around me. Kissing her deeper, I stand up, moving us both to the door, where I lock it with one hand, holding her up and against me with the other.

Pushing her back against the door, she shoves my trousers and boxers down just enough so she can grab my ass. My hand takes hold of her knickers, moving them to the side.

"You're always ready for me." Her knickers are wet from how much she needs me right now. I position myself at her entrance; she gasps and her head snaps back as I push myself into her, burying myself deep with her fingers digging into my shoulders through my shirt.

"Fuck me Jack, I need it, I need you." Her head leaning back on the door as I start to move faster, in and out of her beautiful body. My hand rested on the door beside her head, kissing her, nipping at her lips.

"Harder Jack," she moans in my ear. This woman…fuck. I do as I'm told, fucking her with everything I have. As I am slamming myself into her, she screams my name. Fuck she feels so good.

"I'm never letting you go, Millie, you're mine."

"Yes, fuck…Jack," Her eyes close, leaning back as I feel her pleasure clamp down on me, I slam into her again.

"Don't stop." I would never, I'll always give her what she wants. Keeping up the pace, I feel her body go tight as she releases around me, pushing me over the edge. I spill myself into her, feeling her orgasm again, but this time with me. Taking me higher as we fall together. My head slumped on her shoulder, her head on mine, our breathing rapid, our bodies fixed together.

After a few minutes, I guide us over to the sofa, where we part only to make ourselves decent again. She comes back into my arms and we sit for a while, not saying anything. Just letting the whole shit show sink in.

"Okay." That's all she says before she stands and starts working on the ball again.

"What are you doing? There's no need to do any of that now. I'm going to cancel it." It makes sense until we can find him and put him away.

"I need a distraction if you want me to stay. I need to take my mind off this mess I have caused. You're not cancelling it, your employees have spent money on stuff for this event, and you are not letting them down because of me. Who's Owen?" It's like she just remembered the conversation with Dan. He should be back soon.

She sits at my desk now, lists in a shaky hand, ready to get it all done.

"I'm cancelling it Millie, end of discussion."

Raising an eyebrow at me, she says. "Really? End of discussion? I don't think so. You may have your ways of bossing others around, but not me. If you cancel this, he will know he has gotten to you, and he wins. And I don't want him to win. We are having this ball," she says, slamming her hands down on the desk.

I come around to her side, drawing her to me. "Okayyy, he won't win Mil, I won't let him. And Owen is the head of my security team. We will make sure we get him, that we are all safe. I promise," I say, kissing her again.

Chapter Twenty-Six

Full of Surprises

Millie

Keep to our normal routines, that's what Owen had told us. Owen is the head of security, like Jack said, but he was nothing like I had expected. He was tall and muscular but looked nerdy, with glasses and unruly hair, a proper geek, but on all accounts, you can't judge a book by its cover. He doesn't stand out and just fits in, unlike his second in command. His name is Leon and he is fucking huge, like brick shit house huge. Massive…ha, I had to laugh when we were introduced; it was nervous laughter, but again, he was like a teddy bear. Like I said, never judge a book by its cover.

Between the pub, my day job and building my business, oh and doing the events' work, I have not stopped. And to be honest, I don't want to. I know if I do, I may break; the guilt I feel about this whole situation is eating me alive. The more I think about it, the more I feel literally sick to my stomach that these people have been put in danger and may still be in danger because of me. I've not been able to sleep; how can I when I know he did this?

It's one thing hurting me but how could he set fire to the club? He could have hurt hundreds of people. It's all my fault. I've not been able to eat properly either. I just can't. And I seem to have people watching me all the time, I hate it. Everywhere I go, they are there, following me. I understand why Jack wants them around. We all have security, Dan and Em included. But he should be using them on his family, not me.

Some members of staff have figured out something is wrong; they don't know what, but keep asking why I have two men following me around all the time. I need to talk to Jack; it's only three days until the ball, I need to be able to relax a bit and I can't do that with them around me like this.

When we spoke to the police, I had to tell them everything, and Jack and Em were by my side when I did, reassuring me it would all be okay.

The following day, the police informed us that Glen had flown out to Ibiza the week the story was leaked about me and Jack to the press. They said he has since flown to mainland Spain, where he is hiding out, but they are not able to locate him.

I'm scared, I feel like I'm being watched; I know it's Owen and his team watching but something is giving me the creeps. I've not told Jack he would make me have someone with me 24/7, although I already suspect they are. I just can't see them. I just can't shake this feeling like someone's watching me.

I'm also slowly losing my marbles. No, seriously, I keep misplacing stuff. The other day, I could have sworn I got my stuff out ready for the following day: a white blouse with a navy pencil skirt, leaving them on the chair in my room. But when I went to get them off the chair the following morning, where I thought I had laid them, they weren't there, only my bra and thong were there. My skirt and shirt were still hanging in the wardrobe. Maybe I dreamt about it. Or maybe I got distracted. I know it's me, my head is all over the place and not sleeping is making it worse.

Jack wants me to move into the Manor with him, but I won't. If I had my way, I would have left already, making sure it was only me Glen could hurt. I've come to love them as my family, and yes, that includes Jack. I've not told him though, I'm still dealing with my own shit to be able to say the words out loud. But I do love him, my whole body aches for him, he's all I think about. He is the only ray of sunshine in my life right now. But now I can't help but think Glen will hurt them all. It's like I can feel my heart breaking, like it's being torn into pieces. About to shatter, I can't stop it. I know what I need to do, and I'll do it after the ball on Saturday; if he has not been found by then, I can't risk them. Especially now Em is pregnant, she has her surprise for Dan set for after the wedding in just over two weeks' time. That's another thing, how can I put the happiest day of their lives at risk? I just can't, I don't want their special day to be consumed by worry about what might happen. I can't do that to them.

They will all be better off if I wasn't here; I know I said to Jack I would stay that day in his office. But I can't. So I've made my plans and during Jack's speech, I will leave. I'm not taking anything with me; I'll just disappear. That way, they will all be safe. I've written my letters to each of them explaining why. I just hope they understand.

Wiping away yet more tears, I click on my laptop. It's only 5 am but I can't sleep any longer. Dreams invade my mind, and not nice ones. Having Jack next to me each night is a huge comfort but I still can't get it out of my head enough to sleep well.

"How long have you been awake for?" Jack says, resting his head on my shoulder, his arms weaved around my waist as he kisses my neck.

"A while, why don't you go back to bed? It's still early." I say, my fingers feeling the scruff on his chin.

"Only if you come with me.," he says, kissing my neck more, his hand slipping under my top. I'm fully dressed and ready for work.

"You see I've just had this dream," cupping my breast through my bra, "more of a fantasy really," he says, finding my already hard nipple and rolling it between his thumb and finger. A pure shot that spirals down to my core, making me moan.

"Oh, and what was this fantasy?"

"I'll show you if you come with me." Standing up, I wrap my arms around his neck, bringing his lips to mine.

"Always eager, but right now I need you back in the bedroom," and like a dizzy schoolgirl, I laugh and head for the stairs, his hands grabbing my ass as we go.

When I reach our room, he stops me, pulling my back against him, his hands trailing down my front, and skimming over my blouse, teasing me. Pressing me into his already hard erection makes me moan. The man is only in his boxers, there is nothing left to the imagination.

Moving me to the end of the bed, he steps back, sitting himself on the chair opposite me.

"Strip, and do it slowly," he says, the smile on his face is almost cheeky, teasing me. My toes curl with excitement at the thought of stripping for him. When he stands and removes his boxers, leaving himself completely naked, I can't help but look at him, biting my lower lip. I have to squeeze my thighs together to try and relieve some of the tension I have building in me. He leans back, showing me his well-sculpted body, tanned chest, his tattoo touching everywhere I want to. My eyes drift down to his abs and the perfect V that forms at his lower abdomen, trailing down to his cock. I'm wet already, just looking at him. He runs his hand through his blond hair, pushing it back away from his face.

"Millie, I said strip." I move my hands to my waist, untucking my shirt, while standing there in front of him. This is hot. My shirt falls to the floor, revealing my lace bra; he moans and shifts in his seat, taking his length in his hand and moving it slowly up and down, while his eyes remain on me, unwavering.

I slowly turn around and undo the zip at the back of my skirt, bending down slightly as I glide it over my hips and down my legs. Turning my head slowly, I watch as he eyes my backside. He moans, holding himself a little harder; I know he loves it when I bend over, only wearing my thong, my ass and centre on show just for him.

Straightening back up, I remove my bra and slide my thong, slowing down my legs. Flicking them at him when they reach the floor.

"Umm..." His eyes close as he catches them, still touching himself. I start to walk over when he shakes his head.

"Stay there. I want you to touch yourself." My cheeks flame red instantly. I know we did this over the phone, but with him watching, it is so intense, my breath is slow and shaky.

"Feel yourself, play with your nipples for me." I trace the outline of my breast with my fingers and slowly start to circle my pink bud, letting out a moan as a wave of pleasure zips to my core, taking one in-between my fingers and rolling it. My back arches and I lower myself onto the edge bed.

"That's it…" I glance at him and he is staring intently at me. I decide to take it into my own hands, keeping one hand on my hard nipple, while I trace my other hand down my stomach, making small circles as I go. I have never felt so sexy in my life, the way he looks at every move I make, it's passionate and powerful. I feel like I could come right now, just from the burning look in his eyes. When my hand reaches my lower abdomen, I part my legs for him, showing him just how wet I am, without yet touching myself there. I lean back on the bed, holding myself up with one arm, with which I glide my free hand from my knee to my inner thigh. I tremble under the fierce sensations taking over my body as he watches my hand move closer to where he wants to be, and I open my legs a little further for him. Running my fingers up and down myself, a moan escapes my lips and I tilt my head back. God this feels amazing. I know I'm doing the work but fuck…I need more, pressing my finger to my aching clit, my back arches as warm desire spreads through me.

"Put a finger inside you Millie. Let me see you."

I want to watch him when I do, lifting my head up and my gaze lands on him, touching himself, stroking himself a little harder. His eyes filled with the same desire as mine. The air around us crackles with tension. Without moving my gaze, I slide my finger in, moving it slowly in and out, feeling myself getting higher, and just how this makes me feel. My emotions hit me all at once but I hold them back; I wanted to give him this…this moment. I add another finger, needing more when he stands up and walks towards me.

"No...that's my job." He kneels down in front of me, removing my hand and replacing it with his, his fingers sliding into me, his other hand coming to the back of my head. Kissing me with such force it's overwhelming; a tear slips down my cheek when I can't hold back my feelings anymore. He takes me higher, moving his fingers in and out faster, bringing me closer and closer to exploding around his fingers. He leans me back, moving an arm around my waist and edging me back up the bed.

"I love you Millie," he says as he removes his fingers and slides his full hard length into me.

"Oh god! Yes!" I scream, "Jack!"

I all but combust around him; my emotions are so raw another tear slips down my cheeks as he slowly makes love to me. Kissing me tenderly, letting my hands roam his back, while I hold on to him. This is something else, this feeling—his eyes on me, watching me. It's beautiful. And I know my heart is his, so I let go with my orgasm taking over as he thrusts into me over and over again. My heart and soul explode with love for this incredible man. He comes with me, lowering his head into my neck as we ride out our pleasure together. My tears leak from my eyes, and I can't stop them, I don't want to. That was pure. There are no other words to explain it.

We hold each other for what feels like an eternity, not moving, our arms wrapped around each other. Unwilling to let go of this moment.

"Did I hurt you Millie?" He whispers in my ear after a while. "I'm so sorry, if I did…"

"Jack..you didn't hurt me, you could never hurt me." Moving his head, he kisses me lightly on the lips.

"Then why…why were you crying?" He looks into my eyes, confusion etched all over his face.

"Because that was beautiful, perfect, hot, sexy, mind-blowing and loving…it was everything to me."

Later that day, Mary walks into my office holding a huge bouquet of red flowers, every kind you can think of.

"These were delivered for you!" She almost squeals at me, "Who are they from? Open the card!" She demands in a flurry.

"I think we both know who they are from," I chuckle. As she places them on my desk, I take the card out and open the envelope, a little embarrassed.

"Emilie, I'll never forget what you did."

That's a little odd, I wonder, *what did I do?* I've been so absent-minded lately, it's easy to think I've missed something. The flowers are beautiful, not something I thought Jack would do though, huh, I guess I was wrong.

"We were right, they're from Jack," I smile, taking the flowers and placing them on my desk,

"He has it bad for you young lady. In all the years I've known him, he has never acted like this with anyone. It's about time, and so lovely to see." She winks at me and walks back out of the office, closing the door behind her. I sit looking at the flowers for a while, remembering last night. As I reach for the phone to call and thank him, it startles me when it rings before I have the chance to dial his number.

"Hello, Manor Hotel, how may I help you?" I say, my eyes wandering over the flowers once again.

"Hello, may I speak with Miss Emilie Munroe please?"

"Yes, speaking, how can I help?"

"This is Joshua Davenport, family friend and estate attorney from Davenport and Dooly Associates in London. I'm calling to arrange a meeting with you, regarding your inheritance." *My inheritance?* It takes longer than it should to realise what he's talking about. In just over a week's time, I turn twenty-eight—the age my parents set for me to inherit everything they worked so hard for. I'm taken aback slightly; I don't know how I feel about this on top of everything else.

"Oh, um…yes sure, when would you like to meet.?" I'll deal with it, I'd rather have my parents back then the money, I'm not saying it won't come in handy, but I already have the money from the house when that finalises. I feel overwhelmed that they are taking care of me from wherever they are now.

"This week, if possible, I can come to you, if it works out better for you". He says matter-of-factly.

"That would be wonderful, thank you, what day is best for you?"

"Tomorrow? I can be there in the afternoon at 2 pm?" he suggests.

"Yes, I can do that, I'll need to move a few things, but that should be fine." I feel a little silly forgetting about it all. And that my birthday is so soon.

"Very well then Miss Munroe, tomorrow it is." He hangs up the phone and I just sit for a few moments, taking in what he's just said, remembering my parents, and how much I miss them.

Today is full of surprises already and it's only 11.30! What else can today bring? I laugh to myself when someone knocks on the door.

"Come in, you don't have to knock," I shout, as the door creeps open, revealing a very welcome face and just the company I need right now.

"I'm here!" Charlie bursts into song. I laugh and move in for a hug. I may hold her a little too long, but I need this.

"Everything alright there Millie? Did you need a hug this morning?" I nod and pull back, resting on my desk.

"You are just what I needed. What are you doing here?" I ask.

"Well, that's a long story I want to tell you over lunch. Can you spare me a few hours?"

"I can do more than that. I'll give you lunch and drinks after work. How does that sound?"

"Amazing, but why can't you ditch work? You're dating the big handsome boss man; there have to be some perks. Right?" Grabbing my bag, I lead her out the door.

"There are plenty of perks, believe me, but none of them I can do this week. We have the Summer Ball on Saturday, and prep is well underway yet a little behind. So I can't take time off, not this week, and well with everything else going on, I don't want to. I need the distraction."

"What are you on about? It's been like a week since we have spoken. What's happened?"

"I'll fill you in over lunch," I say as we walk out the door into the restaurant. I fill her in on everything.

"Shit!" That's all she has said for the last few minutes, on repeat. "I need to tell you something on that note." She takes a big breath in. "Do you remember the notifications we set up on the security system for the house?" I nod. I've never looked at it; I turned off all the notification reminders. I also know what's coming next: "Well, shit hit the fan, the video notification came through, and I've never seen him that angry…" Oh fuck.

"I don't want to know anymore," I say, stopping her dead. I know exactly what he's like. I don't need to know anymore. "That's why I now have a security detail, well, we all do. I bet you can't spot them?" I know I'm ignoring the point she just made, but if I saw the video, I'd lose what little control I have left of my emotions if I saw it.

"Okay…Oh wow, really, I bet you I can…" she starts looking around, and spots Leon immediately pointing him out; he nods at her and continues to look around.

"There are two of them…you will never guess the other." I know where he is, he is sitting on the table next to us. He can hear every word, and no doubt ready to pass on this new piece of information. So I have to be careful what I say.

"You're right, I have no idea, I think it's only big Ted over there."

Owen stands up. And Charlie doesn't even glance at him, when he stands behind her, leans down and whispers something in her ear. Her cheeks instantly go red. It's not often Charlie gets flustered, but right now, she has no idea what to do. I start laughing when he walks away, moving towards the bar.

"That's Owen, what did he say to you? I don't ever remember seeing you go red, or being flustered."

She starts fanning herself with the menu, and I can see Owen smiling, looking towards us from the bar.

"Um… well…I'm not sure I can say it out loud." Her cheeks flush again. I hand Charlie her glass of wine, she drinks it in one go.

"I need something stronger, he just told me…he…no I can't say it, some things are meant to be kept between two people. But I think I'm going to like it down here," she says, her fingers lingering on the glass.

"What do you mean?"

"Well…I've quit my job, and I'm moving down here to be closer to you. Plus, I have nothing left in London. My family is all down this way. I hated my job, it got a little too serious for me. The hours sucked, and I want to be a florist."

My mouth is quite literally hanging open—so much information in such a short amount of time. My brain is trying to catch up.

"But…what… you worked so hard to become a solicitor. Wait, what about Andrew?" Andrew was the love of her life, well I thought he was; they got married a few months after our trip to Ibiza, six years ago. I thought they were happy, I guess I was wrong.

"Being a high profile solicitor is not worth the drain on your life. Andrew got bored of waiting to have kids, slept with someone else and got her pregnant. Blamed it all on me for working too much. The little prick. Although to be honest, I worked like eighty plus hour weeks and weekends. So I filed for divorce just over seven months ago. I need a change, I've been doing a floristry course on the side for a while now, and I can't tell you how much I enjoy it." She sighs filling up her drink. "Oh and I bought a shop on the high street."

"I don't know where to start with all of this information Charlie!" I put my head in my hands, still processing. "Right now is possibly the worst moment to be closer to me. Until Glen is in custody, you would be better off staying in London. He knows you." This has just got so much worse; my heart is in shreds, she's moved down here to be with me. Everyone I love is all in the same place. I can't take it!

"Are you crying?" Charlie asks, her hand reaching for mine.

"No." This is too much.

"Yes you are…there are tears running down your cheek, it's a sure giveaway," she says, giving my hand a squeeze.

"This last week has been a lot, and now you have decided to move to be with me, I just feel…I don't know." I wave my hand flippantly; I can't tell her what I'm planning. If I run, they will be safe.

"It's okay, I get it, it's like you're living in a movie, psycho ex, arson, finding the man of your dreams." She winks at me and I can't help but burst out laughing.

"You're ridiculous, you know that." She winks at me again, laughing.

"I'm only telling the truth. Anyway you need to get back to work, and I have plans to make."

"Well if you're staying, why don't you come to the ball on Saturday? Where are you staying?"

"I'm staying here, at the Manor. Even booked myself a spa day for tomorrow."

"That sounds amazing, I'll book one for myself when this week is over." I sigh, standing up and making my way back to the office. Then I realise I won't be here next week.

"Seven pm. You're all mine Millie!" she shouts as she heads out the door.

"My poor feet, why do they make heels hurt so much?" Since we arrived at the club, all we have done is dance and dance. It's been amazing, but my feet feel like they are on fire. I've taken my shoes off and I'm never putting them back on. Ever. Charlie laughs at me, linking arms as we head back from the bar with another cocktail in hand. I'm going to feel like shit tomorrow, it's already past midnight, and we are still going strong.

When I met Charlie in the pub at seven, we both burst out laughing. We had almost identical outfits on, short black leather skirt, mine a little longer than hers, with a silk cami that cut low in the back and front, only in different colours, and both of us opted for black stilettos. It's like we planned it. I even offered to go home and change but she insisted we just carry on. So here we are.

"Do you realise how much Owen has been staring at you all night?" I tell her, but she refuses to look in his direction.

"Don't be silly. He is doing his job, looking out for you."

"Don't you like him? I have a feeling he really likes you, you never did tell me what he said to you at lunch. Spill!" nudging her a little.

"Ugh… okay. He said, he knew everything about me, and that Andrew was stupid to ever let me go, and that I would be screaming his name for the rest of my life." Her face turns red just at the thought of it. That was creepy and sweet and sexy all at the same time.

"I have no words for that…oh yes I do…that's fucking hot! And maybe a little weird, but mostly hot."

"It was, but the more I think about it, the more I feel like running. I don't need a man in my life right now, not serious anyway." That was fair, she has been through some shit in the last few months. And I have a feeling I don't even know the full story. After what Andrew had done, I can't blame her for wanting to be single for a while.

"I understand, but you could also have some fun, it doesn't have to be serious. When was the last time you had sex?"

"Too long ago for me to remember, and it wasn't that good." A sad smile on her face.

"Well tonight will be different, you can have any man you want in this room, pick one and have some fun."

I scan the room looking for a cute guy, one you know will only want a one-night stand. It's not hard to miss them, their eyes land on every single girl in the place like they are looking for prey.

"What about him?" I point to a guy over at the bar, tall, dark hair, handsome. "Go and chat him up!"

"What would I even say…do you realise how long it's been since I chatted someone up? I'll just make a fool of myself."

"No you won't, I'll walk over with you. All you need to do is be you. Come on, drink up, we need to get another," I say, placing my empty glass on the table.

As we walk over, the guy glances over his shoulder, looking our way. As we get a little closer, I notice him looking at Charlie, so I move away, letting her walk to the bar while I move to a different spot. Charlie slides in next to him at the bar, and within a few seconds, he is not only chatting her up, but has also bought her a drink. Mission accomplished. I know she won't sleep with him, but it won't hurt to feel good for a while.

As I take a sip of my drink, I get an uneasy feeling in the pit of my stomach, like i'm being watched again. I look for Owen and he is still there keeping watch, mainly on me, but with thunderous glances over to Charlie, still talking to Mr Handsome.

Why can't I shake this feeling? Maybe it's the drink, and with that, my stomach churns. Placing a hand on my stomach, I glance at Charlie but she is deep in conversation with Mr Handsome. When I stand up, my head spins, and I have to grab the bar to steady myself. I'm going to be sick; holding it down as much as I can, I walk to the bathroom. I don't want to make a scene, my head is spinning and I can feel a darkness edging in. If I run, I know I'll fall, and the way my legs are right now, I'm not sure they would support me. Pushing the bathroom door open, I glance around quickly and lock it behind me; the room spins and seems to be tilting to one side. My mind races but all I can do is watch as my body feels heavy and gives way to the floor, blackness flooding my vision.

Banging, that's all I hear around me. *What is that noise? Why is it so dark?* My eyes flutter open but I can't focus. *What is that noise? Where am I?* When my eyes finally focus I realise I'm still in the bathroom of the club, on the floor. I must have passed out. Bang! *What is that noise?* Sounds like someone is trying to get in.

I still feel sick, I need to get up, but my body has other ideas. I don't know how long I have been out. I have a feeling that's Owen trying to get in. My head is so fuzzy, when I eventually stand up, I sway a little, just as the door bursts open and in fly Owen and Leon, looking worried and pissed off at the same time.

"Millie?" Owen shouts, looking round, finding me leaning against the wall for support.

"What's happened? Are you hurt?" I look at him a little confused, shaking my head at him and instantly regret it as I almost lose my balance again. He grabs my arm and leads me to the sofa by the large mirror.

"Millie, what happened?"

Kneeling down in front of me, I look up and see Leon checking the stalls and blocking the door, glancing over at me.

"I don't know, I think I drank too much. I must have passed out when I got in here, sorry…I…don't know, how long?"

"Shit, Jack is going to kill me! I didn't think you drank that much. You were in here for almost fifteen minutes." Owen looks over at Leon for confirmation. He nods again, then says, "Three glasses of red, four cocktails and some water in between." I'm glad someone has been keeping count. Mixing my drinks is never a good idea. Owen lifts my head and checks out my eyes, nods at Leon and helps me stand.

"What did you just do?" I say, looking at him.

"I checked your eyes to see if there was any sign of dilation, but you're fine, they look normal. I'll ring Jack and tell him what happened." He sighs, reaching for his phone.

"You think I was drugged?!.." My eyes popped out of my head. "Don't tell him…please, I wasn't drugged, it's my own fault for mixing drinks. Plus I've been a little stressed. Just take me home." I plead, "Jack's away tonight and I don't want to worry him anymore than I need to. He has so much on his plate already, I don't want to add to the stress-load he already has on his shoulders after everything I've caused." I can't let him tell Jack.

"I have to tell Jack, Millie he's my boss, and it's my job to make sure you're safe. And right now…I'm not sure you are."

"Please, please Owen, I don't want him to worry, this is all my own fault. He doesn't need to know. There was no way I was drugged…I mean I got the drink from the bar myself. No one could have got to them, if they had, you or Leon would have seen." I have a feeling this will reassure him.

He eyes Leon again, and they seem to share some sort of silent conversation. In the end, Leon shakes his head, then says, "Your call."

"Okay, but if he even asks you if anything happened tonight, you tell him the truth. I'll get shit for it. But I hate keeping secrets. Especially ones like this. Even more so because it's Jack. Are you sure you're okay?" His eyes are all over me, checking me again for any injuries.

"Apart from feeling a little foolish and a tad nauseous, I'm fine. Let's go and grab Charlie, and go home." I say, starting to stand up.

A little smile crosses his lips when I mention her name, but a frown soon descends when we walk out and he spots her still being chatted up by Mr Handsome, although now, his hand is on her lower back and he's pulled her closer to him, so they're almost touching.

Leon holds me steady, even though I think I'm fine now, if not feeling a little sick still. Owen heads over to where they are standing and whispers something in the man's ear. His head spins around to face Owen, removing his hand from Charlie like she is on fire and has just burnt him. He holds his hands up and walks away as quickly as he can.

Both me and Leon chuckle as Charlie glares at Owen, looking like she is ready to explode and rip his head off. But her demeanour changes when Owen tells her about me. She moves away from him, coming to my side and gives me a hug.

After the club, Owen and Leon dropped us back at the cottage; Charlie made herself comfortable on the sofa, insisting she stay the night at mine, even though I told her there was no need. I think she wanted to make sure I was okay. It was nice to not be alone that night, especially when I still couldn't shake the feeling of someone watching me. It was odd.

Closer

I'm watching you Millie. It's laughable how gullible people are. How someone you have never met will do anything for some cash. Even as they watch over you, I can get to you.

I'm here Millie. I know you feel it.

Chapter Twenty-Seven

Uneasy

Jack

"Dude it's two days until the ball, Millie has given me a list of things that need to be done today, and it's huge!" he shakes the list in my face. "She's working all day and then tonight at the pub, she can't help, we have to decorate today so the final touches can be put in place tomorrow, ready for the photographers on Saturday morning." Then, pausing for a few seconds, he says, "She has even arranged for the couples who have booked weddings with us to come round and have a look on Saturday afternoon. The woman is mad! But also awesome," eyeing me.

    I've been listening to this for the last two hours; our train ride back down from London has been slow. Well, it feels slow, with Dan groaning on like he is. I want to see Millie so badly; I know she's not dealing with all this like she should be. I just want to see her to see if she's truly okay. Owen called me and told me about the security system stuff; Charlie showed him everything. But Millie's not even mentioned it. She knows I know, but she's holding it all in. It's not good. I won't get a chance to see her until after her shift tonight. So I've been bombarding her with messages and photos of Dan stressing out. She sends me one's back of how her day is going; it's mostly coffee, painkillers and water, while she sits in the office.

Although, her pictures from last night of her and Charlie were nice to see. I got an update from Owen when they arrived home, I'm sure he's not telling me everything. Something was off when he called me, after he dropped them back at the cottage. He and Leon took off and left the B team to cover the cottage. But his update was a little shorter than normal. Something isn't right, I know if it was important, he would tell me or should tell me but I also have a feeling he is hiding something, and it's frustrating.

"We'll get it done Dan. *We* do this every year, *you and me. We* don't normally have a Millie to help us either. Remember it's our treat to all of our employees, that's why we organise it." I say, emphasising the "we" while pointing from me to him, looking down at the list she has done for us. It's a lot to do on top of the other meetings we have today.

"I've got to go and see Mike this afternoon when we get back, about the licences for the pub. There is also an issue with the brewery that he needs my help with. Will you be able to handle the Ball decorations and this list? I'll ask Mary to get a few helping hands in for us." I say to Dan as he huffs at me.

"Dan, what's wrong? You've been edgy for the last two days, what's going on?" He's my best friend. I know when something is up, even though we have seats in first class on the train, he wouldn't sit down, he's pacing and driving me insane.

"Nothing."

"Liar, tell me or I'll add about that time we went to Thailand in my best man speech." That should make him spill. It was a good story, maybe I'll add it anyway.

"Fine, but if I hear one word of that story in your speech, I'll tell Millie about the time in Wales." He grins at me, knowing I'd kill him if that ever got out. Shit, that's the only downside to him being my best mate, he knows too much!

"So… what's up with you?" I prompt him, eyeing the seat for him to sit down.

"There is something off with Em, I don't know what it is, but she has asked if I'll stop drinking with her until the wedding. It's weird, I don't like it, plus she is like horny as hell all the time. Not that I'm complaining but it's like every time she sees me. And that's a few times a day, yesterday we did it like four times. I'm literally knackered. And I have a really bad feeling in my gut about this Glen dude. Something is not sitting right with me."

"Well, that was too much info, she's my sister dude! And that's something you will have to sort out between you and her! I never want to hear words like that again from you!" I wince, moving to an easier subject. "Why doesn't she want to drink? She loves a glass or two…?" I add.

"I know right, she says it will just be better if we have a clear head over the next few weeks with everything going on."

"Umm, makes sense, but still doesn't sound like her. Do you think she is okay?" She would have told us if something was wrong. She's never been any good at faking it.

"She seems fine, her normal bossy, workaholic, organised, sexy self. I just have a feeling like something's off, I can't explain it." Sitting in the chair opposite me, he puts his head in his hands, like it's the only puzzle he can't crack.

"I'm sure it's just wedding stuff. Maybe she has a surprise planned for you? Do you have a gift for her for the morning of the wedding?" He sits up straight with a massive smile on his face, nodding at me.

"Yep, but I can't tell, she is going to fucking love it!"

"Good, now what's this feeling you have about the fuckwit Glen then?" In all the years I've known Dan, I have to admit when he has a feeling, it's usually right, he can never pinpoint what it is, but the feelings he has normally mean trouble or something unexpected. So I trust him when he tells me something doesn't feel right.

"I don't know what it is, just that it's not right, I know the police say he's in Spain, and can't find him. But I'm not so sure."

"Fuck, I hate it when you have a feeling…" My heart sinks.

"I know, but I need to voice it," he cuts me off.

An hour later, I'm on my way to see Mike. I've left Dan to his own devices with ball stuff, I just can't handle it right now. I still want to cancel but Millie refuses to let him win. I get it, but I have the safety of everyone coming to think about and it's stressing me out. I have a meeting with Owen and Leon later to talk through the final prep for the security for night, and with Dan sharing his feeling about the whole Glen thing, it has me even more on edge.

When I walk into the pub, Mike waves me over and we sit adjacent to each other at the bar. He hands me a stack of paperwork and we slowly make our way through the new licensing agreement, and the new brewery contract.

"How's Millie?" He asks when he stands to grab us both a drink from behind the bar. I know what he's getting at; everyone knows there is something going on, and Mike knows more than most about Millie's past.

"She's okay, I think. Doing what she normally does, burying herself in work, trying not to think about it," I say honestly.

"So what's happened…I know something has changed, she's putting on an act again, I can tell. Over the last month or so, she has been so different, I mean in a good way." He hands me a coffee and sits back down.

"Well to put it in a nutshell, her ex, the guy that beat her, he knows about her and me. He was the one behind the arson attack on the club in Ibiza. The police think he is in Spain but I don't know."

"Jack, that's tough! No wonder she is edgy, and working so much. I can only imagine how she feels about it all."

"Yeah, she tried to leave when she found out it was him, and it was only by accident that she saw his picture on my desk. She said it was the only way, if she left then everyone else would be safe."

"But you managed to convince her otherwise?" He sounds worried, and he should be.

"I did, for now at least," I say glumly. I'm not sure what she will do if he's not found soon.

"I'll keep an eye on her as much as I can. She is working tonight, and tomorrow night, but I'll let her leave early Friday.

She needs some rest, maybe you can plan something for the two of you?"

"That sounds like a brilliant idea, thanks Mike. And sorry to offload onto you." I shrug at him.

"It's all in the job description boss! Plus I've known you a long time. I think you're good for each other." Smiling, he picks up all the papers and puts them into the file.

"I'll send these off and get it all sorted, that should be it from now on, everything else I should be able to sort out myself."

"Thanks Mike, you're making it easy, I wish all takeovers were like this." I laugh and head for the door. The idea of doing something with Millie tomorrow night sounds great, but I think she needs to be reminded of who she has around her, of who cares for her. And with that, I dial Em's number. She always takes so long to answer the phone, it's irritating.

"Finally!" I say when she answers. And I hear her laugh.

"You know I only do it to bug you right? I know how much it annoys you." She laughs again.

"I should have known, you okay? What's this about you and Dan not drinking before the wedding? Is everything alright?"

"Everything is perfect, I just want us to have our heads together with everything going on, that's all."

"Umm…" She's lying, I can tell; something is definitely up, but she sounds happy enough, so I won't push it.

"What do I owe the call for anyway? I have a client in a few minutes." Always to the point as usual.

"Just wondered what you and Dan were up to tomorrow night? I was planning on bringing Millie around, and getting a takeaway? If that's okay?"

"Absolutely, we'll order pizza, bring pudding! What time will you be around?"

"Ace, about eight? What pudding do you want?"

"Chocolate…anything chocolate, maybe lemon?"

"I'll buy a few then, something for everyone." I laugh.

"Perfect, see you tomorrow." And she hangs up. Yep there is definitely something up with her; I'll figure it out eventually.

Just as I'm about to put my phone back in my pocket and climb into my car it rings again. Recognising the number, I answer immediately.

"Hello, Jack Lucas," I say, holding my breath a bit.

"Mr Lucas, this is DCI Rivers…"

I've tried to call Millie a few times since speaking to the police earlier but she's not answered. When I spoke to Owen, he said she had been in and out of her office all day, but she is now in a meeting with someone called Joshua Davenport. Apparently he's a fancy lawyer from London. This has me worried; *what would a big lawyer want with Millie?* Maybe it's to hold a function, but they wouldn't come down and organise it themselves; they tend to have people for that.

So when I walk into the Manor reception at two-thirty, I want to speak to Millie, I want to see her. I want to make sure she is okay, but as I walk around the desk towards Millie's office, Mary stops me in my tracks.

"Jack, you can't just walk in, she's in a meeting," she says, standing in front of me so I can't walk in.

"Mary, I own this business, I can just walk in…"

"No Jack, this meeting is personal. She asked for privacy and to not be disturbed. The guy turned up early and they have been in there ever since, well over an hour now."

"But..."

She cuts me off. "No, go and grab a coffee and I'll let her know you are here when I can."

"Fine, but let her know the police will be here at three. They have some information they want to talk to us about together."

"I'll let her know, and Jack...is everything okay?"

"It will be." I give her a small smile, then head to the ballroom to check on Dan. My phone beeps, it's a message from Owen.

> **O:** *He checks out. A family lawyer from London, a firm called Davenport and Dooly. Specialise in handling large estates.*

> **Me:** *Thanks O*

My annoyance settles a little, knowing it could be related to her parents. I don't know much about them; I know how they died, and I also know how hard it can be to lose both parents, but both at the same time must have been tough; it left her all alone.

When I reach Dan in the ballroom, he looks in a flap again, but has a smile on his face this time. I swear he lives off the drama. The place is starting to come together, tables are laid out and being set and ready to be decorated with flowers on Saturday morning, for the photographer and couples viewings in the afternoon. Our theme for this year is Masked Jungle vibes. We pick something related to music each year. Our employees are flying in from all over the world, randomly picked, so we have someone from all levels of employment. It works well, there will be almost five hundred people here on Saturday—some flying in early to make the most of the company-funded event.

"Well what do you think?" Dan says, walking over to where I stand by the door.

"It looks good, this is way more than we have ever done before. I think it's set to be our most themed event yet."

There is so much stuff going on; fake life-sized animals have been randomly placed around the room, they look amazing. The DJ Booth is a hut in the corner of the room; Max, one of our resident DJs from the club, has flown over early to set up and help out. Jeff and Audrey from the Manor are helping to set up the photo booth, and the gift bags for each guest. Millie had even hired living plants to be bought in. It's going to look awesome when it's done.

"Yeah, I know, Millie has really gone to town with this."

"I think it's been a good distraction for her. We have a meeting with the police in a bit. Let's hope it's good news, although he didn't want to tell me over the phone, and I've not been able to get in touch with Millie to tell her about it." Yes, I'm still annoyed, *why didn't she tell me?*

"Oh, the lawyer dude, yeah, they have been in there for a while. I tried to get to see her to take her to lunch but Mary is a force to be reckoned with. I was not going to get on her bad side."

"She was the same with me." I slump my shoulders a little. "Want to grab a quick drink before the DCI arrives?" He eyes me like I've gone mad, "I mean coffee, not the hard stuff, you dick." He laughs.

"I really want a beer. It's only been eight hours since she asked me to not drink with her, and it's all I can think about."

"You have issues." I laugh, lighting my mood a little.

Fifteen minutes later, with two coffees in my hand, I'm sitting waiting for Millie to come out of her office when DCI Rivers walks in the door with another officer in tow. I'm about to greet him when the office door opens and Millie steps out. It looks like she has been crying; immediately changing directions I walk over to her and wrap her in my arms..

"What's happened...are you okay?" I whisper in her ear, when I notice an older man trying to move around us. Stepping back from Millie, I extend my hand.

"Jack Lucas." He nods, and takes my hand, shaking it firmly

"Joshua Davenport, It's nice to meet you Mr Lucas, Miss Monroe has told me a lot about you, and all of which I am grateful for." I can see Millie blush, so I wink at her and she rolls her eyes at me.

"Thank you for coming all this way to see me Mr Davenport, and thank you so much for everything." She goes to shake his hand, but he pulls her in for a hug, that's odd.

"Your parents were good friends of mine, and it's good to see you looking so well. Look after yourself, I'll be in touch when it's all complete." And with that, he walks out and leaves us to it. I wrap my arms around her waist, and pull her closer, kissing her neck.

"Care to tell me what that was all about?" She shakes her head at me.

"Umm...Not yet, I need to process, but it's good, I promise." She laughs, wrapping her arms around my neck and placing her soft sweet lips on mine.

"Miss Monroe, Mr Lucas...." I hear the DCI interrupt.

She looks at me, moves back a little to look over my shoulder, "DCI Rivers, I'm sorry I didn't know you were coming?" She looks a little confused, looking between me and the officers.

"Umm...check your phone, we tried calling a few times," I tell her with a smirk. Not that I want to, but I step away from her, and gesture for the officers to walk into the office, myself and Millie follow. Millie sits at her desk and I move behind her, leaning against the wall. I'm not sure what they have to say, but I don't want it to be bad news. I can already feel the nerves coming off of Millie. DCI Rivers takes a seat opposite us, while the other officer stands in the corner.

"DCI Rivers rang a few hours ago saying he has some news on the case." Millie stands up and comes to stand next to me, and I lace my fingers with hers, feeling her tremble slightly.

"Thank you Mr Lucas, we wanted to let you know that we have found Mr Cadwell."

Millie looks at me, her eyes wide, like she is looking at me for confirmation of what they just said. Squeezing her hand a little tighter, I nod. I need more information than that, they have told us this before, yet still no arrest.

"Where was he? Do you have him in custody?"

"We don't have him in custody yet, but the Spanish authorities have arrested him. We have lots of things to deal with before we can get our hands on him, but I wanted to let you know the situation before the papers got hold of it." His face looks almost a little relieved.

"That's amazing, I…I can't believe it, I know it's not over yet, but…" She is smiling like I have never really seen before. She is beautiful. "Thank you," she says, her eyes starting to shine with tears.

I feel like a huge weight has been lifted; the pressure I was feeling over it all was almost too much to take. I can't even imagine how Millie has been handling it all. Hopefully now, we can move on. Yes there is still so much to do but if they have him, then Millie can relax and truly be herself again.

We spend the next half an hour going over what will happen next; all the while Millie holds my hand, gripping like I'm her life support, it's like she can't get her head around that it's over. She is free, from him, from her past, free to be herself without worry, free to be mine.

When DCI Rivers takes his leave, Millie tries to get back to work, but I refuse to let this moment pass by without some sort of celebration.

"Wait, Millie, just take a few minutes, let this sink in, it's over!"

"I'm not sure I quite believe it yet, I know what he said, it's amazing, but for so long….he…dominated my life, every waking moment, and even in my dreams he was there turning them to nightmares, it's hard to think that it's over just like that!" The emotion in her voice says it all, everything she has been through, everything she has tried to escape from, it is hard to believe. I can't explain the relief I feel, so I can't imagine how it is for her. Pulling her up from the chair, my fingers lace with hers, looking her in the eyes and holding her gaze.

"You don't have to worry now Millie, it's over, take tonight off? We can do something that's just for us? What do you say?" She frowns at me; I know she hates letting people down, but then she smiles.

"But there is so much to do with the ball we can't take the time off."

"I'm the boss and yes we can. Dan will handle it, we will work this afternoon, then tonight we do what we want, I'll organise it all…you need to enjoy this moment."

"Well as you're my boss in both my jobs… Okay, if it's just us. I'll ring Mike, I need to tell him I quit anyway." My face must say it all, because she smiles and pulls me in for a kiss that sets my world on fire.

"Really, you're quitting the pub?" I say as I pull away briefly.

"Yes, Oh and I should also let you know that… I'm also quitting working here too…" She kisses me again to stop me from talking, but I have to know why, so I pull back.

"What? Why?" It's all I can manage. Thoughts of her leaving run through my mind, but I wait for her answer, pushing the fear back out of my head.

"A few things have fallen into place at just the right time. I'll explain more tomorrow, but now I feel we need to celebrate in a way only we can." She leaves me hanging and walks over to the door, locking it. I'm sitting in her office chair and I watch as she turns around slowly, her back leaning against the door. Her hands come up and let her hair down, it falls like silk onto her green blouse. Her hands trail down her breasts and she undoes a few buttons just to give a peek of the black lace bra she is wearing underneath. Walking over to where I'm sitting, she unzips her skirt at the back and lets it fall to the floor, revealing stockings and suspenders, and the smallest piece of fabric covering her most intimate area. I've never seen anything so sexy in my life—the black and green making her a pure vision of beauty. Placing her hands on the arms of the chair on either side of me, she straddles me, bending over to kiss me. Her tongue slides over my lips, parting them, I let her in, loving the taste of her. My hand tangles in her soft hair, pulling her closer and deepening the kiss. Sliding my hand up between her thighs, tracing the line of her stocking with my fingertips, her moan is all I need to hear to know she wants more.

"This is the best way to celebrate with you, if you'll have me," she whispers between kisses.

"You know you're mine, Millie." My fingers trace the lace on her panties, pressing firmly to feel how wet she already is. Moving them to one side, I slide my finger inside, making her gasp and start riding my hand, as I add another finger, moving it in and out. She steps back, shaking her head at me.

"No, it's my turn." She bends down and unbuttons my trousers, tracing my hard length with her fingers, slowly pulling my zip down. I shift slightly so she can pull them down, and then she's between my legs, teasing me, her hair brushing the inside of my thighs, turning me on, making me harder. She looks me in the eyes as she takes me in her mouth, so deep it takes my breath away. My hand tightens on the arms of the chair and I watch as she sucks me, bringing me so close with every touch of her hand, tongue and lips.

"Fuck…Millie…" She sits back and I feel the loss of her lips around me. She slides her panties down her smooth legs; all I can do is watch this intelligent, beautiful woman. I know what I have to do tomorrow.

Chapter Twenty-Eight

It's Over

Millie

The last twenty-four hours have been overwhelming, confusing and the best of my life so far. My emotions are all over the place; I'm smiling one moment, and the next, I feel like crying. I can't focus on anything. I keep going back to the conversation we had with the police, everything they said. I still can't get my head around that they have him. I keep repeating it to myself to make it seem real, but until I see him in cuffs in this country, I don't really think I will believe it's happened.

The difference in Jack has been amazing, you could see him relax as soon as DCI Rivers told us. He called off the security detail that follows me and his family, and loosened the security for the ball, only having a few on standby for other reasons. Leon and Owen have been formally invited to the ball as a thank you. I know Owen is looking forward to seeing Charlie again; as for Charlie, I'm not so sure. She seems irritated by him for some reason, but it's clear he knows what he wants, and that's Charlie.

I rang Mike last night to tell him I was quitting. He was happy for me, but asked if I could still work this evening just until the night shift came in. I've given two weeks' notice at the Manor, giving Mary enough time to get someone else in. Then it's all me, my life…is my own again. Wow, just that thought alone is overwhelming. I don't have to worry about him anymore… and I'm crying again. Nope, still not real. Last night after we finished setting up for the ball, Jack whisked me off to a private dinner at an Italian restaurant called Milo's—it was stunning, old-fashioned decor but romantic as hell. He pulled out all the stops just like he did when we went strawberry picking; it was just us, and it was just what I needed.

I think I fall in love with him more every time I see him. I've never met, let alone been with anyone like him before. I'm in awe of him—he's successful, *really* successful, kind, loves his family. He's not interested in money, although he has plenty of it and he just wants the best for everyone around him. I just need to tell him how I feel, and I will tomorrow night, when we dance at the ball. I'll let him know everything, because when he looks at me, I see my whole world looking right back in those tantalising blue eyes. The whole evening was perfect. We got a little bit too excited in the restaurant; he was teasing me under the table, so we left a little early, walking home hand in hand.

I still can't believe this man wants me, but he does, so I'm taking it, well, taking him with both hands and my whole heart. We finished off with a few drinks and an early night, although there was nothing early about it.

After the last time I drank, I've kept to a limit of just a few drinks. I can't be passing out again, not like that, and if Jack finds out, well, I know he will take me to the doctors to have me checked out for every possible illness. I know what it is, it's the stress of the last few months and years all accumulating into one moment. There is nothing more to say, I've ploughed through work to keep me occupied and keep him out of my head, but now I have no reason to. I can try and enjoy my time, being me. No limits, no restrictions and no one bringing me down. I let out a deep breath, it's been so long since I was able to just breathe, without all the overwhelming thoughts that would follow. It's nice to have the space, or will be when the ball is over.

I feel a little stupid for planning to leave this weekend; I honestly thought it was the right decision. I've moved the letters to the drawer in my bedroom, to keep them safe. They don't say anything about leaving, but they show each and every one of my new friends how I feel about them and how I consider them family. Jack's is the most personal one. I know he knows a lot more than the others already, but this letter is everything I feel, everything I am unable to express after Glen crushed me. I'm not sure they will ever see the light of day again, but it was worth writing to them, even if it was for my own benefit at this point.

"Millie?" My attention snaps back to the room in hand. Like I said, I can't concentrate; I'm in a room full of people all working their asses off to help with the ball. Food has arrived and needs to be taken care of; flowers are arriving and need to be refrigerated and ready for tomorrow; guests are arriving, and my list is getting longer.

"Yes...sorry Dan...a million things running through my head right now, what do you need?" I say, wiping my eyes.

"You, Jack and Charlie are coming over to our house tonight, right?" He says like an excited puppy. This was news to me. He doesn't even mention why I was wiping my tears away. I've been doing it so much lately. "Um...yeah sure, do Jack and Charlie know?"

"Yeah, it was Jack's idea. Be there for eight? Also do you know why Em's decided we aren't allowed to drink before the wedding? I thought once I told her Glen had been caught, she would let up and give in, but she still wants to see it through."

"No idea," I cut him off, "maybe she feels like she still needs to have a clear head with all the wedding stuff. You know once this ball is over it's all wedding again, you only have two weeks left." I don't like keeping it a secret from him, but it will be worth the surprise and the look on his face when he finds out.

His face lowers, unsatisfied with my answer, and he huffs and walks off to help with the food delivery coming in. Chuckling to myself, and watching him walk away, I feel eyes on me.

"You know, don't you?" Jack sneaks up and wraps his arms around my waist, kissing the side of my neck.

"Know what?" *Play dumb Millie! You know nothing,* I say to myself with a smile.

"You know why she's not drinking don't you? Don't play games with me Millie, I can see the flush in your cheeks, it's a giveaway that you're fibbing." *How can this man know me so well already?* He spins me around to face him, looking deep into my eyes, trying to get an answer from me, seeing if I'll crack.

"I have no idea what you're talking about Jack." He kisses me, then moves his hand down to my stomach.

"Maybe one day it will be us." He rubs my stomach, chuckles and kisses me again.

"What the..." *Did he just say he wants kids with me? Oh my god, he knows about Em.* "Still no idea what you're talking about. But for us one day...yes." And he kisses me so passionately that Dan has to separate us. After trying to get our attention for what he said was at least ten minutes; I couldn't believe it. Jack just smiles at me, and that smile just gets me—how happy he is to be with me, me of all people; he loves me, for exactly who I am. For the rest of the afternoon, I watch as all the plans we have made for the ball come together. Everything is prepped with only a few small details left to put in place tomorrow morning for the big night.

When four-thirty rolls around, I watch as Dan and Jack sort out the signature cocktail for the ball. Dan looks really pissed that Jack gets to taste them while he watches. There is a twinkle in Jack's eye, knowing Dan will be ecstatic when he finds out about Em being pregnant. It warms my heart to know he will be the best uncle to that baby.

When I arrive at the pub for my last shift, Mike greets me with a huge hug, handing me a glass of champagne.

"This is to celebrate everything you have overcome in the past few months. I'm so proud of you, but I'll miss you working here," he says as we clink our glasses together.

"Mike, if you ever need me to fill in a shift, you only have to ask, you know I won't mind. You won't even have to pay me."

"That's ridiculous, how could I not pay you?" His arm flies up in the air. I watch for a minute, sipping my champagne while he rants that he would never take advantage of me like that. "I could never...and Jack would..."

I cut him off.

"Mike, I don't need the money. I've just sold my parents' house for a hell of a lot of money and I found out yesterday that the trust fund my parents set up for me, takes effect as of next week. I can assure you I don't need the money." I chuckle, feeling so secure in myself for once, I can't stop smiling.

"Are you serious? Really?" Mike's kind eyes look directly at me for confirmation; he must like what he sees because he hugs me again.

"You deserve it Millie," he whispers. "Right then, your last shift awaits you, kitchen duty, bar and glasses, if that's okay?"

"Perfect," I say, hugging him back. "Thanks for everything Mike. I mean it, you have become like a dad to me." I shrug at him and he hugs me again.

"Right, that's it, get to work before I cry, and I can't be seen crying." He gives me a brief kiss on the cheek and walks away to the office. I can't stop smiling, even as the pub becomes busy and I'm run off my feet, trying to help where I can. A few of the regulars chat with me, as I collect glasses and then suddenly, a shiver runs up my spine, that feeling's back. It's uncomfortable, creepy, almost like I'm being watched; I can't shake it as I walk through the pub.

When I walk back out from the kitchen, I can't help but actually look around—it feels so intense I can't ignore it. Picking up a few glasses from the bar, I see a glimpse of something, my stomach sinks as my hands shake so badly that the glasses drop from my hand and shatter when they hit the ground. When I look back, what I thought I saw is gone; I look round the room, but nothing. That feeling is gone and replaced with confusion and gut-wrenching fear. There is no way it could have been; standing there frozen, my reasoning kicks in; my head is all over the place, and I'm tired and emotional. Bending down to pick up the glass, I cut myself in the process. Mike comes over, taking the glass from my hand and tidying up the mess I made. I can hear him talking to me, but I don't know what he's saying. He hands me something for my hand, and wraps it around to stop the bleeding. It can't have been, there is no way it could be; I need sleep, and rest and a large drink. Putting it to the back of my mind, I carry on. *There is no way it could have been him,* I think to myself, shaking my head and those thoughts far away. *My mind is playing tricks on me. It has to be.*

Twenty minutes later, I'm saying a quick goodbye to Mike and making a call to get a taxi to take me to Em and Dan's. I wait in the bar while it arrives, trying to put what I think just happened to the back of my mind and forgetting about it as best I can. But the feeling in the pit in my stomach is still there.

I'm the last one to arrive; Em answers the door and pulls me to one side before I can get a word in.

"Does Jack know? Did you tell him?" she says, holding my arm lightly.

"I think he guessed. He's not said it out loud that he knows, but I think he does...why?"

"He's been winding Dan up since he arrived a few hours ago, supporting my decision to not drink, and he just keeps looking at me like he is about to explode." She laughs and I can't help but join in.

"Well, I best go and join in, you may have to tell him sooner...otherwise one of them will burst." We walk into the kitchen, where Charlie, Dan and Jack all sit around the island, eating pizza and drinking beer. Em offers me a glass of wine and

I take it eagerly; I drink it in one go and walk to the fridge to get a refill.

"Now I thought Jack was being mean, but you...Miss Millie...I expected better," Dan says, reaching for a beer, when Em swats his hand away. Jack just looks at me, eyebrows raised.

"It's been a weird few days, I needed that," shrugging it off. "Anyway I have a few things I need to tell you all, and I need some courage to do it." All eyes turn to me as I settle on one of the bar stools. I wasn't going to say anything but while they are all together I might as well. I sit next to Jack but look at Charlie and she comes to the other side, like she knows it's going to be hard. Jack just looks confused, but I think Charlie gets it. Taking a deep breath I let it all out.

"I want to say I'm sorry..." Jack goes to say something but I stop him. "Let me finish. Like I said, I'm sorry, all of this was my fault, I brought him into our lives, not intentionally but I did and I'm sorry, I put you all in danger. You have all become my family, my closest friends and so much more," I say, looking at Jack. He takes my hand, then frowns, noticing the new cut, but he kisses it and looks back up. "I would never want anything to happen to any of you. Over the last few months, you have all been so wonderful. You have taken care of me even when you didn't know me, and I can't thank you enough for that. It's been a crazy few days, some of the worst and best of my life, and I need you to know a few things about me."

I look at Charlie and take her hand in mine. "A year after I met Glen, both of my parents died in a car crash. It was a tragic accident, it left me vulnerable and on my own. But they left me their house in London, the house I grew up in. A few weeks ago, I sold it for more money than I ever thought possible. It was the last thing my parents gave me, but after what happened there, I could never have gone back. Then yesterday I had a meeting with my family's lawyer, where he told me I am now worth approximately…" I giggle because I still can't believe it. "Well, let's just say I'm never going to have to worry about money again." I watch as their faces turn from sympathy, to shock, to happiness. "They owned a chain of high-end department stores across the country. Little did I know, they sold them just before they died, planning on retiring early. They set up a fund for me. So here I am…this is me." The room is silent; Charlie turns to me, a massive smile on her face, and hugs me so hard.

"I'm sorry I wasn't there for you when you needed me, never again though." She smiled.

"Thank you, it was never you, I know what he said to you, and you will never apologise for something he did." I say as sternly as I can.

"Well, damn…that has to be the best ending to a story I have heard in a long time. Dan you can have one beer…" Em says. I've never seen him look so happy, or move so quickly.

They all take turns to hug me, Jack being the last. He holds my hand, playing with my fingers; he doesn't say anything, just looks at me and says, "You're going to really want to buy the cottage now aren't you?" I laugh and kiss him.

"What happened to your hand?" I just shrug and tell him. "I dropped a glass, and cut myself picking it up, clumsy." He just smiles and kisses me again.

"Sorry to interrupt things, but can we talk about weddings please? I have so much left to do, I need help." Em says. Dan's eyes light up and he grabs the wedding folder.

"Whatever you need, we'll get it done." The boys are tasked with labelling the personalised men's favours, while we do the ladies'. We are all settled in the living room when suddenly, Em picks up her phone and starts crying.

"This can't be happening! It's two weeks before the wedding, how can she do this!"

"Babe, what's wrong?" Dan looks really worried; Jack stands up and goes to sit by her.

"The florist just cancelled our order, she double booked and has gone with the other couple, how could she, what are we going to do?" She puts her head in her hands and starts crying again. Dan looks lost. I look at Charlie, I think she feels a little uncomfortable, she doesn't know them that well, but I have an idea.

"We'll sort it out Em, don't worry," Dan says, eyeing Jack.

"Charlie, help me get a few more drinks?" She looks a little suspicious but gets up and follows me to the kitchen anyway. When the door closes behind us I grab her and just look at her.

"You're acting weird, why are you looking at me like that?" She moves to the fridge and gets out more wine and beer for us all.

"You can help," I say, and take some of the bottles from her, putting them on the island.

"I am helping, I've got the wine."

"No, I mean you can do the flowers for her!"

"Oh…um…you're right, I can, I know I could, do you think she would let me?" I smile, getting excited for her, her first job as a florist.

"There is only one way to find out, walk in there and tell her you can help." She is nervous, I can tell but this would be amazing. "She will love that it's you!" My smile widens, the more I think about it the more excited I get.

"Okay!" She picks up the wine, and I take the beer for Jack and the cokes for Dan and Em.

Charlie walks in first and sets the wine on the table, I refill our glasses and hand Em her Coke. She's still upset, I can't blame her, I'd be if it were me. Charlie sits on the floor in front of Em, and places her hand on her knee; when she looks up all she says is, "I'll do it, I'll make your wedding flowers." Jack, Dan and Em all look up at the same time.

"What?" They all say together

"I'll make your wedding flowers, that's why I quit my job in London, I've been training to be a florist, I've bought the shop in the town, I have all my suppliers ready and waiting for orders, I just need to set it all up. You would be my first official client and I'd be honoured if you would have me." Wow, I'm going to cry, I'm so proud; with everything she's going through, to do this is so kind of her.

"YES! I'll have you, oh my...fucking hell...you're a wedding saver!" Em shouts and we all laugh, pleased the situation has been resolved so quickly.

"Right girls we have stuff to organise, I'll show you what I'm after, will you have enough time?"

"I have plenty of time on my hands, I got the keys and have moved into the flat above the shop, so I can start tomorrow. Show me what you need." The smile on Em's face says it all.

With that, Em jumps up and grabs another folder. Inside are all the decorations and ideas for the wedding day—buttonholes, flower arches, flower displays, centrepieces, bouquets and flower crowns. There's so much, I would have no idea where to start; Charlie on the other hand, just takes pictures and nods like it's nothing. She even starts to add suggestions about alternatives and add-ons that Em could have, and she agrees to it all.

"I'll cover the cost of it all Charlie, just send me the bill. Do you need anything upfront?" Jack chimes in, a while later.

"I'll speak to my suppliers first and let you know, thanks Jack."

"If this goes well Charlie, we would consider you for the Manor's flowers. We have a weekly order with a company about an hour away, but I'd rather use local if I can." Jack adds, making the whole situation feel even better. Her face lights up, like she can't believe her luck.

"Wow, Jack, that's amazing, thanks!" We all settle into the sofa, still doing the favours, adding labels to bottles, chatting about nothing when Charlie says, "I hear you own a club in Ibiza Jack?"

"Yep, sure do, it's under refurbishment at the moment, but hopefully we'll open in a month or so."

"I love Ibiza, we went once, do you remember Mil? It was a while back, but we had the best time. Dressed up as superheroes one night too, it was hilarious." I can feel my cheeks flush, oh I remember all right, Jack just smiles that smile, knowing Charlie has no idea, it was him I slept with, I hope to god she doesn't.

"I remember you disappeared for an entire day." *Oh god, no.* "The night after we dressed up, we were going home that day too. I had no idea where you were, only a text from you saying you were okay, and you would be back later." *Please don't say anything else.* Jack is trying his hardest to conceal a smile, it's not working.

"Where did you go Millie?" Jack smirks, I'm not sure it's possible but I can feel the heat in my face. I must be bright red.

"Well, all she told me was that she went to see the guy that helped her out the night before, and ended up having the best sex of her life…" *Why oh why,* I bury my face in my hands, this woman, *I'm going to kill her.* But I can't help but giggle so I'll play along. "I mean can you imagine our Millie, sneaking off and having hot sex with a total stranger?" She smirks at me. I'd really forgotten how inappropriate she could be sometimes.

"Well it was one of those one-time things." Jack raises his eyebrows at me as I say it.

"A one-time thing, really?" he questions.

"Yep, he was hot, but he knew it, wasn't like he was relationship material."

"Oh really?" he says mockingly, "not relationship material, but the best sex you ever had?" Of course he picked up on that bit.

"Well I'll never forget that day we had together, it was incredible."

"A whole day together?" He questions again, it's so hard not to laugh.

"You sound jealous, Jack," Dan says, eyeing the pair of us.

"Jealous? Me? Maybe," Jack smiles, winking at me. I head into the kitchen and listen to them all talking. Dan and Em are in deep conversation with Charlie once again.

Leaning against the sink, I take a long drink of water. I need to cool off and get my head back together after tonight. We have a long day tomorrow, and I want to be on top form, just in case something needs to be done, or has been forgotten to be done.

"So best sex you ever had?" Jack says, walking into the kitchen.

"Like I said it was incredible, a day I won't ever forget. Do you know how often I dream of that day? I push myself off the side and walk over to him, placing my hands on his chest, warm and hard.

"You're not the only one Millie."

"Do you remember this?" I ask, lifting my top and pulling my jeans down a little to reveal my tattoo.

"I do." He traces it with his finger, sending electricity through me.

"Well, do you remember what I said about it?" Stealing his fingers, I hold them over my lizard tattoo.

"Yeah. It's been bugging me, trying to figure out what the lizard could mean. It represents one of the most amazing times of your life, I just wish I had been part of it." I brush his fingers with mine, looking down at where our hands touch.

"You were, this represents Ibiza, you, of what you did to me that day, what we did. How you made me feel, I've never felt like that with anyone else." His hands grip my hips, pulling me against his hardness; I can feel him already and I want him now. I slide my hand between us, taking him in my hand through his trousers; he groans, and presses into me harder. I look up and kiss his jaw, feeling the day's stubble beneath my soft lips, the warmth of his skin sending shivers down to my core.

"The way you made me come, over and over again," I whisper to him, gliding my hand up and down his erection. His hands move me away just enough so he can undo my jeans, and as soon as they are open, he slides his skilful hand down inside my panties. I'm wet, *really* wet, ready for him and only him.

"Fuck…come with me," he says, removing his hand. He leads me to the door on the right, and as soon as we are in, he wastes no time. His hands pull my jeans down to my knees, working his own just as quickly. Pulling my t-shirt up and the cup of my bra down, he takes my exposed nipple in his mouth and sucks so hard, it takes my breath away. His skilful fingers work my clit in a smooth circular motion, my grip tightens on his cock and he groans louder with each stroke; he feels smooth and hard as steel, it's intoxicating. The way I feel about him, I never thought it would be possible, but he is everything.

"I need to fuck you Millie, turn around." I do just that, bracing myself against the wall, ready for him. His fingers ease into me from behind. "Jack!" He speeds up, pulling my hips back slightly to get a better angle. I feel the loss of his fingers but as quick as they are gone, he pushes his cock against my wetness, making me moan, teasing me. His finger presses my clit the same time he slams into me—I see stars, the pleasure, the feeling I have, the sensations, it's all too much, I can't hang on.

"Fuck, I love that you have that tattoo. It's like my mark on you, it's the sexiest thing you have ever said to me." I feel my walls clamp down around him, and I have to bite my own lip to stop myself from screaming as my orgasm takes over, wave after excruciating wave of pure bliss. He thrusts into me with his own need coming faster; tears come to my eyes, with the overwhelming feelings I have been needing to get out. In just a few short months, this man has turned my life around, and been there for me in ways I could never imagine. And just when I think it couldn't get any better, another wave hits, and tears spill over— I'm lost in him. As he finds his own release, he braces himself on the wall with one hand, supporting me with the other; I'd fall if it wasn't for him. My legs tremble, my breathing ragged. He pulls out and spins me around, kissing me so slowly, his hands cupping my face, while pressing me into the wall.

"I love you, everything about you, I'd do anything for you." His words come out in whispers against my lips. And I feel them deep in my soul. But just as I go to say them back, he steps away, helping me pull my jeans back up. My face is still wet with tears that he can't see in the darkness of the room.

"Jack…I…" Once again I just can't say them out loud. And more tears fall for the unspoken words, what I have.

"Are you crying? Oh shit Millie, are you okay? Did I hurt you?" He cups my cheek, wiping the tears as they fall.

"No…God no…I just…I…"

"I know you love me Millie…"

"You do? But…"

"I also know how hard it would be for you to say those words to me. Like I said, I'll wait forever if I have to." His thumb brushes my cheek and wipes the tears away. He kisses me again, and I melt into him, hoping he can feel just how much I want to say those three simple words to him.

"Now…we need to get out of this room before anyone sees, and knows what we did in my sister's laundry room." I chuckle and leave the room, Jack holding my hand, then giving my ass a quick squeeze before I head for the toilet, to compose myself for the remainder of the night.

Chapter Twenty-Nine

A Split Second

Jack

The sunlight hurts my eyes when I open them. We were a little distracted last night when we got back, we must have forgotten to close the blinds.

I stretch out and find Millie's warm, naked body wrapped in the bed sheet. She looks beautiful and so at peace when she sleeps now. There had been times when she would wake from a nightmare crying and panicking, but now her face is restful, buried into the pillow, her flaming red hair splayed out and slightly tangled. The crisp white sheet wrapped around her legs, leaving her top half exposed, her soft breasts begging to be touched, her rose bud nipples, wanting to be teased. She looks like a goddess, and all I want to do is worship her. I watch for a while, just taking her in. *Beautiful.*

"It's creepy when you watch me sleep," she smiles, not opening her eyes, moving towards me, her head resting against my chest.

"I enjoy it though, I love watching you look so peaceful, and beautiful." Her hand trails circles over my chest, her fingers light against my skin.

"Mmm." I can't resist her, pulling her in close. I match what she is doing, trailing my fingers over her shoulder, waist, hip and over the curve of her stomach.

"Mmm...that feels good, if you carry on like that, we'll have a repeat performance of last night," she giggles as I slide my hand down her thigh, lifting her leg so it's draped over mine. My cock is already hard, just thinking about what we did last night.

"I wouldn't mind a repeat of last night…" I position myself so she can feel how hard I am against her, but she wiggles away from me.

"We have way too much to get through today, plus if we repeat what we did last night, I won't be able to move afterwards." She smiles and climbs out of bed; I watch as she walks naked to the bathroom. Cold shower it is then or I could join her in the shower. I quickly get my ass out of bed and walk to the bathroom; the shower is already on. I stand in the doorway, watching as she washes her hair. Everything she does turns me on, it's hard to concentrate on anything else when she is around.

Opening the shower door, I step in, just as she is rinsing the shampoo out of her hair. She smiles at me when she sees me, shaking her head slightly, she knows she wants me just as bad as I want her.

"You're relentless," she says when I take her in my arms, hot water soaking us both.

"I know, but everything you do makes me react like this, so it's your own fault really." She laughs when I poke her with my erection. It's music to my ears, I'll never tire of that sound. Her laugh trails off when I kiss her, my hand instantly finding the hot wetness between her thighs. Pushing her up against the shower wall while kissing down her neck to her chest, I take a hard nipple in my mouth and graze it with my teeth. When I slide two fingers into her, her gasp just makes me harder and more determined to make her come, twice if I have my way. Pressing my thumb against her clit I move my fingers slowly in and out, building her up, tugging on her nipple, she moans my name and I can tell she's close. Curling my fingers slightly inside her, I reach that spot that takes her over the edge. Gripping my shoulders, she leans her head back against the wall, while she rides the orgasm, moving her hips in time with my fingers,

"Jack...oh god..." When I tug her nipple one last time, she explodes around my fingers. She's so god damn sexy when she comes, I love it. I love her.

I replace my fingers with my hardness. Lifting her up, her legs wrap around my waist. Teasingly, I slowly push myself into her; I can feel the aftershocks of her orgasm around me. With one hand on the wall and one hand wrapped around her waist, I thrust deeply into her, savouring the moment. When I start thrusting into her, I'm lost in the pleasure, with my own need taking over, and Millie taking me as deep as she can. It's fucking heaven.

"I'm not going to last long, Millie...fuck you feel so good."

"Harder…" she says. "I'm so close, harder!" I slam into her, feeling her walls tighten around me with each thrust, my own cock twitching, aching for release. I'm a goner; nothing makes sense anymore, the feeling of her, fucking her, loving her. Spilling myself into her as she comes with me, I lean against her, taking her mouth with mine, as she drains every last drop from me; I can barely stand. Hell, I can barely breathe. That was…fucking hell…perfect. Hot, sexy, wet and mine, in all the best ways. "Fuck…this is what you do to me," I say as we untangle our bodies. She kisses me, like she never wants to let go.

"That's what *you* do to me," she says. We spend the next few minutes lazily washing each other. I know we have a shit ton of stuff we need to do today, but fuck me, I never want to leave this woman's side. I hope one day she realises just how much she means to me, and how I could never hurt her. Tonight, might just be the night.

The day passes in a flash of frenzied activity—everyone is doing something, from photographers to wedding couples, more guests arriving and last-minute prep. Millie has been on top of it all, making sure everything is perfect. Everyone knows what they need to do, and by three o'clock, I see it's all done. Millie's at one of the tables off to the side of the room, looking over her lists to make sure everything's done. Dan and I have been working on my speech; it's one of the few times I actually get to speak to some of my employees in the same room. So it has to be good; some of these people have been working with me for years, while others, only a few months.

Dan says my speech is too serious, which is why he adds in what I can't, a lighter side to my serious nature. Always has done, in any situation. Even when my mom passed away when I was eight, leaving me and Em with Dad, who did his best. Or when Dad was diagnosed with cancer when I was seventeen, and passed away two years later, leaving me and Em heartbroken. But Dan was always there making me feel better, in the way only Dan can, witty and clueless.

"All done. You need to practise so you don't have to look at it too much. What time's the speech?" Placing a printed copy in front of me, I fold it and place it in the inside pocket of my suit jacket. I'll look at it later.

"Eight, just before everyone's seated for dinner." Millie chimes in, "We need to head off soon and start getting ready, I'm so excited. Oh, you need to be one of the first to welcome everyone," she says.

An hour later, Millie climbs back into my car, after getting her things to get ready at Em's. Dan and I have to go back to the hotel for six to start welcoming everyone, and hand the gift bags as we go, so the girls are getting ready at Em's and coming together later on.

"Sometimes I think I've lost my mind." She laughs to herself when getting back into the car.

"What makes you say that?" I turn to frown at her as I start the car back up.

"Lately, I've been misplacing things, well not really misplacing things, but I could have sworn I got all my stuff ready for tonight, all ready on the bed, just to pick up and go, but I must have dreamt it as nothing was as out. I hadn't done it. It's weird, but I've had a lot on my mind lately. It's not the first time either," she sighs, fastening her belt as I pull off the drive.

"That's true, what else has happened?" She spent the next fifteen minutes telling me all the little stories about the coffee, her stuff being in odd places, the key bowl moving and clothes being put back when she thought she got them out ready. She laughs at herself, but the information sits in the pit of my stomach, making me feel uneasy.

"Well, in two weeks I won't have to worry so much, I'll be full-time self-employed launching Milliecan." *I love the name of her business, it's everything it needs to be, and it's a big fuck you to Glen,* I think internally, smiling to myself.

"You have had a rough few weeks, it makes sense. Tiredness and stress can do strange things to a person, even one as smart and beautiful as you," but even as I say it, something feels off. I don't like the feeling I have about what she's said.

Arriving back at the Manor, Dan heads to check in with the events team and the staff on duty tonight, while I head over to Owen and Leon in the bar. I need to check the security for tonight. It won't get out of hand, but we need to make sure everyone is safe, drunk or not. They are still my employees, and I'm responsible for them all.

As I approach, I can see they are having a hushed but heated discussion. Leon, looking really pissed off, sat on the edge of the chair, leaning over his knees. He was pointing an accusing finger at Owen, who had his head in his hands, looking sorry for himself. I only catch the end of the conversation.

".... you're in the wrong, you need to tell him the truth…" He stops when he sees me. *What is that about?* You never see the two of them like this, that's why they make such a good team, and why I hired them.

"Everything okay? Tell who what?" I ask. Owen just looks at me, sighs and asks me to sit down.

"Shit man, I fucked up." Owen's head lowers, running his hands through his hair and over his face. My stomach sinks a little more, he never fucks up.

"What's happened, tell me now!" My voice only raised a little but enough to let them know I was already pissed. I knew something was up, I should have…

"It's Millie," Owen interrupts my thoughts "The night she went out with Charlie, well, something happened, I should have told you, but she asked me to keep it quiet."

"I fucking knew you didn't tell me everything. What the fuck happened Owen? It was your job to keep her safe!" I grind out through gritted teeth, clenching my hands into fists. I watch him as he takes a deep breath and gives Leon a nervous look to the side.

"I think she was drugged in the bar; I don't know how. We were watching her all the time, no one other than her and the bartenders touched her drinks. When she went to the toilet, she locked the door behind her, when she didn't come back out a few minutes later, we had to break the door down to get in, she had been unconscious on the floor…" There are too many people around for me to lose my shit right now, but I can feel my temper rising.

"Outside, now!" I almost yell at them, pointing to the door leading to the garden. They both rise and follow me out; once outside, I lose my shit. Grabbing Owen by his shirt, shoving him hard against the wall and getting in his face. "What the fuck, man! You prick!" I scream in his face. Leon places a hand on my arm, but the look I give him has him stepping away. I know deep down these two would beat my ass, I'm a big guy, but these two are trained Soldiers, but the way I feel right now has me imagining I could kick their ass.

"How could you let that happen?" My mind is racing with all the possibilities of what could have happened to her.

"She said she wasn't drugged and that she just had too much to drink, but we checked and she hadn't had that much, she said she just felt sick. She locked the door for some privacy, but before she did anything, she blacked out, only waking up when she heard us kicking the door in. I checked her over, it was weird. Her eyes were normal, but there was definitely something not right. I'm sorry we…I should have told you, but Millie didn't want you to worry, she said you had other things on your mind, much bigger things than her passing out." I can't take in the words he's just said… *what if she was drugged, what if there is something wrong with her…I couldn't handle it if she…Fuck.*

"You should have told me, what if there is something wrong with her, what if she's ill? Was it drugs? Can you be sure?" I let go of him, and he leans back against the wall in defeat. I can't have my staff seeing me like this, so I step away.

"No, I can't be sure, but what else could it be? She didn't have that much to drink."

"If you would've told me, I would have found out, taken her to hospital, got her checked out."

"She didn't want to go to the hospital, I get the feeling she hates them." She does, I know she does, but it's inexcusable to have not told me about this, to have put her at risk like that.

"I can't do this now, I'll deal with you tomorrow, just make sure the B team is on it." I walk away before I do something I regret; Leon catches up with me, before I walk through the doors.

"It's been killing him not telling you, but Millie didn't want you to know. Don't be too hard on him. I'm sorry, mate." He plants his huge hand on my shoulder and walks back over to Owen, who is sitting down on the outdoor sofa, head in hands.

Fuck, I've got a few minutes before my speech, and I need to calm down. I've been talking to anyone to get my mind off what Owen has just told me. But I just can't let it go. Everything seems to be making me think that something is not right. Dan's bad feeling, Millie's misplacing and forgetting stuff, now Owen and Leon admit that Millie might have been drugged. I know I can't do anything about it now, but I think I'll have Owen and Leon look into the police case for me, see what they can find out. I quickly send them a message asking them to do so, and head towards the back doors of the stage.

Millie and Em arrived about an hour ago and I've not been able to speak, hold or even touch her all night and it's driving me crazy. I know she's here but we keep missing each other, getting pulled in different directions. I keep watching her from across the room, she looks like the goddess she is in that emerald green dress, fucking sexy as hell. Images of what we did while she wore the dress last time flick through my mind, her bent over in the kitchen, her smooth skin against mine. My dick is already straining to get out of my tux trousers. I can't think about that right now; going on stage in front of my employees with a hard-on is not ideal. And god help it if I see another man try and chat her up, if it carries on, I'll have to make an announcement in my speech, telling everyone hands off she's mine. She would hate it. I smile.

I'm backstage when Dan stands by my side. "Ready for the speech of the year?" he teases.

"I should be, I do it enough," I respond, pulling the speech out of my pocket. I walk on stage when the MC announces my name, and the music turns down low. There are wolf whistles, friends shouting my name, and even some whoops. Makes me smile every time. I love this bit of my job.

In the sea of faces, I spot Millie, as soon as I walk to the front of the stage. My hand reaches for the small box I have in my pocket. Checking, for what feels like the hundredth time, it's still there. When I look around the rest of the ballroom, I'm surprised I can't see Em, she loves to heckle me when I do these things and she said she would be there in the front row.

As the speech goes on, I've already thanked everyone for all their hard work, I've given them jokes, told them how well we are doing, and that it would not have happened if it was not for them. I've already presented the funny award, for the person who makes the most stupid mistakes, and the best dressed of the evening. Everyone seems to be having a good time. My eyes have been on Millie for most of the speech. I watch when she tenses up, looking at her phone, as all of the fun leaves her eyes. She glances at me and then I watch her walk out of the room, phone pressed against her ear. I feel my phone vibrate in my pocket, frowning a little, is she calling me? Why would she do that? Nodding over at Dan, I nod towards Millie; he just shrugs and carries on listening to my...well, our speech.

Just as I'm about to announce the employee of the year a few minutes later, I look at Dan and see he's not there; it's odd we always present the award together. The next moment, I see Owen and Leon running through the crowd. Owen looks at me and mouths, "It's him, he's here." My world stops—it all happens in slow motion—my heart stops, then speeds up again. I run but my legs won't move fast enough, leaping off the stage, everyone moves out of my way, and the room goes silent. Running in the direction of the door, following Owen and Leon through the crowd, Leon splits off in a different direction, heading to the front of the building through the side door. He's big but my god, can that man move! Still running, my heart is racing at a million beats a minute, I don't know what's happening or what to expect, but then I hear a loud bang! *Fuck was that a gun shot?* Everyone around me screams and people hit the floor. They push away from where the noise has come from; it's making it harder for me to get out. When I manage to get through, I slam into the door, sending it almost off its hinges, almost falling as I turn towards the noise. That's when I see them.

He has her.

The only thing I can think is, I need to get to her, keep her safe. I run for him, but I'm held back by Owen.

"You son of bitch…" I scream, but stop when Owen whispers in my ear.

"He has a gun. Don't piss him off any more than necessary, we'll handle it. Leon's out front, everyone is coming." Looking around, I see Dan, Em wrapped in his arms, crying.

"It's okay Jack," Millie says, looking at me. Her voice is calm, but I can see her hand clenched at her side, knuckles white. *What should I say?* I feel helpless, the woman I love is in deep shit right now, and I can't help her. *I have to help her, I'll never forgive myself if she…if anything happens, no I can't go there, it won't happen.* I try my hardest to fight against Owen again; he is stronger than he looks, but I have to try. I can't just watch this happen; I know he wants to hurt her.

"Jack...Stop..." she says, looking me in the eye "Don't." How can she expect me not to fight for her.

"Did you get my flowers Emilie? I wanted you to know I was here. I've been here all along watching you, as soon as I found out you were fucking *him.*" He looks me up and down like I'm a piece of shit on his shoe.

"You don't get to be happy Emilie, you took everything from me!" He grabs her harder. *What does he mean? She took everything?* She had nothing when she got here. I saw it for myself.

"You humiliated me! You'll regret leaving, you ruined everything! You'll fucking pay for everything you've done!" Glen's eyes are wild, he spits the words like they are pure venom on his lips. He's lost control. The hate he has for her shows in every way, with every word he speaks.

Something has to happen now, before he can hurt her. Then I see it, I see blood—the deep gash running down her side. That bastard! He's fucking cut her...badly. My blood runs cold; I start shaking, my anger and fear coming through! He's going to kill her.

Chapter Thirty

Sickness

Emma

"I'm so excited you're here, I've missed getting ready with the girls," I say, hugging Millie as soon as she walks through the door. Not giving her a chance to even breathe a word.

"I'm in need of some serious girl time, not being able to talk about the baby is killing me. I'm not sure I can hold off telling everyone much longer. Plus I'm starting to feel sick, morning sickness is kicking in, but luckily it's not that bad, yet." I know Dan knows something's up, I think to myself but he has no idea, it's funny really. I see him watching me, trying to figure out what's wrong. Jack knows, I know he does, he's not said anything to me yet, but the way he has been on my side about not drinking is a definite giveaway. Plus he's been winding Dan up and it's hilarious to watch them banter the way they do. They are going to be the best Dad and Uncle this kid could possibly ever wish for. I'm so lucky to have them in my life.

"I've got a bottle of Prosecco ready upstairs for you, and some Nosecco for me, nibbles and snacks too, I may have gone overboard just a little," I say, pulling her behind me up the stairs. She laughs at me. I'm like an excited kid at Christmas. I've not really been out much since the hen do, or the dress fitting. Only to the pub, but after the whole Jane situation, I've not wanted to. It's put me off going out, I mean, if she can do something like that to Millie, then what is she capable of doing to me? If it wasn't for Millie, then she would have hit me when we were having drinks after the dress fitting. Why Millie stepped in, I have no idea, I'm grateful she did, but I could have handled it. Janes tried to get in touch a few times since then, but I've not answered. I don't want or need someone like that in my life. Or making trouble for Jack and Millie. They both deserve to be happy.

"Wow, really? That's awesome, let's start shall we? I need a drink after the week I've had. Can I take a shower before we pop the Prosecco?"

"Sure, the last door on the right, towels are in there," I say, pointing to the door and heading to mine and Dan's room. I've set up my room so we can both use the mirror and hair stuff, nibbles and prosecco chilled on the bedside table. I'm just finishing my makeup when she walks in, wearing joggers and a vest top, her hair wrapped in a towel at the top of her head.

"Perfect outfit for the ball." I laugh, handing her a glass of prosecco.

"That's what I thought, I might add some fluffy socks, maybe some slippers. At least I know no one will be wearing the same as me." She giggles, twirling around like she's showing her outfit off.

I love the lightness she has; she makes everyone around her feel welcome. It's slightly unreal how close we have become since she moved down here. It's like she has always been part of our lives.

"Hit me with all the baby talk!" she says after taking a long sip of her Prosecco. "I know it's been killing you not being able to." She says, and that's all it takes, it flows out while we get ready, everything I've been secretly reading, cute outfits I've been buying and hiding. I know it's only been a few weeks but I never realised how much I wanted to be a mum. A mini-Dan would be amazing.

"I've even started sorting out the smaller spare room, it's almost empty. And Dan's not even questioning it," I complain, shaking my head, like he should figure it out.

"He must think you want to decorate it," she states, taking the towel off her hair.

"Yeah, but this time it will be cute stuffed toys, cots and rocking chairs." I laugh, knowing Dan will be just as excited as I am about the baby's room.

"Men! Sometimes I wonder what goes on in their heads," Millie says and we laugh together.

"I need more snacks," I say as I stand up and reach over for the crisps.

"You do realise we are having a massive three-course meal in less than two hours, right?" I should be offended really but I'm not. I'm hungry and it keeps the sickness at bay.

"Oh my god, I know, but the hunger never stops, it's like they say, I'm eating for two now." She smiles at me, shaking her head and sets about doing her hair. Catching a glimpse of the dress bag she brought in; I wonder what it's like.

"Can I see your dress? And then can I do your hair? Is that weird?" I feel like she's my younger sister! I've always wanted one. I tried to dress Jack up when we were younger but he was having none of it.

"No, it's not weird, and yes you can do both." Standing up, she walks to the wardrobe where she hung the dress bag and unzips it. The most beautiful emerald green silk dress hangs there. It is stunning, vibrant and so soft. The perfect colour to set off of her hair.

"Wow, it's stunning Millie. So soft. I bet you look a million dollars in it, and that slit up the side, well we all know what Jack's going to think. Oh shit, I shouldn't have gone there. That makes me feel a little sick. I forgot he's my brother for a moment." She laughs and blushes next to me. I take it down from the wardrobe and hold it in front of her.

"Can I see yours? Would that be okay?" she says, nodding at the other garment bag on the back of the door.

"Sure, go ahead, it's nothing like yours, in fact I think I'm a little jealous." I shrug.

"Don't be ridiculous, you would look amazing in a bin bag, I'm sure it's spectacular." When she opens the bag, I remember just how much I love that dress. It's not the first time I've worn it, but it's been a long time. It's pale yellow, and very fitted, it has a bodice in a sweetheart neckline, with diamonds running down from the top left to the bottom right of the dress.

"Em, it's magnificent! I'm lost for words at how beautiful this is!" And she really is; her face is taking it all in, tracing the diamonds with her fingers.

"I thought I would get it out for one last wear, I do love it," I say, running my fingers over the satin material.

"Anyway, enough chit-chat, we need to get ready…Shall we put your hair up?" Waving her towards the chair by the mirror. "I may even have some bling we can put in for you."

Just over an hour later, we are all set and ready to go, looking like we have stepped out of a movie set. There is a beep outside, just as we take the last sips from our glasses and apply a little more lipstick, letting us know the car Jack ordered for us is here. I can't believe how quickly that went.

Stepping out of the car, we walk up the few steps that lead to the main door, our arms linked. It's such a beautiful night, warm and still bright outside. When the light dims later on, Millie tells me they have set the terrace up to have fairy lights and lanterns. I can't wait to see it; it's going to look magical and so romantic.

As we walk into the reception area, some of the staff nod in our direction, as Mary comes over looking amazing in a floor-length deep red gown.

"Well, don't both of you look absolutely beautiful!" She beams, giving us both a small hug.

"The boys are still greeting guests as they arrive in the ballroom. I've just seen your friend as well, I'm sorry I can't remember her name."

"Charlie?" Millie Says

"Yes, that's it, she's just gone to the bar."

"Thanks Mary, you look so elegant in that dress." She rolls her eyes a little

"Elegant is not a word I would ever describe myself as, but thank you Em. Now go and have some fun, you both deserve to let your hair down a little". She smiles and waves us off.

We catch small glimpses of the boys for the next half an hour, but don't get a chance to talk to them—everyone wants to talk to the boss. And as Dan is second in command, they love him too! Charlie walks up to us at the bar, wearing a dress that blows your mind. It's fitted at the top, strapless, then flows down over her hips, where it falls shorter at the front and trails behind her, in a sea of pastel blue and gold. She orders a double gin and tonic and drinks it in one go. We share a look that says, *oh shit*.

"Something wrong Charlie?" Millie asks

"Nope nothing, just need to renounce men for a while, they are all dickheads," she replies, then orders another along with a few shots, and drinks them all. Millie looks at me apologetically. So I take the hint and leave them to it.

"I'm off to find Dan, make sure he's not drinking and all that." I think Charlie needs her friend right now.

Ten minutes later, I find Dan in the DJ booth, chatting away. When he sees me, his eyes widen, he stops talking and walks towards me, looking me over like he can't believe what he sees.

"How did I get so lucky to have a beautiful woman like you agree to marry me?"

His arms lace around me, bringing me in for a kiss that sets me on fire within seconds.

"Carry on like that and we won't make it to the dinner," I say, while he twirls me around, taking me in.

"You look hot in that tux, I think you need to wear it more often." He smiles and kisses me again, holding me close.

"I'm sorry but I have to find Jack, I need to get him on stage in ten minutes," Pulling a sad face, I step to the side, gesturing for him to pass.

"Make sure you find me after the speech, I'll be the one heckling him in the front row." He lets out the laugh I love. He intertwines his fingers with mine, bends down and kisses my knuckles, looking up at me.

"Em, I'll find you." Those words are full of want, his lips twitch into a sexy smile as he leaves me standing there, I hear him whisper to himself, "Luckiest man alive", when in reality, I'm the lucky one having him in my life. Then I realise I'm standing by myself in a ballroom full of people. I need to find Millie, get her to come and stand next to me while I heckle Jack during his speech. It's something I have always done, he can be so serious sometimes, I like to lighten the mood, tease him. A perk of being his sister I suppose, I can get away with it.

The bar is almost empty when I walk in, just a few stragglers waiting to get a drink before heading into the ballroom. I can't see Millie. I must have missed her. I sigh, it's no fun being at a ball by yourself, and not drinking. I know when the speeches are done, it will be all of us together, but right now, I want to have some fun. And just like that, it's like my body says…fun, *you do realise you're pregnant, don't you?* A wave of nausea hits me, worse than I've felt before; it's different from being sick, it's like you feel it in your stomach, but it stays in your throat. I thought it was called "morning" sickness, for goodness sake. Grabbing a glass of water from the bar, I make my way outside, through the double doors, to the patio area. The breeze cools my skin as soon as I step out, soothing me a little. I place my hands on the wall, leaning my head against the cool bricks, taking slow, steady breaths, it won't last long, a few minutes and it will go hopefully, I don't want to miss Jack's speech.

"Hello Emma," a voice I don't know says from behind me. No one calls me Emma anymore; it was always something my parents called me when I was in trouble, and that was a lot. Lifting my head up a little, I start to turn around when a hand shoves me against the wall. My head grazes the brick with the force he's using, my cheeks stinging from pressure.

"What the fuck, what do you think…" My words die out, when I not only see but I feel the cold hard nozzle of a gun pressed to my side. I freeze, I don't know what to do, my body shivers, but this time it's not from the cold, it's from the uncontrollable fear that runs through me.

"You may not know me, but I know all about you and your sweet fucking little family." He breathes down my neck pressing the gun harder into my side, his words are like ice on my skin, spiteful and venomous.

"Wh…who are you?" That's all I can manage.

"It's time for her to pay, and you're going to get her for me." He laughs in my ear, but there's nothing funny about the way he says it.

"Who..?…I don't know what you want…b…but…"

I stop as his hands clutch the back of my hair, pulling me backwards. It stings as he pulls it harder, reaching around with the gun in his hand and grabs my purse.

"Get your phone out and unlock it," I reach for my bag, but my hands are shaking badly.

"Hurry up!" he demands, "otherwise it won't just be her I get rid of tonight." His words make me rush, *who does he mean?*

What if…no I can't go there, oh my god, my baby…Dan doesn't even know.

Tears start to spill over my cheeks as the seriousness of the situation sets in. When I finally find my phone in the bottom of the bag, I unlock it and go to hand it to him. But he presses the gun harder into my side, twisting it a little "No, send a message to Emilie…Tell her I'm here, and that if she loves you and wants to see you're not hurt, she will trade places."

"No…" It's not a protest, it's disbelief that the man holding a gun to my side is him. Glen.

"Oh yes…Even better, let's take a good old picture, shall we? What better way to surprise her, her life for yours!" He takes the phone from my hand, slides his hand from my hair and moves it slowly, wrapping his cold hand around my neck, turning me around to face him. I close my eyes, I don't want to see this, but curiosity gets the better of me, and when I open them, the look of pure evil stands before me. Dark hair, dark eyes, pale skin, he looks like he's not slept, the redness around his eyes; he's dirty too, like he's been sleeping rough. Then the words come out before I can stop them.

"You piece of shit…I won't do it, she's happy…I won't let her do it. No." I cry, this can't be happening, not now.

"She doesn't deserve to be happy." He raises his hand with the gun and strikes the side of my face with the handle of it. I try to scream but he shoves his hand over my mouth, and pushes me against the wall so hard all the breath leaves my lungs. The gun moves up, coming into contact with the swelling of my cheek and he takes a picture of me, pressed against the wall. I don't know what's happening, but I feel so unbelievably sick, but this time, it's not the baby making me nauseous.

"Now send that message to her, tell her it's your life or hers…or you'll see what the other end of this gun can do." Pure hatred for her, that's all I can hear. I try to protest again, but he moves the gun under my chin, closing my eyes for a brief second. I wish or even pray that someone finds us, so I don't have to bring Millie out here. But when they open, it's still just me and him. The evil that stands before me and his gun, pressed so hard under the soft skin of my chin, I can feel the bruise forming already. He presses the phone into my hand; I don't want to do this. I cry silently, *I'm so sorry Millie, I hope you forgive me.* I find the picture and type the words with blurry eyes.

Em: *I'm sorry…he said it's my life or yours.*

It's all I could manage; I can't stop the tears now. *What have I done?*

Chapter Thirty-One

Shit Hits The Fan

Dan

Standing at the side of the stage, leaning against the wall. I watch Jack walk out to the centre of the stage. He always gets a good cheer and even the odd whoop when he does these, especially when it's the employee ball. They love it, it's such a testament to the type of boss he is. I can see out to the crowd from here, they can't see me though. I can't see Em. Odd, maybe she's got held up with something. There are so many familiar faces in the crowd. We had all the staff from the club in Ibiza flown in last night. They have all worked so hard to get the club back up and running, and it's paid off; we open the new and improved version next month. Now that's going to be one hell of a party. We're making a pit stop during the honeymoon to celebrate the reopening too. I know it's work, but it's the best kind of work.

I say the speech word for word as Jack says it to everyone. I can't help it. We'll be handing out Employee of the Year in a bit, and this guy deserves it. Issac has been with us a few years now, but this year, he's really proven himself, worked hard, helped when he was needed, and has been an amazing help to other members of staff, even letting us know when one of our own was struggling, he stepped up. And that made us proud to have him on our side.

I get drawn back to Jack as he looks around and frowns at me, nodding for me to look out; I watch Millie walk towards the doors, I shrug back at him, she's probably just going to the loo.

My phone buzzes in my pocket a few minutes later. Reaching for it, I see it's from Millie…my heart plummets.

> **Millie:** *Em's in trouble, you need to take her to hospital…*

It's like all the air gets sucked from my body, just seeing those few words. *What the fuck!* My heart races as I race out the stage door and down the steps. Taking them a few at a time. I don't know where she is. She never said, I have no idea what's happened. *Why didn't Em call me herself? Oh god, maybe she can't, is she unconscious?* A million scenarios run through my mind. But nothing prepares me for what I see next. I'm just coming out the stage door that levels into the reception area when I see them, my heart sinks. Fuck. It's him, a little rougher looking but it's him.

"Em!" I shout and she looks at me with fear in her eyes. My eyes run up and down her body to see if she's hurt, I can see marks on her face. He's holding her by her hair. Walking her towards me. Em's eyes dart to her side, I follow them and see a glimpse of what he's holding to her side. Although I can't see what it is, not from here.

"Hey! Let her go!" I yell, running forward to meet them. When I spot Millie, she steps directly in front of me, her hand stretched out towards me to stop me. *What's she doing?* Looking directly at me. She takes a deep breath and moves towards them. Stopping in my tracks.

"I'm so sorry, Dan. Just do what I asked okay?" She says, her eyes full of fear and regret. *What's she talking about?* I try to pull her back but she pushes me off, shaking her head.

"There she is, I knew it would work, you can thank Emma for getting you out here," Glen says, eyes on Millie.

"Millie…don't, he just wants to hurt you…" Em shouts as Millie walks towards them. Millie shakes her head again, "it's ok" she says, "I won't let him hurt you, I promise" she raises her hand in front of them.

"Let her go, take me…" her breathing evens out "I won't let you do this to them, she's pregnant."

What…she's what…did…she just say…it all makes sense… pregnant, my world almost shatters, my wife-to-be and my unborn baby…in his hands. I'm stuck, I don't know how to deal with this, I can't let Millie do this, but I also want Em out of that shit heads hands and safe in my arms. My body takes over, my fingers move and I speed-dial Owen. We have a code for shit hits it the fan. "RED" it's all I say down the phone, I don't hear anything else. I focus my attention back on Millie and Em, I need to stop this…

"I don't care about her, I'm here for you," he shouts, his voice full of anger.

"It's ok Em" Millie says, like she knows how it's going to end. She's so calm. My eyes darting between them. Reaching out, I say, "Millie, please think about this…" my words are cut off. Owen comes rushing through the door, stopping next to me and holding me back just as I make up my mind to take him down myself. He tries to reach for Millie, but she's further forward and just out of his reach.

"Take me, Glen, I know you don't want Em," she says firmly, moving forward slowly.

"I don't fucking want you either bitch, but you have to pay for everything you've done," he says, pressing whatever is behind Em's back into her harder; she whimpers biting her lip, trying not to cry. He then shoves Em so hard she almost falls over, but Millie catches her, telling her to "go." A tear slips down Millie's cheek, her shoulders sag slightly, almost like she's relieved. Em tries to grab her and pull her back but Millie shakes her head, "I'm done running," she says as Glen grabs her. Em runs to me, as Owen steps in front of us, trying to get to Millie. I take Em in my arms, my hands wandering all over her, checking she is okay and then finally wrapping my arms around her and holding her close. Closer than I think I ever have before. She's okay, I can't help but hold her as tight as I can. *She's okay,* I think looking into her eyes, *she's safe.*

"You're okay, I'll get you to hospital." She shakes her head and turns her tear-stained face to watch as Millie's grabbed by the throat and pulled towards Glen; he turns her around and puts the gun in his back pocket.

"I should have dumped you in the river when I had the chance." From behind his back, he pulls out a knife, pressing it into Millie's side, covering her mouth with the other. He slides the knife down her hip, slicing her dress and her skin with it. Her stifled scream emanates from behind his hand, tears running down her cheeks. Glen presses the knife harder into her side, causing Millie to scream again, then throws it on the floor behind him. He reaches back and pulls out the gun, seeing it, Millie goes silent.

"Millie, don't move…" Owen says from behind me and we all watch as Glen presses the gun to the side of her head.

"Millie…" Em screams and sobs into my chest, clutching my hand like I'm the only support she has. I'll never let her go. *Where the fuck is Jack?*

Her eyes close for a long second before opening again, like she's trying to gather all the courage she can. He holds the gun up and fires it into the air. A warning shot for us to stay back. Just then, the ballroom door slams open, and I watch as Jack comes flying through. Owen runs at him, stopping him, but Jack keeps fighting to get to her. The pain on his face is indescribable as he watches what's happening, realising Glen's got the love of his life.

"You son of bitch!" he screams, "if you lay one finger on her, I'll kill you myself," but stops when Owen whispers something in his ear. Owen continues to say something to him, but all my focus is on the need to get Em away from this, but I know she won't go. Not while Millie and her brother are faced with this.

"It's okay Jack," Millie says, her voice cutting through my thoughts, her voice edging on the side calm.

Chapter Thirty-Two

Fears & Nightmares

Millie

I've never felt fear like this, it feels like all my fears and nightmares rolled up into one. I should have known he would never stop until he got what he wanted. I should have known he was devious enough to trick the police. Watching Jack do his speech was amazing, god I love him so much, it's like falling in love with him never stops. He caught me at my weakest of moments, he saved me, he loves me. And what do I bring? Nothing, other than the pain of his family being in danger, and right now as Jack makes his speech in front of all his employees and friends, this world he has built, that danger is right outside.

The picture of Em chills me to the bone, and I stand frozen in place for what feels like forever. I know what I have to do. I love them all like my family, I can't let this happen to them. As I walk out the room, I need to let Jack know how I feel and how sorry I am that I have to do this. I know what Glen wants, and it won't end well for me, but Em's worth more, her and the baby.

I know Jack won't answer, but that's okay, if he did, he would never let me do this for him, for them. So when his phone clicks to voicemail, I'm already walking through the crowd, everyone is full of smiles, cheers and love for the man and company they work for.

"Jack…I want you to know just how much I love you, I fell for you the moment I laid eyes on you six years ago. I'm sorry it's taken me so long to say those three words to you. I'm sorry Jack, I have to do this, I won't let him hurt you, or your family. Thank you, for showing me I could have it all again, but I can't let him do it. I'm sorry… I love you." My voice breaks as I reach the end, and walk out the door.

I can't see them, I don't know where they are, the photo looked like it was outside. But as I run towards the back doors, I spot them walking towards the ball room, from the corridor. I need to make sure Em gets to the hospital as soon as possible. So before I step out I send Dan a quick message, that will have him here within a few seconds.

> *Me: Em's in trouble, you need to take her to hospital…*

I watch them walk slowly forward, when I see Dan running out of the stage door, heading towards them, I won't let him get hurt either, this is all my fault.

"Em!" he shouts. "Hey! Let her go!" running forward to meet them. He spots me as I step in front of him, I stretch out my arm, my hand stopping him, looking directly at me, confusion setting in. I take a deep breath and move towards them.

"I'm so sorry, Dan. Just do what I asked okay?" My voice was almost breaking at the pain in his eyes. My eyes are full of regret for what I've bought for this family. They don't deserve this. I should have left, when I first had the chance to go. I could have prevented all of this. If I had stayed and never left him. These wonderful people would be out of harm's way, living their life, none the wiser.

Em stares at me, fear and panic written all over her, as Glen shoves something into her back. I edge forward.

"There she is, I knew it would work, you can thank Emma for getting you out here," Glen says his eyes trained on me.

"Millie…don't, he just wants to hurt you," Em shouts to me, but I shake my head, "It's okay," I say, "I won't let him hurt you, I promise." It's far from okay, but he can't hurt me anymore than he already has by coming here and threatening my new family. I take a deep breath, raising my hands in front of them as a gesture for him to look at me and away from Dan.

"Let her go, take me," I say, my words coming out as steel, as I gain confidence. "I won't let you do this to them, she's pregnant."

All of my focus is on the two people in front of me; I have to get Em out of his hands, and back into Dan's.

"I don't care about her, I'm here for you!" Glen yells at me, and it brings back all of the memories I have of him. And at that moment, I think I shut down. I feel numb, I won't let him do this anymore, I'm ending this right now, so I step forward with only one goal in mind, this ends today.

"It's okay Em," I say quietly, trying to remain as calm as I can. I've got myself between Dan and Em now, at least that's something, I think.

"Millie, please think about this." I hear someone rush in, but don't look around, my eyes on Em. I can see the gun in Glen's hand now, my heart rate picks up, thinking of what she might have been through already.

It's all my fault.

This has to end.

"Take me, Glen, I know you don't want Em," I say moving a step closer nodding to Em that it's okay.

"I don't fucking want you either bitch, but you have to pay for everything you've done!" Em whimpers, biting her lip as he presses the gun into her back, trying not to cry. A split second later he shoves Em so hard away from him, she stumbles and almost falls, I manage to catch her just before she hits the floor, lifting her up. "Go!" I say as she tries to take me with her. Shaking my head, "I'm done running," I say, letting her go, when he grabs me by the throat, his fingers digging deep, causing me to wince, I can feel his nails breaking the soft skin on my neck as he pulls me into him. But all I feel is relief as Em runs to Dan, taking her in his arms; she's safe and I let out a sigh of relief.

"I should have dumped you in the river when I had the chance," he says into my ear, his voice laced with hate, his cold skin on mine. I can smell the alcohol in his breath mixed with dirt. *Has he been sleeping rough?*

His hand comes up to cover my mouth when I feel a sharp blade cutting into the skin over my hip. It burns as the pain radiates through my lift side. I let out a scream but it's almost silenced by his hand. I can feel my tears spilling over as he moves the blade down, digging deeper into me.

"That's just a taster of what you deserve." He throws the knife behind him. "You're worthless," he says pulling out the gun, his other hand tightening in the back of my hair. I can't move.

"Millie, don't move!" Owen says from somewhere, as Glen presses a gun to the side of my head. So this is it, I thought it would be worse than this. More painful. If he does it at least it will be quick. And Jack's not here to see it happen. Something in me clicks, a wave a calm takes over.

"Millie!" Em screams, it's like I'm not here, and I'm watching it happen before me.

My eyes close for a long second before opening again. Taking the gun from my head, he holds the gun up pointing it at the ceiling and fires it into the air. The sound is deafening, making me flinch backwards. The room falls silent around me. I watch as everyone stills.

The door to the ballroom bursts open, I watch Jack come flying through as Glen places the gun back at the side of my head. Owen runs at Jack, stopping him, but Jack keeps fighting to get to me. *He's safe too,* I think to myself, *As long as Owen can hold him back.*

"You son of bitch!" Jack shouts, his eyes all over me, trying to tell me something. "You lay one finger on her, I'll kill you myself!"

"It's okay Jack." My voice is calm, the pain in my side getting worse the more he shoves me around, I can feel the blood dripping down my thigh, Jack spots the wound on my side and tries to break free of Owen's grasp to get to me again. I can't let that happen.

"Jack stop!" I say, as his eyes locked with mine. "Don't."

"Did you get my flowers Emilie?" I can feel his warm breath on my skin, and it makes me feel sick. "I wanted you to know I was here, I've been here all along watching you, as soon as I found out you were fucking *him*. You don't get to be happy Emilie, you took everything from me. You humiliated me! You'll regret leaving, you ruined everything! You'll fucking pay for everything you've done!" I ignore him, nothing I say now will make any difference. He's lost it, the anger just pours off him, every fibre of him screams hate, and it's all aimed towards me. *For what? Money? Is it really worth all of this?* But it all makes sense, the stuff I was telling Jack on the way over here thinking I was going insane, losing my mind. It was all him, watching me, taunting me. He's been here all along. I was never free of him.

"Jack, it's okay. Don't." My words trail off when Glen pushes the gun back into my neck, harder this time and I wince as it pinches into my skin. He starts to move backwards, dragging me with him. Painfully pulling my hair to make a move. I almost stumble at the unexpected movement.

"You're coming with me." He laughs in my ear. "You thought you'd got away from me, you thought last time was the worst, you haven't seen anything yet." He spits into my ear, moving us towards the door. I know if I get out of this room, they will all be safe, that's all I care about right now. This is all my fault, I have to end this, but I don't know how. So I walk with him, I just need to get myself free and then…I have no idea. I don't want to die like this, not by his hand, he will have won if I let him do that. I just don't know what to do. We're still moving backwards,

I have no other option but to go with him, whatever he has planned for me, it won't be nice. *If I don't go, what would he do? Hurt them? I can't risk it.*

"If anyone's tries to come after us, I'll hurt her quicker than you can call her name!" I watch as everyone stands back, Jack still fighting to get to me, looking at me, every emotion crossing his face, while Owen tries his best to hold him back, almost taking him to the floor. Em looks between me and Jack, anxiety written all over her face. Dan is watching Em, like he will never let her go again, his hand firmly on her tummy. I smiled inwardly, I suppose it wasn't the best time for him to find out, but look at him. He's happy.

"You're going to hurt me anyway." I mumble, my thoughts coming back to what he might do to me. His laugh chills me, how could I have ever liked or even thought I loved this man? There is no emotion in him, just pure hatred for me, for what he thinks I have done to him.

"True," he says as the door closes behind us, I feel such a weight off my shoulders knowing they are all safe inside, the relief I feel is overwhelming, tears roll down my face. He can't hurt them if I'm out here with him.

"Five years of my life I wasted with you," I say "when I could have been with Jack all that time." His grip tightens on me as he moves me closer to the steps. What I don't expect is for him to throw me down the steps, I reach out a little too late as I land on the bottom step, my face in the gravel. The hard stone digging into my legs and hands, the burn of the gravel from the force in which I fell. There is no relief, when I feel his foot connect with my arm as he kicks me.

"I was only with you for your money, I knew how much your parents were worth, I knew you would be getting the money someday." He smears as he aims for me again.

"Ha!" I let out a small laugh. It's so clear now, why he beat me, he thought I would be getting the money as soon as they died, not years later. He kicks me again when I try to stand up and get away from him.

"You can't even do that right can you?" he says through gritted teeth, pulling me away from the steps. "You can't even get the money from your dead parents!" The third blow comes and this time I see it coming but I'm too slow to move. He punches me over and over again, each blow hitting my back as I try to turn away from him. He's losing control, like he always does. I'm on the floor again, facing down when I hear the door being pulled open; I hear Owen and Jack shouting and footsteps moving my way.

"No," I say, trying to stand again, getting further away from them all. "You would never have gotten a penny from me, you still won't. Jack is a million times the man you are." I manage to stand up and he knocks me back pushing me. Collapsing to the floor again, I let out a cry starting to feel the pain creeping in. I know I shouldn't have said that to him, not while he holds a gun on me, but I'm done being afraid of him. He can hurt me all he wants, I won't cower away from him again. I'm so much stronger now than I ever was with him. I have a man who loves me.

"Millie!" The fear in Jack's voice scares me; I know he can see what's happening, I didn't want this. And that's when it all happens at once. I feel the gun against my head as Glen pulls me up and shoves me towards a car, opening the door I'm shoved towards. My vision blurs as he strikes me again, this time just below my eye.

"Get in!" he shouts, shoving me further. Refusing to go I lash out, one attempt to get free of him. I hit and kick him back with everything I have, managing to get him in the crotch; he doubles over, I punch him in the neck just as I hear running and shouting, but I can't focus on who it is. The voices mingle together. Suddenly I'm not alone, I see what looks like Leon tackle Glen to the floor, pushing me away from them as they fight. Owen joins them trying to contain Glen, the gun drops from his hands, as Glen reaches for it trying to get back to me. I hit the ground with a thud landing on my knees and I watch as Jack races towards me, "You will pay for this, I'll fucking kill you, Emilie!" Glen shouts. That's when the gun goes off, I hear shouting and a scream, I feel something hit my side, a heaviness takes over my body, my already blurred vision darkens, I try to fight it, I want to tell Jack how much I love him before I die, it wasn't meant to be like this. "I love you, Jack," I try to say. I think my words fail me and I'm lost in darkness, just hearing the sounds around me slide into nothing, I fade to emptiness.

Chapter Thirty-Three

Waiting

Jack

"Millie, hold on!" I can't get to her quick enough. The bastard locked the door. It took everything in me and Owen to knock it open. I watch as Leon leaps on Glen, pushing Millie away as he fights to keep him back. She falls to her knees on the floor, I'm running, racing past as Owen joins Leon to get Glen under control, trying to get the gun away from him.

"You will pay for this, I'll fucking kill you Emilie!" I watch as Glen reaches for the gun, I run faster but it's too late, the gun goes off.

For a split second everything goes still, a smile spreads over Glen's face, Leon and Owen pinning him down, and I watch as Millie falls back, her eyes drifting closed, her hands coming to her stomach. Sliding to the side of her, I catch her before her head hits the floor, cradling her to me. What's happened...why is she...then I see the blood, he shot her. That prick shot her!

I hear the sound of sirens coming down the road, she's still breathing but it is shallow, there's blood everywhere, I place my hand over her side, putting pressure on the wound and I just hold her. Fear penetrating my soul and taking over. I can't lose her, I've only just found her again.

"I love you Jack," she whispers as she loses consciousness, I try to wake her, but nothing works, "I love you more than anything Millie, don't leave me, not like this."

After we arrive at the hospital, we wait as the doctors do what they need to do to fix her. She's been in surgery for hours; I feel so helpless just waiting around. I don't like it, Dan and Em both join me in the waiting room. I can't sit down. How can I? I don't know if she's okay.

"Are you and the baby okay?" I ask Em and she nods, she looks exhausted.

"Perfect, if it wasn't for Millie, I don't know what would have happened to us," she says placing a hand on her tummy.

"Mate, I owe her everything, she...she saved Em's life, and my baby's life. She put herself in that position for us!" Dan says, sitting down pulling Em onto his lap.

"I don't understand? What did she do?" Looking between them, "I thought Glen had just grabbed Millie, what are you on about?" Em takes a deep breath and motions for me to sit down next to her, then she takes my hand, giving it a reassuring squeeze. When I look at her I realise she's been hurt, and I never even noticed.

"Oh my god, your face…did he?"

"A wave of morning sickness hit and I needed some air, so I went out. Glen found me there. He hit me with the gun and made me send a picture to Millie to get her to come outside, to trade places."

"That must have been when she walked out of the ballroom, I just thought she was…" Em cuts me off.

"Well, she came out, but not before sending Dan a message telling him I was in trouble and he needed to get me to hospital," she says looking at him lovingly.

"When I got out there he had Em, the gun in her back…mate, Millie switched places with her, she just did it, before I could wrap my head around what was happening."

"She caught me when he pushed me away, I tried to get her to come with me, but I think she knew he would hurt us all, she said she was done running, so she stepped in my place. Then he grabbed her." She closed her eyes at the memory.

"That's when he drew the knife on her and did what he did, Owen had to hold me back, I tried but…" You can see the guilt he feels about it all, I don't know what I would have done if our roles had been reversed.

"She saved my life Jack, even after everything she has been through, she held her own against him and protected us," Em said, letting out a heavy sigh.

She did that for my family, she put herself in harm's way for my family, knowing what he would likely do to her, she still did it. I don't know if she is brave or stupid, but it certainly makes me love her more, if that's even possible.

"When she left the ballroom, she was on the phone, who did she ring?" Dan and Em both frown at me, but then I remember my phone vibrating during the speech just before it all kicked off.

"She rang me, didn't she...?" Taking my phone out of my pocket, I see it. One missed call and one voice mail. Placing it to my ear I listen to her voice. She sounds scared, but sure. "Jack...I want you to know just how much I love you, I fell for you the moment I laid eyes on you six years ago. I'm sorry it's taken so long to say those three words to you. I'm sorry Jack, I have to do this, I won't let him hurt you, or your family. Thank you, for showing me I could have it all again, but I can't let him do it. I'm sorry... I love you." Her voice breaks as she ends the voice message.

"She knew what she was doing." Em takes the phone from me and listens, "She didn't ask for help, she never even went to Owen or Leon!" I say.

"She's going to be okay Jack, I just know it, she can't leave us now, not when everything is just starting between the two of you."

"I think she knew she might die, that's why she called me." The last words she spoke to me were "I love you" —the first time she said them to me might be the last time I ever hear them. I don't say that out loud, I don't want to believe she might not make it, but the bullet wound was in her stomach, adding in the other injuries she got from him tonight, will only make it harder for her to recover.

A few hours later there's a knock on the waiting room door; Leon, Charlie and Owen all come in.

"What's the news?" Charlie asks.

"No news yet, she's still in surgery," I say glumly.

"She's stronger than she looks Jack," she says, squeezing my shoulder then sitting down with Dan and Em.

Owen sits next to me, and Leon on the other side. "We have news, he's been arrested, at least six charges against him so far, and that's not including the arson charge for the club, assault & battery, assault, attempted kidnapping, stalking, possession of an illegal firearm, possession of a deadly weapon with intent.... he'll be going away for a very long time, with no hope of release any time soon." He looks almost pleased.

"Well, it's not long enough, for all the stuff he has done to her!" I say, anger seeping out, I can't help it, none of this should have happened.

"We managed to give him a good kicking before the police arrived," Leon said beside me, a smile coming across his face. I suppose that's something.

"How did he manage to escape the police in Spain?" I ask Owen, wanting answers.

"They never had him, they had someone who looked a lot like him, he flew back to the UK after the arson attack, and has been camped out here ever since, watching her and messing with her head. He has even admitted getting someone to add something to her drink when she passed out in the bar with Charlie, and breaking into the cottage. That guy is fucked up!" he adds at the end.

An hour later we are all still waiting, Charlie has fallen asleep on Owen's chest and Em on Dans. Leon has been on countless coffee and snack runs, just to keep himself occupied, I think.

There's another knock at the door and the doctors walk in.

"Are you all Miss Monroe's family?" she asks, looking at us all.

"Yes, I reply, how is she, is she okay? Can I…" I ask.

"Miss Monroe's surgery went well, she is and will be okay, if not sore and in some pain for a little while. She is sleeping off the anaesthetic right now, and needs her rest."

"Can we see her?" I stand up "I don't want to wait any longer I need to be there when she wakes up."

"I can't let you all in, just one for tonight, and I shouldn't even be doing that, but given the circumstances one of you can go in." Everyone looks at me at the same time and nods, the doctor moves to the door and I follow.

Chapter Thirty-Four

Awake

Millie

My eyes feel so heavy, I want to wake up and I have to force them to move. When they finally drift open, I realise I'm in a hospital. I feel groggy and so tired. My whole body feels heavy like I've had too much sleep. That feeling keeps overtaking me, my whole body struggling as I try to stay awake, staring at the ceiling. I shift a little to get comfortable, and take stock of what's going on. Taking in a sharp breath as the pain that runs through my side hurts like hell. It's excruciating. So I stay still, I don't want to feel that again. I'm trying to remember. *What the fuck happened?* It takes me a while for the memories to come flooding back. But when they do, it's like living them all over again. The last thing I remember was…oh my god, I think I was shot. My hand instantly goes to my side, where the pain is. I could have died, *fuck* I could have died. He tried to kill me, in front of everyone, letting out a shaky breath while a single tear slips down my cheek, as I try and stay calm.

In reality I think I knew what I was getting into. I knew Glen wanted to really hurt me, if not kill me—he was willing to hurt anyone to get to me. That's what scared me the most. In all his anger to hurt me, he could have hurt so many people. I wonder what happened to him. There was no way I was ever going to let him hurt the people I have come to love in such a short period of time. I would never let that happen. Em and the baby, how he could've hurt them, even killed them. What if Dan had got to them before me, and Jack…what if Owen hadn't been able to hold him back? Thank fuck that man is stronger than he looks to be able to hold Jack back like that. I remember the pain in his eyes as he fought Owen trying to get to me.

Things could have gone so differently; my heart feels heavy for what could have happened. The beeping of the machine draws me back from my swirling thoughts for a moment before they come back again. The events of the night run through my mind, I remember Leon and Owen fighting Glen, I remember Jack shouting my name, then seeing him running towards me as the gun went off, then nothing. I must have blacked out, I don't remember Jack reaching me. I have a million questions I want to ask about what happened. *Is Em okay? Did they get him? Where is he? Was anyone else hurt?* I take a few deep breaths; I need to calm down, even that hurts. The fact that I'm here right now and in what looks like a very nice hospital, all the questions can wait a while.

When I eventually look down, I find Jack by my side holding my hand, fast asleep with his head on the bed. He's still the sexiest man I've ever seen, his man bun is all hanging loose, that sun kissed dirty blond hair falling over his face. He is one of the only men I know that can look that good with bags under his eyes, wearing those grey joggers I love so much and dark green hoodie like a second skin. Shit he looks good in everything, it's a little annoying. Looking around the room, I can see some flowers and cards, a few bags, and snacks around. I could do with a drink, my throat feels dry, but it's too far away for me to reach without waking him up.

It's dark outside when I peer out the window. I don't want to wake him. So I just watch and stroke his hair while he sleeps. He looks so peaceful; I wonder how long he has been here. *How long have I been here?* I slowly move the bed sheet covering my stomach to take a look at the wound on my side, to see where it is, but my side is covered with bandages so I can't get to it without taking them off or waking Jack up.

So I settle in and watch him sleep some more, enjoying the quiet the room brings. I love that he is here by my side. The last time I was in hospital like this…well, there was someone by my side but he just wanted to make sure I never told anyone what really happened to me. Jack even looks worried in his sleep; his eyes are moving like he's dreaming. I hope it's a good dream. My fingers glide over his cheek feeling the rough stubble that has grown while I've been here.

I hope he's not pissed that I did what I did. I had the best intentions; I hope he realises that. In the time I have been here, they really have all become my family, Em and Dan like the brother and sister I never had and always wanted. Dan is always making light of any situation, the funny man who wears his heart on his sleeve, making me laugh even when he doesn't realise it.

Em just being there, someone I'm able to share everything with, no judgements. No matter what happens. And Jack, my eyes well up, my heart almost bursts just at the thought of how he has allowed, no that's not the right word, how he has supported and helped me be who I want. He has encouraged me, teased me a little and showed me how love should be. He loves me for who I am, the good, the bad and the psycho ex. *How did I get so lucky?* And that's when I see it, a sparkle that sits on my other hand, a huge emerald stone, resting on a gold band sits on my ring finger, I lift my hand up, watching it glitter in the dull light, moving my hand around to make it sparkle more in the dim light that surrounds us. This man has some explaining to do when he wakes up. I can't contain the huge smile that spreads across my face. This man is everything. My new beginning, my soulmate, my friend. The love of my life.

When the nurse walks in a while later, her eyes go wide when she sees I'm awake. When she goes to say something, I shush her, moving my finger to my lips. "I don't want to wake him," I whisper. She smiles and shakes her head, but carries on doing what she needs to do without making a sound. After she hands me a glass of water, she heads back out of the room. I sink my head back into the pillow and must have drifted off to sleep as when I wake up again, Jack is still there, holding my hand fast asleep. I feel a little better, well less groggy anyway.

When the sun rises, I squeeze his hand and he stirs. "Jack," I whisper softly, stroking is cheek. He grumbles a little, I don't want to startle him, but his eyes fly open sitting up as soon as he realises where he is; he looks around the room as if looking for someone else. I smile and chuckle, then wince and groan at the movement in my side. When his eyes land on me, a smile spreads across his face. His eyes run over me, like he can't quite believe what he's seeing.

"Oww, morning sleepy," I say, with a hoarse voice, shifting slightly and wincing at the same time.

"Millie…you're awake?" he says in disbelief, his hands flying to my face, cupping my chin in his hands, like he needs to touch me to make sure he's not dreaming.

"Yep, have been for a while, but I didn't want to wake you, you looked so peaceful." He just looks at me, doesn't move, just looks into my eyes, with those deep blue ones trying to read me, making sure I'm not a dream. His eyes wander over me again, taking all of me in, from head to foot. "Are you okay?" I ask when he doesn't move.

"I should be asking you that very question. I'm great, now that you're awake. How do you feel?" He asks, moving his hand to rub down his face, while sitting on the edge of the bed.

"I feel sore, in a bit of pain, groggy and tired, but okay apart from that. How long have I been asleep for?" What he said about being awake, how bad was it?

"You've been asleep for almost a week Millie, we've been so worried about you, you went into surgery as soon as we arrived, and they said you would be okay…but you never woke up when they thought you would." He reaches for my hand and when he takes it, I pull him closer. I can see the stress and exhaustion written all over him. His eyes still do not believe I'm awake. I have to ask the question…

"Did he shoot me?" His eyes reach mine, and I see the answer in them.

"I tried to get to you…but…" He starts, I know what he was trying to say, and I won't let him think it. I let this happen, not him.

"Kiss me please." I don't need to ask him twice; he moves closer and gives me the most loving and tender kiss I think I have ever had. His soft lips take mine, moving slowly, taking his time, savouring each moment, passionate and all encompassing. The warmth of his lips on mine is calming. When he pulls away, he whispers, "I thought I had lost you Millie. Don't you ever be that stupid and brave and amazing again!" Moving his hands to cup my face, he kisses me again, deeper this time.

"You can't get rid of me that easily, it's going to take so much more than a psychopath ex-boyfriend with a gun and a knife to make me leave you." The look he gives says that was too soon, but I don't care. "Now get on the bed properly, I want you as close to me as possible for a while." I smile when he shakes his head at me.

"It's over Millie, you never have to see him again."

"Good, because I never want to see him again… I also think you have some explaining to do?" I say lifting my hand up to him, shining the ring at him.

"Oh shit!" He laughs. "I must have left it on and fell asleep…"

"Ask me," I cut in.

"What…" he says looking at me like he's excited and scared. I want him to ask the question, I want to see the worry on his face gone when I answer him.

"Ask me Jack," reaching for his hand, "Ask me to be your wife." His smile is striking, but I think it matches my own. Jack takes both my hands in his, bends down resting his forehead on mine. Then whispers the words I have only ever wanted to hear from this man.

"Millie, will you be mine, for the rest of our lives?" I feel the tingles throughout my body as his words wash over me—words I will never forget.

"Yes," I whisper back. He climbs on the bed, hovering over me, but careful not to move me too much. We kiss for what feels like an eternity. All of our emotions over the past few weeks came to the surface and combined in one perfect, unimaginable moment.

"I love you so much Millie," he says taking a breath,

"I love you, Jack," I say it back, kissing him again, I never want him to let me go.

Jack eventually slides into bed next to me, holding me carefully. After a while we sleep, wrapped up in each other, feeling free and at peace for the first time in a long time, until the nurses come back needing to do their checks.

Jack only left the room that day when the police arrived to take my statement, they answered some of the questions I had, but weren't that willing to give much out.

Over the next few days, Jack answers all the other questions I had, all while holding my hand or kissing me. He hardly left my side. And when he did it was to make calls to everyone to tell them I was awake or updating them on my progress. With that information floating about in the world I had visitors all day, and every day until I was allowed to go home. Jack never left my side. He was attentive, caring and everything I have ever wished for in the man I love. Huh sounds funny really when I say it now, I don't know why I never told him as soon as I knew I loved him, he is the best thing that has ever happened to me.

Em and Dan visited the day after I woke up. When they walked in, Dan almost jumped on me giving me a hug and crying thank you's into my ear. Em stood back and watched with tears in her eyes as she rubbed her tummy, giving me all the evidence I needed to know that they were okay.

When we were done crying and "hugging it out" as Dan called it, they told me they had postponed the wedding. They said they wanted me there and to be able to enjoy the day. So it's next summer, another twelve months away. Guilt filled me from the inside, I know how much effort they had put into it. And it was all my fault it had been taken away.

"I'm so sorry, it's all my fault, if I..." I say but Em just looks at me.

"Don't even say it! Me and Dan have decided to postpone, not just because we want you there with us, but I don't want to be pregnant when I get married, I want to really enjoy myself and have a drink! God I miss wine, Mike says his sales have gone down since I became pregnant." She laughs and I laugh with her, holding my side a little.

"Sorry, are you ok?" She scrunches her face up knowing it hurts like hell when I move. They didn't stay long and were replaced by Charlie. Jack left us to it, to head off to find something for dinner. Charlie just sat with me, hardly spoke, but held my hand. She looked so sad.

"Charlie, please don't blame yourself for this. This was not your fault." She shakes her head, lowering it slightly, looking at her hands.

"If I had been a better friend and just stuck with you all those years ago, then you being hurt again could have all been avoided."

"If that had happened then I would never have met Jack again, I wouldn't wish what happened to me on anyone else Charlie, but it's made me who I am." She looked up at me, tears in her eyes, and guilt being replaced by admiration.

"You are pretty amazing!" She laughs a little. "He does really love you, you know. Did you know he never left your side once while you've been in here. He stopped working and left Dan in charge of everything. He even had Dan, Em and me running around picking things up for him and you to bring in, he refused to leave you on your own. He wanted to be there when you woke up, you scared us Millie." I had guessed as much, and it makes me love him back so much more. I need a change in conversation before we both end up crying.

"Enough about me, how are things with you?" We fall into an easy conversation about Owen, and how hot and cold he has been with her. She said that was it for them, she didn't need the hassle of it. She's concentrating on her new flower shop and giving men a miss for a while. I have a feeling there is more to the story than she's letting on. I'll ask her again when I'm home.

When she leaves, Jack comes back with dinner, we watch a movie, a rom-com, his choice I may add. When he climbs into bed with me, his hands sneak beneath the covers and hold me tight. Well as tight as he can with my wounded side.

"I can't wait to get you home and fully recovered. I'm not touching you anymore than this, until the doctors have said you are good as new." His hands tease my thighs, sending those delicious tingles all over me.

"Well, that's disappointing, I was hoping for some hospital fun," I joke, kissing his cheek I sneak my hand down into his joggers, but he pulls it back out before I can even wrap my hand around it.

"Believe me, it's not easy, all I want to do is wrap you around me and...nope." He stops abruptly, his voice husky and low, like it's taking all of his control to hold back. "I now need a cold shower." I laugh but I know how he feels.

The day I left the hospital, Jack said he had a surprise for me. I don't need surprises, not after everything that's been going on, then waking up to find an engagement ring on my finger. *Huh...I guess I like some surprises more than others.*

We both agreed I was never going back to the cottage; it held weird memories for both of us. Good and bad I suppose after we found out Glen has been letting himself in and moving things around, messing with my head. It's a shame but Jack has said he'll be able to let it out as part of the manor hotel. I didn't want to be in the hotel either so that didn't leave us with a lot of options.

We have been talking about places I or we could stay, or live or even buy now that the money had gone through from my parents' estate, but Jack had another idea. He told me about his parents, and how after his father died, they sold the house they had been brought up in, and that he and Em both bought houses with the inheritance once the sale had gone through. It's how he managed to start his business.

The drive from the hospital to the house is only half an hour, and as we pull up in front of it, well my mind has been blown! It's beautiful.

It's like the cottage I was staying in, but ten times the size, and twice as unique, he's been working on it for years apparently, restoring all the original features, but updating everything else. Bringing it back to life. It's stunning. Set in the middle of a huge garden, trees and flowers surrounding it, with a gravel drive, walking around I take a peak round towards the back, I can see it even comes with a sea view. Just from the outside, the cottage has me feeling relaxed already, it feels like home.

"This is it…Happy Belated Birthday!" He gestures towards the huge cottage, while holding me tight against his side. "This is for us, if you say yes, we can live here together, you and me, just us. What do you think?"

I just smile, taking in the house and then him, this man, he is everything I have ever wanted and everything I didn't know I needed in my life. All wrapped up in one sexy as hell package just for me. I take in a deep breath, turning around a little more to face him.

"Yes, yes, yes!" I cry at him, planting my hand on his firm chest. "But I'm paying for half!" I smile at the man in front of me, happy tears rolling down my face this time. He engulfs me in his arms, careful not to hold on too tight, kissing my tears as they fall.

"I wouldn't have it any other way Millie."

This man has a way of taking control that makes me feel loved, safe, secure, alive and free all at the same time. I don't know how he does it, but I'll spend the rest of my life loving him and showing him how utterly grateful I am to have him in my life.

Epilogue

A While Later...

I still can't believe it's all mine, this building, my business, my company, my space! Every time I walk in, I get that nervous, excited feeling all over again, like the day I got the keys. When I look around, I see it all, all my hard work, the reception area where Mary works part time for me. Jack was a little shocked that she wanted to leave the Manor, well go part time. I think she loves the change, plus I love having her here, she's become like a mom to me over the past twelve months. I would also never eat if it wasn't for Mary, a fact I know Jack is grateful for, now that he can't get Marco to cook for me every day. It's not like I do it on purpose, I just get a little too involved and when I look at the time, well it's been hours. I guess that's what happens when you love what you do. My design company is my world, as well as Jack of course.

What I have created took off a little quicker than I expected. After I had designed a range of bright, positive affirmation screen prints, and made them into wall art, bags, t-shirts and jumpers, it all went online and my dad's old friend, Eric got in touch after seeing them. He wanted to put them in all of his stores throughout the country. I was overwhelmed with his generosity, but he also said, it's what my dad would have done. It was so unexpected I cried. He has since formed a fond friendship with Mary. Who knows where that will lead!

I love every second of every day I spend here. I've decorated the place just how I wanted it, the office area feels modern yet feminine with pinks, gold and blacks. I have a lounge for clients when they want custom work done, a showroom, my production area and my very own office.

Em gave birth to the most stunning little girl I have ever seen. She has all of Dan's dark features with Em's bright blue eyes—that girl is going to run the world. I thought Dan was emotional before, well you've not seen him since. He is devoted to both of them, you can see the love shining through with everything he does for them. They got married two months ago now, with little Daisy right by their side. I cried for most of the day, I couldn't and still can't believe how lucky I am to have these people around me.

Oh I should add, Jack and I also got married six months ago. We had the perfect small ceremony on the beach in Ibiza, short and sweet. It was everything I had ever dreamed of, it's where we met, where we fell for each other, where I started to find myself on that crazy hen weekend, where the life I was supposed to have started again. That's now my happy place, the warm sun on my skin, with the most amazing man next to me and the family I love surrounding me.

It's still hard dealing with everything Glen did, but I've had some help to deal with it, and I can honestly say, it's working.

Well that brings me back to today, and I have a small surprise for Jack planned for tonight when everyone comes around to ours. It's become a bit of a routine to get together on a Friday for pizza night. I'm so excited I can't wait!

"Jack, will you check to see if they are here please?" I say to him, busying myself in the kitchen, I'm a little nervous about what I'm about to do.

"What are you up to?" He sneaks in behind me, making me jump, but wrapping his arms around me in the process.

"What do you mean? I'm not up to anything." I can't lie for shit and he knows it.

"Hmmm…Let's make them wait, I want to have you right here in the kitchen, I've been thinking about you all day, bent over this very spot!" His hand slid down the front of my legs, teasing me while slowly lifting my dress up, slipping his fingers inside my panties, finding my clit with ease. My head instantly falls back onto his chest, letting him have a little more room.

"Do it," I say, and the very next second, I hear the zipper of his jeans as I wiggle my ass at him while he continues to touch me in all the right places. I make quick work of pulling my knickers down, feeling his hard length against me as he pulls his boxers down just enough.

Leaning over me, he holds my waist and turns me around to face him. Lifting me onto the kitchen's cold stone surface, pulling my panties off and placing himself in between my legs. Kissing me as he holds me close, he slowly enters me at the same time. The pleasure is almost instant, as shivers run up my spine, just taking him in. A small gasp escapes my lips. I'm not sure I will ever get used to how good he feels inside me. He moves faster, gaining more friction. "Fuck...every time Millie, I will never tire of being with you!" He starts moving his hands, gripping my ass. I feel every inch of him, gliding in and out of me; my temperature rises, I feel hot all over as he continues to reach my most sensitive spots, knowing they will send me into a frenzy of heated passion just for him. I'm holding on to him, my nails digging into his back, his head resting on my shoulder. His breathing is harsh and ragged, as he reaches into my hair holding me impossibly closer.

"Fuck!" we both say together as we feel the high of our movements coming closer. I'm coming hard, clenching around him, when I feel him still and let go of his own orgasm, holding me, kissing me as we both reached the end of our high.

Panting and a little sweaty, I place my hands on his shoulders and lean back a little to see his face. Flushed, and so god damn handsome, that small smile creeping up his lips.

"You know that doing *this*," I point at the two of us still joined blissfully together "is what got us into this little situation." I point at my stomach.

"What?" He looks a little confused but I smile and let out a small nervous laugh. "What are you trying to tell me Millie?" I can see it in his eyes. He knows what I'm telling him. So I just nod and kiss him. He pulls away a little.

"Are you saying we are...we're...Pregnant?" He's nervous to even say the words.

"Yes. We have a little one just in here," I say pointing to my stomach again.

Well, that leads us to round two, and they have to wait for us to open the door when they arrive twenty minutes later, with Jack and I crying happy tears. Jack immediately tells everyone the good news, not even waiting for them to sit down or have a drink, and we are engulfed in a mass of arms, words and so much love, I cry all over again.

Life isn't a fairy tale. It's a journey and you have to make it.

The End

If you have enjoyed this journey with Millie and Jack, you can find out more about Em and Dan, in More Than Tempted – a FREE eBook short story, just for you.

Follow the link below here:

www.subscribepage.io/Tempted-eBook

Follow me for more on

Website – https://author.bekkivowles.co.uk/
Instagram – www.instagram.com/author_bekkiv
Facebook – www.facebook.com/bekkivowlesauthor1
TikTok – www.tiktok.com/bekkivowles_author

Love,
Bekki xx

About the Author

Bekki Vowles is a romantic, always has been and always will be. From the first day her nan handed her a Mills and Boon book, she never looked back. She divides her time between her two sons, her husband, fur baby and being a life coach, helping other mums to navigate the changes and challenges of becoming a parent. Writing is her escape, her happy place, just like reading. Process is a big part of her writing – only when she writes she can determine what happens, who falls in love with who, and how it ends. Giving an edge to the story you may not have seen coming.

Milton Keynes UK
Ingram Content Group UK Ltd.
UKHW010721050224
437294UK00019B/923